the sense of adventure and intrigue that grabs you right up until the final gut-clutching finale."

—*East Side Monthly* (Providence, RI)

"A wild, no-holds-barred thrill ride with nothing less than the fate of the United States hanging in the balance.... Land's latest doesn't so much redefine the genre as reassess it. Indeed, *Blood Diamonds* might well be the first great thriller spawned by the Post–9/11 age. A jewel of a book that sparkles enough to read with-out the lights on."                     —*BookCrossing*

"Mr. Land is a master at creating many subplots and intrigues, all of which are occurring simultaneously.... Action addicts should be in heaven."                     —*The Mystery Reader*

### Keepers of the Gate

"A strongly plotted, impressively solid new entry."
                     —*Kirkus Reviews*

"This is a big, complex mystery propelled by a genuinely compelling plot and its likable lead characters. We enjoy watching these smart, efficient detectives sort out what's what and we enjoy watching the author have fun with his bigger-than-life plot, carefully calculating how far he can go without turning his story into a cartoon.... A lively and well-told yarn, sure to please fans of high-concept thrillers."                     —*Booklist*

"A labyrinthine tale of conspiracy and deception.... Land is adept at gauging the unique effects the Mideastern culture and history will have on the emotions and motivations of his protagonists."                     —*Publishers Weekly*

"Land's pacing is masterful, giving the reader a sense that he is watching an action movie. And he depicts the very real Israeli-Palestinian conflicts with clarity and poignancy.... Another spectacular, fast-paced, suspense-filled thriller from Land, one that will keep you up at night turning the pages. *Keepers* is a keeper."                     —*The Providence Sunday Journal*

"Land is coming into his own with the Ben Kamal series, reflecting a maturity of craft most authors struggle to convince us they have and fail. With *Keepers of the Gate* Land hits his stride. . . . Land stands head and shoulders above his competition in creating—down to the smallest detail—characters who provoke both our caring and interest. The devil is in the details, as they say, and in this case Jon Land has done better than give the devil his due—he's given us genre that manages to capture the elusive human factor."

—*The Boston Book Review*

"Few writers capture the conflict and turmoil of the Middle East like thriller author Jon Land. Land has done it again in *Keepers of the Gate*, a novel of suspense about the Palestinian-Israeli conflict, murders, Nazi hunters, Holocaust survivors and biotech research. . . . Land captures the complex and tumultuous nature of the Arab-Israeli conflict without making sweeping indictments on either side. . . . Land gives the reader a little more in *Keepers of the Gate*, an engaging thriller with a more personal touch than his previous works."

—*The Charleston Post and Courier*

"Jon Land writes exciting and believable political thrillers in the tradition of Clancy and Cornwall. . . . The theme of *Keepers of the Gate* is universal, yet heart-wrenching so that readers will understand the motives of the key players, whose flaws make them so human. Mr. Land is a great storyteller who enriches his audience with every novel he writes."

—*The Midwest Book Review*

"International intrigue and double feints are par for the course in this thrilling tale. Be advised, when you think you've figured it out, Land has more surprises in store. . . . A white-knuckled read. Land has packed eight days of action into this tersely written, well-plotted work which races towards its surprising conclusion."

—*BookSense*

## OTHER BOOKS BY JON LAND

\*Published by Forge Books

# JON LAND

# BLOOD DIAMONDS

FORGE®

A TOM DOHERTY ASSOCIATES BOOK
NEW YORK

## September 11, 2001

The friends we lost,
The heroes we found.

This is a work of fiction. All the characters and events portrayed in this book are either products of the author's imagination or are used fictitiously.

BLOOD DIAMONDS

A Forge Book
Published by Tom Doherty Associates, LLC
175 Fifth Avenue
New York, NY 10010

www.tor-forge.com

Forge® is a registered trademark of Tom Doherty Associates, LLC.

ISBN-13: 978-0-7653-6112-7
ISBN-10: 0-7653-6112-4
Library of Congress Catalog Card Number: 2001057516

First Edition: April 2002
First Mass Market Edition: April 2003
Second Mass Market Edition: May 2008

Printed in the United States of America

0  9  8  7  6  5  4  3  2  1

# A C K N O W L E D G M E N T S

If you've been looking for *The Dragon at Sunset,* the book I promised you last spring, you've found it. Same book, different title. These things happen and, if you love the cover as much as I do, you can see the reason for the change.

One thing that hasn't changed is much of the list of people I am beholden to on every book, a list that starts with the wondrous Toni Mendez, an agent who both shares my vision and enriches me with her own. Twenty years together now and she's better than ever.

Also better than ever is the terrific publishing family at Tor/Forge headed by Tom Doherty and Linda Quinton and backed up in publicity by Jennifer Marcus and Jodi Rosoff. I don't have the space here to thank all the sales and marketing people who actually placed this book in the store where you bought it, so I'll do so collectively with the biggest thanks of all to Natalia Aponte, a brilliant editor who returned from maternity leave just in time to make this book what it is. Meanwhile, the influence of Ann Maurer, my editor for all twenty-four books, can be seen on every page.

I'm also *especially* grateful this time to Rabbi Jim Rosenberg, who provides incredibly insightful literary advice with the same aplomb he helps me with Israeli and Jewish culture. Our lunches are starting to rival my lunches with

Natalia at Bolo for major plot refinements. Richard and Sharon Smith (whom I met at a book signing), Cathy Brown, and Carol Hatfield helped greatly with the St. Louis scenes, while Pnina Levin and Amir Mica joined Nancy and Moshe Aroche in lending their expertise about Israel. Unfortunately, those who helped me with Palestinian subjects and locales prefer, in the current climate, not to have their names mentioned, but that makes me no less appreciative of their efforts. So, too, Emery Pineo, still the smartest man I know, Bob Burgess, and Irv and Josh Schechter.

For those of you who like surprises, I hope you enjoy the first chapter of *The Blue Widows*, the next Ben and Danielle adventure. It's available now in hardcover for anyone who can't wait for the paperback. As always, I'd love to hear what you think. E-mail me at JonLandauthor @Netscape.net. In the meantime, there's a tale to tell, so turn the page and let's begin.

So rejoice, you heavens,
And you that dwell therein!
But woe to you, earth and sea,
For the dragon has come down upon you!
His fury knows no limits,
For he knows his time is short.

Revelation 12:12

# PROLOGUE

TONGO, SIERRA LEONE, 2000

I f you'll follow me, gentlemen," Colonel Masio Verdoon said to the representatives from Parliament, as they huddled in the thin shade of their truck, "we'll get started."

The six representatives, personally chosen by President Kabbah, followed Verdoon back into the heat of the midday sun. Tongo was located in the Kono region of Sierra Leone, well east of the coastline's cooling ocean breezes. The representatives walked with Colonel Verdoon up the slight hill through the steamy air, their shoes crunching over pressed gravel and their noses wrinkling at the stench of sun-baked mud rising from the shores of the river beyond. Perspiration darkened their shirts in widening blotches that looked like huge insects clawing their way through the fabric.

"As you know, we retook the Tongo diamond fields from the Revolutionary United Front over a year ago," Colonel Verdoon resumed near the crest of the hill. He wore his coarse black hair cropped close to his scalp, his face dappled with scars and his stoutness further exaggerated by a belly that hung over his gun belt. "This, of course, has nearly crippled the rebels' ability to purchase arms on the black market and has allowed the government to use the profits to make substantial investments in our nation's infrastructure."

The six representatives exchanged frowns. Evidence of such investment remained nearly nonexistent, leading many lawmakers to question the functionality of the once diamond-rich fields. Hence, this tour.

A trail had been flattened at the top of the hill, angling down toward a narrow ribbon of water. Government soldiers stood at their posts all along the riverbank, overseeing dozens of workers busily dipping large sieves in the water and scooping up whatever they could. The workers shook the sieves to sift out sediment and dirt, then inspected whatever lay trapped by the screen. The toilsome motion had a choreographed flavor to it, as if it formed the steps of some well-practiced, synchronized dance.

"These are alluvial diamonds, of course, and the method for mining them has remained unchanged for centuries, with a few exceptions."

As the tour group approached the river, more workers hurriedly collected the contents of the sieves into wheelbarrows and brought them to a conveyor belt on which the stones and rocks were placed.

"The conveyor is covered with axle grease," Verdoon explained. "Rough diamonds, we've learned, stick to such grease while regular stones do not." Verdoon failed to add that this had been learned from the rebels who had mined Tongo far more successfully when it had been in their possession.

The conveyor belt ferried the stones scooped up from the river to a central location of tables squeezed amidst several high piles of excavated dirt. There, another group of workers, under the even more watchful eye of soldiers, stored the potential diamonds in wooden pails.

"There have been no incidents here in Tongo since I took over security," Verdoon said proudly. "We believe the rebels have totally vacated the area, but we have placed mines and traps in the surrounding woods in case they return."

Suddenly an uncovered truck packed with men and

women clad in tattered shorts and frayed shirts rolled down a service road cut from the surrounding forest. The truck parked at an angle off the steep grade and a pair of soldiers armed with M-16 assault rifles climbed down from the cab.

"The next shift of workers has arrived," Colonel Verdoon told the government representatives clustered around him. "Shifts are eight hours long from sunup to sunset." He checked his watch. "This shift appears to be a little early, but . . ."

His voice tailed off as the soldiers herded the workers from the truck, prodding them with the barrels of their M-16s. Near the back several had collapsed from the heat, and the soldiers mounted the truck's bed to rouse them.

Verdoon cleared his throat uneasily, hoping to be saved the embarrassment of one or more of the workers being found dead. He actually breathed a brief sigh of relief when they stirred; brief because the motion was too sudden and abrupt. Verdoon squinted into the sun and saw the dark gun barrels being hoisted from beneath the workers and tossed outward to be snatched out of the air by those workers who had already climbed down.

*Rebels! It was the RUF!*

The shooting began as Verdoon struggled to shepherd the government representatives back up the hill to safety. Random and wild, punctuated by piercing screams as the rebels fired across the riverbanks, downing soldiers and workers indiscriminately. The prospecting workers tried to run from the river. The soldiers who could fled into the woods.

Verdoon drew his pistol, sidestepping up the hill, and fired on the rebels the moment they turned their attention upon him. A pair of the representatives went down screaming. Below, on the riverbank, some rebels whipped machetes from sheaths hidden by their shirts and set off after the workers struggling to flee.

Blades whistled through the air. Blood leaped upward. The screams bubbled in Verdoon's ears. He realized he couldn't swallow, realized his pistol's slide had locked empty and ejected the magazine in favor of a fresh one only to remember his ceremonial gun belt didn't hold any extra clips.

A wave of rebels surged up the hill, their raised machetes fragmenting the sunlight. Verdoon was still trying to shove the last standing representatives over the hill when bloodied blades split the air around him. He sank to his knees and absurdly raised his hands to cover his head.

Verdoon felt a stinging pain, like ice poking into his flesh, and looked down to see his right arm laying on the dirt. He screamed and gazed up at the tall, lithe figure of a woman looming over him, the machete in her hand soaking the ground with fresh blood.

"Dragon," he uttered, recognizing her as the blade rose skyward and then chopped down toward him. "I spit on—"

A flash exploded before Verdoon's eyes before he could finish, dragging a sea of red behind it that swallowed the rest of his world.

# DAY ONE

# THE PRESENT

# CHAPTER 1

The ancient truck rumbled down the street toward the open warehouse. A bearded Palestinian wearing a *keffiyah* rose from a chair set in the shade of an adjacent alleyway and stepped to the curb, watching as the truck's bald tires scraped to a halt atop the rubble-strewn street. None of the residents of the West Bank town of Beit Jala could remember the last time the roads had been cleaned; not since Israeli tanks had left them cracked and broken in a parade-like show of force months before, that was certain.

The passenger side of the truck faced the warehouse, and a burly man with bulging, hairy forearms leaned out the window.

"Vasily Anatolyevich at your service, comrade."

Anatolyevich extended a meaty hand out the window and grasped the Palestinian's in a powerful grip that belied his years. He appeared to be between sixty and seventy with a shock of sterling silver hair brushed straight back and light blue eyes that looked strangely joyful. His skin was smooth and unfurrowed, pale except for a spider web of purplish veins that crisscrossed his nose and stretched across his cheeks.

"Any problems at the checkpoint?" the tall and sinewy Palestinian asked Anatolyevich. Just as his face wasted no expression, his frame carried no extra fat or flesh.

"I told you, comrade," Anatolyevich said with a wink and pulled his hand away, "we paid a premium for these papers, one of the advantages of being Israeli citizens. The officers at the checkpoint believe we're carrying supplies for Gilo," he added in his thick Russian accent, referring to a nearby Jewish West Bank neighborhood that had been annexed to Jerusalem. "Your name, comrade, I don't think I—"

"Abu."

"That's all?"

"It's enough."

Anatolyevich smiled again, a bit forced this time. "So long as the payment you brought is enough, eh, comrade?"

"Once I inspect the goods." The Palestinian who called himself Abu ruffled a hand through his thick beard. "Inside."

With that he gestured to the front of the warehouse where two other Palestinians wearing thin jackets had slid open a large bay.

Anatolyevich squinted into the dark interior and nodded. "Whatever you say, comrade. We need to hurry, though. I have another appointment I can't be late for."

"Business must be good."

Anatolyevich smiled. "Better than ever."

The Russian's driver backed the truck inside the warehouse in a series of fits and jolts. The man who called himself Abu walked beside the passenger window the whole time, as if to act as guide. His two companions slid the bay door closed behind the truck, sealing the large single room from all light except for a few old fixtures dangling from the ceiling, the bulbs of which flickered reluctantly to life. Shafts of sunlight spilled in through some scattered windows and a few rays penetrated the crumbling ceiling as well. Pierced months before by stray shells fired from Israeli helicopter gunships that had strafed the street after Palestinian machine gun fire shattered windows in nearby Gilo.

Anatolyevich and his driver climbed down from the cab

and joined one of the Palestinians at the truck's rear. Anatolyevich hoisted open the rear hatch to reveal a number of wooden crates and plastic tubular-shaped containers, innocuous save for the Russian markings along the sides.

"As promised," Anatolyevich beamed at Abu who had reappeared by his side.

The Palestinian reached past him and drew one of the crates forward.

"One hundred and forty-four Kalashnikov assault rifles," Anatolyevich narrated, as Abu popped the crate open, "packed one dozen per crate. Ammunition included in separate boxes, as requested. I threw in some extra as a sign of good faith."

Abu ignored the Russian's smile and tested the weight of the Kalashnikov. "Freshly oiled," he noted.

"And why not, comrade? After all, the guns are brand new. Never fired. Russian military issue, of which there is now extremely little need. Bad for the military of my former country. Good for business."

The Palestinian looked up at the arms dealer from where he squatted next to the rifles. "Apparently."

The Russian shrugged. "The military's loss is our gain, eh, comrade? They will never miss something they never had."

"What about the rocket launchers?"

Anatolyevich reached past him into the truck's cargo bay and yanked one of the plastic containers forward. His bulging stomach pressed against the hold of the truck as he strained against the container's weight, finally succeeding in bringing it to the edge at the expense of a slight scratch on the face of his gold Rolex watch. It didn't seem to phase him. Abu watched silently as the Russian peeled back two latches and then popped the container open.

"This is our latest model," he proclaimed proudly. "Not even issued to the Russian army yet." He grinned again. "Shipment has been delayed. Apparently my former government is behind on their payments!"

The Palestinian happily examined the tubular launcher

and the rocket fitted into a tailored slot just beneath it.

"The Israeli tanks and helicopter gunships have finally met their match, eh comrade?"

Abu returned his attention to the rocket launcher. "I might want more of these."

"As many as you like! Buy ten, I'll throw in one for free. Business is good. I can afford to be generous."

"With the prices you charge, I'm not surprised."

"Speaking of prices, comrade . . ."

Abu signaled one of his two subordinates who stripped a tattered rucksack from his back. "In American dollars, as instructed," he said, as the man handed it to Anatolyevich.

The Russian held the sack by his side, not bothering to open it.

"You're not going to count it?" Abu asked.

"Later over a vodka, while I go over your new shopping list. You should join me."

"Israel's borders are still closed to us."

"Precisely why I brought a bottle with me. I have it in the cab."

Anatolyevich started round the truck, brushing past the Palestinian who'd been holding the rucksack full of money. The man's jacket was pulled back slightly, exposing a pistol held in a shoulder holster. The Russian smiled at him, then at Abu again before climbing back into the cab.

He reached quickly across the seat, ducking his hand down and scraping it across the floor mat.

"Looking for this?" the man who called himself Abu asked from the window, holding a submachine gun up for the Russian to see.

"The vodka, comrade," the Russian said and forced a smile. "I was reaching for the vodka."

"It was in the glove compartment," the Palestinian said, holding the bottle up in his other hand.

"I—"

"You saw the pistol in Sergeant Khaled's holster. A Beretta nine-millimeter you recognized as standard issue for the Palestinian police. We used to get them from the Israelis."

"You . . ."

"I am Inspector Bayan Kamal of the Palestinian police." Ben Kamal laid the bottle of vodka on the warehouse floor. Still holding the submachine gun, he used his free hand to strip off his *keffiyah* and fake beard. "And you, Vasily Anatolyevich, are under arrest for illegal trafficking in firearms."

CHAPTER 2

Danielle Barnea had been following the man since his arrival in Israel the day before. According to his papers, his name was Ranieri and he was traveling on a Swiss passport. Danielle didn't think he was Swiss; German maybe, perhaps Italian.

She imagined he switched nationalities as often as names.

At the airport Ranieri's two suitcases had been searched in a private security section of Ben-Gurion reserved for diplomats and registered couriers. Danielle noted that he left the section carrying the same two suitcases he had brought in.

Ranieri had proceeded straight from the airport to a jewelry store called Katz & Katz on Dizengoff Street in Tel Aviv, just past the sprawling thirty-one-story complex of stores and apartments in Dizengoff Center. He carried the smaller of his two suitcases inside with him. Danielle kept her distance and watched from across the floor as he disappeared into a back room with a curly-haired man she guessed was one of the store's proprietors, her mind flashing back to the previous morning when she had awoken to find her former special operations commander, Dov Levy, seated in the corner of her bedroom.

"GOOD MORNING, Lieutenant," he said, just after she shut off her alarm. "Or should I say *Pakad*. Chief Inspector."

Danielle snapped upright, trying to push the cobwebs from her brain. "General Levy?"

"I was going to wake you," Levy said casually, bathed in the dark shadows cast by the drawn blinds. "But then I decided to wait. It's been a long time, hasn't it? Your father's funeral, I believe."

Danielle nodded, keeping the covers pinned to her body.

"What was that, five years ago now? My God, you haven't changed a bit."

Danielle ruffled a hand through her shoulder-length auburn hair, trying to tease it into shape, suddenly embarrassed by her appearance. She wiped the sleep from her eyes.

"So sorry to intrude like this," Dov Levy continued, "but I had to make sure we weren't seen together."

"My security system," Danielle started.

"Yes, state of the art. Your locks, too. It's good to see my old skills haven't deserted me." His voice sombered. "I was sorry to hear of your recent dismissal from National Police."

"Administrative leave," Danielle corrected, embarrassed by Levy's knowledge of her misfortune. "I've filed a grievance," she added even more lamely.

"I wouldn't expect it to accomplish much with Moshe Baruch in charge. You're too well known, too accomplished, too much of a threat to him in the high-profile position of a lead investigator. I never liked the bastard. If I was still in the government . . ."

"You mean, you're not?"

"Not anymore."

Danielle tried to smile. "I guess that makes two of us, then."

Levy looked down, then up again, his eyes sad. "I should never have dismissed you from the Sayaret." He shook his head. "Twelve years ago and it still pains me just as much."

"What happened in Beirut didn't leave you any choice," Danielle said, trying not to show that it hurt her even more.

"That doesn't make me feel any better. I feel I let you down, your father, too."

"I felt I let the two of you down."

"Then perhaps this is the chance for both of us to make amends. How would you like to return to special operations?"

Danielle felt herself about to jump at the opportunity, but pulled back. "I'm even more damaged goods than I was back then, General. With all that's happened . . ."

"You're a detective, Danielle, and a detective is what I need now."

"Why me, an outsider?"

"Because the insiders can't be trusted with this." Levy leaned back stiffly. "How much do you know about diamond smuggling?"

"A few cases have crossed my desk over the years."

"I'm talking about diamonds being used to finance civil wars in developing countries all over the world, and to fund terrorist groups like al-Qaeda."

Danielle shook her head.

"They're called blood diamonds," Levy continued. "Rough, unfinished stones smuggled into Israel from Africa and exchanged for huge amounts of weapons and ordnance."

"Where are the weapons coming from?"

"That's what we need to find out."

"We," Danielle echoed pointedly.

"This is a cabinet-level assignment," the former head of the Sayaret explained. "I can't tell you anything else because none of it is official. You won't find anyone in authority able to confirm anything. It's that way for a reason and that's the way it's got to stay until you bring me the proof I need." Levy leaned forward again, his knees creaking and a slight grimace spreading across his face. "All I have is the identity of a courier, and a report that he's due to arrive back in Israel tomorrow. It's a simple surveillance operation."

Danielle watched as Levy studied her with his still forceful eyes.

"What's wrong, Lieutenant?"

"Nothing."

"Have I come to the right place? If you want me to look elsewhere, if you have any doubts, just say the word."

Danielle had said nothing.

THE PROBLEM was, Danielle had realized in the past forty-eight hours, was that she *did* have doubts. Thirty-six had seemed so old a decade ago, ancient by Sayaret standards, yet now that birthday had come and gone. She had spent the morning of her birthday three weeks before filling out yet more papers in her attempt to return to active investigative status, believing she could be the same person she had always been. The same person who had served under Dov Levy in the Sayaret.

But she wasn't that person anymore. Too much had happened in the years since, too much baggage accumulated. Danielle felt no older physically. Still wore no makeup and could easily pass for a woman ten years younger. There was an edge, though, she recalled from that night in Beirut twelve years before that was missing now. Difficult to define. The way her heart could hold steady when bullets filled the air. How she could keep her breathing controlled when dug into the dirt or hiding in the back of the truck. Danielle couldn't remember the last time she had felt that edge. Certainly not since her return from New York almost a year ago.

*If the baby had survived, how old would he be now?*

Danielle did the calculations every day.

Yesterday Ranieri had reemerged from the jewelry store's back room before she could complete them. But he was no longer carrying the suitcase he had brought in, which made no sense to Danielle. So far as she knew, he had come here to pick something up, not drop something off. Clearly there was something going on here neither she nor Dov Levy had considered.

That night she had meticulously searched Ranieri's hotel room at the Dan after he left for dinner. She found nothing of note, certainly nothing to suggest he was carrying the large sum Dov Levy had told her to expect.

Then this morning Ranieri had returned to the same jewelry store on Dizengoff Street he had visited yesterday, and picked up something at the counter Danielle lingered too far away to identify. Outside the store, she kept her distance, aware that Ranieri was constantly scanning for tails and altering his step in an attempt to trip them up.

He drove to Jerusalem from Tel Aviv, and she followed him undetected through the Old City into an East Jerusalem square, or *souq*, dominated by the pungent smells of falafel, spicy kebab, and smoking ears of corn being sold from pushcart grills by smiling vendors. But Ranieri bypassed these in favor of a seat at an outdoor table on the patio of Café Europe, located on As-Zahra Street in the center of the square.

The quirky menu, featuring both Arabic and European fare, was posted on the café's stone façade. A waiter came and took Ranieri's order, returning a short time later with a small pot of coffee, tray of pastries, and a newspaper. The remaining tables were unoccupied, save for a Palestinian wearing a *keffiyah* and puffing clouds of thick white apple tobacco smoke from a chambered, water-cooled *nargeileh* pipe. A young boy maneuvered between the empty tables, pushing a broom across the cobbled surface.

Danielle's nerves jittered. She shrank back further amidst the shops and kiosks across the wide, pedestrian-only square, feeling the exchange Ranieri had come here to broker was about to take place.

*But how was he going to pay to obtain the weapons Dov Levy had spoken of?*

She watched Ranieri fumbling with his eyeglass case, taking the glasses out and then putting them back in. She was certain they hadn't been in his room the night before and she'd never seen him with them before. Ranieri opened the newspaper and began to read, returned the glasses once more to his pocket.

*Of course!*

Danielle felt revived, recharged, everything clear to her as she pretended to browse through various leather goods, handmade jewelry, and assortments of knickknacks dominating the storefronts, waiting for the contact the courier was expecting to arrive.

# CHAPTER 3

In the side view mirror, Anatolyevich watched as Sergeant Khaled and another Palestinian policeman took his driver into custody. He looked at Ben expressionlessly. "I've heard of you. . . ."

"Likewise." Stripping off the beard had taken the harshness from Ben's face. He had blue eyes and wore his dark hair still parted to the side seven years after his return to Palestine from the U.S. His angular face emphasized his high, ridged cheekbones that cast shadows over his eyes and left his gaze perpetually somber.

"You're the American . . ."

"I'm Palestinian."

". . . who came here to help train the Palestinian police. Your men are worthless," Anatolyevich said, and made a spitting motion.

"We caught you."

"You betray your own people in the process, comrade."

"That makes two of us."

Anatolyevich smirked. "Israel is not my country. Just a place to do business."

"Too bad the right of return includes Russian thugs."

Anatolyevich seemed unmoved. "We are much more than just thugs. You must know that. You think you'll have me in custody long?"

"You think Israeli officials will fight for your release?"

"No."

Ben nodded, understanding. "Your associates in the Russian mafia, then."

Anatolyevich scoffed, puffed air through his mouth. "There's no such thing, comrade. Don't be naïve."

"The same thing used to be said about the American version. Now, get out of the truck and keep your hands where I can see them."

Anatolyevich eased the door open and climbed down. "You're wasting your time."

Ben handed the submachine gun to the second of his officers and fastened handcuffs around Anatolyevich's wrists.

"You have a family, Inspector?"

Ben spun Anatolyevich around and glared at him. "My family is out of your reach."

"You really think anyone is out of our reach?"

"They're dead. Murdered by an animal even worse than you."

The Russian resisted slightly. "Pity."

"Let's go," Ben said, leading him toward the warehouse's bay door, as Sergeant Khaled hoisted it upward.

Ben nudged Anatolyevich and his driver into the street where another four Palestinian policemen were standing beside a pair of jeeps with guns drawn. A crowd had gathered, seeming to tense when Ben led Anatolyevich toward a waiting van. The crowd was composed of people of all ages, women as well as men. A few jeered him. Others thrust threatening fists into the air. Ben sensed trouble even before the jostling began, followed swiftly by the shouts, growing in cadence and intensity with each chorus.

"*Khay'in!*"

Traitors.

The stone throwing started next, stinging Ben's face and smacking his legs and torso. A larger rock struck Anatolyevich in the face and crumpled him. Ben hoisted the Russian up and calculated the remaining distance to the police van; even if they could reach it through the hail of rocks, he knew they'd have to drive over the crowd to get through it.

Ben held his ground briefly, shielding his face with an arm. More stones raked his head and shoulder. The crowd was approaching the police now, chanting the whole time.

"*Khay'in!*"

These uniformed Palestinian policemen who stood in their way seemed no different from the Israelis they had come to hate. The officers continued to backpedal, only the line of jeeps separating them from the crowd now. Some of the crowd began to rock those jeeps, trying to tip them over. The rest continued to advance, which left the officers no choice but to raise their weapons.

Before Ben could yell out not to fire, a rock struck his jaw, stunning him. His mouth filled with blood and the world went fuzzy and dim. The return of clarity brought with it the sight of assault rifles appearing at the front of the mob, thrust toward the pair of policemen who leveled theirs in kind.

"*No!*" Ben screamed, but the first shot drowned out his cry.

More shots followed, sounding like Fourth of July firecrackers. Ben watched two Palestinian police officers go down, followed by a third just after Anatolyevich's driver collapsed. Ben dragged the Russian toward the warehouse and yanked him back into the steamy air as soon as he jerked the door up along its squeaky rails.

"Come on! Come on!" he shouted to Sergeant Khaled and a single uniformed officer who were following him, slamming the door as soon as they were inside.

"What do we do, Inspector?" Sergeant Khaled huffed breathlessly.

"The back! We get out through the—"

Ben broke off his words when he heard glass shatter in a hail of bullets in the warehouse's rear. Then more gunfire slammed into the bay door, flooding the room with sunlight pouring through fresh holes dug out of the wood.

"A wonderful country you're building here, comrade," chided Anatolyevich.

# CHAPTER 4

Ranieri was on his fourth cup of Arabic coffee, still picking at the crisp *barazak* biscuits from his pastry platter. Danielle had been watching him for two hours now, having found a spot at the counter of an outdoor coffee bar across the square amidst a small group of American tourists. Her back was to the courier but she angled her chair to watch him in the glass of an adjacent storefront. He had begun checking his watch frequently. But it wasn't until he began pulling bills from his pocket to pay the check that Danielle took a deep breath and strode straight across the square.

Ranieri had just counted out the proper amount of bills when she casually took a seat opposite him at his table.

"I think there must be some mistake," he said, looking up in surprise.

"Since you were expecting someone else, of course. They've been detained," she bluffed. "I've come in their place."

Ranieri tilted his thin, almost skeletal face to the side. He tried not to appear rattled, but his brow furrowed and he pricked his bottom lip with his front teeth. "I don't know what you're talking about. You should leave. There are police about."

"Yes, I know," Danielle said and slid her identification across the table.

Ranieri sat back down and looked at her identification very briefly, fighting not to show a reaction. Danielle hoped he would not notice that the effective date on it had expired.

"I want to know who you were supposed to meet here," she said, hoping to distract him.

"No one."

"Where are the diamonds you brought into Israel?"

"I don't know what you're talking about," Ranieri said confidently, and shoved Danielle's National Police identification back at her before lighting a cigarette.

"Then you won't mind letting me take a look at your eyeglasses."

The man stopped puffing. "I don't wear glasses."

"They're in your right-hand jacket pocket. I saw you fiddling with them before I came over."

The man lay his cigarette down on the sill of the ashtray. "Why not arrest me then?"

"I'd rather we just talked . . . after you've given me your glasses. You must have picked them up at Katz & Katz in Tel Aviv this morning. I almost missed it."

"You have no idea what's going on here, do you?"

"I'm guessing it has something to do with that suitcase you left with the jeweler yesterday."

Ranieri started to reach for his cigarette, then changed his mind.

"How did you get your blood diamonds past customs?"

Ranieri's lips trembled. "If you know so much, you must know how far out of your league you are right now."

"We'll see about that."

"I can't give you the eyeglasses, or say anything about what I left with the jeweler. I'd be killed if I do. You think you know so much, you must know that."

"In that case, I'll just take the glasses after I place you in custody. Then the two of us will take a trip to Tel Aviv and see what they have to say at that jewelry store."

Ranieri shook his head very slowly. "They'll kill you, too, Chief Inspector."

Danielle didn't so much as flinch. "They won't be the first to try."

The courier's eyes flashed with fear, uncertainty, for the first time. But he didn't move, didn't even budge. Then, slowly, he reached into his pocket and removed a hard eyeglass case.

"Can I consider this a negotiation?" he asked, laying the case down on the table before him.

"Why don't we—"

The first bursts of gunfire made Danielle break off her words. She lurched up from her chair and spun in the same motion. Her initial thought was they must be aimed at her, the bullets fired by men providing backup for her quarry.

Then she saw armed figures rushing about the street, clacking off rounds wildly with their pistols as they ran. Two fell to the pavement and began to crawl off, fingers digging into the asphalt trying to pull themselves clear. Danielle kept her gun steady and swung back to the table.

Ranieri lurched forward and made a stab at the eyeglasses. But Danielle yanked the table back and toppled it over before he could reach them. She watched the case clatter against the asphalt at his feet, watched him lean over to grab it, and then kicked Ranieri hard in the stomach before his fingers could find the case. He crumpled backward into another table and spilled it over, scrambling away as soon as he regained his feet.

Danielle had started to reach down to retrieve the eyeglass case herself when she saw the boy with the broom standing in shock amidst the bullets whizzing past him. She dove through the air and tackled the boy, covering his body with hers as another burst of fire sprayed shards of broken glass from a nearby table over her back.

She twisted off the boy and lurched upward, pistol in hand, and found herself face-to-face with the glazed expression of a detective she recognized from National Police. He staggered forward, a pistol held loosely in his hand. Then his spine arched and he dropped to the curb, a victim of the wild spray of bullets.

*What was this? What was happening?*

More gunfire sheared the air around her as Danielle swept toward the detective, ignoring the danger. Stooped low over a spreading pool of blood to better cover him, she looked across the street just in time to see another figure steadying a submachine gun directly on her.

# CHAPTER 5

I think they're on my side, comrade," Anatolyevich taunted, as the siege on the warehouse continued. "I told you I wouldn't be in custody long."

Ben checked his watch out of habit. A rock had smashed its face, but he guessed a half hour had passed now since they'd taken refuge inside the building. He had tried summoning reinforcements on his cell phone, but the signal wasn't strong enough to reach anyone. The sound of sirens had begun to come and go more frequently in the last fifteen minutes or so, able to do nothing to prevent the crowd beyond from continuing to swell.

"You should surrender," Anatolyevich continued, and Ben did his best to ignore him. He had handcuffed the Russian to a support beam after dispatching one of the two remaining officers to keep the crowd from breaching the warehouse's rear.

"You said your name is Bayan Kamal," Anatolyevich said, as Ben remained poised by the side of one of the front windows. "Was your father the late Jafir Kamal?"

Ben swung back toward the Russian. "How do you know my father's name?"

Anatolyevich laughed hoarsely in response, the laugh of a man with a cigarette pack's impression worn into his lungs. His gaze drifted to the truck full of weapons. "It figures."

"If you've got something to say, say it."

Anatolyevich turned away from the truck and shrugged his shoulders. "Like father, like son. That's all."

"My father was a hero," Ben said, embarrassed at sounding like a child.

"That's what you think?" Anatolyevich shook his head. "You are as misguided as he was."

"I'm almost out of ammo!" Sergeant Khaled shouted from across the front of the warehouse, before Ben could respond to the Russian.

"And you, son of Jafir Kamal," Anatolyevich taunted, "are you out of bullets, too?"

"I'll save my last one for you," Ben threatened, knowing he was down to a single clip himself.

"Be like your father," Anatolyevich said snidely. "Surrender. Then maybe your countrymen won't cut your balls off while you're still alive."

He laughed again and rattled his handcuffs against the pole. Ben ignored him and used the opportunity of a lull in the shooting to snap his final clip into his nine-millimeter pistol.

"You better have a look at this, Inspector," Sergeant Khaled said suddenly.

Ben peered out the window at a pair of Mercedes sedans coming slowly down the street, seemingly oblivious to the gun battle into which they were heading. The cars eased to a halt and three of the doors in the lead Mercedes opened, allowing a trio of broad-shouldered, well-dressed men to emerge. Two held their ground in front of the car while the third opened a rear door, and Ben watched Colonel Nabril al-Asi emerge. The three broad-shouldered men fell into step behind the head of the much feared Palestinian Protective Security Service, as al-Asi buttoned his suit jacket and started leisurely toward the crowd.

The crowd backed off en masse. Those who were armed with more than stones lowered their weapons immediately. A few even began to retreat. Ben could hear the crowd murmuring through the shattered window, knew word must be spreading of just who this man was. Al-Asi never said a word, or made a gesture. Just kept walking, one hand tucked casually in his pocket, ignoring the violence that had been raging mere seconds before and could erupt again at any moment.

Halfway to the warehouse, the colonel stooped to pick up a stray rock and tossed it off the street. Kicked three more aside with his Cole-Hahn tasseled loafers before he reached the bay door and knocked.

"It's all right, Inspector. You can come out." Al-Asi's back was to the remaining crowd now, the three men who accompanied him watching it warily.

Ben moved to the bay door, unhitched the bolt, and slid it open.

"Good afternoon, Colonel," Ben greeted.

"Nice to see you, Inspector," al-Asi said. His salt and pepper hair was brushed neatly back. That and his perfectly trimmed mustache made him look like a young Omar Sharif. He had a smile to match the famed actor as well, but al-Asi wasn't smiling at all when he turned back to the crowd. "You can all go home," he said in a tone that left no room for misunderstanding.

Most of those still left began to backpedal or turned to take their leave. A few stubbornly held their ground.

"Now," al-Asi added, as if they were trespassing on his property, and these, too, started to walk away. "That's better," he said to Ben.

"How did you know I was here?"

"I didn't, until the reports of riot-like conditions in Beit Jala reached me. I had a feeling it might be you, even before your mayor called to ask if I could help."

"Another debt I owe you."

"We'll give this one to the mayor." Al-Asi gazed past Ben at the truck inside the warehouse. "I assume what he said about an investigation involving a Russian arms dealer was true. You should have consulted me."

"I had everything under control."

Al-Asi glanced at the still dispersing crowd. "So I see."

"Would you like to take my Russian friend into custody?"

Al-Asi clamped his hand around Ben's shoulder and steered him away from the open bay. "I'll let my men handle that. I need your help with something, if you don't mind."

"Of course not."

"Good. We'll take a drive. But there's something else that brought me here as well."

Al-Asi saw the blood sliding down from the gash on Ben's temple and handed him a handkerchief.

"It's about Pakad Barnea, Inspector," the colonel continued gravely. "And I'm afraid the news is not good."

# CHAPTER 6

The East Jerusalem police substation shares an old stone building with the local post office across from Herod's Gate and just down the street from the Rockefeller Museum. Danielle found herself the only occupant of the holding cells tucked deep in a damp, cold basement that had the feel of a root cellar and smelled of concrete and old sweat.

She had been alone in the cell for several hours when a soldier ushered an old man down the stifling hall. The old man's dress shoes clacked against the worn stone floor, and he looked distinctly uncomfortable as the soldier unlocked her cell door so he could enter.

"It's been a long time, Pakad Barnea."

Danielle rose stiffly, narrowing her gaze. "I remember you from my father's funeral."

The old man nodded. "He and I were close friends. There were some matters in his estate he entrusted to me. My name is Shlomo Davies."

"You're a lawyer," Danielle recalled. "How did you find out I was here? They wouldn't let me call anyone."

"A man in Shin Bet who knew your father contacted me shortly after your arrest."

"They told me they were going to keep things quiet."

"This is Jerusalem, Pakad. Nothing stays quiet long. Anyway," Davies continued, "they would have liked to keep things quiet to keep you from getting legal representation prior to your initial interview. I assume you've spoken to no one in authority yet."

"Not a word." Danielle fidgeted nervously. "Is there any way you can get me out of here?"

"On bail?"

"*Any* way."

"Not for the time being." The old lawyer frowned grimly. "Probably not at all."

"Then I need you to get a message to someone. Can I have your . . ."

"Of course," Davies said, handing Danielle his pen and legal pad from his briefcase.

She jotted down a name and handed the pad back to him.

Davies raised his eyebrows. "Dov Levy, the famous general?"

Danielle nodded. "He was my commanding officer in the Sayaret."

"I wasn't aware women served in the Sayaret."

"They don't anymore," Danielle told him, the cell feeling suddenly cold. "Not for a dozen years." Her voice lowered. "Not since Beirut . . ."

"*STRIKE TEAM in position.*"

Danielle Barnea heard Captain Ofir Rosen's words waft over the sounds of the sea, as the black rubber raft washed up along the rocky shore of the Mediterranean on the Beirut coastline. They had cut the engine a half mile from land and used paddles to reach the shallows, where they relied on the currents to propel them the rest of the way. The result was to make the black-clad figures huddled inside the raft undetectable in the misty night, even by anyone out for a stroll along the docks of the St. George yacht club just a few hundred yards away.

"*We are a go. Repeat, we are a go.*"

Rosen's whispered announcement would be relayed from the platform ship five miles away to the retrieval team standing by in Beirut to await the mission's completion.

Danielle was the last to climb out. She dropped waist-deep into the cold, choppy sea and pulled the raft up onto the beach after her. The gloves made her hands feel clammy, squishing against the rubber of the raft, and she shed them before rushing to join the rest of the assault team.

The commandos of the Sayaret were among the most elite soldiers in the world. Far more than the mere assassination squads with which they were often lumped, Sayaret operatives specialized in retaliatory strikes against terrorist leaders whose desire to see the destruction of Israel was boundless.

Sheik Hussein al-Akbar, their target that night in Beirut, had been linked with a trio of school bus bombings that had left forty Israeli children dead and another sixty maimed or crippled for life. The sheik had transformed a former luxury hotel across from the Beirut waterfront into his own personal villa. Intelligence from the advance team indicated the villa was laid out like a fortress and patrolled by a dozen soldiers.

Danielle was the only female member of tonight's strike team, and one of only three ever to have been chosen for duty in the elite Sayaret. She and the other commandos piled into an old rusted van, driven by a local double-agent who kept his speed slow along Allenby Street through a downtown Beirut dominated by bombed-out shells and abandoned buildings.

Just past the famed St. George's Hotel, the team pulled the traditional Muslim robes that were waiting for them in the van's rear over their wet uniforms and then checked each other to make sure their Uzi submachine guns, grenades, and pistols were effectively concealed. Danielle had just begun pulling her arms through her robes when Captain Rosen latched a hand on her wrist.

"Don't bother, Lieutenant," he said.

"Sir?"

"You're not coming. We can't take the chance." Rosen didn't give her a chance to respond. "You're a woman. No way a woman in this part of the world would be seen in the company of so many men. If you're recognized . . ."

Danielle nodded, disappointment leaving a heaviness in her stomach and a clog in her throat that made it hard for her to swallow.

"You'll handle backup and communication," Rosen told her.

The van pulled off Allenby Street and parked on El Sayad Street, a side road adjacent to the sheik's fortress. Danielle watched the members of the team spill out through the back of the truck and took her place quickly behind the monitor, put on her headphones, and sat down before a single large television screen. Captain Rosen's glasses were outfitted with a tiny camera that broadcast everything he saw back to the van where it would be taped. On the monitor Danielle could see the sidewalk sliding rapidly past and caught glimpses of other team members as they approached the entrance alongside the ten-foot stone fence enclosing the compound. The television screen showed an armed guard at the front steel gate of the former luxury hotel watching them with a mixture of confusion and consternation.

*"We are here for our meeting with the sheik,"* Captain Rosen said in Arabic.

*"I was not told to expect anyone."*

*"Then please call up to the sheik so this oversight can be corrected."*

The guard thought briefly, then reached for his walkie-talkie. On Danielle's television screen, a puff of smoke fluttered into the air at the same moment the *pfffffffft* of a silenced gunshot filled her ears. The guard's body was dragged aside before the other guards on the fortress grounds were any the wiser. Another of the team members stripped off his outer robes to reveal an identical uniform and took up the dead guard's position while the rest of the team continued on to the house.

Danielle watched Rosen's camera pan from side to side as his head turned to size up the opposition's strength and positioning. She catalogued both herself, playing along, willing the mission to go smoothly.

"Come on," she muttered to herself. "Come on . . ."

As if in answer to her command, the assault team fanned out to their assigned positions and the gunshots began. They came sporadically in short bursts, the sheik's guards picked off one at a time.

On screen the converted hotel drew rapidly into view. Rosen rushed the entrance, joined almost instantly by the two other commandos covering the front. Danielle could see them on either side of him as Rosen lifted his foot and slammed it into the door.

A series of rifle blasts turned Danielle's ears to mush and she stiffened, realizing the assault team had come under fire. The screen became jumpy as Captain Rosen dove to the floor and fired while rolling. The dizzying picture showed another of the sheik's guards hurtling over a second-floor railing.

More gunshots from other points in the house were followed by reports of downed enemy guards. In her mind Danielle kept count of how many had fallen, breathing slightly easier when all but one were accounted for, allowing the team to move on to the second floor for its final assault on Sheik Hussein al-Akbar himself.

An ambush laid at the top of the stairway by a final guard failed miserably and ended with his bullet-riddled body tumbling down the steps. The commandos had no reason to expect any more guards would be present up here, but still moved cautiously after reaching the second floor.

Danielle could see the empty hallway beyond, projected in jittery motion, evidence of Captain Rosen sweeping his gaze about. Suddenly she noticed the lighting change subtly, as if someone had cracked open a door, letting more light spill out from a room.

Danielle grasped her headset. "Pull back!"

"What? Say again," Rosen ordered.

"Pull back. Something's wrong. I think it's a trap."

"Negative on that. We are—"

Rosen's words ended when a figure wearing a long coat and a cowboy hat burst through the open door Danielle had noticed, springing in front of the advancing Israelis at the head of the hallway. Danielle was screaming into her headset in the same moment she recognized the twin submachine guns clutched in his hands.

The dual sprays of gunfire came as rickety clicks in her ears, as Captain Rosen's hidden camera broadcast unbroken flashes bursting from the shooter's muzzle bores.

Rosen went down first. His camera spun wildly before the view locked on the ceiling. Danielle could see nothing else when the continued clacking of twin submachine gun fire was answered futilely by the commandos whose desperate screams echoed in her ears.

"No," she muttered to herself, feeling stomach acid wash up her throat. "No!"

Danielle tore her headphones off and lunged out of her chair to grab a lonely Uzi from the wall. She was almost to the back door of the van when the team's Arab driver and local intelligence source grabbed her from behind.

"You can't!"

"Let me go!" Danielle ordered and threw him aside.

"You know what you have to do! You have your orders!"

Hand on the latch now. "Shut the fuck up!"

But she stopped. The man was right: There was an exact procedure to follow when things broke down, and that procedure dictated that she take flight to properly report the situation.

"All right, just get us out of here," Danielle ordered, turning away reluctantly from the door.

The Arab clambered back behind the wheel. Danielle returned to her station, prepared to shut the system down and secure the tape. The van had just pulled out onto Allenby Street, speeding away, when a face appeared on the television screen from inside the fortress. Cocked at a strange angle since it was clearly looking down at the body of Ofir Rosen, but clear enough for Danielle to recognize the cowboy hat she had glimpsed before and a face she would never forget.

Then the man smiled and tipped his hat, discolored along the brim by long-dried sweat, before the sole of a boot rose over the camera and swooped down with a thud that ended the transmission.

"I WAS discharged from the Sayaret upon my return," Danielle finished. "Reassigned to Shin Bet."

"You did nothing wrong."

"Procedure, unfortunately, in such matters."

"Your father couldn't . . . intervene on your behalf?" Davies posed tentatively.

"He was one of the men who wrote the procedure." She refocused her thinking. "But none of that matters now. You must tell Levy what's happened, if he doesn't know already."

Shlomo Davies rubbed his hands together, his eyes suddenly evasive as if seeing Danielle a different way. "Are you saying Levy had something to do with what you were doing in East Jerusalem?"

"Just contact him. Please," Danielle implored the old lawyer, fearing she had let the legend of the Israeli intelligence world down once again.

"Very well." Davies shrugged and flipped to a fresh page on his pad. He had been practicing law in Israel for four decades, semi-retired from a firm of which he had been a founding partner. "I have informed the Jerusalem police there will be no further discussions with you unless I am present and until you are formally processed," Davies told her. "That will probably take place tomorrow, at which point you will be transferred to a jail in the city center. I will be informed of that formality, now that I am your attorney of record." Davies tightened his expression, taking on the glare that had wooed Israeli juries for forty years. "I have the criminal division of my firm already working on motions and have subpoenaed all statements taken from witnesses at the scene."

"Thank you."

"For now, if you could just tell me what happened in East Jerusalem," the old lawyer said, readying his pen. "What led you to shoot and kill your superior, Moshe Baruch?"

# CHAPTER 7

W hat else?" Ben demanded, seated next to Colonel al-Asi in the back of his Mercedes.

"I told you, Inspector, it's—"

"She *killed* Commander Baruch. That's all you know?"

"Calm down, Inspector."

Ben fought to steady his breathing. Heat brewed beneath the surface of his skin. "I'm sorry, Colonel."

"No need to apologize. I understand, believe me. The cooperative ventures you and Pakad Barnea worked on were symbols of peace when it still seemed possible," al-Asi said grimly.

"I thought being together was still possible for us."

"And you have both paid a great price for making the effort."

"You've got to know something more about what happened. *Anything*."

Al-Asi shook his head. "I'm afraid not. Not yet. My contacts are working as we speak. Give them time."

"But—"

"We'll wait at my house, Inspector, while you lend me a hand with something."

Al-Asi had his driver take them to the Kharja neighborhood on the eastern edge of Jericho where a group of well-guarded homes, reserved for the highest officials in the Palestinian government, were clustered within view of the

Jordan River. Ben had never been to the colonel's home before, but was somehow not surprised to find it uniquely western in design, especially the lavish and exquisitely manicured grounds, when the vast majority of homes in the West Bank could barely squeeze gardens into their tiny yards.

Al-Asi led Ben around to the rear of the house. In a grassy area not far away from a decorative fish pool lay the disassembled clutter of what looked like an elaborate children's combination swing set and jungle gym.

"I was hoping you could help me put it together, Inspector. I'm having trouble reading the directions."

"You read English better than I do, Colonel."

Al-Asi frowned. "Not this time, apparently. Come, I'll show you," he said and headed toward the wood and steel components mixed indiscriminately with various tools atop the ground.

"We've got to put the base together first," Ben told him, picking out the largest posts.

"You haven't even looked at the directions."

"I've put a few of these together in my time, Colonel."

Al-Asi looked relieved. "Then my intuition was correct. I could have workmen assemble it, but I've been trying to immerse myself more in day-to-day things. Family life and so forth. I expect to have more time on my hands soon." He looked over the clutter and shook his head. "This was to be my first project."

"We'll have it put together in no time," Ben promised, starting to separate the pieces, as he had done on three separate occasions back in Detroit for his own family.

Al-Asi's cell phone rang and he excused himself to talk beneath the shade of a trio of young olive trees. When the conversation was over, he flipped his phone closed and returned to Ben, his expression grim.

"It happened in East Jerusalem. Commander Baruch was leading a detachment of plainclothes police on a security detail."

"What was Danielle doing on such a detail?"

"By all accounts, she wasn't supposed to be there—at least, not as part of Baruch's detail."

"You're saying she was there specifically to assassinate him?"

"I'm not saying that at all. That's what the *Israelis* are saying."

Ben fought to cool his emotions again. "How did you learn even this much, Colonel?"

Al-Asi stooped down, careful not to dirty his trousers, and began dragging his tools into a common pile. "I generously provided the Israeli authorities with the locations of two Palestinian dissidents to arrest in exchange for the information."

"If that's all you know, you were shortchanged."

"Not really. I've been trying to get rid of these dissidents myself for some time. In any case, this is all my counterparts in Israel know at the present time. Everything remains clouded. Pakad Barnea herself is not answering any questions."

"She doesn't deny the charges?"

"No, but neither does she affirm them."

Ben shook his head vehemently. "Danielle's not capable of such a thing."

"She's been under a great deal of pressure lately, Inspector."

"Don't you think I know that?"

"I was speaking of the past several months. When was the last time you saw Pakad Barnea?"

"You wouldn't ask that if you didn't already know the answer," Ben said and fit a pair of boards together, lining up the holes. "Hand me one of the bigger screws. One of those over there," he said, indicating the proper item to al-Asi.

"Twelve weeks ago," the colonel said, handing him the screw. "And much has happened since then, starting when Commander Baruch refused to reinstate Pakad Barnea to her former rank and position."

"That much I know about."

"Sed a grievance. I think it's still pending."

"It is. But the board is packed with Baruch's right-wing cronies."

"The mentality that currently prevails in Israel, unfortunately," al-Asi noted, sounding profoundly distressed. "There is no longer any room for an appeaser. The desire to work cooperatively is seen as a sign of weakness."

"Danielle and I haven't worked together in almost a year," Ben reminded the colonel. He slid the wooden dowel into place and then accepted a tack hammer from al-Asi to gently knock it into place.

"Pakad Barnea's reputation precedes her everywhere, Inspector."

"You're blaming me, my relationship with her?"

"I'm not assigning blame, merely explaining it."

"Our relationship is over."

Al-Asi watched as Ben turned the two assembled pieces over and handed him a second wooden dowel. "Is that what you told John Najarian, the businessman from Detroit so interested in employing you?"

"Another question you must already know the answer to, Colonel."

"You've decided to take his offer."

"I'm giving it strong consideration, yes." Ben leaned the first two pieces of the swing set against his thighs. "I should have known my phone was bugged."

"Not yours, Inspector," al-Asi said, flashing his typically wry smile. "His. Back in America by a colleague of mine in the CIA. I trust this unfortunate news about Pakad Barnea will force you to stay among us a bit longer," Colonel al-Asi added, after Ben had pounded in the second dowel.

Ben reached for a third piece of the base to join the first two. "I need to see Danielle."

"More chance of me putting this swing set together by myself than getting you into an Israeli jail as anything but a prisoner."

"Please, Colonel."

Al-Asi shook his head. "I'll do the best I can." He tightened his gaze, uncharacteristically seeming to search for words. "But after what happened in New York, losing the child and everything, I thought you were finally ready to let her go. You know, move on, as the Americans say."

"Could you, under the circumstances, Colonel?"

Al-Asi frowned. "I suppose not."

"Neither can I."

# DAY TWO

# CHAPTER 8

The trucks thundered over the rise and descended onto the village like stampeding cattle. Chickens scurried from their path and women scooped up small children, clutching them to their breasts and running for their mud shacks. A jeep led the convoy, followed by a pair of open troop carriers packed with military-clad men whose uniforms were a nondescript combination of fatigue and camouflage styles. A few had trimmed the sleeves from their shirts. Others wore only T-shirts stained dark with sweat. The second troop carrier had a covered wagon in tow, the kind of wagon that would normally be used to haul produce to and from the nearest markets.

The vehicles, old with loud clattering engines, rattled to a halt in the village center. Immediately the armed occupants of the trucks spilled out and began sweeping the town, herding the residents they came upon into the center of the street. The villagers cooperated without protest, their eyes wide with fear.

The village of Katani lay southwest of the larger town of Masiaka at the foot of Sierra Leone's Occra Hills. The temperature this time of year often stretched into the low hundreds and swarms of flies buzzed the air, attacking in bold and relentless droves that left people tired from the efforts to swat them. Flies were nothing new in this part of West Africa, but they seemed to thrive in the heat that had grown oppressive, lingering beyond its predicted end to turn the day air steamy and the nights too thick and soggy to offer any relief.

The troops continued to herd the town's inhabitants into the town square. A few, either blind or missing legs, lagged behind the others. Muffled sobs sounded. Women clutched babies tighter to their breasts, as soldiers poked at them with the muzzles of their rifles. Other soldiers began a methodical search of the village's structures, doing their best to destroy everything in their path.

Finally, a tall figure emerged from the back of the lead jeep. Her high combat boots kicked stones and debris from her path as she walked straight down the street, flanked by soldiers holding Kalashnikov assault rifles. A pistol was holstered on her hip, but she walked briskly with hands clasped behind her back. Her rigid posture further enunciated her over-six-foot frame. Her gait was more glide than strut, her motions smooth and light. Her skin was a rich brown color, unmarked by scars. Her hair, tied tightly atop her head, was the same black shade as her piercing eyes, which seemed almost whiteless in their intensity.

The woman, whose uniform identified no rank, walked past the decaying and decrepit buildings in disgust, ignoring the flies and wrinkling her nose at the stench rising from the poor sanitary conditions. She shook her head, her expression honestly pained as she watched the last of the villagers squeeze against each other atop gravelly, clay-colored dirt marred with tire ruts in which fetid water steamed in the sun. Several were missing hands; still more, entire arms.

The woman moved to the center of the throng, stopping briefly to stroke the head of a baby before she moved on and began to speak.

"I am General Latisse Matabu, leader of the Revolutionary United Front, voice of the people of Sierra Leone. I know you have all heard of me. Most of you probably fear the RUF. You have probably heard stories of our ruthless-ness and cunning."

She stopped and aimed her next words at a man supported by makeshift crutches with a stump for a right leg.

"As some of you can attest, these legends are correct. I have very likely done all the things you have heard about at one time or another, but I have never done them without good reason. And many of the atrocities for which I am blamed occurred before I took over the Revolutionary United Front that fights on your behalf." Matabu continued walking amidst the crowd, hands clasped casually behind her back. "Still, President Kabbah's government would have you believe I am a villain."

General Latisse Matabu stopped and hardened her gaze, meeting the stares of those she passed and watching them cower before her.

"Perhaps they are right. But this is war. And your village stands at a crucial junction between the Occra Hills and our RUF strongholds in Kono. I have heard the government troops have been using your town as a staging post to launch operations against my forces. I have heard they are planning an offensive that would make your village a stronghold."

Matabu pulled a foil pouch from her pocket and held it high overhead for the villagers to see. "This was found two days ago just outside Katani. A chewing tobacco pouch, its remnants still fresh. *American* chewing tobacco." She stopped directly in front of a toothless old man. "Is it yours?"

The old man shook his head.

"Yours?" to a younger man.

The young man shook his head.

A woman next with a baby in her arms. "Yours?" And, without waiting for a reply, Matabu backed away, nodding. "I didn't think so. But if the tobacco does not belong to anyone in this village, who does it belong to? Who drank the whiskey from bottles we found smashed in the woods?

Who ate the rations from the cans my soldiers found in the marsh?"

Matabu began moving again, stopping before a number of terrified villagers and prompting, "You?"

Not surprisingly, she received no response.

"So what am I left to think? That a peaceful village like yours is harboring not only my enemy, but your own? Interlopers, invaders from the outside hired to do the devil's work."

A strange smile crossed her face, as if she thought of something shared only with herself. "Perhaps the devil is not so bad. In many parts of my country, I am referred to by another name:

"The Dragon," Latisse Matabu finished.

She stopped in front of the crowd, her soldiers standing their posts diligently several yards away. "If this is how my enemies choose to think of me, then so be it. But the people of this village do not have to be my enemies. If you are my friends you will tell me what you know of the soldiers you have been harboring. Their weapons, their number, and their movements." She kicked at some brownish water that had pooled in a rut. "Your streets tell me they have driven their vehicles down them. Your farmland tells me their boots have trampled your land. The Revolutionary United Front does not seek your involvement. We seek only your cooperation in ridding our nation of the pestilence the United Nations and the United States have forced upon it. So what will it be? Who will speak?"

A few of the villagers exchanged glances. None spoke.

"Your silence confirms my suspicions," Latisse Matabu resumed, "and that confirmation means your village must be punished unless I am satisfied. Punished in a way that will destroy it forever. So speak now or pay the price."

Still no one spoke. Matabu shook her head and looked up to the sky, as if for guidance.

"I provided a chance for your village to survive and you squandered it. I gave you a choice, something the government troops did not." Latisse Matabu shook her gaunt, angular head. "Now you must pay for your obstinacy."

With that, she gestured toward a pair of soldiers nearest to her. Instantly the men hurried to the wagon hitched to the second troop-carrying truck. One of them yanked back a tarpaulin to reveal a large steel-colored crate; coffin-sized, only higher. The other approached the crate, only to lurch backward when it seemed to move, as if something were shifting about inside.

The two men looked at each other, exchanged a nervous glance, then unhitched the wagon and dragged it toward their leader.

"You think I do not know what loss is? You think I do not know what it is to suffer?" Latisse Matabu challenged the villagers clustered before her, eyes bulging in terror as they watched the soldiers stop the wagon holding the crate directly in front of the Dragon. "I know these things all too well, better than any of you will ever know them. That is where my strength comes from, a strength I would have used to liberate each and every one of you." She shook her head in honest disappointment. "But now you have betrayed me, and you have betrayed your country. And for that you must pay."

Matabu reached for her gun belt and the villagers shrank back in fear, whimpering en masse. But all she grabbed was a chisel with which she began to pry open the crate, as one of her captains approached from the structures her soldiers had been dutifully searching.

"General," he began softly, "there is no trace of the Americans."

"Of course there isn't. They only passed through here, never intending to stay."

He looked at her quizzically. "But I thought—"

"What you thought doesn't matter. What matters is I am setting an example to make sure none of the villages between here and Kono dare support our enemies again."

Then Latisse Matabu returned her attention to the residents of Katani.

"Behold the end of your world," she said and started to lift off the top of the crate. "Behold the sight of hell itself."

# CHAPTER 9

Shlomo Davies steadied the legal pad atop his legs. "Where should we begin?" he said, seated on the cot alongside Danielle.

True to Davies' prediction, the night before she had been transferred to this six-by-eight cell in Megrash Haruseim, the newer of the two police stations on Jerusalem's Jaffa Road and the only one equipped with a jail. The concrete had been cold to the touch then, but baked quickly under the heat of the morning sun. The cell stank of urine and sweat and the last occupant's misery.

"Is General Levy coming? Did you get him on the phone?" Danielle asked eagerly.

"I'd like us to talk about what happened in East Jerusalem first," the old lawyer said instead of responding. He kept dabbing his nose with a handkerchief, as if that might do something about the stench. "You were not part of the team led by Commander Baruch?"

"I told you that yesterday. What about General Levy?"

"And Baruch had no knowledge of your presence?" Davies asked, instead of responding.

"No, at least as far as I know."

Davies made some notes and looked up. "Was your presence in East Jerusalem authorized by someone other than General Levy?"

"No."

"It was an independent investigation then."

"I suppose so, yes."

"Which your current status strictly prohibits."

"Technically."

This time the old lawyer made no note. "Let me explain something, Pakad. In order to build your defense, I need to establish the totality of the picture. For instance, if we can show you were in East Jerusalem pursuing legitimate concerns, as opposed to a reckless pursuit of Commander Baruch, we will find ourselves on much firmer ground."

"Reckless pursuit . . . Is that what they're calling it?"

"It's a legal term."

"Which means premeditated murder."

Davies let Danielle see him flick his pen closed. "Is that what happened?"

"Not in any way."

"Then we need to introduce the true purpose for your presence somewhere you didn't belong."

"I keep telling you, General Levy can corroborate everything."

Davies shook his head slowly. "No, he can't."

"But you said—"

"I didn't finish, Pakad. General Dov Levy died six months ago."

# CHAPTER 10

Ben looked at the clothes spread around the living room floor of his small apartment in Jericho. Neat piles with the creases perfect, the briefs and socks folded. It was the only order Ben felt he was in a position to enforce.

There were six other apartments squeezed into the building, all of them occupied by families. He was the only person who lived alone and, come to think of it, he couldn't think of another Palestinian who did not share his home with others. Mostly family, and sometimes friends. Sometimes out of convenience, but increasingly out of necessity.

As the Israelis bulldozed more homes and raided an increasing number of towns in search of suspected agitators, more and more Palestinians were forced to seek shelter with family and friends. The result was a society layered upon itself and clustered in tiny, fearful pockets. Children seldom played outside anymore. The few businesses that remained open lacked customers capable of paying for their wares.

Things had been different when Ben had first returned to Palestine almost eight years ago. There had been hope then. For the first time in generations, maybe ever, the Palestinian people could look forward and see a future. But that future had dissolved in an endless cycle of violence that seemed to know no end.

Eight years ago, upon his arrival, it had taken Ben weeks

to muster the resolve to unpack, and now it was taking him a similar amount of time to pack up his meager belongings to leave. He kept putting it off just as he kept postponing the phone call to John Najarian in Detroit to accept Najarian's offer to work for his personal security firm in the United States. But Ben couldn't leave now, not while Danielle was in an Israeli jail, and so his clothes would remain stacked on the floor and furniture in a kind of limbo trapped between coming and going.

In spite of their recent estrangement, Danielle remained the only thing keeping him in Palestine. Somehow he couldn't bear the thought of being half a world away from her; certainly he could bear being that distance from anything else he had found here. Enemies almost entirely. Very few friends, although Colonel al-Asi more than made up for that.

While the colonel could keep Ben safe from his many enemies, he couldn't make the Palestinians Ben had returned to help accept him. From the ones who could never bring themselves to trust an outsider to those who hated him for his knowledge, skills, and relentless efforts to modernize their thinking. Palestine, though, was no place for modern police work. The need was there, yes, but not the desire on the part of those charged with the duty. The Palestinian police, he had found, could not separate themselves from the masses out of which they had risen. The vast majority had stopped patrolling the streets in favor of leading violent attacks upon those same streets, in many cases taking up arms supplied by the Israelis against them.

As for the detective force Ben had envisioned as elite enough to rise above this fray, too many of the recruits he had personally selected had taken their skills to the paramilitary Tanzim or President Arafat's elite Force 17, or been transferred to more prestigious security services. They, too, had turned their weapons and training against Israel instead of the criminal element in Palestine they had been conceived to control.

Ben began to feel he had been used, a public relations

tool toyed with for a time and then discarded when public relations ceased to matter. The final straw had come when the Israelis shelled the police academy outside of Jericho, destroying the one thing that gave him hope in his own pursuits.

Danielle was all he had left, even though he didn't really have her at all anymore. The irony of coming home to Palestine only to fall in love with an Israeli . . . Ben would be leaving with more than he came with; it just didn't feel that way.

Ben paced the small apartment, careful to avoid the neat stacks of clothes. Only one other time in his life had he felt this helpless, and that was the night he had come home in Detroit to find a serial killer called the Sandman had slain his wife and children. He had shot the Sandman dead and felt no better as a result. Returned home from his family's funerals to find he had worn two different color socks, accounting for the anal nature of the clothes piles lining his living room like speed bumps to slow down his emotions.

His cell phone rang. Ben plucked it off the desk and pressed it against his ear.

"Yes?"

"How is the packing coming, Inspector?" greeted the voice of Nabril al-Asi.

Ben resisted the urge to draw back the blinds to see if the colonel was standing down in the street, watching him.

"Very slowly."

"Good. I'm glad. You won't need much for where you're going tomorrow anyway."

"And where's that, Colonel?"

"Jerusalem, Inspector, to see Pakad Barnea."

# CHAPTER 11

That's impossible!" Danielle insisted, her breathing suddenly rapid. "Levy *can't* be dead!"

"I'm afraid he is."

"But I *spoke* to him!"

Shlomo Davies shook his head. "It couldn't have been Levy. Perhaps you were being set up, Pakad."

"I wasn't being set up," Danielle insisted, recalling the conversation in her bedroom just four days earlier. Could the man she thought was Levy have been an imposter? No, it *had* to have been him. She took a deep breath, feeling the cell's musty stench coat her throat. "I'm telling you, Levy's *alive!*"

Shlomo Davies frowned. "And it was what the man claiming to be Levy said that led you to East Jerusalem?"

Danielle nodded. "Yes."

"Go back to the start of the gunfight. Could you tell where the gunfire was coming from?"

"All directions, it seemed."

"Palestinians and Commander Baruch's people exchanging bullets."

"That's what I assumed."

"There's a problem."

"What?"

"Not a single Palestinian gunman was found on the scene; none arrested, wounded, or killed."

Danielle looked baffled. "I don't see how that could be."

"According to the reports I've read, that's what it is. When did you first see the commander?"

"I saw other National Police officers I recognized first, in addition to the one I dragged to safety after he'd been shot."

Davies made a notation on his legal pad. "That detail was left out of the scene reports."

"The officer was badly wounded. I saw Commander Baruch for the first time while I was crouched over him."

"Did Commander Baruch see you?"

"We looked directly at each other. Then he raised his gun and pointed it straight at me. He was getting ready to fire. I could see it in his eyes. I thought when he realized it was me, he would . . ."

"Go on," Davies prodded.

"He was about to shoot me. I'm sure of it."

"And you . . ."

"Fired after he did."

"That's not what the witnesses say."

"What *do* they say?"

"That you fired at Baruch first. That you shot the policeman you claim you were protecting."

"No! Ask the policeman, for God's sake! Just ask him!"

Davies swallowed hard. "I can't. The last of the wounded died in surgery last night."

Danielle felt her heart skip a beat.

"Is there anyone else who can corroborate your version of the events? What about this man you came to East Jerusalem to see, the one in the café?"

"He got away."

"It occurs to me that he may have witnessed at least a part of this."

Danielle almost laughed. "He's not about to testify in my behalf."

"Who was he, Danielle?" the old lawyer persisted. "What was so important about him that you risked everything to pursue an unauthorized investigation?"

Danielle stopped, remembering something. It had slipped her mind up until now, clouded over by the terrible reality of what had taken place the day before.

*The eyeglass case! The courier, Ranieri, had placed it on the table just before the shooting started! Danielle remembered tipping the table over to keep it from his grasp. . . .*

Danielle looked back up at Shlomo Davies. "What if I could prove the validity of what I was doing in East Jerusalem?"

The old lawyer seemed to perk up. "Anything that can prove you did not go there with the express purpose of killing Commander Baruch would be extremely helpful in making our case."

*The eyeglasses had spilled off the table when she shoved it aside once the shooting started. Danielle was certain of that, just as she was certain that Ranieri had run off without retrieving them!*

"Do you have the name of the café in East Jerusalem?" Danielle asked Davies.

He flipped through his notes awkwardly, suddenly confused. "I'm sure I must have written it down somewhere . . ."

"They may have found a pair of eyeglasses on the ground in a black case."

"Eyeglasses?"

"Please, just ask them. But don't call. Go there in person."

"To East Jerusalem?"

"Or send someone you trust. Tell him to say the glasses were his, or yours, and he's come to retrieve them."

Davies narrowed his gaze. "What's so important about these glasses?"

"They're the key, Mr. Davies. They can prove everything I'm saying is the truth."

# CHAPTER 12

Relax," said one of the guards, trying to reassure Ranieri, "you have nothing to worry about. You're safe. Have some food," the guard added, hovering over a luscious tray of seafood which included chilled whelks and periwinkles layered next to tiny *crevettes grises* and lobster tails.

"No, thank you," he responded meekly.

The big man was one of four assigned in three separate shifts to watch him at the Antwerp Hilton, the city's newest, and most secure, luxury hotel. Following the gun battle in East Jerusalem, Ranieri had fled Israel and flown to Antwerp by way of Athens, seeking refuge. He had no idea what had gone wrong yesterday, only that the meeting's disastrous results would leave him a marked man since he had lost what he had come to exchange.

Antwerp was his best possible destination because the only item of value Ranieri had left was information that would be of extreme interest to powerful forces headquartered in the city. Enough interest, anyway, to assure he was kept safe and alive long enough to tell his tale.

He had met them early this morning in the Grote Market located in the heart of the Old Town district. As instructed, he stood near the huge fountain set in the center of a triangular square lined on two sides by beautifully restored guild houses and on the third by the ancient Town Hall.

Ranieri didn't like the feeling of being enclosed, especially after yesterday's incident in the East Jerusalem *souq*.

But the men he was expecting showed up on time and brought him straight to the Hilton, where he had been safely under guard ever since. His debriefing was scheduled for first thing tomorrow morning. Ranieri had the terms for his cooperation well rehearsed, hoping he could summon the strength to issue them forcefully.

Ranieri retreated into the suite's bedroom to change into some of the new clothes his guards had obtained for him, but hesitated at the sight of a window washer wearing a strange hat busily scraping at the windows with his rubber squeegee.

"I have to use the bathroom," he said, back in the living room.

The head guard looked bemused, winked at his fellows. "Be my guest."

Ranieri entered the bathroom and closed the door behind him. He splashed water on his face and, embarrassed, left the water running when he sat down on the toilet, wishing he had brought something in with him to read.

*It's nice to worry about something unimportant*, he thought, looking forward to tomorrow. He washed his hands carefully before opening the door and stepping back into the living room section of the suite.

An unfamiliar man sat on a chair turned to face the bathroom, a pair of workman's boots crossed casually before him with the heels digging into the carpet. Ranieri assumed the man was part of the next security detail.

Until he saw the four men assigned to the last detail sprawled upon the plush carpeting, dead.

Ranieri cowered back against the wall.

The stranger stretched his legs and arms comfortably, revealing a pair of semi-automatic pistols holstered beneath his jacket. He had a face as worn as drum-dyed leather. Stringy dark hair peeked out from beneath a cowboy hat, the brim of which was darkened by sweat.

*The hat!*

Ranieri had seen it before, just moments ago in the bedroom.

*This man was the window washer!*

"Got in through the bedroom," the man explained, as if reading his mind. "Cut through the window glass with a little laser thing and climbed inside. Your baby-sitters never knew what hit them. Shoulda had a man posted in the bedroom, too." He pulled his legs in and leaned forward in his chair. "You know why I'm here?"

Ranieri remained still.

"People I work for can't have you go blabbing everything to the folks here in Antwerp. That'd make things uncomfortable for everyone. Now, let's try again. You know why I'm here?"

Ranieri nodded fearfully.

"That's better. You got something that don't belong to you. People I work for want to take delivery."

"I was in East Jerusalem as planned!" Ranieri ranted. "They never showed up!"

"Yeah, a real cluster fuck's what I heard. But we can put all that behind us now soon as you turn over the eyeglasses."

"I—I—"

"You—you *what*?"

"I don't have them."

"Really?"

"An Israeli police detective followed me to East Jerusalem. She approached me at the café."

"She?"

Ranieri nodded. "A woman."

"Most 'shes' tend to be."

"She knew about my meeting. She knew everything."

"Not my problem."

"I'm not making this up! I *couldn't*! She was holding a gun on me. I placed the glasses on the table. Then the gun battle began. The table toppled over. I tried to retrieve the glasses. But I couldn't find them. If I had stayed any longer, I would have risked being caught."

"That was just the down payment anyway."

"Right."

"People I work for are more interested in where they can find the balance."

Ranieri swallowed hard. That was information he had intended to save for the officials he was supposed to meet tomorrow, the leverage he needed.

"I'm waiting," the cowboy said.

Ranieri looked at the widening pools of blood beneath the four men the cowboy had already slain. "Why should I tell you anything? You're going to kill me anyway."

The cowboy nodded slightly. "Maybe."

Then in a blur of motion, from a seated position, he drew his weapon and shot Ranieri in the knee. The courier's legs collapsed and he crumpled to the floor, staring in shock at the blood spreading down his leg through the hole in his pants.

"Then again," the cowboy said, "maybe not."

Ranieri waved his hands frantically before him, unable to take his eyes from the still-smoking gun held casually by the cowboy. "Please! Please! I'll talk!"

"I figured you would."

Ranieri gasped in pain, trying to recover the breath the shock had stripped from him. "I followed the usual procedure! Made the drop at a jeweler on Dizengoff Street in Tel Aviv. Katz & Katz this time. The shipment must still be there!"

"That all?"

"It's the truth!"

"Okay," the cowboy said, and raised his gun barrel just enough to shoot Ranieri in the forehead.

The courier's head snapped backward and cracked into the wall before his body slumped, spasmed once, then stiffened.

The cowboy stood up and pulled a cell phone from his pocket. As he dialed a number, he wandered over to the tray holding the assortment of seafood.

"It's Black," he said when the line on the other end was

answered. "Things are all wrapped up here."

"Very good, because you're needed back in Israel."

"I know. Jewelry store in Tel Aviv's apparently got the rest of what you're looking for."

"There's something else that requires your attention first."

Jim Black swept a pair of tiny things that looked like shrimp off the tray and into his mouth. "Fuck!" he gasped, spitting them out.

"What?"

"Nothing. Goddamn fish tastes like shit, that's all. You can buy me dinner when I get back."

"Just hurry."

"No problem. What else you need me for?"

"An Israeli detective. A woman. Is that a problem?"

"Depends how good she is."

"She's in jail."

"Then it's not a problem," said Jim Black.

# DAY THREE

# CHAPTER 13

M r. Davies will see you now, sir."

Ben Kamal rose from the couch in the reception area of the Tel Aviv law firm located in a small renovated building across from the Hilton Hotel. He smiled and followed the receptionist to an office down a long, sweeping hallway. She had already inspected his identification papers and, not surprisingly, didn't give them so much as a second look. After all, the documents Colonel al-Asi had provided were perfect in every way; more than forgeries or reproductions, they appeared to be authentic.

The receptionist escorted Ben into the office of Shlomo Davies, the lawyer representing Danielle Barnea, and closed the door behind her. Davies did not rise upon seeing Ben enter. He looked harried and worn, an old man long past the age of coping with high stress and sleepless nights. The wisps of hair that clung to the side of his head were poorly combed, his eyes drawn and blotched with red as if he'd been looking at too much he didn't need to see anymore.

"Thank you for meeting me, Mr. Davies," Ben greeted.

The old man frowned and didn't bother offering him a chair. "I got a call today from a high-ranking government official telling me that you were coming and I should see you. Very well. I've seen you. Now, if you'll excuse me,

Mr. Kaplan, I have another matter urgently requiring my attention."

"I know. That's why I'm here."

"Why *you're* here?"

"My name isn't Kaplan, sir, it's Kamal. Inspector Bayan Kamal of the Palestinian police."

Davies started to stand up, then abandoned the effort. "What is the meaning of this? What is this about?"

"Danielle Barnea."

The old man peered at Ben, narrowing his eyes. "You said your name was Kamal?"

"Yes."

He nodded. "I think I understand."

"I doubt very much that you do, sir."

"You and Danielle Barnea . . ."

Ben let the comment stand as it was.

"You must have very powerful friends, Inspector Kamal."

"One, anyway."

"Often that is all a person needs. But believe me when I tell you there is nothing you can do to help Pakad Barnea."

"I just want to see her."

"I'm afraid that's impossible."

"Unless I was an outside counsel, retained by your firm to lend assistance. Check my papers, Mr. Davies. It's all been provided for," Ben said, and slid the documents Colonel al-Asi had given him across the table.

The old man flipped through them, suitably impressed. "This powerful friend of yours?"

"One is all it takes, just as you said."

Davies snickered, raising his lip enough to reveal a missing bridge on the left side of his mouth creating a toothless gap. "I don't want Pakad Barnea distracted."

"I want to help."

"And I already told you there's nothing you can possibly do."

Ben held his ground directly in front of Shlomo Davies's

desk. "Your inquiries have turned up certain rather striking discrepancies in Danielle's story, haven't they?"

"How did you—"

"The policeman she rescued died in surgery, didn't he?"

"His wounds were grave."

"Or maybe he died because he was the only one who could confirm Danielle's story about what happened."

"There were other policemen on the scene I intend to subpoena."

"You won't be able to interview them any more than you'll be able to find any of the Palestinian gunmen who opened fire."

"Are you saying Danielle was framed?" Davies posed incredulously.

"I'm saying someone is doing their best to cover up the truth. And there's something else," Ben continued, repeating what al-Asi had learned the previous night. "There's no log of Commander Baruch ever entering East Jerusalem."

The old man's eyes widened, his expression losing its resolve. "I haven't had time to check those records."

"It doesn't matter. The logs will be altered by now to account for the commander's presence, I can promise you that."

"And can you tell me why?"

"Let me speak to Danielle, and maybe I'll be able to."

"She's already told me everything she knows, even about—" Davies' face paled. "My God . . ."

"What is it?"

"I just remembered something. Pakad Barnea told me to check it out. It just slipped my mind . . ."

"Check *what* out?"

"The café in East Jerusalem she was sitting at when the shooting started. Pakad Barnea said something about a pair of eyeglasses in a black case, that they were the key."

"Eyeglasses?"

Davies nodded. "Belonging to this man she'd been meeting. She asked me to go back there, see if anyone had found them."

"Then what are we waiting for?"

# CHAPTER 14

I have the results of your latest blood test," the doctor said, as he entered General Latisse Matabu's office inside the Revolutionary Unified Front's headquarters in Kono.

The RUF controlled this region of Sierra Leone and made no effort to distance themselves or hide. If anything, under Matabu's guidance, the RUF had become increasingly open in their dealings, preparing for the political legitimacy that would come with their eventual rise to power. Now that peace talks had broken down, President Kabbah would not be able to stem the tide forever and sooner or later the American-led peacekeeping effort would tire of ineffectuality and senseless loss of life. They would leave and there would be nothing standing in the way of the RUF taking Makeni, Freetown, and the other more populous areas. The power in Sierra Leone would be returned to its rightful heirs.

Matabu rose slowly from behind her desk. "It is not like you to be so abrupt, Doctor Sowahy."

The doctor, a wizened old man with skin like worn tar and a shock of white hair, handed her a piece of paper. "I want you to read this for yourself."

Matabu scanned it quickly. "This is supposed to concern me?"

"It should."

She handed the paper back to him. A broken back suffered many years before had left Sowahy permanently hunched over and made reaching for anything an effort. "I have more important things to worry about now."

"I want you to start taking the medications."

"Why?"

"So you can live to rule this country."

"I already rule this country. I only lack the title."

Dr. Sowahy's gaze was as grave as his voice. "You're dying, General."

Matabu smiled. "If I could be killed, Doctor, I would have died many times by now." Her voice faded slightly. "Once in particular, as I'm sure you recall."

The old doctor scolded her with his eyes. "I treated you afterwards."

"A shame you couldn't heal what was truly broken inside me."

"You continue to punish yourself for something you had no control over, that wasn't your fault." The doctor grabbed the edge of Matabu's rattan desk to support himself. "Well, I am as stubborn as you are, and I am also older and more patient. I brought the medications with me."

"And you can take them with you when you leave."

Sowahy tightened his gaze. The whites of his eyes were streaked with red lines. He blinked rapidly. "You see that man, that animal, in everyone you kill, General. But you can only kill him once."

"It didn't last long enough the first time, Doctor."

A loud knock sounded on the door before Sowahy could respond.

"Enter!" Latisse Matabu ordered, holding her gaze on the old doctor who still saw her the same way he did the day she'd been carried into his office and laid on his examination table a decade before.

"General," an RUF sergeant said, barging in, "we have just heard from our contacts in Israel. There was a problem with the exchange in East Jerusalem two days ago. A very serious problem. . . ."

# CHAPTER 15

"I f you don't mind, Inspector," Shlomo Davies said on the West Jerusalem side of Damascus Gate, "I'll wait for you here."

"I don't blame you," Ben Kamal said, as the old lawyer took a seat on a stone bench.

The violence of two days ago had led to a substantially stepped-up presence of Israeli soldiers in that section of the ancient city. The result, effectively, was to close the last bastion of tourism still available for Palestinians. Even though East Jerusalem was not technically under their sphere of control, it was Palestinian shopkeepers and store owners who would pay the price for fear, intimidation, and warnings from Israeli authorities for shoppers and tourists to stay away.

Ben passed through Damascus Gate into the main *souq*, typically lined with food and trinket vendors. The potent smells of spices and ripe fruit, pungent and sharp, were usually enough to advertise their presence. But the streets of East Jerusalem were virtually barren, the operators of kiosks, storefronts, and the produce market prohibited from entering the city for the second day in a row.

On an adjoining street, Café Europe, where Danielle had h the man she had refused to identify for Davies, ty, too. Its wooden outdoor tables, covered in colorful cloth, were all unoccupied, not a single waiter in sight to serve them.

Ben took a seat at one of the tables, imagining Danielle sitting here just before the gun battle. He tried to picture the case containing the eyeglasses that were so important to her spilling off the toppled table. He looked beneath his table just to make sure the glasses weren't there, bemused by the act's futility as he tried to wait patiently for a server to approach him. So far there was only a young boy wearing a man-sized apron sweeping up areas that clearly did not beg to be swept. The boy smiled and Ben flipped him a hefty coin.

"*Ahlan*," a smiling waiter greeted Ben in Arabic, looking surprised to have a customer.

"*Blackran*," Ben replied, returning his welcome.

The man beamed at being addressed in Arabic and readied his pad. "What can I get for you?"

"A cup of Turkish coffee and a portion of *kunafeh*," Ben ordered, referring to a pastry of cheese topped with wheat flakes and soaked in honey.

"Right away, *sidi*."

"A question as well. I left my glasses here a few days ago. I was hoping you could check to see if they'd been found," Ben said, and slid a healthy tip across the table.

The waiter took it gratefully. "I will check for you, *sidi*."

"They were in a hard case."

"I'll look as soon as I place your order," the waiter promised and hurried back inside, leaving Ben alone with the boy who continued sweeping.

Ben's cell phone rang and he quickly snatched it to his ear.

"Good afternoon, Inspector," greeted Colonel Nabril al-Asi in his typically jovial tone. Background noise blurred his voice to the point of being virtually unintelligible.

"I can barely hear you, Colonel."

"Hold on a second."

The noise vanished.

"Is that better, Inspector?" al-Asi asked, his voice crystal clear.

"Yes. What'd you do?"

"Switched off my new riding lawn mower, a John Deere from the United States. I'm really starting to enjoy involving myself in the domestic side of things. Plenty of time on my hands to master such skills now that my duties have been curtailed. Although I'm having trouble getting the blades to work . . ."

"How's the swing set?"

"Works perfectly, thanks to you. I only called to see how you were making out."

"Very well, thanks to you."

"I was concerned because I wasn't expecting to find you in East Jerusalem. My guess is you're probably seated in the same café where Pakad Barnea was when the shooting started. Am I correct?"

Ben leaned forward, then shifted his legs to make room for the boy's broom. "How did you know I was here, Colonel?"

"The Americans have this remarkable technology that enables them to latch onto the location of any cell phone user when his phone is in use. Supposedly developed to pin down the whereabouts of someone dialing 9-1-1."

"Supposedly."

"In fact, it's an offshoot of a more complicated system using global position satellites meant to aid in the pursuit of terrorist cells. They're all using wireless phones these days, you know."

"You got this system from the Americans?"

"From the Israelis, actually, before the start of our current conflict. *They* obtained it from the Americans. Amazingly useful for keeping track of friends, I must say. Unfortunately, I will not be nearly as useful to you, if the Israeli friends I've been able to maintain desert me."

"I understand."

"So let us hope it doesn't come to that. You'll stay in contact with me."

"Of course."

"Good." And Ben heard the riding mower switch on again before the colonel broke the connection.

Moments later, the waiter reappeared holding Ben's coffee in one hand and plate of *kunafeh* pastries in the other. He set them down and then added a napkin and silverware from his apron. Ben could smell the warm honey topping and felt suddenly hungry, realizing he hadn't eaten anything since Colonel al-Asi had phoned him the night before.

"I'm afraid no eyeglasses have been found, *sidi*."

"Thanks for looking," Ben said, stirring his coffee. He knew it had been a long shot. Worth following up, but still a long shot. Leaving without at least sampling the coffee and pastry would draw attention to him, which gave Ben an excuse to gobble up the *kunafeh*. It was freshly baked, the crisp pastry and sweet cheese warm out of the oven.

Suddenly the boy who'd been needlessly sweeping the outdoor portion of the café appeared by Ben's side smiling. Ben smiled back, wondering why the boy was still standing there when he saw the boy was holding something in his left hand:

An eyeglass case!

# CHAPTER 16

Mayor Anton Krilev was presiding over his morning senior staff meeting when one of his assistants burst into the conference room.

"Sir, I'm sorry to interrupt, but . . ."

"Catch your breath, Constantine, and tell me what's wrong."

The young man tried to catch his breath but failed. "Sir, I have just heard from the hospital."

Krilev nodded. "Which one?"

"*All* of them, sir. One after the other."

Anton Krilev felt the prick of panic, like ice sliding down his spine. Around the conference table at Dubna city headquarters, his senior staff exchanged nervous glances.

The young assistant finally managed to continue. "The hospitals are being flooded with patients, sir. They are asking that you declare a state of emergency."

"An epidemic?" wondered Krilev, already considering his options.

"People are dying, sir, *dozens* of them."

DR. ASHAR Levin, chief of staff of Dubna City Hospital, was leader of the city's small but thriving Jewish community. Mayor Krilev found him waiting outside the emergency room entrance where an adjunct triage unit was being constructed on the street with the help of hastily placed cones and rope strung between trash cans.

"We can't keep up with this," Levin said brusquely, checking his clipboard to make sure the proper procedures were being adhered to.

"Keep up with *what*, Doctor?"

"It started three hours ago. Old people and children mostly, but now all ages in increasing numbers as the morning has gone on."

As Krilev listened, a convoy of ambulances screeched to a halt behind a makeshift barricade where harried hospital workers struggled to unload patients who had been packed three-deep into the vehicles' interiors. The mayor felt queasy as the stretchers rolled by, each carrying a victim soaked in their own blood and vomit.

"What caused this?" was all he could ask Dr. Levin.

"You can see the symptoms for yourself. Vomiting, bleeding through all body orifices, secretions, seizures, and ultimately nervous system failure. The ones I've spoken with all claimed they began to feel sick around dawn or shortly before. None of them exhibited any symptoms whatsoever prior to that. Whatever this is, it came on fast." Dr. Levin looked from the endless line of stretchers back at Krilev. "You can see why we need that state of emergency."

The mayor of Dubna struggled for words. "What do I tell Moscow? A disease, a plague, some sort of outbreak . . ."

Levin shook his head in frustration. "Tell them we don't know yet. Just tell them to get here."

# CHAPTER 17

Jim Black entered the closed wing of the Jerusalem jail building which housed Danielle Barnea's cell. He chose a circuitous approach that would keep him as far as possible from the guard room, even though he was wearing the proper uniform. The entry door to the block was locked from inside, but locks proved only a minor impediment to Black.

Killing, of course, was impossible without access. The true key to his profession was familiarizing oneself with the proper uniforms and identifications. People seldom asked questions when those checked out. Access codes had complicated matters somewhat, but there were ways around those as well, and such sophisticated systems, he knew, had not been installed in this ancient building.

Black approached the head of the corridor containing Danielle Barnea's cell. He'd studied her file and found himself surprisingly impressed. Danielle Barnea was an extremely skilled operative who had killed many in her own right. Shit, she was almost as good as he was. Practically grew up in the Israeli version of the American Special Forces that had spawned him.

Black began to wonder if he could equalize things. Give her a gun and let her draw it out with him. She might even make for decent competition for a change.

The logistics, of course, ruled that out. But considering

the possibility made him feel less bored. Black hadn't come up against anyone he considered a worthy opponent for a long time now, and was beginning to wonder if there was anybody good left out there. Barnea had possibilities. He'd like to compare notes with her, swap stories of their exploits.

Since this was a jail, though, he'd have to get in and out fast. Go right up to the bars of her cell, stick a silenced gun through, and start shooting.

Almost too easy to bother with.

Jim Black much preferred the tougher jobs that came his way occasionally. Hostage rescues or political assassinations where he'd have to elude a hundred guards. Those were challenging. Black was no idealist. He'd never done a single thing in his life simply because he believed in it. If the money was right, he got the job done. Simple as that.

Black wasn't expecting additional security on the wing and didn't care much if there was. Nor did surveillance equipment particularly bother him. He was good at avoiding cameras and would be out of the building before any forces could be marshaled to pursue him.

Black continued walking, Danielle Barnea's cell directly ahead now. No guards in sight, besides him.

Black slid one of his Sig Sauer pistols from its holster and screwed in the suppressor. Held the gun low by his hip as he neared the jail cell, bringing it up an instant before he reached the bars.

The cell was empty.

# CHAPTER 18

S he'll be up shortly, gentlemen," the watch commander told Ben Kamal and Shlomo Davies, after ushering them into the interview room they would be using.

The two men sat side by side behind a single, bare table. Ben zipped open his briefcase and removed a yellow legal pad. The briefcase had been Davies' idea. Otherwise, the old lawyer warned, Ben ran the risk of not fitting in. All lawyers carried briefcases, after all. Davies had sent an assistant out to fetch one when they returned to his office from East Jerusalem, and then packed it with the kind of standard materials that would raise no eyebrows when it was searched by the guards.

The only thing Ben had added was the case of eyeglasses he'd recovered that morning at Café Europe, which he now took out and placed on the table.

A lump rose in his throat when the door opened, and a guard led Danielle Barnea into the interview room. Her hair was a bit mussed, yet the natural auburn waves still tumbled naturally past her shoulders. Her eyes widened when she saw him, flashing with the deep richness forever locked in his mind. She looked worn, though, and her face was pale and drawn beneath the bright fluorescent lighting.

For her part, Danielle tried not to appear surprised when she saw Ben seated in the interview room next to Shlomo

Davies. He rose stiffly, pressing his palms against the table-top. She realized she had never seen him dressed in a suit before. Standing there, he looked more American than Palestinian and that, she guessed, must be the point.

"Pakad Barnea," Davies began, and Danielle reluctantly turned her eyes to him, "I want you to meet Mr. Benjamin Kaplan, an American criminal attorney we use in these matters from time to time. Mr. Kaplan—Pakad Barnea."

Danielle's escort backed out through the door and closed it behind him, freeing Danielle to approach the steel table. She shook hands with Ben but pulled away quickly, long before Ben would have let go on his own.

"Please, sit down. We have much to discuss. First off, I have brought the eyeglasses you requested." With that, Davies accepted the case from Ben and slid it across the table. "The authorities have no problem with this."

Danielle's eyes widened when she saw the case she remembered from the café table in East Jerusalem. She popped it open and removed the glasses, inspecting them briefly as if looking for something before returning them to the case.

"If you don't mind, Pakad," Shlomo Davies continued, "I will now turn the interview over to my associate. Mr. Kaplan."

"I'm not going to lie to you about the severity of the charges lodged against you," Ben said, maneuvering the legal pad just enough for Danielle to see what he was writing. The measure was a pretext due to the fact that both of them were certain they were under surveillance, even in this supposedly private interview room. Israel had no constitution to provide for such matters being disputed in court. "That said, I believe the case against you is arguable."

Danielle nodded and leaned forward so she could read what Ben had written:

COLONEL AL-ASI MADE THE ARRANGEMENTS. I HAD TO SEE YOU.

Danielle showed no response. "You shouldn't have bothered."

"Mr. Davies and I have found certain irregularities in the investigative reports," Ben replied. He went back to jotting, as he spoke. "Mr. Davies has briefed me on the particulars and shared the notes of your interview with him." He stopped writing, so Danielle could read his latest entry.

WHAT CAN I DO FOR YOU? JUST TELL ME WHAT I CAN DO.

"There is nothing you can do. I'm in good hands with Mr. Davies' firm. You should go home."

"I specialize in these kind of cases, Pakad Barnea. The difficult is nothing new for me. I won't let you down."

Danielle ran the eyeglass case through her hands. "Thanks for bringing my glasses. They'll make everything clearer."

Ben wrote, HOW?

Danielle looked away from him.

There was a knock on the interrogation room door.

"I'll get that," Davies offered, his joints cracking as he rose from his chair and moved across the ugly gray room.

Ben stared at Danielle's hands resting on the table, resisting the temptation to take them into his.

"Just a second," Shlomo Davies said when the knock came again. "What's the matter?" he asked, opening the door. "Don't you have a key to your own jail?"

"Musta left it at home," said a tall man with stringy hair. He stuck a gun in the old man's stomach and fired twice, the muffled shots enough to make both Ben and Danielle swing round from the table.

The tall man had already leveled his gun on Danielle when Ben grasped the only thing he could use for a weapon: the briefcase the now dead lawyer had provided him. He picked the case up and flung it wildly across the room, leaping over the table in the same instant.

The tall man tried to twist from its path, but the case grazed his wrist and knocked the gun aside long enough for Ben to pounce on him. The tall man knocked Ben effortlessly aside, stunning him with a blow to the head. By then, though, Danielle had sprung from her chair as well, bounding forward and lunging toward the intruder.

Recognition flashed in her eyes. Her mouth dropped.

The tall man's face was one she could never forget, even though the only time she had seen him before was over a grainy television monitor.

*This was the gunman who had wiped out her Sayaret team at Sheik Hussein al-Akbar's fortress in Beirut a dozen years ago!*

All that was missing was his cowboy hat.

The jail alarm sounded.

Danielle slammed into the man and locked a hand over the wrist controlling his pistol. In the hallway she glimpsed the fallen body of the guard who had escorted her down here, heard the pounding of footsteps rushing down the hall for the interrogation room.

A trio of guards charged into the room, weapons drawn and trained on Ben and Danielle.

"Back off!" one of them, a captain, yelled. "Back off now!"

Danielle refused to let go of the tall man's gun hand. "No! He's not one of yours! He killed the guard in the hall and the old man!"

The captain looked down at Shlomo Davies' body. "Get away from the weapon and back off, or we'll shoot you!"

Danielle saw the harshness in the man's eyes, the way he was holding the gun. Knew she had no choice but to pull her hand off the tall man's wrist.

The tall man fired the gun from his hip, hitting all three guards in a non-stop fusillade that left them no time to get off any shots of their own.

"Come on!" Danielle shouted, taking hold of Ben and dragging him from the room.

She slammed the door shut on the way out, in time to absorb the tall man's next barrage. Another pair of police guards swung round the corner and came face-to-face with them, taken totally by surprise. Their guns were drawn, but they hesitated long enough for Ben and Danielle to pounce on them. A flurry of blows dazed the officers and enabled the pair to wrench their matching Uzi submachine guns free.

"This way!" Danielle signaled, steadying the machine pistol now in her possession.

She had just started to turn toward the rear of the jail building when the tall man rushed down the hall with gun blazing.

# CHAPTER 19

Ben opened fire with his submachine gun. Its power and kick surprised him, sending his shots wildly off mark, but still threatening enough to force the tall man to dive to the floor for cover.

Danielle kept firing back at the cowboy she remembered from Beirut, as she and Ben rushed toward the front part of the jail section of the Jerusalem police station. The alarm continued to wail. Somewhere, not too far up ahead, voices screamed and shouted at each other.

"Put the gun over your head in both hands!" she ordered Ben.

*"What?"*

"Just do it and start walking fast down the hall, toward the front of the building! It's our best chance!"

Ben did exactly as Danielle instructed, while she watched their backs, clinging to the hope that the cowboy might have been hit or retreated by now.

"We give up! We give up!" Danielle repeated, when another team of guards spun round a corner and converged on them just before the main guard post in the jail section of the building.

Danielle felt rough hands strip the weapon from her grasp and thrust her against the wall. She actually had just begun to breathe easier when fresh gunshots boomed down the hall.

The guards twisted in agony, falling one after the other. Ben recovered his Uzi and surged past them, bursting through the heavy door into the main entryway, firing the weapon purposely wild and high to discourage any police guards who might have been lying in wait here.

"Danielle!" he yelled just before she spun through the doorway, which coughed bullet-riddled concrete chips in her wake.

She sprayed single rounds at the cowboy. But he must have ducked into the stairwell for cover, and her bullets clacked harmlessly into the wall.

BLACK SLAMMED a fresh clip into his pistol, doing his best to still his breathing to regain control of the situation.

*Barnea was escaping!*

So many things he had not bothered to take into account: that she would not be in her cell; that she might be able to escape; that she would not be alone.

*Looks like I fucked this one up*, he thought to himself, but glad in a way since it placed him and the woman, a pair of pros, on equal ground. See which of them was better.

Black spun round the corner of the wall firing, trying to keep Barnea and the man from getting outside.

BEN AND Danielle had just reached the vestibule perched before the main doors when the shooting started again. They swung simultaneously and returned fire from behind the thin cover of the wall, trying for a bead on the tall man. A siren wailed, signalling the arrival of the first ambulance to be summoned by the alarm.

"Go!" Danielle said. "I'll cover you!"

Ben darted across the open stretch leading to the exit when Danielle spun out firing. Her bullets held the cowboy at bay long enough for Ben to make it outside and down the steps of the old building.

On cue, the ambulance screamed onto the scene and halted almost directly before him.

Ben leveled his gun straight for the paramedic in the driver's seat. "Out!"

"But we're—"

"Out!" Ben repeated, throwing open the door on his side.

"Okay, okay," the driver relented, exiting with his hands in the air along with the man in the passenger seat. In the same moment Danielle rushed down the steps firing the last of her bullets back through the glass, shattering it to further slow the cowboy's pursuit.

Ben watched her leap into the passenger side of the ambulance and immediately slammed his own door behind him, as policemen poured out of the station from two adjacent doors in the main *Megrash Haruseim* building and opened fire on the ambulance.

"Get down!" he screamed, crouching below the dashboard himself.

Danielle caught a glimpse of the cowboy crashing through the bullet-weakened glass and firing non-stop with a pair of pistols toward the policemen who were caught totally by surprise.

Ben lowered his Uzi to the floor, slammed his foot on the accelerator, and tore away from the jail, the sound of gunshots lost to the screech of the ambulance's tires against the pavement.

# CHAPTER 20

I know him!" Danielle said suddenly, hunched low and staring into the side view mirror. "I know that son of a bitch!"

"Who is he?"

"I don't know his name, only his looks. He took out a Sayaret strike team in Beirut a dozen years ago. I was the only survivor."

"It looks like someone sent him to finish the job."

Ben tightened his hands around the ambulance's wheel, approaching an intersection where a soldier was busily diverting all traffic off the heavily congested Jaffa Road to avoid a protest march just up ahead. The soldier saw him coming, started to raise his hand, and for just a moment Ben thought the soldier was going to order the ambulance to stop. Instead, though, he held traffic up so Ben could continue down Jaffa Road, unencumbered by the yarmulke-clad marchers stabbing the air with their picket signs.

"The eyeglasses!" Danielle realized suddenly.

"I've got them right here," Ben said, pulling the case from his pocket.

Danielle took the case and held it tight instead of opening it. "You can drop me off a few blocks up."

"Why would I do that?"

Danielle's features flared. "This isn't your fight."

"If it's yours . . ."

"It's *Israel's* problem. This is all about military supplies, lots of them, being sold on the black market through brokers here. In exchange for diamonds smuggled out of Africa."

Ben's mind flashed back to his arrest of the Russian Anatolyevich two days before. "Assault rifles, rocket launchers . . ."

"Yes!" Danielle said, her mouth wide with surprise.

"Keep talking."

"I was given the identity of a middleman, a courier named Ranieri, who was coming into the country to close another deal. I was supposed to track the shipment back to its source, destroy the pipeline."

"Which led through East Jerusalem."

"I followed Ranieri there—"

"But his source never showed up," Ben completed for her.

"How could you know *that*?"

"His name is Anatolyevich and he was in Palestinian custody at the time," Ben said flatly, turning to look at Danielle. "I know because I arrested him."

# CHAPTER 21

"Thank you for coming with me, Doctor."

"I thought it might give me more opportunity to convince you to start taking the medicine," Dr. Sowahy said to Latisse Matabu.

They sat together in the backseat, while the driver and Matabu's personal guard sat in the front. This final checkpoint on the road leading to Kono was merely cursory; it had been months since any government troops had dared to show their faces in the eastern part of the country once again controlled by the Revolutionary United Front.

"The problem with that exchange your officer spoke of," the doctor started.

"What about it?"

"He said it was serious."

"It's not like you to involve yourself in my affairs, Doctor."

"Your affairs are having an adverse effect on your health, General. That leaves me no choice."

Matabu weighed Sowahy's words. "The lost shipment is an inconvenience—nothing more. You'll see what I mean when we reach our destination."

Their car neared a clearing that had the look of a tiny meadow sliced in two by the roadway. Matabu stiffened, then reached across the front seat and grasped her driver's shoulder.

"Pull over here." She turned toward Sowahy, not seeming to see him. "This is where it happened . . ."

The old doctor looked, trying to get his bearings.

"Three years ago, after the RUF failed to retake Freetown and lost Tongo, the government told my father they were ready to conduct peace talks, that there had been enough violence, that enough innocent people had died and been displaced. They asked him to pick a spot and he chose to meet here, because it was a place he always felt safe."

Latisse Matabu took a deep breath and stepped out of the car. Her boots crunched atop the gravel. She drifted from side to side, as if searching for something she had lost. Behind her, Sowahy emerged from the car hunched over with a grimace and hobbled toward her.

"The delegations were to meet at this checkpoint. Right here, I think." As Matabu spoke, her hands clenched into fists by her side. Beads of sweat began to form on her forehead. She stood rigid amidst the knee-high grass, ignoring it brushing against her legs. "My father and his top staff came in their uniforms, the government representatives in their suits. They climbed out of their cars simultaneously and approached. When they were halfway to each other, the men wearing suits drew their weapons and opened fire." She stopped and looked at Dr. Sowahy again. "They were soldiers. Mercenaries from the bastard Executive Outcomes hired by the government."

Matabu spat on the ground to enunciate her point.

"My father never suspected an ambush. He thought himself too powerful, too . . . respected. He did not realize that the government knows nothing about respect, only fear. Fear is what they respond to. Intimidation is what they respond to."

Latisse Matabu squeezed her eyes closed.

"The soldiers who came to our house later that morning were in uniform—government troops, not paid mercenaries. They came without fear, because my father was already dead. A lesson needed to be taught to any who might choose to follow in his footsteps. My mother saw them coming and tried to hide my younger brother and sister. But the soldiers found them. They found them and made my mother watch while they cut off their limbs. She threw herself on one of their blades but it still took a long time for her to die. A terrible death she did not deserve, this woman who fought to feed the poor and organized the only welfare system Sierra Leone ever had.

"Of course the government denied they were responsible. They have continued to deny they were responsible right to this day. They blame insurrection on the part of the RUF, rebels who had tired of my father's leadership. The story is all bullshit but that never stopped the international community from accepting it."

Latisse Matabu opened her eyes and stared into the distance.

"You know where I was when all this was happening?"

Sowahy coughed and had trouble catching his breath. "Studying in the United States, where your parents wanted you to be."

"They wanted to spare me being raped again, while the government forces raped this country." Matabu swung toward him with a suddenness that startled Sowahy. "It was you who contacted me, Doctor."

He nodded grimly. "I felt it my duty. But I warned you not to come back."

"You said there was a death warrant on my head, as I recall."

"There was."

She turned again toward Sowahy. "Well, I came home anyway, to find a government publicly advocating peace while privately determined to destroy us. The government troops we captured told us interesting tales when we tortured them. Tales of American Green Berets training and equipping them. Tales of yet more mercenaries who came to their aid in the guise of peacekeepers. No matter how many we killed, it was not enough."

"And it never will be, General. You do this out of hate

for the enemy, not love of the people. After what was done to you . . ."

"I could live with the rape, but it wasn't enough for that monster." Matabu's voice drifted, as if aimed at someone far away. "We tried to hide the truth from him, but he found out. He found out and came to my home. . . ."

"I know the rest," Sowahy interrupted, trying to spare her.

"My parents sent me away and I might never have come back, if they had lived." Latisse Matabu hardened her gaze. "And now that I am back, I intend to win this war."

"How? How can you possibly win?"

Matabu smiled at Sowahy and started back for the car. "Come," she said. "Come and I'll show you."

# CHAPTER 22

"Vasily Anatolyevich," Ben elaborated. "Member of the Russian mafia currently thriving in Israel."

Danielle still couldn't believe what she had just heard.

*Ben had arrested the man Ranieri was waiting to meet with in East Jerusalem!*

"It was an undercover operation in Beit Jala," Ben continued. "Anatolyevich delivered a shipment of guns to me a few hours before he was supposed to meet you in East Jerusalem."

"You're saying he's *in custody*?"

Ben nodded. "At one of Colonel al-Asi's safe houses."

Their ambulance approached a gridlocked snarl of cars across from Safra Square typical of Jaffa Road. Ben waited for the cars in his way to make room for him, gave the horn a few honks to further punctuate his point.

Danielle stuck the eyeglass case into the pocket of the slacks she'd been wearing for three days now. "We've got to get to the West Bank. I need to see this—"

A bullet shattered the side view mirror, then a second spiderwebbed the glass on the passenger side window.

"It's him!" Ben screamed, watching in his mirror as the assassin dressed as a jail guard veered toward them on foot just a few cars back in the traffic that had snarled behind the ambulance. "Your cowboy!"

JIM BLACK realized he should have waited a bit longer before opening fire. Draw a little closer, be sure he had a clear shot. Trouble was, getting that close to Danielle Barnea meant she would be that close to him. Fear was something he never experienced in these situations but risk, risk was something to be avoided at all costs.

Black figured if he got lucky and took out the man driving the ambulance, he'd have a much easier route to Barnea. It was a tough shot, yes, but he'd managed tougher.

Firing as he sprinted down Jaffa Road, he knew almost instantly his shots were errant. But the ambulance remained mired in traffic, and he retrained his aim on its rear tires and clacked off another series of shots.

"MOVE! MOVE!" Danielle roared, ducking low in the seat now.

"The bastard shot out the tires! We won't make it to the next intersection!"

"Turn right, then! Just up ahead onto Shadal Street!"

The assassin was just two car lengths back when Ben jerked the ambulance to the right and gave it gas. The vehicle cracked into a pair of small passenger cars and shoved them slowly aside, shredding its blown-out tires. Ben pulled the Uzi from the floor and started to look toward the driver's side window.

"Wait, how many shots do you have left?" Danielle asked him.

"I don't know! I don't know!"

"Don't waste them!"

"But—"

"Just *drive*!"

The rattling in the ambulance's rear end intensified, as

Ben aimed the vehicle for the entrance to the street that was barely wide enough to accommodate it. Next to him, Danielle twisted round and pushed herself through an opening in the seats into the rear compartment.

"Drive on another twenty yards, then stop," she instructed.

The jarring ride made her clutch the side of the vehicle to keep her footing in the ambulance's rear. The stretcher had already been jostled free of its bonds and kept banging up against the rear doors. Danielle quickly located the four oxygen tanks and turned on the spigots that opened the flow of gas from them. Then she yanked the tubing and masks away, so the oxygen was free to fill the whole of the cramped rear compartment.

Danielle had just finished when Ben jerked the ambulance to a full stop.

"Leave the engine running," she said, returning to the front and then opening the passenger side window. "And give me the Uzi."

Ben handed the submachine gun over and then squeezed himself through the driver's window while Danielle did the same on her side. As he emerged, bullets singed the air beside him. But he clambered over the ambulance's hood and scrabbled away to join Danielle.

She steadied the Uzi and fired as soon as Ben drew even with her, a series of neat shots through the ambulance's grille toward its radiator and engine block. The initial burst sent a burst of flames out of the hood and ignited the oxygen released in the rear of the ambulance

"Get down!" Danielle yelled, and fired the last of the Uzi's bullets into the engine block.

The resulting blast coughed rubble from the buildings lining both sides of the street into the air, scattering it in all directions as well as atop Ben and Danielle like chips of stone rain. A few secondary explosions ignited, further heightening the wall of flaming steel that had been effectively placed between them and their pursuer.

"I guess you're stuck with me now," Ben said, his ears still ringing from the noise, and then ran with Danielle toward the other end of the street.

# CHAPTER 23

I want to see what happened here for myself," Daniel Sukahamin, defense minister of Sierra Leone, insisted.

"The area around the town may not be secure, sir," warned the American colonel who headed the team of U.S. military advisors.

Sukahamin twisted toward him in the rear of the jeep, as the vehicle thundered down the road, approaching the outskirts of Katani. "I believe making villages like this secure was your job, Colonel. Wasn't that what you were sent here to do?"

Daniel Sukahamin had been a close, undaunted ally of Sierra Leone's President Ahmed Tejan Kabbah since Kabbah's forces retook power from the RUF in 1998. It had been Sukahamin who strengthened ECOMOG, an alliance of West African states conceived to keep the rebels in check during the cease-fire. He had also come up with the idea of rallying the Mende kamajors together to form the Civil Defense Forces and defend their own villages against attacks by the Revolutionary United Front. The kamajors were the traditional hunters of the Mende tribe, the main ethnic group living in the southern and western provinces of the country. Their involvement helped splinter the RUF and prevent it from achieving footholds beyond their base in the east.

But the Civil Defense Forces, the CDF, were difficult to

keep under control and, once armed, often did more harm than good. Battles broke out among local tribes, as well as between the tribes and the standing army, and Sukahamin realized that in the kamajors he had created a terrible monster that was sometimes as bad in its own way as the Revolutionary United Front. It became a full-time public relations job to blame the RUF for the atrocities perpetrated by the kamajors.

After the international peacekeeping force dispatched by the United Nations had proven utterly ineffectual, becoming hostages rather than protectors, Sukahamin enlisted the help of American soldiers in the role of military advisors. The role of these soldiers, on the surface, was to train and equip what small organized army the defense minister was able to cull from the ranks of the Civil Defense Forces. Clandestinely, though, the Americans led missions and conducted counterterrorist activities aimed at disrupting, perhaps ultimately destroying, the Revolutionary United Front. As a result, for the first time in longer than he could remember, Daniel Sukahamin could actually envision a time when his country's civil war would at last be concluded.

"Minister," the American colonel started to explain, "my orders—"

"Fuck your orders! My country is dying, Colonel, and the Americans sent you here to save it." Daniel Sukahamin leaned back and stiffly folded his arms, staring straight ahead. "We know General Matabu and her rebel forces are preparing to launch another assault on Freetown. If we fail to hold the capital, or even engage in a drawn-out battle, we risk splintering the Civil Defense Forces into a dozen factions. The Dragon will wear President Kabbah's balls around her neck and proclaim herself leader." Sukahamin turned back to the American. "You have children, Colonel?"

"A boy and girl, sir."

The defense minister's gaze turned cold and steely. "Do you know what would happen to them if they were here when the government fell? The boy's limbs would be hacked off one at a time and he would be left to bleed to death. The girl would be raped by as many rebels as could thrust themselves inside her before she died."

The colonel wrinkled his nose in disgust.

"I do not exaggerate. This is the reality our people face."

Sukahamin was about to continue when he saw the first wave of villagers from Katani coming forward, blocking the road.

"What the hell," the colonel muttered.

The villagers cowered at the sight of the jeeps, most backing away while some shed the meager belongings from their backs and fled into the woods. A few approached the vehicles whining and screaming, too many talking at once to be understood.

The colonel stripped the M-16 from his shoulder, leveling it as he signaled the other two soldiers in the jeep to do the same.

"I warned you this area wasn't secure, sir," he barked at Sukahamin.

But the defense minister was struggling to make sense out of the villagers' desperate pleas.

"It's not the Revolutionary United Front they're running from, Colonel," Sukahamin reported.

The colonel shook his head in confusion. "Then what is it?"

Sukahamin listened some more before responding. "The end of the world, Colonel. They say they are fleeing the end of the world."

# CHAPTER 24

"H is office is in that restaurant right over there," Danielle told Ben, after the bus dropped them in Haifa. "You can wait outside if you like."

"What, your friend Sabi doesn't like Palestinians?"

"Not when they're also policemen."

"I think I'd better come inside with you."

"Suit yourself," Danielle said, her detached tone unchanged from the interrogation room. And New York.

"I'm sorry," Ben told her.

"For what?"

"Do you really need to ask?"

Danielle didn't look back at him. "You know the worst thing? I don't remember. The first thing I recall is waking up in the hospital. Afterwards."

"That's enough."

"No, it's not, because I can't try to figure out what I did wrong, what I could have done different."

Ben suddenly grew calm. "Do you remember what else you told me about the failed raid in Beirut a dozen years ago?"

"No."

"That you kept a copy of the tape for years afterward. Watched it again and again."

"So?"

"To figure out what you did wrong," Ben continued,

"what you could have done different. That didn't help then and it wouldn't now. It's a blessing you can't remember."

"You saved my life; I remember that. I must have let my guard down. That never would have happened ten or twelve years ago."

Ben turned toward the waterfront restaurant they had walked to from the bus stop. "How well do you know this man?"

"We'll see."

Located in northwest Israel, the port city of Haifa was lined with harbors that featured a constant flow of boating traffic, both large and small. From fishing boats to pleasure craft, to expensive yachts, to freighters hauling merchandise in and out of the country, Haifa's port was home to some, a way station for many, and a quick stopover for still more. Its strategic Mediterranean location made it conducive to trade for virtually any European commercial center and convenient for any seaworthy pilot.

But the city enjoyed a thriving business center as well, so the sound of boat horns and the smoky bellows of incoming freighters inevitably battled the noises of traffic inching its way along the city's busy portside streets. All of Haifa was enveloped by a sense of having to get somewhere fast, from the babble of tourists snapping their pictures to the rush of businessmen and the blur of traffic choking the streets.

The city over the years had expanded up the hillside into a series of tiers. The bus had dropped Ben and Danielle off on the lowest tier, the port level, which left them only a short walk to the Banker's Tavern restaurant where the unofficial mayor of Haifa ran his business. Little of that business was legal, since Sabi was as close to a crime boss as Israel had.

A smuggler as well as an Israeli Arab, Sabi was one of the few people who got along with everyone. Palestinians welcomed him because of the constant flow of merchandise he expedited, free of Israeli duties and taxes, into the West Bank and Gaza. And Israeli officials looked the other way, even in these times of the continuing *intifada*, because Sabi's shipping contacts in Alexandria, Port Said, Turkey, and elsewhere remained crucial to the nation's trade. The National Police, meanwhile, left him alone because he kept control of the unsavory characters who came and went through Haifa much better than they could ever hope to under *any* conditions. Sabi could play both sides against the middle and never seem to lose.

"Pakad Danielle Barnea!" he roared excitedly, as soon as Danielle entered the restaurant. "Is that you?"

As always, Sabi sat in his corner booth, occupying most of one side by himself. His incredible girth was part of his legend, and he seemed to grow bigger each time Danielle had occasion to meet with him. His huge jowls hung like slabs of meat from his face. He had a triple chin and a roundish, basketball-sized head that seemed to grow directly out of his neck. The pair of men sitting opposite him in the booth had to pull in their legs for him to shuffle his way out, watching as he swallowed Danielle in a bearish hug when they met halfway across the floor.

Sabi eased her away from him but kept hold of her shoulders, casting a brief glance toward Ben who had remained in the doorway. "I was worried, Pakad Danielle Barnea. After all that I had heard these past few days ... Now, please, what is it I can do for you?"

"You can tell me about the Russians who are moving arms through Israel."

Sabi scowled. "Bastards have no honor. Impossible to do business with."

"You don't deal in weapons, anyway."

"Not for a long time. Too dangerous. Bad for trade. And anything that is bad for trade is bad for Sabi, eh Pakad?"

"Not bad for these Russians, obviously."

Sabi snickered in response this time. "Enterprising criminals Israel was kind enough to take in after they had drained their own country dry. Take my advice and throw them all out on their asses. Come," he said, leading her to the booth his two bodyguards had vacated, "join me."

"I'm not exactly in a position to pass on anyone's suggestions right now," Danielle said, once they were seated across from each other in his booth.

Sabi's thick, oval eyes softened. "You look hungry, Pakad Danielle Barnea. Please, have something to eat," he offered, opening his palms to indicate the selection of food that covered the table. "*Min fadlak*. Help yourself."

"Later, Sabi."

"Just a bite of *tabbouleh*," he persisted, indicating a salad dish. "Or some *melukkhiya* spinach soup. Make you strong like the American Popeye, eh?"

Danielle had to admit the smells were inviting enough to make focusing on the matter at hand difficult. She had barely eaten a thing for three days. Her stomach grumbled as Sabi continued to coax her.

"How about a platter of *mezze*, appetizers, or some fresh baked *mankoushi*. I have some loaves cooling in the kitchen now."

"No, thank you."

Sabi frowned. "It's a bad sign when a hungry person chooses not to eat. Usually means they have lost more than their appetite."

Danielle remained silent.

Sabi hoisted a bottle that had been resting before him. "Some wine, then." He poured her a glass of Cabernet Sauvignon without waiting for her to respond. "The best the Kefraya vineyards of Lebanon have to offer. They send bottles to me special. Would you like to know why? Because I intervened when the Israeli troops were trampling their vineyards during the 1982 invasion. People are not apt to forget such favors."

Danielle left her glass of wine untouched. "I understand."

"Do you really? Then you should work for me." Sabi leaned forward until his huge stomach pushed up against the table. "You would thrive in a world where there are no politics."

"There are always politics, just different kinds."

"And what kind is it that brings you here to me?"

"I need to get into the West Bank."

Sabi looked at her suspiciously, then gazed at Ben. "Does this have something to do with that Palestinian standing in the doorway?"

"He saved my life today."

"I know who he is, Pakad. I know all about him."

Danielle kept her eyes off Ben, on Sabi. "Not as much as you think you do. What about the West Bank?" she prodded.

"Not something I'm often asked to do. Out of the West Bank, yes, but into the West Bank . . ." His words trailed off into a shrug that merged his massive neck into his shoulders. "It shouldn't be a problem. But I will need some time to make the arrangements."

"Take all you need. Can you arrange for me to use the restaurant's kitchen in the meantime?"

Sabi lit a huge cigar, didn't challenge Danielle further. "Of course. Anything else, Pakad?"

Danielle looked briefly toward Ben. "Just one more thing . . ."

# CHAPTER 25

I won't ask," Ben said, as he followed Danielle into the kitchen.

"It's better that you see."

Once in the aromatic kitchen, filled with the luscious smells of herbs and fresh vegetables, Danielle filled a bowl with water. Then she pulled the eyeglass case from her pocket and opened it. After removing the glasses, she carefully popped the large, ultra-thick tinted lenses out one at a time and dropped them into the bowl of water where they quickly sank to the bottom. Next she located a microwave oven and placed the bowl inside it. Danielle set the temperature on high, the clock to the five minute mark, and pressed start.

The microwave began to whir, and Ben could see the water just beginning to boil when his cell phone rang.

"My Israeli counterparts are very upset with me, Inspector," greeted Nabril al-Asi, sounding coarse and impatient, his tone lacking its usual joviality.

"I can ex—"

"They want to know why someone whose identity papers they approved on my recommendation could be involved in a jail break."

"Jail break?"

"That's what happened, isn't it?"

"No. Well, yes, but not that way."

"Is Pakad Barnea still incarcerated?"

"No."

"Is she with you in Haifa?"

Ben recalled the new technology that allowed al-Asi to pinpoint his position from his cell phone signal. "Yes."

"Then you helped her escape."

"Because she would have been killed otherwise. There was an assassin at the jail," Ben said, eyeing Danielle as the microwave continued to whir. "An American assassin Pakad Barnea had met up with before. He struck while we were meeting in the interrogation room."

"And I suppose you're going to tell me he is responsible for the nine dead, eight Israeli policemen and the lawyer who was representing Pakad Barnea."

"As a matter of fact—"

"I believe you, Inspector. The problem is the Israelis won't. The story they are floating mentions nothing about an assassin on the premises. Now I want you to listen very closely to what I'm about to say: If you return to the West Bank now, I can keep you out of this. Protect you. Another day, and matters will be beyond my control. So you must return *now*."

Ben took another look at Danielle. "I'm sorry, Colonel," he said into the phone.

He heard al-Asi sigh instantly. "I am, too. You and Pakad Barnea are about to become two of the most hunted individuals in all of Israel, more so than even the terrorists I deliver to my Israeli counterparts from time to time."

Ben swallowed hard. "What about you?"

"Don't worry about me. I still provide too many services for the Israelis for them to stay mad very long. They'll probably target me for assassination and then purposely bomb the building when I'm not there."

"Thank you, Colonel. I'm sorry I dragged you into this."

"I don't have much else to do these days. Lots of time spent at Rafiq's Supply Store picking up things for the house and our new offices. Every day I go there. By the way, I was wondering if you knew anything about roses?"

"No."

"I'm planting some now in my new garden. I don't think I'm doing it right. I assume Pakad Barnea is with you."

"She is."

"Do you think she knows anything about roses?"

"I can ask her."

Ben could hear al-Asi sigh again on the other end of the line. "Don't bother. I fear I'm wasting my time. Building swing sets, mowing the lawn, playing gardener. We can't make up for what we've lost."

"We have to try, Colonel."

"Yesterday I took a team to arrest an especially nasty militant hiding out in the Jabalaya refugee camp. The residents rose up against us, against me, before we even got close." Al-Asi paused. "I thought our people were standing in mud but it's really quicksand, isn't it, Inspector?"

"I feel like I'm sinking, too."

The microwave oven beeped just as Ben returned the cell phone to his pocket. Danielle removed the bowl from the oven. He could see right away that the plastic eyeglass lenses were no longer visible, having melted into the now boiling water. Still, Danielle peered into the steaming bowl and waited for it to cool before reaching down into it and plucking an object off the bottom.

"An interesting prescription for glasses, don't you think?" Danielle asked, opening her palm so Ben could see the small diamond she was holding.

# CHAPTER 26

General Latisse Matabu led Dr. Sowahy down a trail cut by the government years before through the woods in Sierra Leone's eastern Kono region. The deep, mud-soaked grooves indicated that trucks had used the trail very recently. RUF soldiers were posted at regular intervals and in some of the tallest trees where they wielded binoculars along with assault rifles.

"Don't worry, they won't shoot you unless I tell them to," Matabu said as she walked. "Taking Kono back two years ago gave us the means to buy the weapons we needed to fight the government troops and so-called military advisors from the United States and elsewhere. The troops who killed my father had been trained by the United States, armed by the United States. But soon we will make them all pay."

"What about the peace talks?"

"A sham perpetrated on us by President Kabbah. I released all children and U.N. peacekeepers his government viewed as hostages, but where are the concessions we were promised in return? No, the government asks for much and gives nothing in return. What we want we must take ourselves in Freetown."

"You're talking about waging all-out war again," Dr. Sowahy noted grimly.

Matabu nodded. "The RUF failed in its last attempt to

take the capital and that failure ultimately cost my father his life. I do not intend to repeat his mistakes. Retaking the diamond fields here and elsewhere was only the beginning. The rest will follow in due course."

Matabu stopped at the end of the trail and faced the old doctor instead of going on. "General Treest put this disease inside me, Doctor. God should have taken him before I had the chance. I don't even think he enjoyed the rape. He just wanted to make me hurt. But I returned the pain he gave me a hundred times as soon as I returned. I put an end to him as I will put an end to the others in the government who are no better or different."

Matabu parted a final bit of stubborn brush to reveal the river she had personally seized from government forces two years before. Residents of nearby villages sifted through the murky water with screened sieves under the watchful eye of RUF troops standing on the banks. The scene looked unchanged from that day she had brought a truckload of her troops here in the guise of workers, except for who was in control.

"Welcome to Tongo, Doctor," Matabu said to Sowahy. "The last of our alluvial diamond fields to yield anything significant. The fields at Bo and Kanema are all but drained, and soon this one will be, too. No matter. By that time, Sierra Leone will be ours."

# CHAPTER 27

The diamond glimmered in Danielle's palm. Finely shaped and the size of her pinky fingernail, the stone seemed to rise out of the water that had accompanied it from the steaming bowl.

"*That* was in one of the eyeglass lenses?" Ben asked, still not believing his eyes.

"Encased in a polymer designed to melt at three hundred degrees and hidden beneath the tinted surface. Making it virtually undetectable in the event Ranieri was searched."

"Did Levy tell you that?"

Danielle shook her head slowly. "Only that diamonds were being smuggled into the country to purchase weapons."

"How did you figure the rest out?"

"Ranieri made two trips to a jewelry store in Tel Aviv, the first straight from the airport after his arrival and the second on his way to East Jerusalem two mornings ago."

"Why two trips?"

"He delivered something on the first trip, must have picked the eyeglasses up on the second. I still haven't figured out how Ranieri got his diamonds past customs. In any case, I followed him from the time he arrived at the airport. My plan was to pick up Anatolyevich, or whoever showed up to meet Ranieri in East Jerusalem, once he left the meeting to track down the weapons. Except, thanks to you, Anatolyevich never arrived."

"Sorry to have ruined things for you. Again."

As Ben watched, Danielle grabbed a second bowl and drained the contents of the first into it, turning her hand into a catch as the water ran through it. He heard a soft clacking sound each time Danielle caught another diamond in her palm, almost two dozen small but impressive stones in all. She dropped them in the same bowl and watched them glisten beneath the kitchen's harsh fluorescent lights.

"How much are they worth?" Ben asked, recalling the diamond engagement ring he had bought for his wife fifteen years ago with most of his savings. The thought left a lump in his throat, as the familiar wave of sadness rose deep inside him.

"I'd say between a half and three-quarters of a million dollars. Enough to buy lots of bullets and bombs."

"Which are still unaccounted for."

"They don't have to be for long," Danielle said. "Why don't we pay Anatolyevich a visit?"

# C H A P T E R  2 8

Mayor Anton Krilev tilted his eyes upward toward another flood of airplanes flying over the downtown section of Dubna, when the convoy of trucks rumbled down the central avenue. He watched an officer emerge from the backseat of an army-issue vehicle and hurry over to him. A short, barrel-shaped man with a thick head.

"Thank God you've come!" Krilov said, as armed soldiers began to spill out from the four trucks. "It's gotten worse since I contacted Moscow!"

The officer looked about, seeming to study the air, then signaled his troops to disperse. "I am Colonel Yuri Petroskov. In charge of internal security for this region."

"Anton Krilev. I am mayor of Dubna," Krilev greeted, extending his hand.

Petroskov brushed past him and left the outstretched hand hanging there. "You will take me to your office now so I may establish my headquarters."

"Good idea. Then I can brief you."

Petroskov continued to scan the street. "I do not need to be briefed."

"The phones, though. Suddenly they don't work anywhere in the city."

The colonel stopped and faced Krilev. "I know. They were shut off on my orders."

"*Your* orders?" Krilev repeated in befuddlement.

But Petroskov had already continued on, leaving the mayor to struggle to keep up. "How many dead so far?" the colonel asked.

"I've lost count, the reports are coming in so fast. A few thousand perhaps, many of them children." Krilev gazed at the fully armed soldiers continuing to fan out through the streets, disappearing between buildings. "I had requested doctors, additional medical personnel and supplies."

"And you will get them." The colonel swung toward him again. "Once the city is secure."

"Secure? I don't understand what you—"

Petroskov arched his head slightly backward, exaggerating his perpetual grimace. "Dubna is under quarantine, Major. Until further notice, no one will be allowed in or out without proper authorization from myself or one of my officers. Is that clear?"

"When I called Moscow—"

"Is that *clear*?"

"Yes, sir. It's clear."

"Then after I establish my headquarters, you will take me to your hospitals. I will want to speak to the doctors charged with treating the infected. And the other city commissioners, I will wish to meet with them as well."

"Of course," Krilev said, huffing now from the effort of trying to match the colonel's rapid stride. "But there is new information. Several witnesses report small planes flying very low over the city for the past several days. Other witnesses have reported a strange smell coming from the woods at the same time. My thinking is that . . ." He let his voice tail off when it was clear Colonel Petroskov wasn't paying any attention. "Colonel?" Krilev said, trying to rouse him.

"Please leave the investigation to me, Mister Mayor."

Krilev stopped in his tracks. "You already knew what happened here," he realized. "You expected this."

"I am prepared for it."

"For *what*? My city is dying, Colonel, and this is what Moscow sends for help?"

"Moscow sent what is needed, Mayor, so that things cannot get any worse. Now, where is your office?"

# DAY FOUR

Vasily Anatolyevich leaned forward in his chair, grinned at Danielle and snarled at Ben. "So the son of Jafir Kamal returns." He gazed around him at the well-furnished appointments of his guarded room in Colonel al-Asi's safe house in the relatively plush suburb of Al-Bireh north of Ramallah. "Tell me, Inspector, do you Palestinians treat all your prisoners this way? It's no wonder you have no country of your own."

"I notice you're still in custody," Ben chided.

"And I finished my last bottle of vodka yesterday." Anatolyevich smoothed his hair back with his hands. His face was freshly shaved and a lilac scent rose off his flesh from the kind of soap sold in fashionable Tel Aviv boutiques. "Where is your Colonel al-Asi, by the way? He promised to bring me another one so I would talk to you, Inspector."

"You can be a free man today if you help us," Ben said, ignoring Anatolyevich's words.

"I will be a free man anyway; it will just take a little longer."

"But not a rich one," Danielle interjected.

Anatolyevich eyed Danielle lasciviously. "You bring such a pretty woman with you. I'm amazed, Inspector."

"Pakad Barnea was kind enough to take your place at the meeting you missed in East Jerusalem on Monday," Ben told him.

"My place? You think I know what you're talking about?"

"These," Danielle said, producing a small pouch containing the diamonds that had been embedded in Ranieri's eyeglasses. She opened it and produced one of the beautifully finished stones. "You were supposed to receive them in exchange for weapons."

Anatolyevich's eyes bulged. He stretched a hand upward, as if to reach for the diamond, then pulled it back.

"Now," Ben said, "would you like to cooperate with us or not?"

THE NIGHT before Danielle had cut her hair short, slicing off her tumbling waves and smoothing what remained into a shaggy, layered look. She added a pair of non-prescription eyeglasses and some shapeless clothes Sabi had purchased for her at a flea market to complete her disguise.

"What do you think?" she had asked Ben.

"On you, everything looks good."

"You're giving me too much reason to question your judgment."

Ben shrugged, missing the familiarity of her appearance. "It's a good thing your hair will grow back."

"Now it's your turn . . ."

She brushed his hair straight back and colored it black, adding some glaze to give it a waxy sheen.

"No shaving for a while," she instructed, after working a bronzer into his face, concentrating it on Ben's cheekbones to enhance them. Looking in the mirror when she was done, he had to admit his appearance had been radically transformed.

"You're very good at this."

"I had lots of practice at one point."

"Your days in the Sayaret?"

"Everything seemed so simple then."

"There was nothing simple about the mission where you first met our cowboy."

"He could have been killed in the ambulance explosion yesterday."

"But you don't think so, do you, Danielle?"

"Men like him don't die so easily." She looked at Ben more closely, as if to inspect her handiwork. "Or you."

"Is that a compliment?"

"What do you think? You saved my life in New York. . . ."

"But not our child's."

"You didn't let me finish. You're stronger than you think you are, Ben. You had to be strong enough for both of us."

"I'd been there before, that's all."

"A terrible place."

"Yes," Ben said, eager to change the subject. "And if you're right about the cowboy still being alive, we'll undoubtedly be seeing him again."

"I should have killed him in Beirut like I wanted to," Danielle followed reflectively.

"Reliving the past again."

"You said so yourself: It's a habit with me."

"You were, what, twenty-four years old at the time?"

"Twenty-five."

"A kid."

"Old for special operations."

"Young for Shin Bet, though, where you were reassigned."

"To provide me a graceful exit."

"There's no such thing," Ben said, knowingly.

THEY HAD made the trip into the West Bank just after dawn, hidden in the back of a truck packed with refrigerators and stoves bound for Ramallah. Sabi's government-approved transfer visas rendered the Israeli checkpoints mere inconveniences; the truck was not searched once during any of three separate stops. It dropped them in the center of Ramallah and a cab brought them the rest of the way to Colonel al-Asi's safe house in Al-Bireh where Anatolyevich was still staring at the diamond Danielle had pulled from the pouch.

"We want to know exactly what weapons Ranieri was buying," said Ben. "For whom, as well."

"And where we can find these weapons," Danielle added.

Anatolyevich leaned back comfortably. "Talk and I go free?" The Russian snickered. "Is that the deal you came all this way to offer me?" He shook his head. "I'm afraid you'll have to do better."

"No," Ben told him, "we've got a better idea." He looked toward Danielle.

"We want to purchase the same merchandise you intended to sell to Ranieri," she added.

"And where would that leave my original client, comrades?"

"Your original client is no longer in a position to pay you," Danielle reminded, pouch in hand. "We are."

Anatolyevich looked at the pouch. "You'll have to do better than what's inside that."

Ben and Danielle exchanged a glance.

"You don't know, do you?" the Russian taunted them.

"Know what?"

"Those diamonds in your pouch were only a down payment."

"*Down payment*?" Danielle asked incredulously.

Anatolyevich nodded. "A considerably larger sum is waiting at whatever jeweler Ranieri was using as a conduit this time."

"How much?"

"Ten million dollars."

"What were you selling worth *ten million dollars*?" Ben demanded, not believing what he had just heard.

Anatolyevich folded his arms comfortably. "Set me free, let me keep that pouch of diamonds, and I might tell you."

"Not good enough," Danielle told him. "We want to see what you were selling for that kind of money."

"Why not?" Anatolyevich smiled. "I have nothing better to do." The Russian turned his gaze on Ben, as he stood up casually. "Let's go, Inspector. I'll tell you the truth about your father on the way."

# CHAPTER 30

From the safe house in Al-Bireh, they were driven down a dusty road, pitted by stray ordnance blasts, to an abandoned building twelve miles away in Ramallah as instructed. Ben and Danielle left Anatolyevich with al-Asi's guards while they went inside.

"Pakad Barnea," Colonel al-Asi greeted joyously, "how good to see you."

He took her hands and kissed her lightly on both cheeks. The colonel was wearing carpenter's pants and a dress shirt but no tie. The inside of the building smelled of paint and sawdust, and Ben could see one of al-Asi's fingers was bandaged.

Turning to Ben, the colonel swept his hands across the scope of the building. "What do you think of my new headquarters, Inspector?"

The old one in Jericho, Ben knew, had been destroyed by Israeli shelling a year before.

"It seems to be coming along."

"Not as quickly as I had hoped," al-Asi conceded, gazing at his hands. "This building was going to be razed to make room for yet another hotel. I appropriated it when the outbreak of violence changed the owner's plans. I'm not much good with a hammer and nails, as you know. With my budget cut to the bare bones, though, I must learn fast." Al-Asi hooked a hammer over the loop of his carpenter's pants. "You should know that my Israeli counterparts remain especially determined to catch you both."

"They've contacted you?" Ben probed.

"A polite phone call with an oh-so-carefully cloaked warning to turn you over should our paths cross. Disappoint them and I was politely warned this building would not be here tomorrow morning."

"What did you say?"

"That I am the only thing standing between Israel and another dozen suicide bombers every month."

"You sound bitter, Colonel," Ben noted.

"These have been difficult times, that's all. Honesty is missing from the new Israeli administration. Our working relationship is gone. So much wasted. We've lost everything we gained."

"Again."

"You understand."

"My father would have."

"He was ahead of his time, Inspector," al-Asi said reflectively.

"Because he wanted peace."

"And because he understood that to get peace, we must deal with the Israelis. That the other Arab countries will forsake us the moment it best suits their needs and interests."

"Then why was he killed, Colonel?" Ben asked, while Danielle continued to look at them in silence.

"I've told you what I know."

"That he was murdered by my former commander in the Palestinian police, Omar Shaath. I would like to hear more."

"Regrettably, there is none."

"So you have no idea *why* Shaath killed my father. What my father did upon his return that led to his assassination."

Al-Asi sighed. "Your father advocated that the Palestinians make their own peace with the Israelis or risk losing far more than they had already. His was the lone dissenting voice against a violent response. Even a man of his stature and position, though, could not by himself sway the rest of the council."

"What kind of council?"

Al-Asi looked uncharacteristically uneasy. "An ad hoc group of Palestinian leaders that formed in the wake of the Six-Day War. All of them men who had lived through 1948 and didn't believe it could get any worse. The Six-Day War in 1967 proved them wrong. They gathered to discuss what could be done about it."

"You're saying my father was a part of this council," Ben said, vaguely recalling his father's departure from Michigan around that time. Jafir Kamal had said he was going away for a while on business, not saying how long exactly, nor where exactly he was going. Ben and his mother had driven him to the airport. Ben remembered a kiss and warm embrace. It was the last time he'd ever seen his father.

Al-Asi nodded. "The members initially welcomed Jafir Kamal with open arms, believing he had returned to retake his place as a hero to our people and lead them in the struggle to take back our land."

"He disappointed them."

"His was the voice of reason in a time that did not call for it. His comments fell on deaf ears."

"Shaath was a member of this council."

"Yes."

Ben swallowed hard. "When he murdered my father . . ."

"He could have been acting on his own," al-Asi said, anticipating Ben's question. "Or following orders."

"So my father was killed, and yet the council still failed to mount the kind of violent response to the Israeli occupation he tried to stop."

"Strange, isn't it?"

"Yes," Ben replied, realizing in that instant that al-Asi knew far more than he was saying.

# CHAPTER 31

W here in Gaza is the merchandise?" Ben asked Anatolyevich from behind the wheel, once the three of them were on their way. Colonel al-Asi had supplied a sedan with rare diplomatic plates that would assure safe passage along the road that connected the West Bank to Gaza, as well as provide clearance through the volatile Eres checkpoint.

"The fishing piers on the Mediterranean coast," the Russian replied, disinterestedly.

"The shipment is on a *boat*?" Danielle wondered.

Anatolyevich smiled. "Something like that, yes." He looked back at Ben. "Interesting that you returned to your homeland, just as your father did before you. Two of a kind. Two fools. Two cowards."

"I think it's time you told me what you know about him."

"We met once," the Russian nodded. "In 1967, when he came back after the Six-Day War...."

"I CALL for a vote!"

The shouting and thrusting of fists had reached a frenzied pitch when Jafir Kamal rose from his seat at the table occupied by Palestinian council members and waited for the other men to quiet themselves.

"I wish to be heard before we vote," he said sternly.

"There has been enough talk, Abu Kamal! It is time for action!" a council member exclaimed.

"Enough of our people have died! If we do not respond forcefully now against the Israelis, the lessons of *al-Nakba*, the catastrophe, will remain lost upon us," a second council member insisted, referring to Israel's founding in 1948 that had cost thousands and thousands of Palestinians their homes.

"*Min al nahr ila al barh*," the leader of the council intoned. "This land will be ours, *from the river to the sea!*"

"Yes!" Jafir Kamal agreed, turning toward him. "My point precisely: Enough of our people *have* died."

"So you would sit back and do nothing, while the Israelis steal our land, burn our homes?"

"How does he know?" another of the council members challenged bitterly. "He has no home here any longer. The great Jafir Kamal has come from his new home in America to save us all."

"He should have no voice, no vote!"

"Agreed!"

More voices added their acknowledgment until the chorus of shouts aimed at him rang in Jafir Kamal's ears. Through it all a young boy dressed in a shapeless, worn-out shirt and tattered trousers struggled to distribute a tray full of tea to the council members. The jostling hand of one smacked the boy as he was handing a cup to another, and the warm liquid spilled over the man's robes. The council member backhanded the boy in the face and sent the remainder of the cups flying.

Jafir Kamal helped the boy to his feet and watched him scramble back toward the kitchen before responding to the criticism leveled at him. "It is true I moved my family to America. It is true I came back in the wake of the war, leaving my wife and two sons behind." He hardened his gaze. "And it is also true that the land on which I was raised, and raised my family, now serves as an Israeli military outpost. I'd say that entitles me to a voice and a vote."

"You speak the language of an ass, Abu Kamal."

"Yes, because that is what all of you have become. You chastise me for being an outsider," Jafir Kamal said, turning toward the stranger who stood still and silent in the corner of the room. "And yet it is an outsider to whom you turn for help."

"Our friends in Egypt sent him to help us," another of the council members added.

"You mean our friends in Russia, don't you?" Kamal argued, staring at the stranger.

"What's the difference if it gets us the weapons we need?"

"Of course," Jafir Kamal said cynically, regarding the stranger with disdain, "so we can fight the Egyptians' and the Syrians' war for them, a war they have already lost."

The council members looked at each other incredulously.

"You would have us make peace with the Israelis, then, Abu Kamal?" the leader challenged.

"If favorable terms can be arrived at, yes, I would. I would like to propose sending a delegation to meet with the Israeli leadership."

"Madness! They would never hear of it! They don't even recognize our right to our own land," another voice insisted.

"The American life has turned you soft," the council leader added, "while you tell us to be hard. You would have us betray our heritage, our faith, even encourage the inevitability of our own destruction. Your people, Abu Kamal, your people."

The young boy returned with another tray full of tea and began to distribute the cups more carefully.

"You heard the man," said a young soldier named Omar Shaath, who towered over Jafir Kamal when he stood to face him. "Once a hero, you are a hero no more. You are a disgrace to your people who should be gone from here now."

Jafir Kamal refused the boy's offer of a cup with a slight

smile and a shake of his head. "Not until I've cast my vote, whether you wish to count it or not. But first I'd like to hear the substance of this plan."

"We've already heard enough!" Shaath bellowed, feeling for the pistol wedged into his belt. "Now, be gone from here before I—"

"I don't mind explaining myself again," a new voice interjected from a darkened corner of the back room. The windows had been covered up and, without electricity, the sole illumination came from lanterns which cast a murky glow over the new man's sallow face. He was a young man, late twenties or early thirties judging by his looks, but his raspy voice bore the brunt of experiences well beyond his years. "In fact, I welcome it. My country holds Abu Kamal in the highest esteem and would welcome his support."

The man from Russia directed his next words toward Jafir Kamal.

"We are prepared to bring the shipment in through Jordan, as soon as the final approval, and arrangements, are in place."

"You do not expect payment?"

"Your victory over Israel will be payment enough. The weapons are strictly top of the line and not limited to small arms. Enough to equip a small army. Five truckloads to start with, already waiting across the border for you to give me the go-ahead."

"You wish us to do your country's dirty work for you," Jafir Kamal accused.

"My country is the only true ally of your people, of all the Arab peoples. For us to openly help you take back what is yours would lead the United States into taking an even more active role on behalf of the illegal Israeli state. It must be done this way, in darkened rooms and secret shipments, until the tide has turned and you have your land back."

"Do you have anything more to say, Abu Kamal?" the council leader asked.

Jafir Kamal shook his head and met the hateful stare of the hulking Omar Shaath.

"Then the call for a vote is accepted. All in favor, raise your hands."

All the members, save for Jafir Kamal, raised a hand. In the darkened back corner of the room, the Russian smiled.

"How fast can you manage the delivery?" the council leader asked him.

"Give me a few days," the young man promised. "Then you will have all the guns you need."

BEN SAT behind the wheel dumbstruck. Sweat glued his hands to the wheel. More perspiration soaked his shirt and rolled down his face. The Russian's tale made him feel as if his father were in the car with him. He felt hot, shivered anyway.

"How do you know all this?" he asked.

"Isn't it obvious, comrade?" Anatolyevich grinned. "I was the young man in the corner."

# CHAPTER 32

Still grinning, Anatolyevich looked to Danielle. "Surprised, Pakad?"

"Not at all." Danielle fixed her eyes on the Russian, as she stroked her cheek theatrically. "What might you have done in the former Soviet Union, let me see . . . I'll bet it was KGB, or GRU—military intelligence. No, how about GRU and *later* KGB. Attached perhaps to Middle Eastern affairs. You would have been what, twenty-five years old in 1967?"

Anatolyevich smiled like a man who'd been found out. "Thirty."

Danielle turned from him to Ben. "The Russians had military advisors and support personnel all through the Middle East back then, especially Egypt. Word is the Egyptians sent them into Israel in the wake of the Six-Day War to stir up the opposition."

"Very good, *Commissar* Barnea," Anatolyevich complimented sharply.

"The Egyptians wanted their Russian friends to support a guerrilla war waged by the Palestinians against the Israelis," Danielle continued. "And if the Israeli government learned today you were one of those Russians, you'd be in danger of being deported. Back to Russia."

Anatolyevich looked flustered for the first time. His lips trembled with rage. A vein bulged at his temple. "You think

I don't know who you are, the two of you? Your lives are a joke. You're both frauds." Anatolyevich swung toward Ben, spittle dribbling from both sides of his mouth. "Just like your father was a fraud."

"Why, because he didn't want to fight your battles for you?"

"Our plan might have *worked*!" the Russian raged. "If a man like your father had signed on to lead it. Imagine my disappointment when he alone voted against the Palestinian council's plans for what would have been the original *intifada*." The Russian shook his head. "The routes, and diversions, everything arranged. I was ready to have the guns brought in."

"But you never did. Otherwise, the council would have used them. So what went wrong in 1967? Why were your weapons never delivered?"

Anatolyevich steadied himself with a single deep breath, then yawned and stretched comfortably. "I think I'll take a nap. Wake me when we reach the Gaza seaport and maybe I will finish my story."

# CHAPTER 33

"We're closed," Jacob Katz said to the man who'd been rapping on the door of his shop. "It's the Sabbath."

The man stuck his foot in the door before Katz could shut it. "Yeah, well we got an appointment, you and me." An American accent, not quite southern.

Katz took a longer look at the man; big and broad with eyes glittering like the diamonds that filled the store's display cases. One of the man's ears was bandaged and his cheek was blistered, as if from sunburn. The rest of his skin was leathery rough. He held a cowboy hat in his hand, a hat that looked shiny around the brim.

"I don't have what you want," Katz managed. "I've got it stored somewhere else."

"Figured you would," said the cowboy. "Just as I figured you were likely thinking about keeping it for yourself."

"No, I was just waiting—"

The cowboy pushed open the door and Katz backed off, not resisting.

"I've done everything they asked," Katz insisted, trying to sound confident. "Give me until tomorrow. I'll have it here then."

"Yeah," Jim Black said, looking around, "that's what I told them you'd say. I told them to cut you a break. What the fuck you want from him, I said?" He faced Katz. "They weren't as sympathetic as me."

Black walked on, inspecting the contents of the cases. "Nice stones."

Katz said nothing.

"I hear you do a lot of finish work on them right here."

Katz nodded. "In the back."

"Could you show me?" Jim Black asked, sounding genuinely excited.

"What?"

"Could you show me how you do it?"

Katz realized he didn't have a choice. "Sure. Right this way."

Katz moved through the shop into an alcove where he pressed in the proper combination into a keypad. He had maneuvered himself to block his actions from view, but the cowboy didn't seem to be paying attention, looking disinterested until they entered the work area.

"Hey," he noted, "looks like a science lab."

"We have to keep it as clean as possible."

Black looked up at the walls. "Nice security cameras. Bet they set you back a shit load."

"Yes, they did."

"I did some security once for the Israeli Diamond Exchange in Ramat Gan. They got maybe a thousand cameras and more metal detectors than an old whore's got crabs. Fortified doors, too. Take a tank to blow through them."

"I've been there," Katz said, trying hard not to sound condescending. "The exchange attracts twenty thousand visitors a day."

The cowboy walked past him. "The guys who do the finishing for you, they sit at these funny desks?"

"Yes."

"Don't look too comfortable."

"They get used to it."

Jim Black looked back at Katz. "Guess a man can get

used to just about anything. So how's it work, the process I mean?"

"With very fine tools, manufactured specifically to be used on diamonds."

The cowboy pulled an object that looked like an electric toothbrush from a slot tailored for it on one of the desks. He pressed a button on the handle and a tiny polishing wheel began to turn with a mechanical whir. He pressed harder on the button and the wheel spun faster, its tiny engine whining now.

The cowboy mocked a sweeping motion near his mouth. "Got any paste? I could use a polish."

"That thing would cut through to the pulp in a second. It's a polishing tool we use to bring the diamond's color out. Last stage of the process."

"Thing's that sharp?"

"Yes."

"Let me see."

The cowboy's free hand shot out in a blur of motion and captured Katz by the throat. The next thing Katz knew he was bent backwards over the worktable and the cowboy was lowering the churning finishing wheel toward his face.

"Don't worry," he said, "I'm not going to mess up your teeth."

Jim Black aimed the tool for Katz's cheek and started it downward.

# CHAPTER 34

As expected, the papers Colonel al-Asi had provided eased their passage through the Eres checkpoint, and Ben continued on to Gaza City. Once there, he passed Palestine Square and the airport on the way to Gaza Port. He had spent little time in Gaza since his return and hadn't realized how the contrasts of life in Palestine were even more striking here than in the West Bank. The degradation of the refugee camps had grown worse as the closing of Israel's borders forced more and more residents into poverty. Social services had clearly broken down, evidenced by the huge volume of trash left to steam and stink beneath the hot sun.

And yet the square, Midan Filisteen, bustled with activity and hope, as credit was extended and goods were bartered. Even more striking was the perfectly kept, grassy, flowered walkway that formed the median between the lanes of Sharia Omar al-Mukhtar Street. Locals walked upon it as if headed for somewhere better, ambling past robed women who tended the gardens with makeshift watering cans and rakes.

The last stretch of the drive was made along the coastal road called Al-Rasheed. The beach rimmed its entire length to the west, the restaurants and hotels overlooking the coastline all looking lonely and desolate. It was easy for Ben to close his eyes and visualize what might have been in a world of peace. But the smells of raw sewage rising off the Mediterranean and rank garbage strewn about the shoreline quickly destroyed the illusion.

"We're almost there," Danielle said to Anatolyevich, who was still feigning sleep in the backseat.

The Russian left his arms crossed and eyes closed. "I know." Anatolyevich's eyes emerged through narrow slits. "I was hoping to overhear more of your pleasant conversation."

"The port is just up ahead," Ben announced. "What now?"

"We find a boat."

WITH LESS demand for their catch at the markets, there were many small fishing craft to choose from at the dilapidated and nearly abandoned port. Israeli shekels remained the currency of choice in Gaza, as opposed to Arab dinars, and Danielle had more than enough to rent a thirty-six-foot trawler that looked as if it hadn't been scraped or cleaned for a decade. The deck was marred by splinters and rough gouges cut from the wood, many of the screws holding the railing in place long stripped.

Once the three were on board, Danielle took the wheel and edged the trawler at a creeping pace through the harbor, keeping her speed down even in the open waters of the Mediterranean until she familiarized herself with the boat's sluggish controls. The one time she tried to open it up, the engine clanked and sputtered, belching dark oily smoke through the exhaust baffles, which had forced her to ease back on the throttle.

"I need a course, a heading!" she shouted down to Anatolyevich above the grinding rattle.

"You're doing fine. Just keep going straight." The Russian turned and winked at Ben. "I tell you too much too soon, maybe you just shoot me and dump my body overboard."

"*You know we won't do that,*" Ben said in Russian.

Anatolyevich looked shocked. "You speak my language, comrade."

"I learned it before I learned English. My father taught me."

"Interesting he should do so, don't you think? Perhaps it was because he was dealing with my countrymen long before he left for America. Because we were the ones bringing in food and supplies when the Israelis left you with practically nothing. He must have known your future lay with us."

"Did you use the same routes for the food and supplies that you intended to use for the guns?"

"You see a difference?"

"Don't you?"

"It was a question of survival in both cases. Your father knew that, too."

"What changed?"

"He left. It is never the same when you come back." Anatolyevich paused. "Is it, comrade?"

"*This isn't about me,*" Ben responded in Russian.

"Your father taught you Russian because he thought one day you would take his place, fill the role that he had once filled. You, a people of no chances, cast your lot with us."

"My father?"

"Most of all. Before he left for America."

"The other leaders didn't give him a choice, did they? They wanted him out before the Six-Day War."

"He was making waves."

"And then they begged him to return."

Anatolyevich looked surprised. "Is that what you think?"

"It's what my mother told me—the only thing."

"It's what he wanted all of you to think."

"Why?"

"Because it was easier to accept than the truth."

"What is the truth?"

"What do you think, comrade? You think leaving when he did, so soon before the Six-Day War, was just a coincidence?"

"He knew it was coming?"

The Russian nodded. "A small number of Palestinians were informed in the hope they would join the attack from within."

"But my father refused to lead the guerilla war in Israel," Ben picked up, realizing. "That's why he was forced to leave Palestine. That's why he moved us to America. But why didn't anyone else take his place?"

"There was no one else who was able to lead, comrade. Oh, a few tried. Omar Shaath, for example."

"The man who assassinated him."

"Your father knew what he was walking into when he came back. He was relying on the mistaken assumption he could make a difference, just as you did." Anatolyevich started to fish through his pants pocket. "Speaking of which, I have something to show you."

His hand emerged finally with a crinkled black-and-white snapshot. He smoothed it out as best he could before handing it to Ben. Pictured was a boy serving tea from a tray to an intense-looking man who appeared to be declining the offer of a cup.

"You look quite a bit like him," Anatolyevich noted.

Ben felt his chest tighten as he studied the photograph. "You took this?"

The Russian nodded. "That night during the meeting of the Palestinian council. My superiors always insisted upon documentation. Tiny, hidden cameras were usually unreliable in those days, but I got lucky."

Ben continued to stare at the picture, realizing with a strange sense of melancholy that it was likely the last one taken before his father was murdered just a few days later. In 1967 Vasily Anatolyevich had come to the West Bank, representing the KGB, with an offer to bring truckloads of guns for the Palestinians to use against the Israelis. The offer had been accepted, Jafir Kamal the lone dissenting voice. A few days later his father was dead and the guns, by all accounts, never arrived. Anatolyevich was likely the last person left who could tell Ben why.

Then again, there might be another person, Ben thought, shifting his gaze from Jafir Kamal to the boy holding a tray of tea at his side. The room's ambient light was just enough to show a thin, frail figure, his face dipped downward submissively and thus bathed in shadows.

"Who was the boy?" Ben asked Anatolyevich.

"Funny," the Russian said, "I never thought to ask. I assumed he was the son of one of the council members. I thought it might have been you when your Colonel al-Asi gave it to me."

Ben looked up from the picture. It was the kind of grainy shot Ben recalled from the old Polaroid cameras he'd had as a boy that spat out unformed worlds that stank of bitter chemicals long after they took black-and-white shape.

"Al-Asi gave this to *you*?"

The Russian nodded. "Apparently it fell into his possession after he took over your Protective Security Service; many of our old files did. We enjoyed a close relationship with your people for many years." Anatolyevich looked as if he suddenly found something funny. "Interesting how I found myself procuring arms for the Palestinians once again, with considerably more success, I might add."

"Until Tuesday."

"Thanks to you."

"Considerably different circumstances, too."

"Yes, profit instead of politics. I much prefer profit. We have something else in common, you know."

"I wasn't aware we had anything at all in common."

"How old were you when your father left to come back here?"

"Seven."

"About the same age I was when my father left for World War II. I never saw him again either. It is a terrible thing to lose a father that way."

Anatolyevich waited, perhaps expecting Ben to respond.

When he didn't, the Russian gestured to the picture still held in Ben's outstretched hand. "Keep it if you wish. I have no use for it."

"Colonel al-Asi must have thought you did."

"I believe he just wanted me to understand the scope of his reach. That he had the measure of me."

"The colonel is like that."

"A good friend to have, comrade. He made it very plain what would happen if I did not act in good faith on our little journey."

Ben looked at the snapshot again and then eased it into his pocket, trying to keep it smooth. "What happened to my father, Anatolyevich? Why was he killed?"

"Ben!" Danielle called from the bridge before the Russian could respond. "Off the port side, look!"

# CHAPTER 35

The freighter listed atop the sea, bobbing gently in the waves. Even from this distance, her weathered exterior gave her the appearance of a ghost ship adrift through time and water. An ancient and rusted medium-range haul relic, no more than two hundred feet in length, abandoned to her own demise.

"Your ten-million-dollar shipment's on *that*?" Ben posed.

"There's something wrong," Anatolyevich said softly, when they drew to within a few hundred yards. He lowered a pair of binoculars salvaged from the trawler's supply closet from his eyes. They trembled in his hands. "There are no guards on deck."

"Guards?"

"We should turn around now, go back to Gaza."

"We're not going anywhere until we've seen what's on board."

"Didn't you hear what I said? There's no one on deck. It might not be safe."

Ben took a step closer to the Russian, strangely unmoved. "What's on board, Anatolyevich?"

"Turn this boat around, I beg you, before it is too late!"

Ben eased his hand to the pistol he'd kept hidden in the car through the drive to Gaza from the safe house, suddenly wishing for something with more firepower.

"It looks abandoned," Danielle called down to them from the bridge. "Anchored astern, but, he's right, I don't see anyone on board or inside the tower."

"Her gunwale's only thirty feet above the surface," Ben said back to her. "I saw a grappling hook and rope in the supply box we could use to reach the deck."

Anatolyevich grabbed hold of Ben's arm. "Please, comrade, I beg you. You don't understand!"

"Make me."

"The guns in Beit Jala, where do you think they came from?"

"You told me: Russia. Army surplus."

"In the Russian army, *everything* is surplus, because there is no Russian army to speak of these days. But the guns still exist. As merchandise now, to be sold to the highest bidder; sometimes, *any* bidder. But not just guns." Anatolyevich paused. "Other things."

"What kinds of things?"

"Just because we lost the Cold War, comrade, does not mean we didn't fight. Our scientists were as busy as yours figuring out how to win. But missile shields and space-based ray guns were beyond our capabilities," the former KGB man said, the derision clear in his voice. "We needed to find other means to defeat you. And once we lost, all those means would have been wasted.

"Until we discovered a market for them," Anatolyevich finished.

"Palestinians?"

"Among many others."

"Not many others can afford to pay ten million dollars."

"Unless they are in possession of considerable resources."

"The diamonds . . ."

"Rough diamonds lifted from African mines and passed to middlemen, delivery boys who bring them to Israel to exchange for armaments."

"But you're saying there's more than just guns and bullets on that freighter."

"Considerably more, comrade. That's why you must tell *Commissar* Barnea up there to turn this boat around!"

Ben's features flared. "What's on board? Is it nuclear weapons? Biological? *Chemical*?"

"You don't want to know, believe me," Anatolyevich said and cast his gaze over the bow, as Danielle edged their boat ever closer to the looming steel hull of the freighter. "Tell her to stop. Before it's too late."

"Answer my question first."

"Not nuclear, not biological, not chemical! No, what's on that freighter came from a secret program I oversaw in Dubna while I was with KGB and later when I served briefly with the Federal Security Service. Kept active until the very last days of the Soviet Union by leaving them in the dark about the extent of our progress. Looking toward the future, you understand," Anatolyevich added with a touch of irony. "Already planning for it."

"Preparing to sell the results of your program, in other words."

"Waiting for the right time, the right offer, the right party."

"To sell *what*?"

Anatolyevich's eyes were furious, emblazoned with desperation. "I can make calls. I know people! We must arrange for the freighter to be blown up. Before it is too late."

Now it was Ben who latched on to Anatolyevich, shoving him backward against the cabin. "Not until we see what's on board."

# CHAPTER 36

U
p close, Cyrillic letters scrawled in fading, peeling paint identified the freighter as the *Peter the Great*. Danielle eased their trawler close to its side and dropped anchor.

Ben threaded the grappling hook through the accompanying rope and hurled it skyward. Remarkably, it locked on to the gunwale on the first try and he began to climb instantly. He needed both hands to manage the effort, leaving the pistol provided by Colonel al-Asi stuck uselessly in his belt. He could feel the muscles in his arms twist into lean cords flared with veins and ridges, more glad than ever he'd been religious about staying in shape since his return to Palestine. Police headquarters in Jericho had a small gym in the basement, but mostly his exercise regimen came down to push-ups in his apartment living room, sometimes with his feet propped up on the couch's thin fabric.

Anatolyevich went next and for him the task would have been impossible if not for Danielle's efforts at helping him make the climb. Ben neared the top of the rope well ahead of them and peered over the side of the ship. He found the deck deserted, just as it had appeared from their boat. Breathing easier, he eased his body up and over the gunwale, then helped Danielle and Anatolyevich climb over to the deck of the *Peter the Great* as well.

"You see what I mean?" the Russian charged fearfully.

"It's just like I told you. Now let's get out of here before it's too late!"

"I think we'll have a look below first," Ben insisted.

Danielle panned the deck. "The lifeboats are all still in place." Her eyes reached Ben. "So where's the crew?"

Ben scanned the freighter's deck. Close up, the *Peter the Great* looked older and in even worse disrepair than it had from sea. Surfaces blistered and bubbled everywhere with rust. The paint, in two or three different patchwork shades, was faded and peeling. Tack welds covered the deck and surrounding structures like scars from jagged knife wounds. Orange streaks of corrosion crisscrossed the deck, like a cancer slowly eating away at the freighter's body. The air stank of dried oil, and the entire deck was filthy with a film of it that Ben realized had already covered both his hands.

"Let's see if we can find them," he answered finally.

ALL THREE moved toward the entrance of the stairwell that ran just beneath the *Peter the Great*'s deserted bridge. The steel door that led to it was closed, and Danielle drew her pistol before they got there. Anatolyevich hovered well back on the deck, while Ben and Danielle took up positions on opposite sides of the door. The door opened inward and Ben used hand signals to indicate he would handle the task of forcing it ajar. Danielle nodded and watched as he sprang the latch and threw his shoulder into the door in a single, swift motion.

The force of the thrust caused Ben to slip on the wet deck. Danielle watched him going down when a gunshot exploded from within the stairwell, the noise deafening because of the echo. Danielle dove and slid across the deck, firing high into the darkness to make sure she avoided Ben. She heard a grunt, then the thumping sound of a body tumbling down the stairs before she slid to a halt.

"Ben!" she screamed.

"I'm all right! What about . . ."

Ben's voiced trailed off when he glanced at the deck and saw Anatolyevich lying on his back, blood spreading beneath him across the moist deck. His chest had been caved in by what could only have been a shotgun shell, explaining the volume of the shot that had left a terrible ringing in Ben's ears.

Danielle spun into the doorway over Ben, gun aimed down the narrow steel stairs. The body of the man she had shot lay twisted at the bottom of the first flight, shotgun poking out from beneath him.

"Crew member?"

"Dressed like one, anyway."

"But who did he think we were?"

Danielle reached down to help Ben to his feet. "Only one way to find out."

# CHAPTER 37

G eneral Latisse Matabu was dreaming of a ship. A great ship that carried the last of her hope within its holds. But her sleep quickly turned restless, because this ship that should have been hers was not. Strangers patrolled its decks, threatening the last gift she intended to leave the world.

Strange how the gifts she had been blessed with could not help her heal herself. The great powers she had inherited from the original Dragon were powerless against the disease that was ravaging her body. And the revenge she had extracted on General Treest upon her return to Sierra Leone could change nothing. Latisse Matabu knew this, just as Dr. Sowahy did. She could lie to herself no longer. To take his medication, though, meant accepting that she was not unique, no different from anyone else. Accepting that science could help where the gifts that defined her could not.

The doctor had come again today, looking grave after he completed his examination.

"What's wrong?" she asked him.

Dr. Sowahy came round the desk and faced Latisse Matabu in her chair. "I have heard tales about your trip to Katani two days ago, General." He narrowed his gaze and shook his head slowly. "What have you done?" the doctor asked, not bothering to hide his disgust.

"Only what an ancestor did long before me. You knew my grandmother?"

"We were born in neighboring villages."

"There is a tale she used to often tell me, a tale of one of our ancestors they called the Moor Woman. It starts in Anatolia, now Turkey, in 1347. . . ."

ORHAN, SON *of Osman I, founder of the Ottoman Empire, reached the top of the ridge and halted, staring down into the valley through the swirling mist that had appeared out of nowhere. There, rising out of the gray vapor clouds clinging to the ground, appeared the ruins of an ancient fortress.*

*Most of its walled structure had crumbled long ago, leaving only a single port of entry through a still-standing archway. Its color must have been once that of polished white granite. But the years had reduced its remnants to a clay red hue, blackening the fortress in the places the sun no longer touched. All three of its towers had been sheared off at varying heights by time. Its dome was cracked, but whole. The battlements that had once housed the fortress's guards had collapsed upon themselves in near matching piles of rubble.*

*Orhan ordered his troops to hold their ground and started down into the valley, choosing his way carefully. The path seemed to narrow, all but the ground immediately before him lost to the mist the further down he climbed. Dead, leafless branches looking like hands poked out of the muck.*

*Finally the ruins of the fortress appeared directly before him. Orhan stopped near the fallen rubble of an archway and peered ahead into the darkness before stepping through.*

*"Come in," a wizened, crackly voice called from inside. "I've been waiting for you."*

*Orhan continued until the shape of an old woman was directly before him and sank to one knee in reverence. "I am—"*

*"I know who you are. Orhan, son of Osman I, conqueror of the Byzantines. Orhan, ruler of the Ottomans."*

*Orhan's eyes adjusted to the darkness and saw before him a dark, lithe figure cloaked in shapeless black rags the same color as her mottled, wrinkled skin. She was more shadow than person, seated on a straw mattress dimly lit by the thin light struggling through cracks in the structure's walls.*

*"Now tell me what has brought you to my presence," the Moor Woman said, her milky gaze locking on Orhan. "Tell me what leads you to come to a witch for help."*

*"I must complete my father's work. There is a world beyond Anatolia that awaits our rule."*

*The Moor Woman smiled, revealing the stubs of rotting teeth and purplish gums. "That world will cost you a great deal."*

*Orhan took a step closer, stopping as if an invisible barrier had sprang up in his path. "My armies are not strong enough to fight all of Europe."*

*"You will not need your armies, if you follow my instructions. But the price is a great one."*

*"I am willing to pay you anything!"*

*"Not my price—the one you must live with for all your remaining days."*

*"I do not care how harshly the world judges me."*

*The Moor Woman offered a pair of bony, withered hands to the leader of the Ottomans. "Then sit with me, Orhan, and listen while I describe your task. . . ."*

"I'VE HEARD enough!" Dr. Sowahy blared, interrupting Matabu's retelling of her grandmother's often-told tale.

"The story isn't finished. The Moor Woman sent Orhan

to a dying village on the Black Sea. Told him to gather rats and sail on to a number of ports where he was to release the rats onto dozens of Italian merchant ships still in their harbors. These merchant ships would later dock at various European ports of call to empty their storage holds. And at each port the rats, thirsty and ravenous, emerged carrying a pestilence that changed the world forever.

"The Black Death, of course, spread throughout Europe and any threat Orhan and his successors may have faced from the west was eliminated, his enemies neutralized. The Ottoman Empire was born. The Moor Woman had been true to her word. And Orhan was true to his as well, securing her passage on a merchant ship bound for Africa where she made her true home. No longer known as the Moor Woman, though. In Africa her powers and visions earned her a new name from those who feared her:

"The Dragon."

Matabu smiled thinly. "What if I was in possession of a comparable means to establish my empire, just as Orhan established his?"

Sowahy shuddered. "I won't listen to this!"

"You should, Doctor, because what happened then is going to happen once again. Our enemies are going to be vanquished, just as Orhan's were—"

Matabu felt a hollow pang building behind her eyeballs, a stinging pain that surged into her cheeks and left her dizzy.

"What is it?" Dr. Sowahy asked, reaching for her hand to take her pulse.

Matabu pulled it away. "Just a spell."

"You can't let yourself get so worked·up."

Matabu smiled slightly. "I am remaking the world, Doctor. How can I not?"

B en and Danielle descended the steel stairs slowly, listening for any stray sound other than the echoes of their own steps. Beyond the soft clacking of the freighter's still idling diesel motors and the rhythmic lapping of the water against the freighter's hull, though, there was only silence.

They searched the first two decks and found nothing. Just empty berths and staterooms, and a mess hall littered with half-eaten meals. Whatever happened here, then, had clearly happened in a hurry.

With each descent the air grew staler and hotter. The third sub-deck was located in the deepest livable bowels of the ship, containing access to the various cargo holds. The first two holds Ben and Danielle checked offered only a few stray remnants of machine and auto parts, discarded refuse from a previous cargo.

A dripping sound and a door that creaked slowly back and forth had them approaching the third hold warily, each tightening their grasps on their pistols. Ben peeked inside and then eased open the door as Danielle joined him.

The hold was lined with the bodies of the *Peter the Great*'s missing crew members, strewn from wall to wall. A dozen at the very least.

"My God," she mumbled and slipped past him.

"Shot?"

"Yes," Danielle replied, needing only a cursory inspection to reach that conclusion. "And all at about the same time, by the look of things."

"When?"

Danielle found a patch of dried blood and did some quick calculations in her head. "Last night sometime."

"Killed and then dragged here to be hidden," Ben assumed.

"No," said Danielle, inspecting the blood pattern. "Most of them were brought here and *then* killed. You can tell by the way the bodies fell that they had been lined up."

"A massacre," Ben said, and backed out of the hold.

Even more tense than before now, he closed that cargo hold door behind them and moved on to the next. The air grew cold as they drew closer, downright chilly, owing to the fact that this final hold was obviously refrigerated.

This time Danielle entered first, spinning her way through the large archway with gun drawn.

The hold was empty.

Danielle lowered her gun, shivering from the supercooled air as mist formed before her face.

"Look at this," Ben called.

He had passed her upon entering the deserted hold, and had crouched down in the center of the floor.

"There was something here, all right," he continued, pointing at the floor. "Based on the dust pattern, anyway."

Danielle shined a flashlight she'd brought from their trawler across the floor, looking for any signs of what might have been stored in the hold. "Crates of some kind," she presumed. "Big ones, maybe three by six feet."

"Stolen, obviously. But by whom?"

"Good question," a familiar voice said from the doorway leading into the cargo hold, and Danielle swung to find herself face-to-face with General Dov Levy.

# CHAPTER 39

Professor Deirdre Cotter held her hat to her head as the jeep thundered down the narrow road carved out of the jungle.

"You still haven't told me where we're going," she said to the Sierra Leone cabinet minister seated next to her in the jeep's rear seat.

"The village of Katani, Doctor," Daniel Sukahamin replied.

"It's 'professor,' not 'doctor.' "

"Whatever you say, miss."

"Fine. Then tell me why the hell you're taking me there."

"Because you are needed, miss."

"You're defense minister of the Sierra Leone government and I'm a botanist, an agriculturist, working for the U.N. mission."

"We're well aware of what you do, miss," Sukahamin assured her.

*"Then what in God's name do you need me for?"*

"You are the same Deirdre Cotter who came to my country with her husband three years ago?"

Cotter stiffened. "Do you really need to ask?"

"Your husband was taken hostage and murdered by RUF rebels two years into your stay."

"For Christ's sake . . ."

"And yet you stayed. You did not run. You stayed even beyond the time expected of you. Why?"

Deirdre Cotter swallowed hard. "Because I thought I could make a difference. I *wanted* to make a difference."

Sukahamin remained utterly calm. "You are about to get your chance, Professor."

"WHAT DO you know about the villages in this region?" the defense minister of Sierra Leone resumed as the road narrowed and the jeep drew closer to the town of Katani.

"Fishing- and farming-based. Pretty much self-reliant."

"Until yesterday, Professor."

The jeep slowed as the first awkward signs pointing toward the village appeared on the side of the dirt road, haphazardly nailed to a tree. But as yet no people had appeared even though the jeep had already passed the stream from which the villagers drew their water. Normally there was a constant parade back and forth of locals toting large drums and containers. The anomaly made Cotter even warier than she already was.

The jeep wound its way into the village, which was composed of little more than a collection of slipshod and ramshackle structures. Some of the larger, better-kept ones had windows and arched roofs, while others qualified merely as huts fashioned from hard-packed, dried mud. These huts, mostly homes for the villagers, formed a semi-circle around the town center.

With the town center empty, Deirdre Cotter expected frightened faces to be peering out from behind doors or curtain flaps fashioned out of burlap or other scraps of clothing, but there were none.

"The village is abandoned," she realized, feeling their jeep bump across the uneven landscape, not stopping at the abandoned town.

"Since yesterday," Sukahamin acknowledged. "They had

some unwelcome guests the day before that: the RUF."

Cotter's features flared. Her lips trembled. "What are you dragging me into, here? I told you, I'm just a *botanist*! The U.N. sent us here to help educate your people on how better to work the land, not get involved in your civil war."

"You have been involved since your husband was murdered, miss," Sukahamin said gravely. "In Sierra Leone, *everyone* is involved."

The jeep halted and Sukahamin climbed out, shadowed instantly by his driver and bodyguard, who shifted their weapons round to be within easy reach.

"This way," the defense minister beckoned when Cotter finally exited the jeep, wiping the sweat from her hands on her cargo pants. "Their fields are clustered in a valley just beyond this ridge."

Swarms of bugs nipped at her flesh and Cotter kept swatting at them to no avail. They seemed immune to insect repellant in this part of the world. The only thing that worked was a mixture of mud and leaves a villager had shown her months before. But the pasty mixture stank horribly and left a grayish residue on the skin that was almost impossible to wash off, even with hot water and soap.

Sukahamin took the lead, picking up the pace as the group neared the top of the ridge. Suddenly a stench pierced the breeze, something bitter and acidic like nothing Deirdre Cotter had ever smelled before. She slipped at the ridge's steepest point and had to be helped to the top by the defense minister's guards, who maintained a firm hold on their weapons as well. Her breath tasted bitter, made her want to retch. She finally drew even with Sukahamin and gazed down into the valley with him.

"The devil has come to my country, Professor, hasn't he?"

"Close enough," Cotter said, not believing her eyes.

# CHAPTER 40

Ben had drawn his pistol when Danielle shouted, "*No!*" She took a step closer to Dov Levy, former head of the Sayaret. "This is General Levy, the man who gave me this assignment."

"Unofficial as it may have been," Levy affirmed. "Thank you for not shooting me, Inspector. Don't worry," he continued to Ben, "introductions aren't necessary."

"You forgot to tell me you were dead," Danielle said.

"Amazing how dying frees up one's movements," Levy replied. He must have been in his mid-fifties now. But his hair remained thick, his body hard and angular. "It allows me to look into things, with nobody the wiser."

"Or have others do it for you," Danielle added.

"Difficult to assemble an actual staff under the circumstances, Lieutenant."

"I'm not a lieutenant anymore."

"Just as I am not a general, and yet we still fight the same war we have always fought." Levy stepped out of the hold into the murky light cast by dangling bulbs in the corridor beyond, followed closely by Ben and Danielle. A dark scruffy beard painted his face gray, as if he hadn't shaved since the last time Danielle had seen him. "What has become of the guns, Lieutenant?"

"Not guns," Ben said before Danielle had a chance to.

"Pardon me?"

"He's right," Danielle explained. "This freighter wasn't carrying guns; it was carrying something far more deadly. Tell him, Ben."

And Ben did, summarizing Anatolyevich's evasive comments about the now missing cargo for which he would have been paid upwards of ten million dollars in diamonds.

"This is all your fault," Levy scowled when he was finished.

"*My* fault?" Ben asked.

"If all had gone according to plan, Anatolyevich would have led Lieutenant Barnea here from East Jerusalem three days ago." Levy turned toward Ben, scowling. "Thanks to your arresting Anatolyevich, though, we have no idea what has become of that cargo, or even what it is."

"How did you find us?" Danielle asked Levy, suddenly suspicious.

"I picked you up in Haifa. Sabi's sources are not always as discreet as he would have you believe. In any case, I followed you into the West Bank."

"And after that?"

"Your friend Colonel al-Asi had planted a bug on the Russian, and I was able to home in," Levy said to Ben. "The colonel seems to like keeping track of you."

"Just as you like keeping track of me," interjected Danielle.

"I shadowed you to Gaza and then followed you out to sea."

"You used her," Ben charged. "This is your fault, not mine. If you had used traditional authorities instead of Danielle—"

"Only I couldn't."

"Why?" Danielle demanded.

"Go back to East Jerusalem, Lieutenant. Tell me what went wrong."

"Commander Baruch was there."

"Coincidence?"

"Yes."

"No," Levy corrected.

"*What?*"

"Think!"

"There was no record of Baruch ever going to East Jerusalem," Ben remembered. "Nothing in the logs."

"Of course not, Inspector, because he was not there in his capacity as head of National Police." Levy refocused on Danielle. "The position of his men, how they were spread through the square, what did it make you think of?"

Danielle tried to recall the precise sequence of the deadly events in East Jerusalem, how they had unfolded.

*. . . she saw armed figures rushing about the street, clacking off rounds wildly with their pistols as they ran. Two fell to the pavement and began to crawl off, fingers digging into the asphalt trying to pull themselves clear. Danielle kept her gun steady and swung back to the table. . . .*

"Oh my God," she thought, realizing.

*. . . She twisted off the boy and lurched upward, pistol in hand, and found herself face-to-face with the glazed expression of a detective she recognized from National Police. He staggered forward, a pistol held loosely in his hand. Then his spine arched and he dropped to the curb, a victim of the wild spray of bullets.*

The way Baruch's team covered the East Jerusalem square, the way they were spread, indicated a protective operation, not an assault. There was only one person, though, they could have been there to protect: Anatolyevich.

And only one person who could have posed a threat to him.

"The police were shooting at me," Danielle said distantly, as if not believing her own words. "They were shooting at me. . . ."

# CHAPTER 41

I think you see my point now," the former head of the
Sayaret told her. "Understand why I needed you, Lieutenant?"

"After Beirut . . ."

"*Because* of Beirut. Reassigning you afterwards was
mandated, but it was wrong. I knew that and so did your
father, yet there was nothing either of us could do."

"The man who wiped out our team was the same one
who tried to kill me in the jail. A cowboy."

"His name is James Allen Black. Impressive record in
American Special Operations. Liked his work a little too
much for the military's taste. Very good. Very expensive."

"You know this and he's still *alive*."

"I learned about him after the Israeli government had
already made use of his skills on a number of occasions.
From everything I know about Black, the two of you are
very lucky to be alive."

"So is he," Danielle said, and stepped forward into a thin
shaft of light directly in front of Levy. "But I could just as
easily have been killed in East Jerusalem, couldn't I?"

"Something I could never have foreseen occurred, remember? Inspector Kamal arrested Anatolyevich. And
when he didn't show up in the square as planned, and you
did, Baruch panicked."

"Because he thought *I* was the one who intercepted the

Russian, not Ben," Danielle realized. "That I had penetrated the network Baruch was a part of."

"And had discovered his involvement. I suspect Commander Baruch was trying to cover his own ass when he ordered his men to fire on you."

"Because Baruch was being paid off."

"Not him alone. Believe me. This is a huge conspiracy in which many, many Israeli officials have gotten very rich, Lieutenant."

"Are you saying *they* know what was on board this freighter?"

"No! No! Guns, rockets, plastic explosives—the less they knew about the shipments, the better." Levy turned his attention back to Danielle. "Commander Baruch must have thought you were in East Jerusalem investigating *him*. He must have felt he had no other choice."

"Wait, you're forgetting something," Danielle said rapidly, her mind back in East Jerusalem. "During the gun battle, *Palestinians* opened up on Baruch's men from all angles."

"Palestinians no one could find any trace of, because there was only one shooter. And he wasn't Palestinian."

Danielle's eyes widened. She felt herself shudder, more memories of what had transpired in the square flooding back. The wounded detective, the bullets strafing the café . . .

"It was you who shot the policemen," she said, her voice barely audible, "including the one I tried to save."

"Only to stop them from shooting you."

"Just before I killed Moshe Baruch."

"Not exactly," Levy said, softer.

"What do you mean?"

"You didn't kill Baruch; I did."

"THE BALLISTICS report would have proven that," Levy continued, "had one been ordered. That's why no trace of any Palestinian gunmen were found in the area."

Danielle found herself speechless, a mixture of relief and confusion flooding through her.

*She had killed no one in the square that day!*

"So what do we do now?" she managed.

"Find someone in the government we can trust with what we've learned, Lieutenant. There's too much at stake now to sidestep a scandal. Let the truth come out." Levy thought briefly. "Stay in Gaza tonight. Meet me first thing tomorrow morning at the fish market."

"How will we find you?" Danielle asked.

"Just be there," Levy said to both of them. "I'll find you."

# CHAPTER 42

Mayor Krilev and Colonel Petroskov made their way along the corridors of a converted maternity hospital in the center of Dubna, squeezing past the dead and the dying.

"You promised me more medical personnel," Krilev accused. He realized Petroskov couldn't hear him and yanked the surgical mask from his mouth. "I said you promised me more medical personnel," he repeated, finding his bravado after nearly two days of enduring the colonel's overbearing manner and brusque orders. "You promised me experts, vaccines, *help!*"

Petroskov interrupted the silent count of bodies he was making. "None of which would have made any difference at all."

"Your soldiers have turned my people into prisoners in their own homes."

"It's for their own good."

"Why wasn't I consulted about the curfew?"

Petroskov stopped and swung toward the mayor of Dubna, scowling in impatience. "You are no longer in charge here, Mayor Krilev. I thought I had made that abundantly clear. Martial law has been declared."

"By *you?*"

"By forces far beyond both of us."

"You're telling me Moscow knows what's going on."

"They know everything, believe me."

"And still they do *nothing*!"

"They sent me."

"And the citizens of my city keep dying. Thousands now, more sure to follow."

"The worst is over."

"I am still Dubna's highest elected official, Colonel. I have a duty to my people."

"Your duty is to Moscow, Mayor, as is mine."

Krilev and Petroskov flattened themselves up against a wall to allow a flood of orderlies to push dollies carrying sheet-covered corpses past them. The line stretched as far down the hall as they could see.

"You said you had something you wanted to see me about, Colonel."

"Yes. My men rounded up dozens of your 'people' trying to flee Dubna through the woods. Three were shot when they refused to comply with the order to stop."

"Shot?" Krilev could scarcely believe what he had heard. "That's monstrous!"

Petroskov looked unmoved. "Your detention facilities are inadequate for the number of those we will need to incarcerate. Other arrangements must be made."

"What would you have me do, Colonel, build another jail?"

"Any civic facility will suffice. Please select one for us to appropriate. And please warn your people that any further attempts to leave Dubna will continue to be met with the harshest response."

The line of corpses came at last to an end, and the two men continued toward the hospital lab commandeered for the small team of scientists who had arrived the day before. Krilev knew that water samples were being brought here from all over the city on a regular basis. So, too, soil and plants. And the bodies of a few of the most recently departed had gone missing. Krilev had a half dozen hysterical families waiting in the municipal building lobby he was using for an office since his had been commandeered.

"That will be all, Mayor," Petroskov said when he reached the armed guards standing rigidly at attention in front of the door.

Krilev stood his ground. "What do your scientists say?"

"They believe the situation has been contained and stabilized."

"That doesn't help those who are dying, Colonel. Or those who might follow them."

"There will be no further infection, Mayor," Petroskov said impatiently. "Just control your people and let me handle everything else."

Before Krilev could protest, the colonel had disappeared through the door which closed immediately behind him.

# DAY FIVE

# CHAPTER 43

S o how does it feel to be Palestinian?" Ben asked Danielle, as they walked toward the Gaza fish market early the next morning.

Danielle looked about, realizing that she was virtually indistinguishable from the Palestinian women she passed, thanks to Ben's efforts. He had bought the proper clothes at an outdoor market the night before and showed Danielle exactly how to arrange them. The shapeless dress and scarf covering the lower part of her face had thus far been enough to get them past a number of Israeli foot and jeep patrols, none of whom gave her a second glance.

"How far is the fish market?"

"A few more blocks. You can smell it now."

"YOU'LL NEVER be able to go home again now," Danielle had said last night, lying next to Ben in bed. It was well after midnight but neither of them had been able to sleep.

"Which home do you mean?" Ben asked her.

"You should have gone back to Detroit months ago. You didn't because of me."

"And never regretted it for a minute."

Danielle had reached over and flipped on a light. "Precisely why I got something for you from Sabi in Haifa."

Ben and Danielle had found a room in Gaza City at the Al-Amal Hotel located near the end of the beach. The Al-Amal was the last hotel open along the beachfront strip, home to journalists brave enough to come to Gaza and foreign dignitaries able to get clearance to come. It stood alone among other shuttered and crumbling structures built in the brief flurry that followed the signing of the Oslo Accords. Strangely none of the rooms offered a direct view of the sea, but they were spacious with high ceilings. Since there was no air-conditioning, they left the windows open through the night.

The sounds were peaceful, the quiet lapping of the nearby sea, the occasional car horn, the distant din of a voice carried through the silence by the wind. No gunshots, no screams. Palestine at rest, at peace. An illusion fostered by the night that would melt away again come morning.

This was the first night Ben and Danielle had stayed together in nearly a year, since their mission to New York had ended tragically in a hospital. When they first came back, battered and exhausted, there had been ample excuses to avoid each other. First Danielle was in need of considerable mending, the kind that only rest could accomplish. Ben was content to leave her alone, believing this time they could pick up where they had left off in New York when his days began and ended by her side in the hospital. Those had been long, taxing days but he sensed she needed him and that was a good feeling. Ben knew he could not make up for what she—and they—had lost. By just being there, though, he hoped to make his intentions clear.

Just as Danielle had made her intentions clear in the weeks following her recovery by never phoning him.

It would have been easy to blame her, even easier to blame the political climate which virtually closed travel between Israel and the West Bank and all but forbade any contact between Israelis and Palestinians. Even Colonel al-Asi had warned him to avoid contact or risk being labeled a collaborator, for which dozens of ordinary Palestinians now faced death sentences.

But none of that should have mattered to him; at least it wouldn't have last year or the year before. He came at last to realize that the moment he had eased Danielle's wheel-chair from the hospital in New York everything had changed. The gulf that had always been there between them suddenly had no bridge. Instead of looking for excuses to be together, it became easier to look for ones to be apart.

So many times they had succeeded in starting over. Now, since the loss of their unborn child, everything had changed. They were left with nothing much to say to one another, because the shape and essence of their relationship had changed. Ben had taught himself to understand and accept that, until Colonel al-Asi had told him of Danielle's arrest.

Strange how there had been no hesitation at that point, no question that he would act. Danielle *needed* him, after all.

The thought made Ben shudder.

His wife had needed him, and she was dead. His children had needed him, and they were dead, too. Life was about moments. A few earlier and his family would still be alive. A few later and he would be dead, too. Moments had brought him back to Palestine and eventually to Danielle, providing tantalizing glimpses again of a happiness he had forgotten was possible.

But only for moments.

"Identity papers," Danielle continued, referring to what she had obtained for Ben from Sabi, "and a new passport, so you can get away from here now before it's too late."

"Will you be coming with me?"

"I can't leave."

"Then neither can I."

"It won't work, us being together," Danielle said. "We should have figured that out by now."

"Maybe we never really tried hard enough."

Danielle groped for words. "You're fooling yourself,

Ben. Neither one of us has anyone else, and that's the worst thing to base a relationship on. We only stay together when there's no other choice. That's why it's never worked before."

"New York is why it's not working now. If the baby had lived . . ."

"It didn't."

"We can't leave things at that."

"We don't have a choice, Ben, and we both know it."

"No, I won't give up," he insisted staunchly. "I'm done giving up."

"So what happens tomorrow when Levy dumps this whole mess on the government's lap and we're out of it? Ask yourself that."

"I have, and the answer is that I'm tired of losing you to things that seem more important."

"There's always going to be something."

"After this, there doesn't have to be," Ben told her.

THE FISH market had been the center of attention in Gaza for decades, packed with people buying and selling. Lately, though, there were fewer of both. The failing Palestinian economy, coupled with travel restrictions into Israel, had severely reduced demand, while a large number of fishermen had taken up rifles in place of reels.

Still, a decent crowd of customers was moving amongst the rows of iced-down fresh fish, caught at sea just hours before.

"I don't see Levy," Ben said, scanning the market nervously.

"He said he'd find us," Danielle reminded. "Let's just stay on the move until he does."

An Israeli jeep spun onto the street and tore forward, violating the pedestrian-only law. Honking its horn, it surged straight for Ben and Danielle who could do nothing but turn away and hope to avoid recognition.

The patrol jeep reached them and passed straight on by.

"You think they're looking for us?" Ben wondered.

"No," Danielle said curiously. "That was a special military police detachment. It must be something else."

The jeep had stopped close to the docks near a huge tray of ice next to a large scale where Gaza fishermen weighed their catch. Danielle drifted in that direction, pulling free of Ben's grasp when he tried to grab her.

All three military policemen were standing over the huge tray of ice, shaking their heads. One was making notes, another spoke into his walkie-talkie. Danielle reached the front of the small crowd that had gathered around them just before Ben grabbed her elbow.

"What are you—"

"Oh my God," Danielle muttered, before he could finish.

A body lay in the tray covered by ice, visible now only because the policemen had brushed the crystals and cubes aside. Danielle glimpsed the milk-white face of the corpse and felt her stomach flutter.

It was General Dov Levy.

D anielle spun toward Ben
     "Levy," she muttered.
     Ben strained to peer over her, but now it was
Danielle who eased him away.

"Don't let the soldiers see you," Danielle cautioned,
trembling with shock and rage.

"The soldiers aren't our biggest problem anymore. Whoever killed Levy—"

"—could still be around, waiting for us. I know, I know.
That damn cowboy! It was him, it had to be!"

"Keep your face down!" Ben advised, when Danielle began peering up and down the street.

"Black's here. I'm going to find the son of a bitch. Finish
him once and for all."

Ben swung her toward him. "Not now, not while he's
got the upper hand. All we can do is get out of here!"

She shrugged, reluctantly breaking off her search for Jim
Black. "You're right."

"Come with me," Ben said, taking Danielle gently by the
arm.

A tight cluster of trucks and vans, belonging to markets
and restaurants, sat parked just beyond the dock area. Ben
kept walking until he came to one with its engine still rumbling to power the compressor that kept the small truck's
rear hold comfortably chilled. He opened the driver's door

and eased Danielle up into the truck ahead of him.

Ben pulled the truck into the street and squeezed past the congestion of others parked in all directions. Then he pressed out a number on his cell phone.

"Al-Asi?" Danielle asked him, still quivering with rage.

"Who else?"

The phone rang once, then the signal died. Ben redialed, got the same results.

"What's wrong?"

"The colonel's number has been deactivated."

"Try it again."

"I've tried it twice already. He warned me about this. It looks like his enemies may have finally caught up with him."

Ben continued to snail the truck onward, as a convoy of Israeli vehicles sped past him on the other side of the street, heading toward the fish market.

"We've got our own enemies to worry about," Danielle reminded.

"Until we stop them, by fitting all the pieces together."

"The diamonds, Ranieri's trail, whoever hired the cowboy . . ."

"All connected," Ben said. "To Russia."

"Russia?"

Ben nodded. "You heard what Anatolyevich said. Whatever was on that freighter came from Russia, the city of Dubna, he told me."

"You're saying we should *go there?*"

"I'm saying *I* should, while you try to find someone in Israel you can trust."

"I'm more likely to be shot on sight, remember?"

"There's got to be something, someone," Ben grasped.

"Maybe," Danielle said, thinking of something. "Maybe."

# CHAPTER 45

I need to know how long I have," General Latisse Matabu said to Dr. Sowahy.

The doctor finished checking her blood pressure and returned the gauge to the old, weathered medical bag he had carried for as long as she could remember.

"With medication, a year," Dr. Sowahy said flatly.

"And without?"

He shrugged. "A month before you are incapacitated. Another two, maybe, after that."

"Four weeks, then."

"It's beginning to affect your brain. I cannot promise you will be mobile, or lucid, for even that long."

"Then I have much to do quickly," Matabu said, realizing that General Treest wasn't finished with her yet.

She dismissed the doctor and moved to the mirror, disturbed to find how much the furrows and lines on her face had deepened. Her skin looked sickly pale and her eyes had lost their sheen. None of these symptoms were new, only more noticeable.

What was new was the fact that Matabu realized she had misarranged the buttons on her uniform top. And when she tried to rebutton them, her fingers were stiff and fumbling. A wave of fatigue swept over her and left Matabu sitting on the edge of her cot, feverish and light-headed. One of the bad spells that came and went, but had come with increasing frequency and ferocity as of late.

The disease had not been diagnosed until the first symptoms appeared during her final months in the United States. A full battery of tests was ordered and, in the end, the doctors had handed her a pad full of prescriptions.

Matabu had refused to take them, not believing she needed any. She couldn't die because the work her grandmother had insisted she was born to do had not been completed yet:

She was to be the savior of her people. Of course, her grandmother had died before Treest and his soldiers had come to her home that day when she was still a young girl. The guards her father had left had been beaten and maimed. Treest had found her hiding in the vegetable basement among the corn.

Latisse Matabu shuddered with rage, haunted again by the memories of the searing pain tearing at her insides as General Treest had raped her. His men held her down until she gave up struggling and let herself go limp, feeling as much guilt as agony, while he thrust himself into her again and again.

But even the rape wasn't punishment enough to suit Treest. He had returned after Latisse Matabu gave birth to a child his rape had given her. Burst into her home and beaten her for concealing its existence from him, then snatched up the basket in which the child was sleeping and strode from the house.

She had chased Treest and his shoulders up the hill, out of breath by the time she begged the general not to hurt her son, to give him back to her. But Treest calmly explained, half smiling, that she wasn't fit to keep his child. It had taken three of his men to hold her back as the general carried the basket with her son inside to the edge of the hilltop and dangled it high over the river. Matabu remembered Treest grinning broadly before he let the basket go.

Only then did his men release her. The basket had already plunged into the river by the time she got to the edge.

She scrambled down the hillside, clawing her way, the branches and brambles scratching at her. Searched the riverbank, but couldn't find her baby. Hell must have swallowed him up, a punishment for letting him been born.

After rebuttoning her shirt, Latisse Matabu emerged from the small camouflaged shanty that held her living quarters and paused briefly. The world had forgotten what a beautiful country Sierra Leone was and, occasionally, so did she. At times like this, though, it took on the pristine glory of an artist's landscape. Dew coated the leaves of the softly swaying branches which formed a canopy over the richly scented soil. The rivers would be calm now, like green ribbons wrapped around the countryside.

Matabu continued past her ever-present guards to the camouflaged entrance of the complex of bunkers containing the greatest stores of RUF ordnance. She descended the rickety set of wooden stairs and continued down a dank underground corridor lit by single bulbs strung along the ceiling. The air was warm and smelled like mud, not much different from the vegetable basement in which she had hidden from General Treest. The final door down, made of thick wood peeling at the edges, had a different lock for which only Matabu had the key. She opened it, yanked the bolt back, and entered.

A frigid blast of air struck her in stark contrast to the steaming heat outside. She could hear the rumbling hum of the four powerful generators required to keep the storage room below forty degrees Fahrenheit.

Inside dozens and dozens of insulated crates had been stacked halfway to the dirt ceiling. Orhan had found his weapon on the shores of the Black Sea, thanks to the Moor Woman. Latisse Matabu had found hers in Russia, thanks to the Russian underworld.

But the contents of these crates would not be used in Sierra Leone, because her grandmother's tales of Orhan had showed her the necessity of identifying one's true enemies. The Dragon had already made the preparations required to set the final stage of her plan into operation.

Thinking of that day warmed her in the storage room's chilly confines. She imagined her grandmother standing by her side, smiling with approval and pride.

"I won't let you down," Latisse Matabu said softly. "I won't let Sierra Leone down."

# CHAPTER 46

Danielle entered the jewelry store at the north end of Dizengoff Street in Tel Aviv, but waited until the same man with whom she had seen Ranieri meet was available before approaching the counter.

"I'm Jacob Katz," he greeted. "How can I help you?"

"I have some diamonds I'd like to get an estimate on."

It was cold in Tel Aviv for springtime. A light rain fell outside, keeping away many of the shoppers and strollers. She had moved through the street and shops, constantly alert to the fact that she was a wanted person. Her disguise would keep her from being recognized by the casual observer and even a posted soldier or policeman. But it would not do much good against a party out looking specifically for her. Jim Black, for example. Or National Police officials who might have been tipped off that someone meeting her description was seen in Tel Aviv.

Katz & Katz stood as it had for nearly half a century; the sign outside read OUR FORTY-EIGHTH YEAR IN BUSINESS! Inside people shopped with their eyes instead of their wallets, gawking at the magnificent stones displayed behind thick, bulletproof glass.

Jacob Katz, with a curly shock of brown hair that resembled a bird's nest, leaned over the counter. A thick gauze bandage covered most of his left cheek. "You were saying?"

"I was wondering if you might be able to do an appraisal for me."

"We normally get one hundred dollars for that kind of work."

"Not a problem."

"You'll need to fill out a form," the younger Mr. Katz said, and started rummaging through a drawer just to his right.

"I think you may want to take a look before I write anything down," Danielle told him, and laid some of the stones salvaged from Ranieri's glasses on the glass counter. "You recognize these, don't you?"

Katz's eyes bulged. He began to tremble. "What are you doing here? *Who* are you?"

"Let's go talk somewhere more private."

THE YOUNGER Katz's office was a cubicle, windowless and closet-sized. He shut and locked the door behind him.

"They never sent a woman before."

Danielle watched the sweat beginning to form and soak through his shirt. He was breathing hard.

She laid the same diamonds on the desk before them. "These frighten you a very great deal."

Katz touched his bandaged cheek. "After yesterday."

"These were the diamonds you gave Ranieri five days ago. But they were only a down payment."

"And you've come for the rest, is that it?"

Danielle looked at his bandage, dark with dried blood in the center. "I came to find out who else already has."

Jacob Katz slumped into his chair.

Danielle leaned over his cluttered desk. "I'm a chief inspector from National Police."

Katz's eyes widened in fear. "I didn't call you! I have nothing to say to you! If I talk, they'll . . ."

"They'll *what*?"

"My father," Katz managed.

"Keep talking."

"Get out! Leave me alone!"

"Tell me about your father and I will."

"Unless they sent you. Unless they're testing me." He swallowed his face in his hands, then clutched at his hair. "*Anee holeh.*"

"You're not going to be sick." Danielle paused. "What if I were here to help you?"

"That's what the cowboy said yesterday."

"Cowboy?" she asked him, feeling a cold tingle prick her spine.

Katz gestured toward his bandage. "Then he pushed a finishing drill through my cheek."

Danielle hesitated. "Tell me about your father."

"He was arrested for illegal trafficking. The authorities are calling him a smuggler. The people I thought sent you arranged everything because they thought he was stealing from them. And he was, but not that much. Just holding back a few of the rough diamonds."

"How did Ranieri get them into the country?"

"Listen to me," Katz implored. "I can't talk to you. If I do, they'll have my father killed."

"Help me and perhaps I can help your father."

The younger Katz's hands emerged from his hair and he looked up. "You can get him out?"

"At least make sure he's protected so long as he remains in jail."

"They'll kill him if they find out I even spoke with you."

"You were expecting someone else when I showed up," Danielle said.

Katz nodded. "The Russians. To pick up the shipment of rough diamonds Ranieri delivered. I haven't even looked at it myself."

With that, he rose from his chair and moved to the wall. A hefty push revealed a secret compartment. Katz reached inside and removed the suitcase Danielle recognized as the one Ranieri had left here. He laid it down on his desk and lifted the top, angling the case so Danielle had a clear view of its contents.

"Recognize this?"

"It's a Torah scroll," Danielle said, baffled.

"Not just any Torah scroll. This is a *Holocaust* Torah scroll."

"One of the most prized possessions in Jewish culture," Danielle remembered. "Certain never to be searched by Customs officials for fear of damaging it."

"With good reason. The Nazis collected scrolls like this from all over Europe and stored them in a Prague building they called the Museum for an Extinct Race. After the war, these scrolls were taken to the Westminster Synagogue in London to be repaired and later distributed to temples all over the world."

Katz stroked the Torah tenderly. "This particular one is a Czech scroll," he said and unscrewed the tops of the rollers that held the scroll together, called the Trees of Life. "The *Atsei Chayim* have been hollowed out. That wouldn't escape close scrutiny but, as you said, these scrolls never receive any scrutiny at all."

Katz laid the tops of the Trees of Life, *Atsei Chayim*, down on his desk. Then he lifted the Torah scroll up gently and turned it upside down.

Dozens and dozens of various-sized stones spilled out from the hollowed-out tubular compartments, clacking against each other on the bottom of the suitcase. Their colors were disparate, ranging from almost clear to dark gray, from radiant white to dull yellow—not looking like precious stones at all.

"Blood diamonds," Danielle muttered, recognizing the stones in this crude stage before they were cut, polished, and made wildly expensive. She tried to calculate the value of the rough stones piled in the suitcase before her. "How much are these worth?"

"In this condition, five million. Once finished, their value at the Israeli Diamond Exchange will be ten times that."

"So Ranieri delivers the rough stones to you in Holocaust Torah scrolls . . ."

"And in return we give him finished stones worth twenty percent of their finished value."

"Ten million dollars, the diamonds melted into the eyeglass lenses constituting a ten percent down payment."

"Standard operating procedure."

"There's nothing standard about such subterfuge."

"There is with blood diamonds, thanks to Certificates of Origin," Katz answered. "Rough stones can no longer be sold on the open market without them, because of the new registration procedures enacted by De Beers and the rest of the diamond cartel."

"Procedures enacted to prevent exactly what you've become a part of."

"Exchanging legitimate diamonds for illegally trafficked rough ones allows us to circumvent them, yes. Everybody comes out on top."

"No one ever checks the inventory manifests? You're not afraid of the discrepancy showing up?"

"Afraid of who?"

"Your diamond dealers. The syndicate you buy from."

Katz almost laughed. "You think De Beers and the others care about blood diamonds?"

"They don't?"

"Only so far as *they* can set the price. The cartel cares about controlling the market and nothing else. If a glut of these blood diamonds were suddenly released, they could drive the price dangerously low, create instability."

"So they buy them, knowing all this, just to keep the prices where they want them. Maintain control."

Katz nodded. "Is that such a surprise? No one gets hurt, after all."

"Except the people in the African countries where the weapons your diamonds buy end up."

"I told you, I don't have a choice."

"You used to. Your father as well. You're lucky you weren't arrested a long time ago."

Katz almost laughed. "Arrested by who? Don't be naïve. Why do you think I haven't gone to the police myself? Why do you think I didn't care you were a cop?"

Danielle remembered claims made by Dov Levy on the *Peter the Great* that Israeli authorities, like Moshe Baruch, were involved.

"The authorities are being paid off to look the other way," Katz explained. "Keep things just the way they are, the diamond market stable, because the whole business about diamonds being rare is a myth. Prices need to be kept artificially high, and anyone who threatens their game is punished."

"Your father, for instance."

"Weren't you listening to what I said? These people answer to no one. They can keep him in jail for as long as they want."

"Unless you help me," Danielle told him.

"How?"

"What time are you expecting your Russian friends to come by?"

# CHAPTER 47

E njoy your stay in Russia," the customs agent said, stamping the passport Danielle had procured for Ben through Sabi.

"Thank you."

Exhausted, Ben moved through the jam-packed Moscow Airport, wondering how best to reach the city of Dubna, located 100 miles to the north. He had no way of knowing whether there would be any evidence left there of whatever had been packed into the crates stolen from the freighter *Peter the Great*, or where exactly he should look for it. With Anatolyevich dead, though, this was his only potential lead.

Outside Moscow Airport, Ben found a bus headed north and was glad to lose himself in the glut of people aboard. Exhausted as he was, he offered his seat to a woman holding a baby. She didn't bother to thank him, just sank into the seat and held her baby tightly to her as if she expected someone to take it from her.

"Where you going?" an old man standing beside him asked Ben, as the bus rumbled across Moscow's pothole-marred streets, gears grinding and worn-out shocks creating a jarring ride. The stench of hot exhaust fumes permeated the bus's interior and more than one passenger sat with their mouths tucked into their sleeves.

"Dubna."

The old man looked at Ben in surprise. "This bus doesn't go there."

"I must have gotten on the wrong one," Ben said, figuring he shouldn't have trusted his ability to read instructions in Russian.

"Doesn't matter. No bus goes there anymore, not for days now." The old man leaned closer to Ben and lowered his voice. "I heard the old reactor there blew. Worse then Chernobyl. People dying and getting sick. No one from the outside allowed in."

"You know anyone who lives there?"

"Cousins," the old man answered. "I called a few times. Nobody answered. All bullshit. But I don't make trouble. Who would believe me?"

Ben kept his eyes on the old man, waiting for him to continue.

"Twenty years I worked at the reactor station in Dubna. Twenty years and then no job. So if anybody knows, it's me."

"Knows what?"

"About the bullshit," the old man said, snickering. "Because the nuclear plant there was shut down a dozen years ago."

# CHAPTER 48

S ergeant-Major J. Peter Reese of the British Royal Marine Corps, hands clasped behind his back, walked up
and down the rows of uniformed Sierra Leonean soldiers standing at attention.

"Good news, blokes," Reese announced, his husky voice
carrying over the parade ground at the Benguema Military
Training Center located outside the capital city of Freetown. As he spoke, a translator who moved as his shadow
repeated the words in Krio, Sierra Leone's native language.
"My government, in the true spirit of generosity, has decided to re-up its commitment to this messed-up little country of yours by continuing to lead the International Military
Advisory and Training Team. That means you're stuck with
me for at least another *six months*!"

The translator couldn't quite match Reese's volume,
which didn't stop a collective groan from rising through
the crowd, although all five hundred troops gathered continued to stare straight ahead. He also botched his translation of the Sergeant-Major's next comment referring to the
additional five million pounds Britain had committed to the
effort.

"And my job, you bloody incompetent lot, is to help your
country, so when Her Majesty orders us out, it will be considerably less of a piece of trouble."

Reese continued to stride between the rows, his back

arched, chest thrown out, his translator struggling to keep up. In spite of the sweltering heat, Reese was outfitted in his full dress uniform, including the battle sword he had actually worn in the brief Falklands War but never had occasion to draw. That uniform fitted his sinewy frame like a glove and helped distract his charges from his slight limp, the consequence of a training wound that had prematurely ended his active service.

"Now, I'd love to spend the rest of my recently extended stay here in God's version of hell breast-feeding you babes who didn't know a rifle bore from the arse end of your old fat mums five weeks ago. But I've got another couple thousand of you to put through their paces, so pretty soon you're going to be seeing my pretty little face against yours for the very last time."

At that point, for effect, Sergeant-Major J. Peter Reese of the Royal Marines stuck his ruddy, pockmarked, and square-jawed visage right into that of the nearest Sierra Leonean soldier.

"Now I hope that pisses you off mightily," he continued, pulling away and spinning sideways on his heels, "but don't fret, laddies, for old Pete's got some good news for you: You've still got me for another week. Happy about that, ain't you?"

"Yes, sir!" the trainees bellowed in perfect cadence.

"Happy about that, *ain't you*?" Reese demanded, louder. "*Yes, sir!*"

"That's a bit better now," he nodded, tossing a wink at another of the British marine trainers who had just had his stay in Sierra Leone extended. "So good I think we're ready to take the next step, go out and kill some rebels!"

An enthusiastic roar exploded through the crowd as soon as the translation was completed, American-supplied M-16 assault rifles thrust into the air.

"They won't be real rebels, not yet. Back home we call these war games, laddies, but it's a pretty safe bet that if you get yourself killed when we're playing, you'll be among the first to go down when it's for real. So pay attention to the rules and the regs, and stick with your training. That's how you're going to kick the arses of these rebels who like to play hit and run. Well, you can't always stop 'em from hitting, but you can sure as shit stop 'em from running."

Sergeant-Major J. Peter Reese's stride finally brought him back to the front rank of the government troops of Sierra Leone who in one week's time would be sent out to take on the forces of the Revolutionary United Front. His translator stopped the same shadow-length's distance away.

"Here's how the game goes, laddies. The forest beyond the compound has been peppered with blokes from Troop A dressed in the olive drab uniforms of the RUF. The object is to hunt them down, flush them, and blow them to hell with your paint bullets before they can do likewise to you. Now you should know that Troop A, and their paint bullets, are going to employ every dirty trick the rebels are known for, so be ready . . . and let's kick their arse!"

As the translator finished his own rendition of Reese's words, another tumultuous scream rose up through the ranks of Troop B, M-16s loaded with paint bullets again jabbed toward the sky.

"*As yu mek yu bed, na so yu go ledohn pan am,*" the Sergeant-Major continued, using their native language for the first time the recruits could remember. Then, translating on his own, "As you make your bed, so shall you lie on it."

EVEN WITH twenty-five years as a Royal Marine behind him, Sergeant-Major J. Peter Reese couldn't pin down the precise moment when he realized things had gone terribly wrong. Something on the wind, a nagging feeling that hit him as an ache in his bad leg just after he had given Troop A, playing the role of Revolutionary United Front rebels, the order to begin their attack.

Their reply had come back over the radio garbled.

In retrospect that must have been what alarmed him, although Reese couldn't quite identify the reason even as he unsnapped the holster for his sidearm.

"I'm going to call this off, Captain," Reese said to the center's commanding officer who stood proud and stiff-lipped alongside him. The thick cover of the dense woods adjoining the Benguema Military Training Center prevented Reese from seeing very clearly, even with binoculars from his vantage point in the thirty-foot guard tower. Still, he kept spinning the focus wheel futilely in search of a glimpse of something that would tell him he was wrong.

Captain Marks, who had been all of twelve years old for the Falklands War, glared at him. "What?"

"Something ain't right, sir; I can feel it."

Marks turned back toward the woods and pretended to be looking at something. "You'll do nothing of the kind, Sergeant-Major. This is a crucial exercise and we must stay on schedule if we're to—"

The staccato burst of gunfire drowned out the rest of the captain's words. The screaming started as Reese grabbed for the walkie-talkie on his belt. He had the damn thing at his lips just when the bursts of gunfire intensified, only no one answered his call.

"Holy mother of God," Captain Marks muttered, watching funnels of gun smoke drift up from the woods to be caught by the wind.

"Bloody hell!" Reese bellowed, pistol drawn as he moved for the ladder.

Marks peered down at him through the opening in the tower. "What is it, Sergeant-Major? What's happening?"

"We been boozled, that's what," Reese said, taking the rungs downward. "It's the bloody RUF out there for real!"

Reese leaped down the final ten feet and hit the ground running, sword in one hand and pistol in the other as he rushed for the woods as fast as his limp would allow.

# CHAPTER 49

Danielle stood watching the diamond shop from down Dizengoff Street well into the afternoon, waiting for the arrival of the Russians Jacob Katz was expecting. Danielle thought of the cowboy, James Allen Black, drilling through the man's cheek. She could picture him smiling as he did it, enjoying Katz's screams. She hoped it would be Black who showed up today; whoever it was, the plan was for Katz to switch on the shop's outside lights to let Danielle know they had arrived.

The last time she had waited outside Katz & Katz, when she was following Ranieri, Danielle's thoughts had been filled with the lingering doubts that had plagued her for months. That maybe she couldn't cut it anymore. That maybe Moshe Baruch was right about her being best suited for a position in administration. Those doubts, though, had now vanished. Her confidence returned with the realization that she had never really changed; only circumstances had. And once those circumstances required her well-honed skills again, they were there at the ready, the tentativeness she had felt gone. Burned out of her as though it had never been there at all.

While waiting for the Russians to arrive, Danielle busied herself by moving through different shops and cafés, always within easy view of Katz & Katz and never staying too long in any one to attract undue attention. Over the many coffees she consumed, Danielle did her best to put together the substance of the plot she and Ben had uncovered.

Couriers dispatched from Africa smuggled rough diamonds into Israel and traded them for finished ones which were then used to purchase weapons from the thriving Russian underworld. The weapons would be shipped to rebels engaged in brutal civil wars currently ravaging the African continent. Meanwhile, the Russians would then sell their perfectly legal finished diamonds at prevailing rates through the diamond exchange. And the original blood diamonds would then end up finished, polished, and on display in stores like Katz & Katz. Everyone in the process profited. Everyone got what they wanted.

Except for the millions of innocent Africans who had lost their lives or been displaced thanks to civil wars funded by blood diamonds.

Finally, an hour before sunset, the lights outside Katz & Katz flashed on. The younger Katz needn't have bothered; Danielle had watched the dark, slack-jawed pair of men enter the shop and knew instantly who they were. They wore thin jackets that barely concealed the pistols holstered over their hearts. Bulky men with eyes like a rifle's crosshairs. They had parked their car just down the street, and she watched them return to it carrying Ranieri's suitcase with the Holocaust Torah scroll inside after they exited the shop.

Danielle put her car into gear and settled in behind them, as soon as the men pulled out from the curb. It was a typically busy Sunday, people enjoying a day out after the Sabbath, and the traffic was maddening. If nothing else, though, that simplified her task of keeping the Russians' car in sight while she hung back at a safe distance.

Once on the highway, their destination became clear. They were heading straight for Little Moscow, a large settlement outside of Jerusalem on the very edge of the West Bank in the dry brown hills of Achelon. Danielle had only visited it once and recalled that Little Moscow was no different in appearance from the other Jewish settlements scattered throughout the West Bank. It had the same prefabricated bunker appearance shared by so many others. Small, functional homes squeezed together with narrow strips of dirt between them that promised grass someday. Schools built within the cover of fortified security walls complete with bunkers for basements in the event of an attack.

Steeped in controversy, this settlement had originally fallen to the Barak government's determined peace efforts and become a sacrificial lamb before construction was complete. But one of the first orders of business of the new Israeli administration had been to order construction resumed with the express purpose of housing Russian immigrants there. Except for the different climate and background, Little Moscow could have been Russia, so unchanged were the inhabitants, determined to maintain their own culture instead of assimilating themselves into Israel's.

The soldiers at an Israeli army checkpoint outside of Jerusalem accepted the papers Sabi had provided, but Danielle wondered how much longer they would hold up to scrutiny and how much longer her makeshift disguise would hold out. The first time a soldier told her to pull her car over or drew his gun, Danielle would know she was caught. So long as the contents of Anatolyevich's freighter remained unaccounted for, though, she had to risk it. Dov Levy had died because of them. She owed him that much.

Almost to the end of the one road leading into Little Moscow, Danielle noticed a pair of civilians with assault rifles dangling from their shoulders checking the occupants of every car. She could see no simple way to get past them and doubted her papers would satisfy them as easily as they had the soldiers at the checkpoint, leaving her with an option she had hoped to avoid.

She checked her rearview mirror when the men waved her to approach and, thankfully, saw no car behind her. The fall of darkness added to the camouflage she would need. Danielle slumped forward and rested her head lightly against the steering wheel. Through a cracked eye, she could see the guards waving her on again, then approaching when she failed to heed their signal.

Both of them. Good.

They came to opposite sides of the car and peered in at her apparently unconscious frame. The one on her side reached through the open window and tried to rouse her. Failing, he said something in Russian to the guard on the passenger side and then jerked open the door.

Danielle tumbled out, hitting the ground with nothing to break her fall. She could hear the crunch of gravel as the guard on the passenger side scurried around the car. Felt the arms of the other man reach for her, but remained still until she was certain the second one was close.

Then she sprang.

It was over very fast. Flashes exploded before her eyes in the darkness, the sequence of events a blur that ultimately left both guards unconscious on the ground. Static prickled her senses, blows launched and connected at the edge of her consciousness like a memory unfolding in real time that stopped with the bodies of both guards lying at her feet.

Breathing heavily, Danielle dragged them one at a time into a nearby nest of bushes. Her heart thudded against her ribcage. One of her knees ached. A hand throbbed, the knuckles skinned and already starting to swell from a misplaced strike that was part of the blur. She could feel a knifing burst of agony in the ribs down low on her right side with every breath.

But Danielle welcomed the pain. She had felt nothing for so long it was good to feel even this. Years ago, during her tenure with the Sayaret, it was moments like these that had made her feel the most alive. To do that job you had to more than accept violence; you had to welcome it. After Beirut that had all begun to change, culminating sixteen months ago when pregnancy took away her taste for the very work that had defined her. Her own mortality had suddenly become an issue.

Right now, though, she felt free, as if a great burden had been lifted. Not quite a happy feeling, but no longer the feeling of hopeless misery that had dominated every waking moment since she'd lost the baby and her job. She felt renewed, restored, reborn. And not angry, neither at her herself nor Ben.

*Ben . . .*

He would be in Russia by now. Danielle found herself missing him, worried about him. As if now that she had finally forgiven herself, she could forgive him, too.

Danielle saw headlights coming up the slight hill and hurried back to her car, hoping the guards' absence would go unnoticed at least long enough for her to interrogate the Russians who had picked up the Torah scroll at Katz & Katz. Get them alone and discuss their world for as long as it took her to find out where the scroll filled with blood diamonds was going. The next rung on the ladder.

No cars were permitted on the settlement's central promenade and she parked in a lot on the outskirts under the watchful eye of well-armed civilians. Walking toward the town center, she realized the Israeli army presence here was nonexistent; the residents of Little Moscow must have preferred to secure and police the settlement themselves. It was true to form. This most recent wave of Russian immigrants had isolated themselves and transplanted their own culture here—a fact more than borne out by the promenade itself.

Russian music blared from storefronts where older men played cards beneath bright outdoor lighting and younger men drank in bars and cafés that dominated the street. Women were not much in evidence and none, Danielle noticed, were alone. No way she could blend in casually here, while she waited for the opportunity to get the two Russians she sought alone.

Aware of the sharp and suspicious stares cast her way, she saw the men she recognized from Katz's jewelry store enter a bar dominated by a tight cluster of bodies dancing uncoupled on the floor to the tune of a Russian ballad. Danielle sat down at an outdoor café table in direct view of the bar. She wasn't sure yet what her next move would be. She could enter the bar and take her chances, or wait here to follow the two men again when they emerged, make her move as soon as they reached the first dark space offering concealment.

Since she was clearly a stranger, it took almost no time at all before an older Russian man with a thick, white pompadour hairdo and an apron approached and folded a pair of flabby forearms in front of her.

"I don't know you."

"Speak Hebrew. Or English."

The man chose English. "I don't know you."

"No, you don't."

"Nobody here does."

"I don't expect they do."

"Explain."

Danielle leaned forward and lowered her voice. "I'm from National Police, here on official business. So get the fuck away from me."

"You have no business here," he growled, leaning close to her. "We take care of ourselves."

Danielle tried to catch a glimpse of the two men when the bar door opened again. "Not well enough, apparently."

The proprietor chuckled, laughed, then just shook his head as he walked away. Technically, National Police did maintain jurisdiction over all settlements. But Danielle had never come across one report of an investigation undertaken here in Little Moscow.

No one came to take her order. Patrons at several nearby tables moved to others farther away. Their whispers buzzed at her ears.

Minutes passed. The two men she had followed here from Tel Aviv didn't emerge from the bar. Danielle began to debate whether she should trail them inside after all, make sure they hadn't left through another exit.

She twisted her chair slightly away from the table, enough to see a man approaching from the center of the promenade, making no effort to disguise himself. His boots clip-clopped atop the fake cobblestones as he walked. When he removed his sweat-stained cowboy hat Danielle saw that his finely chiseled features were framed by shaggy, overly long hair that had gone a little gray at the temples. Beyond that, and some deep creases dug by a long-worn tan, he looked exactly the same as he had a dozen years before.

James Allen Black reached the table and flashed Danielle a smile. "Mind if I sit down, ma'am?"

# CHAPTER 50

B en took a second bus back to the airport where he rented a car, a small clanky Russian model stripped of all amenities. The weather was typically chilly for spring, but he still left the window rolled down part of the way through most of the drive north to Dubna.

Although he could speak Russian, he couldn't really read it, so the local papers were useless to him in determining what sort of crisis had occurred in Dubna. He was fairly certain the city was not mentioned in any of the prominent headlines, and the rental agent did not hesitate or warn him when he asked for directions to the city from the airport. Instead of the computerized variety Ben remembered from rental stations in the United States, the woman recited the instructions and he jotted them down on the side of a map she provided.

During the drive north across roads almost as poorly kept as those in Palestine, Ben reviewed the little he knew about Dubna, a city mired in mystery since its very birth. Its isolated location, acceptable climate, and convenience to Moscow led Stalin in the wake of World War II to clear a thick pine forest near the Volga and build the Soviet Union's first nuclear research laboratory there. The city itself, which for many years appeared on no map, was built around that and other scientific facilities located nearby.

The Institute for Nuclear Studies was not made public

until Khrushchev unveiled it in 1956. Within the original facility lay the world's first atom smasher. Later, plants and factories sprang up to make aircraft, guidance systems, satellite components, and parts for the nuclear reactors that supplied energy to much of the former Soviet Union. The nation's collapse in 1991 led to the closings of many of these facilities and inadequate security at the rest. The population of Dubna shrank significantly with the loss of the preferred status the city had so long enjoyed. It survived, Ben had read, by converting some of its well-kept facilities into centers for medical treatment and research that had become a symbol of hope for Russian advancement and progress.

If it could be done in Dubna, the saying went, it could be done.

But something must have happened that changed that.

Further north, the forest swallowed the roads and Ben found himself enveloped by woods on both sides. The late afternoon sky was dark and he rolled up the window, trying to switch on the heat before remembering the car was stripped to the absolute basics, which apparently didn't include a working heater.

A light mist began to fall thirty minutes into his drive, and Ben switched on his lights and windshield wipers. The wipers hesitated at first, then scratched across the glass in long choppy swipes. He tried his high beams to better see the road, went back to the regular setting when they only made things worse.

Ben had somehow strayed onto a back road that continued to narrow, then began to bend and dip. He thought of pulling over to better check his map, but there was no shoulder on which to do so safely so he kept driving, trying to trace the map as best he could to find where he had gone wrong.

The tiny car had trouble clinging to the corners, and Ben had just slowed a bit for the next curve when a crack sounded and the car listed wildly across the road. He realized he was spinning and fought with the wheel to pull out of it. Out of control, the vehicle veered off the side of the road and spun down a steep embankment covered by the forest's thick canopy.

Ben's head rocked upward, smacking against the roof and slamming his teeth together. He felt himself jolted against the confines of his seat belt and shoulder harness which locked against his collar bone. Branches raked and scratched at him. A window burst. He felt cold glass coating his skin like slivers of crushed ice, as the world dipped and darted. The nose of the tiny car ultimately turned straight down in the final moment before a wrenching thud that tore Ben's consciousness away.

# CHAPTER 51

B et you thought I was dead," Jim Black said, as he stuck a toothpick into the side of his mouth and clamped down on it.

"Not after Dov Levy's body was found this morning in Gaza," Danielle said bitterly. "I knew that was your work."

"He wasn't bad for an old guy. Put up a hell of a fight."

Danielle felt the blood racing just beneath the surface of her skin. She caught the scent of a mildly sweet aftershave drifting from across the table, the scent inapproriately soft for the cowboy. "Before this is over, I'm going to kill you, Mr. Black."

The cowboy leaned a little forward, seeming to like the prospects of that. He had a relaxed, easy manner about him, but wasted no motion. The kind of man who could control every blink and breath. "No need to wait when I'm right here now. I imagine you paid a visit to Mr. Katz."

"That's right."

"Means that scroll those two boys carried out of his place in that suitcase is empty, I guess."

"Right again," Danielle confirmed. "I've got the blood diamonds you're looking for."

Black looked pleased. "Figured as much." His eyes twinkled. "Like the souvenir I left on Katz's face?"

"Easy to inflict when the subject isn't one to fight back."

Black leaned backwards in his chair. "That old guy—he fought back."

Danielle felt something heavy in her throat and swallowed down some air. "Lucky you didn't meet him twenty years ago."

"Guess I'll have to settle for you." Black tilted his head to the side, sizing her up. "You up for a go?"

"That's your call."

"Right now we're just a couple of pros shooting the shit, enjoying each other's company." He kept staring at her. "I saw what you did to those guards back there." He whistled softly, blowing air through his pursed lips as he shook his head. "Man, oh man, you're good. You get a chance to work with your hands these days, you gotta take it. Everything's guns now. Not much opportunity to settle things man-to-man anymore."

Danielle let him see her sizing him up, too. "Or man-to-woman."

Black winked at her. "Know why you're so good? 'Cause you enjoy what you do." Black tipped an imaginary drink her way. "It was a pleasure watching you work."

"I wish I could say the same," Danielle said, not bothering to disguise the anger simmering under her voice.

Black smirked. "That's right. You seen me work, too, didn't you?"

Danielle tried to hide her surprise that he had figured that out.

"You musta watched the whole thing on television back there in Beirut. Good show, wasn't it?"

"It would have had a different ending if I'd been inside with the others."

"I figured as much when I checked out your background after things went bad at the jail," Jim Black told her. "Figured you were something special and sure enough I find out you're about as good as it gets." He looked her over again. "Least you used to be. That old guy I offed, he was your boss. You got a lot of loyalty to a man who bounced you out of his command."

"He didn't have a choice."

"That's what they all say. Explains why I got out of the official end of things where you got to explain yourself. Account for every bullet and put in for mileage." Black shook his head demonstratively. "Uh-uh, Danny girl, not for me." He flung his toothpick aside and smacked his lips. "Look at it this way. I kill you back there in Beirut with the others and we're not having this conversation today."

"So what's stopping you now?"

"I'm supposed to get those stones back. I can't kill you until you turn them over."

"I get to talk to your boss, he can have them."

"That simple?"

"I need his help."

Jim Black stretched out his legs and folded his hands behind his head, letting Danielle see the pair of nine-millimeter pistols holstered under his jacket. "Man, you are one screwed-up bitch. You got to stop caring so goddamn much. Takes the fun out of everything. My way's better. All the fun and none of the baggage."

Jim Black sat up, his two pistols clacking against his sides. He leaned forward again, hands flat on the table close enough to Danielle's to feel their heat. That's what the cowboy seemed like to her: liquid heat poured into a wrinkled khaki suit.

"What I think we should do now is fuck all these pleasantries and just have at it." His eyes beamed as if a bulb had suddenly switched on in his head. "What say I hand you one of my guns and we get at it right here?"

"Do I get to pick which one?"

"Don't trust me?" He lowered his hand to the table, as if expecting a glass to be waiting there, then pulled it away when there was nothing to close his grasp upon.

Danielle shrugged, could tell the cowboy meant every bit of his offer. "An empty one's not much good in a gunfight."

"Didn't bring one of your own?"

She shook her head. "Left it in the car."

"Got a preference?"

"Beretta."

Jim Black scoffed at her with his eyes. "Too slow and cumbersome by a long shot. Here, try my Sig," he said and yanked one of the pistols from its holster and handed it to her.

Danielle tested the weight and heft of the Sig Sauer, had to admit the cowboy was right. "Nice," she said and handed it back across the table to him when he made no motion to go for his second gun.

He flashed that grin again, as he slipped the pistol back into a comfortably worn leather holster. "Want me to take mine out now?"

"That really what you came here for?"

Jim Black looked disappointed. "You're right. I guess we should get moving."

Danielle watched him stand up, staying in her seat. "Where?"

"You want to talk to the boss," Black told her. "That's good, 'cause he wants to talk to you, too."

# CHAPTER 52

H e's still alive."

Ben could hear the voice, but wasn't sure where it came from. His eyes were still closed and he wanted to leave them that way until a pair of rough hands grasped his shoulders and yanked him forcibly from the crushed confines of his rental car. Pain exploded through one of his arms all the way to the shoulder, and his right leg felt on fire. His mouth was sandpaper dry.

He forced his eyes open.

Four figures loomed over him, impossible to clearly discern through the darkness and mist.

"Why?" Ben managed.

"What's he saying?" a woman's voice asked the others.

"Why did you shoot out my tire?"

"Your Russian's lousy," one of the men said. "And we didn't shoot out your tire."

"Blew out on its own," the woman followed. "Your car's a piece of shit."

"He must have gotten lost in the fog," a younger voice chimed in.

The woman crouched down closer to him. Ben was vaguely conscious of the scents of unwashed hair and skin.

"That the case, stranger?" she asked him. "If it is you're about the unluckiest bastard I ever met, getting yourself stuck in Dubna."

"What's left of it," the younger voice interjected.

Ben forced himself to sit up and felt throbs of agony rack his skull. "Is that where I am?" The words felt like marbles sliding around his mouth, making his teeth ache.

"We were trying to make our way out, when we saw you go off the road," the man said. "Hike through the woods after dark where the soldiers won't follow."

"Soldiers," Ben repeated.

"He's not Russian," the younger male voice decided. "Definitely not Russian."

"Is my son right?" the woman asked him.

Ben felt his head clearing. This must be a family that had stumbled upon him, a family that had stopped to help in the midst of their own flight from Dubna. The parents and two sons, if his eyes weren't deceiving him. The boy who had spoken earlier was in his mid-teens. A younger one, who had remained silent, looked to be eleven or twelve.

"Yes," Ben answered. Adding, "I'm American," because it was easier than saying Palestinian.

"What are you doing out here?" from the man again.

"We can't take him with us," the older son charged. "Don't even think of taking him with us."

"Shut your trap, Misha," the boy's mother snapped. "He was heading into Dubna, not going out."

"What's happening here?" Ben rasped, the words broken and staticky. He realized he was very thirsty.

"Dubna's under martial law," the father told Ben. "Whole city's quarantined."

Ben stared at the man through the misty night. His face was tired and worn, his hands carrying the calluses of hard outdoor labor that in the new Russia paid barely enough to eat. Ben's mind remained a bit lethargic, but the word "quarantined" brought back a flood of memories. The deadly weapon Anatolyevich had refused to identify, the one that had been stolen off the *Peter the Great*, had come from Dubna. And now Dubna was under quarantine.

"People were . . . infected?" Ben posed to the family tentatively.

"Infected? I guess you could say that. Some got it worse than others. Depended on the wind and where they were."

"What was it?" Ben asked them all. "Where did it escape from?"

The family looked at each other.

"I think he must've hit his head," said the oldest son and the younger one twirled his finger at the side of his head.

The father frowned. "That's not why Dubna was quarantined."

"Dubna was quarantined because of what they sprayed in the air to kill it," the mother explained.

"To kill what *escaped*? Is that what you're saying?" Ben asked. As he spoke, a vehicle came barreling down the road above with headlights blazing.

"Why so many questions?" the father demanded, after the vehicle had passed by. "Why does this matter to you so much?"

"Because I'm here to find out exactly what happened."

"You help us? Tell the world what's going on?"

"If I can."

Ben heard a rustling sound and before he could continue, the mother and father latched a hand on either of his shoulders and dragged him into the trees, followed closely by their children.

"The soldiers," the younger son, silent up until now, muttered fearfully.

# CHAPTER 53

Pesident Ahmed Tejan Kabbah of Sierra Leone walked across the blood-soaked center of the Benguema Military Training Center.

"There was nothing I could do, sir, I swear!" insisted Captain Jonathan Marks, his uniform streaked with blood and sweat. "By the time the sergeant-major and I realized—"

Kabbah swung toward Marks fast enough to make his bodyguards stiffen. "What sergeant-major?"

"Reese, sir. The man in charge of the exercise."

"And where is he?"

Marks swallowed hard and shook his head.

Kabbah turned away from the British officer in disgust. The parade grounds that hours before had been turned into a combination infirmary and morgue lay deserted before him, the hard ground a patchwork of ugly purplish stains that from his helicopter had looked like a freakish impressionist painting. The stench of blood and fear hung in the hot air, refusing to relinquish its grasp on the site even after all the bodies had been carted away.

President Kabbah had arrived well after the scene had been secured, but the events that had transpired in the surrounding woods were easy to imagine, since he had seen so many similar ones during his tenure in office.

Men screaming and writhing as rescue personnel struggled to wrap bandages around the gaping wounds where arms or legs had been hacked off.

Cries of fear that the rebels were coming back to finish them off.

Freetown, the capital of Sierra Leone itself, had looked much like this after the rebels' failed attack in January of 1999. Kabbah recalled the slow walk he had made through the Old Market in Susan's Bay, its festive décor replaced by bullet-shattered windows and blast-riddled streets. The marketplace, too, had been turned into a makeshift infirmary, the sights of women and children with their limbs severed by animals with guns and swords but without conscience certain to haunt him for all time. The stench had been the same there then as it was here today, and Kabbah honestly believed the market had never shed it entirely, the smells clinging to the old wood-frame buildings like bad memories.

He had grown up on the outskirts of the capital amidst the shantytowns of Lumley, recalling the much different scents of fresh produce that filled the roadside markets nearby. He watched the country he loved degenerate into an escalating cycle of violence an endless succession of politicians and soldiers was powerless to stop. Believing things could be different, he had entered politics himself and was elected president of Sierra Leone in 1996. Then, after surviving a coup by his armed forces, who installed the RUF in power, he was reinstated by a Nigerian-led opposition force in 1998. From that point, war with the rebels had been more or less constant, broken intermittently by peace talks which offered hope but never amounted to anything.

"How many rebels did we kill?" President Kabbah demanded of Captain Marks, as if that might have provided some solace.

"Sir?"

"How many killed of the opposition?"

Marks shook his head helplessly. "Mr. President, our troops were carrying rifles loaded with *paint*."

Kabbah swallowed hard. "Losses?"

Marks' lips barely moved as he replied. "Three hundred and fifty."

Kabbah gazed over the blood-soaked ground again. "We can assume four hundred, then. Perhaps as many as four twenty-five."

He moved on and Marks struggled to keep up. "That doesn't count the members of the other troop whose places the rebels took."

The President of Sierra Leone sighed. "How many more?"

"One hundred dead and two hundred missing, sir."

"Missing?"

"We, er, haven't found their bodies yet."

"How much of this did you witness?"

"I was in the tower, sir. By the time I got down, it was almost over. Couldn't see a thing with all the smoke."

"I see. And Sergeant-Major Reese?"

Marks gulped down some air. "He joined the battle, sir. Mr. President, if I may . . ."

"Go ahead, Captain."

"I'm told the two battalions being trained by the Americans in Nigeria are ready. Several thousand men, sir. Easily enough to put the bloody RUF down once and for all."

"I'm quite aware of the Nigerian troops, Captain. They are not your concern. This is not your war."

Marks straightened his spine and gazed about the barren yard. "With all due respect, sir—"

"I will take your advice under consideration."

"Again, sir, today's bold and murderous action by the RUF can only mean they're preparing to launch a major offensive. I beg you to take action before it's too late."

"Send the Nigerians into rebel-held areas?"

"They're far better trained than your own troops, sir."

"All the same, that strategy will turn my country into a slaughterhouse."

"With all due respect, sir, but isn't that what it's already become?"

"It is civilians who will suffer the brunt of such an all-out attack. Enough innocent people have already died in Sierra Leone. I ask you to leave the decision of what to do with the Nigerian troops to me."

"Begging your pardon, Mr. President, but I can no longer do that." Tears were falling from Marks's eyes, and he didn't bother to wipe them. "They cut Sergeant-Major Reese's head off, they cut off his head with *his own sword*!"

"He will be avenged. You must trust me, Captain," Kabbah said with an assurance that defied the circumstances.

Before Captain Marks could respond, a jeep sped through the training center's open gate, and defense minister Daniel Sukahamin lunged out. Kabbah watched his most trusted advisor approach in a near trot, his clothes covered in a murky film of dirt and dust. Left behind in the jeep was an American woman Kabbah had never seen before, struggling to light a cigarette in a trembling hand. Sukahamin's stride took him over the ground where men had died or bled mere hours before. But he seemed not to notice, his glassy gaze that of a man who had seen something just as bad or even worse.

"We must talk, Mr. President," the defense minister huffed.

"I quite agree, Minister."

"Not about this, sir," Sukahamin said grimly, surveying the area. "Something else even more important. Believe me."

# CHAPTER 54

Pretty impressive," Danielle commented, after Israeli soldiers waved Jim Black through the checkpoint with barely a second glance. They were traveling together in his car, Danielle having left the one she had appropriated in Tel Aviv back in Little Moscow.

"Yeah, well, Sash bought himself a permanent get-out-of-jail-for-free card."

"Sasha Borodin? That's who you're working for?"

The grin on Black's lips lingered a bit. "And smart to boot."

Sasha Borodin, Danielle knew, was a Russian who immigrated to Israel shortly after being acquitted of charges that he orchestrated the double murder of a cabinet minister and his wife in Russia. Rumors of his connections to organized crime here and in other countries were rampant, but nothing had ever been proven and Borodin's twelve years in Israel had proven remarkably arrest- and incident-free.

He boasted openly of donations he made to those whose interests mirrored his own and, although he professed to have no political aspirations, never shied away from supporting candidates who courted his favor. A number of countries had tried unsuccessfully to extradite Borodin for alleged criminal enterprises he had undertaken, only to be continually rebuffed by Israeli authorities.

After all, Borodin had proven himself a prime benefactor of his own people, responsible for erecting schools and community centers in Russian neighborhoods, then investing in the unfinished settlement and building it into Little Moscow. He had established orientation programs for Russian immigrants and helped find employment for them once they were settled.

Many of those jobs had once been held by Palestinians with work visas that permitted them to enter Israel daily. The violence, unrest, and resulting new administration had changed all that, leaving convoys of cars stalled at West Bank checkpoints into Israel as rocks and bullets flew mere miles away. Often Palestinians hoping to be let through claimed they could smell tear gas when the wind was right and hear the sound of gunshots and rockets even when it wasn't. As a result, car windows often remained rolled up and people hunkered low beneath the cover of dashboards on the worst days.

Some went as far as to suggest that Borodin had encouraged, if not orchestrated, much of the violence and continued to perpetuate it to assure gainful employment for as many of his people as possible. Danielle thought back to the arms delivery Ben had prevented the same day she had been in East Jerusalem. No wonder Israel's Russian mafia was willing to do business with Palestinian militants; it suited their ends as well.

That Jim Black was working for Borodin came as no real surprise. It figured the Russian mafia had the most to lose from the investigation she had been conducting—not only illegally trafficking in arms, but doing so under the protective watch of Israeli officials who had been paid off. What did they care about Africa anyway? It was easy to turn a blind eye to a place you couldn't see and had no desire to.

For Moshe Baruch, the price had probably been different. His tenure as *Rav nitzav*, commissioner of the National Police, had been marked by a series of high-profile arrests that included prostitution and drugs, solidifying his hold on power while Danielle steamed and suffered. She wondered if his relationship with the Russians had been long in the making, whether Baruch's indisputable success came as a direct result of their involvement.

Sasha Borodin, Jim Black told Danielle, made his home in the Israeli beach resort of Netanyah, commonly known as Miami On the Med. Once a center for citrus crops, it had grown into a prime resort area that was home to a large number of both American and Israeli retirees, along with some of Israel's wealthiest citizens of any age. A peaceful community until a recent spell of terrorist bombings left the scents of cordite and sulfur to mix with the lush smell of orange trees.

"If I was a Jew, an Israeli, I mean," Black said suddenly from behind the wheel, "I woulda done what you did. Joined up with the Sayaret and all. What was the training like?"

"Tough."

"No different at Fort Bragg back in the States, I'll tell you that much.

"Working for a man or a country. What's the difference?"

"The man pays a hell of a lot better, Danny girl. I'm just saying you should give it some thought, leave your options open. In case it didn't occur to you yet, you ain't got much of a future here. And that's if you get out of this alive." He worked a piece of gum into his mouth and then looked over at her. "I could set you up with some people I know. Get things going."

"I've got other plans."

"With the Arab who sprung you from jail?"

"He's Palestinian."

"Tough as you?"

"Close enough, yes. In some ways, tougher than both of us."

Jim Black snickered. "You should really think about my offer. Mine might be the best one you get for a while, Danny girl. I'd be truly sorry if I have to kill you."

Danielle thought of Dov Levy's body found covered in ice in Gaza. "I can't say the same."

# CHAPTER 55

Ben and the Russian family clung to the cover of the trees while a pair of soldiers struggled down the steep rise into the gully. Ben watched them check his smashed-up car and then search the area cursorily through the mist. A third soldier tried a slow descent of the hill, holding a handheld spotlight, and ended up flat on his back riding the last stretch down on his butt.

The other soldiers laughed as the man staggered to his feet and brushed himself off before shining the powerful light around in all directions. The beam came close to Ben and the Russian family several times. Movement, above all else, would have given them away. But the parents held fast to their two children, and Ben resisted the temptation to peer out from behind the tree.

After a few more minutes, the Russian soldiers tired of the task and retraced their difficult steps up the hill. Neither the family nor Ben said a word until the truck's headlights flashed back on and its engine groaned to life. Seconds later it was gone.

"We're lucky," the younger son said.

"Lucky?" snapped the older one. "We wouldn't even be anywhere near here if it wasn't for him. We'd be away from here already!"

"They'll be back," the father said, standing over them

protectively. "We've got to get on the move." He looked toward Ben. "We'll take you with us."

"What's your name?" Ben asked them.

"Stepanski," the father responded. "We are the Stepanskis. I am Victor. My wife's name is Shavel. Our sons Misha and Alexander."

"Can you tell me what happened in Dubna?" Ben asked, using a tree to help pull himself to his feet. He still felt shaken by the shock of the car crash.

"A problem at one of the old storage facilities," Victor said. "We never found out what."

"But a few days later," his wife Shavel picked up, "the spraying started."

"Spraying from the air, over the city?"

"No. Just in places like this, the countryside. The wind blew it over the city."

"Then came the quarantine," Ben concluded.

"Because people began to get sick. Everywhere people were getting sick and dying. The spray smelled like household cleaner. What you call it, ammonia? Hospitals full. People driving out of the city drive straight into roadblocks."

"This is the only way out," Victor added. "Through the woods."

"But you have to do it at night," Shavel pointed out. "After the curfew when they're not watching as close."

"Go back to what started this."

Victor looked around impatiently. "We've got to get going."

"The storage facility. What happened there?"

"I told you. Nobody knows. Could have been anything, with no money left for security or upkeep. The spraying starts and the city is closed, which is not too hard to do. Dubna was built that way. Only one road in and out for security reasons to protect the scientists and their labs."

"What about the road up there?" Ben asked him, pointing.

"Ends in a few more miles, easily ten from the city."

"How long ago did all this begin?"

"Five days," said Shavel. "Maybe six."

Ben did some quick figuring in his head, tried to calculate when Anatolyevich's shipment had actually set out for the Mediterranean coast. Between a week and ten days ago seemed like a reasonable estimate. Could there be a connection to what had happened in Dubna in the aftermath?

Suddenly they heard branches snap in the distance, accompanied by the rustling sound of men moving through brush.

"More soldiers," the Stepanskis' oldest son whispered.

"Routine patrol," said his father. "Probably alerted to watch out for someone roaming the woods. We should go now, head back toward the city, before it's too late."

"But—"

Victor slapped a hand across Misha's mouth. "We will try again another night. When things are quieter."

Ben drew up close to Stepanski and spoke in a hushed, but authoritative tone. "I need to see that storage facility. I need to find out what started all this."

Stepanski looked as though he was going to argue or object, then simply nodded his head. "Tomorrow, American. I will take you there tomorrow."

# CHAPTER 56

"Y ou know why you're not dead, don't you, Pakad?" Sasha Borodin asked Danielle, after they had both taken chairs by the pool outside his beachfront property in Netanyah. Sodium vapor lights rimmed the pressed flagstone, drawing flocks of mosquitoes and moths in the night.

"The same reason you're not; we both have something the other wants."

Borodin smiled, clearly impressed but not rattled. "Mr. Black has a gun trained on you right now."

"Are you willing to bet your life he's faster than I am?"

Borodin laughed and shook his finger at her. "You're even better than I was led to expect. Now, let us discuss the rough diamonds you took from the jeweler in Tel Aviv."

"You can have them . . . for a price."

Borodin was tall and thin, much different from what she was expecting. Danielle had pictured him as a big and burly man with a size that corresponded to the vast power he wielded. Danielle recalled the time over a year before when a pair of car bombs exploded in Netanyah. It was Borodin who had learned the identities of the Palestinian bombers and had them executed by the Russian mercenary force which did his bidding. But Borodin had tossed money around first, not bullets. In both cases the perpetrators were given up by those close to them who were now much richer for the betrayal.

Borodin wore a bathrobe over his bathing suit. His hair looked wet. His skin had a watery sheen to it, leading Danielle to believe he had just finished a swim when Black escorted her onto the property.

Borodin folded his arms, a bit chilled in the cooling spring nighttime temperatures. He looked surprised. "Money? Is that all you want?"

"No. I want the cargo from that freighter."

"I understand it was stolen."

"And you have no idea what the cargo consisted of."

"Of course not. I've learned over the years the wisest thing is to keep my distance from such matters."

"Then the shipment of blood diamonds will remain just as distant. Unless you help me."

"Help you what?"

"Find out what happened to the missing cargo."

# CHAPTER 57

I thank you for your promptness," Latisse Matabu said, after the leaders of the Revolutionary United Front were seated. "You all know why you are here, so I will not waste any more time."

They gathered not at RUF headquarters in the Kono region where such a presence could be noted by spies. Instead Latisse Matabu summoned her commanders to a centrally located town controlled by General Yancy Lananga, the one member of her cadre with actual military experience, under cover of darkness when ambushes became a logistical impossibility.

Sierra Leone grew so still and quiet at night that even a moderate force could not expect to disguise their approach. Sound would give them away in plenty of time to make an escape, if not over land, then through the tunnels dug beneath all headquarters on orders from Matabu's commanders. Of the twelve who formed the ruling council of the Revolutionary United Front, the only one missing was General Sheku Karim, the one she trusted least and had clashed with most often.

"The time has come to seize the government," she continued, meeting the stares of all the participants in the spill of the lantern light. Any stronger lighting made too inviting a target from the air, and rumors that the Americans would soon be supplying helicopter gunships had not fallen on deaf ears. "Since failing to take Freetown three years ago, we have employed a hit-and-run strategy that has forced the government troops onto the defensive. Their patrols are pointless, their U.N. peacekeepers impotent children when confronted with our might. They distract us with fake peace initiatives and promised consolations. And we submit because it serves our needs while buying us time. *Fohs ful nohto ful, boht sekohn ful, na-in na ful.* If you're fooled once, you're not a fool, but if it happens twice, then you're a fool."

Matabu knew she had the full attention of her commanders now, an opportunity not to be squandered. This was a fractious bunch, easily given to petty jealousies and animosities.

Indeed, the RUF for all its dramatic successes was little more than a loose amalgamation of tribes and cliques who could just as easily be at war with each other as the Kabbah government's troops. Matabu's most difficult job was to keep them focused on the common goal of seizing a power they all felt was rightfully theirs. The key to such an alliance, she knew from her studies in the United States, was to remain vague about what the specifics of such power would bring. Keep the goal simple and focused. It was pointless to let the spoils of victory be divisive until that victory was achieved. Most of her commanders' concerns were local, or monetary, in nature and they were easily mollified with promises that could be kept or voided later.

The Dragon's long-term plan was to divide Sierra Leone into districts controlled by men like these but answerable to a provisional government with herself as the head. Given her condition, that plan, of course, would have to change, something her commanders had no need to hear tonight.

She worried about reprisals, about turning these men loose on their enemies and the villages that had supported the government. How to control the fury and hate, how to harness them into a positive thing instead of letting them become the precursors to anarchy. They had to win the hearts and minds of their vanquished while leaving them their limbs.

"So as we continue our apparent dedicated efforts toward the peace process, our opposition grows complacent," Matabu resumed. "They believe they have beaten us down, believe their American weapons and troops are enough to make us cower and run. They no longer believe us capable of mounting, or desiring, the kind of attack that can destroy them."

The Dragon stopped to let her point sink in.

"They have fallen victim to the illusion we have perpetuated and will not be ready when our attack commences forty-eight hours from this very moment."

A few of the RUF generals exchanged worried stares. "At night?"

"A night of no moon, by design. The blackest of nights."

"An all-out offensive launched in the dark," noted Lananga, suitably impressed.

Latisse Matabu didn't bother to nod. "Our troops will move as close to the capital as possible during the day, using the woods and hills as cover. As soon as night falls, they will be directed to predetermined areas that will effectively surround and cut off the city. At midnight we will attack in a stunning, coordinated effort from all directions at once. Once the government's resistance is crushed, and President Kabbah and his cabinet officers are taken hostage, we will have won."

"We will execute them, of course," another of the Revolutionary United Front generals presumed.

"In public!" chimed in the crazed leader of the Ganta tribe whose men collected the scalps and ears of their victims.

"Do that, either of those things," Matabu retorted, "and we prove to the world that we really are the barbarians the Kabbah government would have the world believe. No, once the government is in custody, we will engage in peace and conciliation talks. The transfer of power will be restrained and orderly. We fight for the past as we prepare for the future."

"What about the Americans?" Lananga asked. "What do you expect them to do?"

"Once we take Freetown, nothing."

"And before?"

Latisse Matabu clasped her hands behind her back. "This is not their fight. The United States knows if they save the Kabbah government, they will be here forever."

"So you believe they'll lie down like the dogs that they are!" the leader of the Ganta tribe said, speaking with his usual passion and vigor.

"And we will step over them, instead of atop them, if they do. This is not their fight, unless we make it their fight."

"We should attack their quarters at the strike's outset," another of the generals proposed, looking about the room in the hope of gathering support. "Not give them the opportunity to choose whether to fight or not."

"Same thing with the U.N. peacekeepers."

"I volunteer my men!" the leader of the Ganta tribe offered eagerly.

Matabu maintained her air of calmness and authority. "Follow that strategy and our triumph will last a day instead of a lifetime. Provocation is what the Americans and the United Nations want. It gives them the excuse they need to repeat their intervention in Bosnia. The Americans, I tell you, are easy to predict."

"This is not Bosnia, General," Lananga reminded.

"No, General, it's West Africa where American influence and presence is much, much stronger. We must not give them a rationale to intervene, must strike so suddenly and resolvedly that they will have no choice but to recognize the government we establish."

"What about the heavier weapons our diamonds purchased?"

"Each of you will be given an allotment in proportion to the size of your commands. Do your best to make sure those who are provided a weapon are familiar with its use. And check your radios. Be sure you have backup units and batteries. Communication will be vital in the coming hours."

"Someday we will have cell phones," one of the generals mused.

"So the Americans can listen in on our discussions," chided Lananga contentiously.

"By that time," said Matabu, "the Americans will be gone."

The door to the shack's inner room burst open and General Sheku Karim strutted through, a sack suspended from his shoulder, a pair of his lieutenants at his sides. "And if they're not," he boasted, "I will do to them what I have done to the Kabbah government's soldiers."

"And what is that?" Matabu asked, not missing a beat.

Karim, a tall rugged man with a white scar down his left cheek, laid the sack at his feet. "An opportunity I couldn't pass up. I taught those bastards a lesson right in their own backyard. You could smell the car exhaust from Freetown."

"You violated the cease-fire," Matabu accused, trying to stay calm. "You have threatened our entire plan."

Karim spit on the floor between them. "I killed no civilians. Only government troops. And a few British."

"That's all you have to say?"

"I have struck a mighty blow."

"You have forced their hand!"

"So what? Whatever comes, comes."

"You had orders."

Karim spit again. "I spit on your orders. We were better off on our own. Freetown would still be ours now, if your father had listened to me."

"And how many more civilians would have lost limbs in the process, General?"

"You spend years with the Americans, then come back here and lecture *me*? I was making the future while you were still wetting your pants."

Matabu's face twitched slightly. "I meant no disrespect,"

she said in conciliation and looked down at the sack Karim had laid on the floor. "Have you brought me the spoils of your victory?"

The tall man's face beamed with pride as he leaned over and reached into the sack. "A gift, General, courtesy of the British."

And he extracted a sword bearing a head run through with the blade. "The bastard killed six of my men before he was shot. He was still alive when I took his head."

Matabu strode calmly forward, each move followed by the other eleven members of her cadre. "Then your actions were justified and I accept your token with pleasure."

She took the sword from Karim by its hilt and held the blade up so she was looking into the glazed, marble-like eyes of the severed head. "*Kohni-man dai, kohni-man behr am.* When a cunning man dies, it's a cunning man who buries him," Matabu said, looking into the corpse's shriveled face.

General Sheku Karim accepted the compliment with a grateful smile. He was still smiling when the Dragon leveled the sword and thrust it into his midsection just below the thorax. Karim gasped, air rushing from his mouth and severed lungs. Spittle frothed at the corners of his mouth.

Latisse Matabu used her free hand to draw her pistol and shot Karim's two lieutenants as they stood dumbfounded by his sides. Then she jerked the sword in further until the head Karim had severed jammed against his own blood-soaked chest. He crumpled to his knees and fell forward, propped up by the sword's hilt, when the Dragon stepped back.

She wiped her hands together, the gesture more symbollic than practical.

Matabu kicked Karim's corpse so it toppled to the floor. "So much for traitors," she said simply and turned back to the rest of her commanders. "Now, where was I . . ."

# DAY SIX

# CHAPTER 58

The two brothers had shared a sleeping bag so Ben could have one of his own. But it made little difference in the cold night. After midnight the mist turned frosty, spreading an unwelcome frigid blanket of ice particles through the woods. The boys had argued for a fire, but their father shot the idea down quickly, afraid it might draw the attention of any soldiers still patrolling the woods.

"What choice do we have?" Shavel Stepanski asked Ben as they stood near the pile of collected sticks and branches they would not be burning. Her husband sat nearby whittling wood with an old, worn pocketknife. The condition of the blade made the effort considerable. But the pile of shavings before Victor Stepanski continued to grow. "It's for our children we must run. Who can bear to watch them grow sick as so many others have?" She gave him a thoughtful look. "You're not really American, are you?"

"What makes you say that?" Ben's head still throbbed, but the Stepanskis had given him aspirin which had dulled the rest of his pain.

"Your Russian. The accent is different."

"I'm American, but Palestinian, too. I learned Russian from my father when we still lived in the West Bank."

"That explains it," Shavel Stepanski said before she retreated to her own sleeping bag, leaving Ben to his thoughts and ultimately his dreams.

He dreamed of being with Danielle in a scene similar to this, but the air was warmer and a fire burned. And they weren't alone; Ben's two murdered children, the son and daughter slain long ago, were with them in the dream; well, not with them exactly. Just a pair of sleeping bags waiting expectantly to be filled.

In the dream his children would be returning. In the dream he did not question why he was with Danielle instead of his wife, killed that same night almost nine years ago. That's what Ben liked about dreams but what also confused him. How could the unconscious mind so willingly accept what the conscious mind knew to be impossible? There was clearly a gulf between the two worlds and somewhere in that gulf was the happiness he hadn't known since the night that had changed his life forever.

Tonight, though, in addition to dreams, he was haunted by thoughts. Thoughts of his father, spurred by the picture of him taken in 1967 just days before Jafir Kamal's death. Ben slid it out of his pocket as soon as he gave up trying to go back to sleep. He couldn't see the faces of his father and the unidentified boy in the darkness, but pressed the picture with his fingers just the same, imagining the things he remembered best about his father, like the way he drummed his fingers on his chin and the fresh smell of his aftershave. Ben sniffed the picture, as if it might impossibly yield some of that scent.

*You think you can put things behind you, but you never really do.*

Not his father.

Not Danielle.

THE MORNING dawned cold and crisp, leaving Ben reluctant to pull himself out of his sleeping bag which had at last warmed up. The stiffness from the car accident had left his body and most of his headache was gone.

Victor Stepanski knelt alongside him, while the rest of his family went to fill their canteens with water. "It's a long way to the storage facility," he whispered. "I will take you there myself."

"What about your family?"

"We'll meet up later." Stepanski paused. "You have an idea of what was being stored there, don't you?"

"Something left over from the Cold War. A weapon, never used."

"You're telling me that's what got out. But why did the spraying make everyone sick? Why didn't the government tell us what was happening?"

"Because they were afraid," Ben said. "Just like we are."

# CHAPTER 59

**Y**ou asked for an awful lot in exchange for a few stones, Pakad Barnea," Sasha Borodin told Danielle, hours after accepting her terms. "The price was many, many favors called in."

"Ten million dollars worth of blood diamonds with a finished value of more than five times that," Danielle reminded sharply, "should be worth plenty of favors."

The night before Borodin had provided her with a beautiful room overlooking the sea, but Danielle had slept only fitfully. Sitting up with her eyes on the door and a vase propped against it in case Jim Black or someone else tried to gain entry.

"In any case," the Russian responded indifferently, "your tapes are on their way here now. You will not view them until the cowboy comes back with the diamonds." He hesitated, dressed elegantly this morning in a silk sport shirt and slacks which draped neatly over his smooth, tanned skin. "I could have you killed once I have the diamonds. You know that."

"You won't, once you've seen the tapes."

THE TAPES arrived at Sasha Borodin's beachfront home in Netanyah just before Jim Black returned from Tel Aviv with the diamonds. Danielle had left all the gems lifted from the Holocaust Torah scroll in a large box she had rented yesterday at a private postal facility in Tel Aviv. She had secreted the diamonds there well before the two Russians she had followed to Little Moscow arrived at Katz & Katz, where they picked up the emptied scroll.

Such postal facilities, just recently approved and subject to stringent regulations, were springing up all over the more populous areas of Israel thanks to the long lines and slow service at traditional post offices. Security comes with a price and it was almost always one Israeli citizens are willing to pay. But new policies directed at a recent terrorist mail bomb campaign tested the patience of even the most stalwart of citizens.

Danielle had simply given Jim Black the box key and the address, and the rough diamonds Ranieri had smuggled into Israel inside the Torah scroll were waiting for him inside just as she promised. Borodin inspected the blood diamonds only cursorily, while she looked over the video cassette tapes. The cases were marked PROPERTY OF THE UNITED STATES GOVERNMENT—AUTHORIZED USE ONLY, with good reason.

Inside were U.S. satellite reconnaissance tapes of the Mediterranean for the twenty-four hour period preceding the time she and Ben had discovered the crew of the *Peter the Great* murdered and her cargo gone. Danielle had provided the specific longitudinal and latitudinal coordinates required. She was aware of the Americans' incredible technological abilities, thanks to a number of security briefings she had attended over the years. Of course, such tapes never left the U.S. government's possession . . . unless they were vital to someone with the power and contacts of Sasha Borodin. Danielle guessed the favors he paid out were to contacts in Israel who had done the dirty work of obtaining the tapes for him from their American counterparts.

"Very good," Borodin said, his inspection of the rough

stones complete. "Now let us take a look at your tapes, Pakad. . . ."

Borodin led Danielle and Jim Black into a spacious recreation room dominated by a wall of windows, the central air-conditioning humming softly. A flat-screen television had been affixed to the front wall directly across from the glass. The glare from the sun streaming in would have made viewing anything impossible until Borodin stopped at a control panel built into the wall and activated mechanical blinds which descended over the windows, darkening the room and making it feel instantly cooler. The glare was gone. Borodin touched another button on the panel and the television brightened to life. Then he crossed the room to a VCR placed out of sight inside an elaborate shelving system that bracketed the flat-screen television on both sides.

The picture was grainy, lacking so much in clarity that even the high-definition television screen couldn't do much to help. It was good enough, though, to clearly make out the freighter *Peter the Great* anchored at sea, just as Danielle and Ben had found it.

Seeing it from this distance made Danielle think of Dov Levy. His return into her life had provided not only the spark she so desperately needed, but also a last link to the era of her father that had so dominated her upbringing. Now they were gone. Levy, her father, her National Police mentor Hershel Giott. The era was finally over. There could be no more looking back in the hope of seeing something that made more sense, or of finding the support she sought.

The picture on screen moved in splotchy burps, not in real time but in a jump speed created by a computer that extrapolated digital images transferred from the satellites and stitched them together. The only way to judge the passage of time effectively at all was in the length of the shadows as they increasingly fell across the bow to indicate the coming of night.

The picture was also difficult to follow because of the constant stream of data scrolling down the far side and bottom of the screen. Gibberish to Danielle but extremely meaningful, she knew, to someone with a knowledge of how to read these tapes.

Several hours after darkness fell, a boat appeared on the scene. It approached the *Peter the Great* in what looked like stop-action photography enhanced by advanced computer imaging that created visual coherence from thousands of miles up. The boat, a large trawler perhaps a third the freighter's size, anchored nearby. Danielle moved closer to the flat-screen television to better interpret the data scrolling across the picture.

"This is from the night before I got to the *Peter the Great* and found her crew dead," she told Borodin and Jim Black.

They continued to watch as a half dozen figures boarded the freighter, watched from the deck by several armed crew members. Obviously the trawler had radioed ahead, perhaps pretending to be part of the planned exchange or in some kind of distress. Either way, the scattered motion of the tape made the ensuing battle difficult to follow, especially since it was over very fast.

Danielle felt a lump rise into her throat, recalling the bodies she and Ben had found gathered in the cargo hold. The *Peter the Great*'s deck hands had been swiftly overcome and taken below where they and the other crew members had been massacred.

"Looks to me like somebody's carrying stuff across the deck," Black said, shocking Danielle back to the present.

"Crates," she noted, thinking of the freighter's empty refrigerated hold where something heavy had been neatly stacked.

"More like coffins," Black followed.

"Look!" Danielle pointed, as the tape continued to move forward in splotchy fashion. "They're using a winch to lower the crates in a cargo net from the freighter onto their trawler." She turned toward Borodin. "The cargo Anatolyevich was selling to the Africans."

"But who are they?" Borodin wondered.

Danielle returned her gaze to the screen. "Let's see where they take the crates and maybe we'll find out."

# CHAPTER 60

The storage facility is just a mile or so away now," Victor Stepanski said to Ben, as they crouched behind tree cover within sight of the one main road that led into Dubna. "We must be very careful. The soldiers could be anywhere."

"You're not scared to go on?"

Stepanski shrugged. "If whatever got out of that place was going to kill me, I'd be dead already."

It had taken them all morning and well into the afternoon to get this far. The long and strenuous walk had brought the stiffness and pain back to Ben's body. Stepanski never even seemed short of breath, even though he smoked a cigarette every time an opportunity presented itself, careful to bury the butt when he was finished to conceal any evidence of their presence.

He and Ben had covered twelve miles of rough terrain in just under six hours, stopping for water but no food save for a single candy bar they split between them. Without the sun to warm it, the day stayed cold and raw. But sweat still glued Ben's shirt to his flesh, forcing him to remove his jacket on numerous occasions just long enough for the chilly air to cool his body and leave him coughing. His calves kept cramping up. His knees throbbed, and the final hill had taken the last his thighs could give him, while the heartier Stepanksi climbed it effortlessly with a lit cigarette dangling from his lips.

"I have many friends who once worked in these facilities," the Russian said distantly. "They are all gone now, dismissed for lack of money. Some were reassigned. Most remain unemployed. I don't know who is there still. It will be interesting to find out."

Ben reached up and stopped Stepanksi before he could lead on. "You've done enough. Go back to your family. Get them away from here."

Stepanski nodded reluctantly and frowned. "Whatever is there, why didn't they destroy it? Why did they just leave it here?"

"Maybe because they thought someday they might need it."

BEN LOOKED back at Stepanski once he was across the road. The Russian slowly waved a callused hand. Ben waved back and felt his fingers stiffen in the cold before he ducked into the woods. According to Stepanski, he had another half-mile to go before reaching the storage facility where whatever happened in Dubna had started. Mid-afternoon and the gray sky gave up no warmth, as if in anticipation of another chilling night. Ben zipped his jacket all the way up, suddenly cold again.

He picked up his pace, hoping it would help recharge him. The path through the forest was easily recognizable and well trodden. Brambles and low-hanging branches scratched at him. Thick vines tried to trip him up.

It felt so strange being here. His father's death had been directly connected somehow to arms smuggled into Palestine from the Soviet Union. Now his own life was in danger because Russians were selling off wares stockpiled during the Cold War. In 1967 the arms were offered for free to Palestinians by the Soviet government. Today they were offered for profit on the black market by the Russian underworld. Ben shook his head, contemplating the irony.

He trudged on, thinking once again of his father's final days. Anatolyevich died before telling him the rest of what had happened. Why the guns had never reached Palestine, why that had somehow led to Jafir Kamal's assassination. He felt the path he was walking now would lead to those answers as well. That there was an eerie connection between these dual pursuits. Alone in the woods with no one to back him up, Ben thought he understood why:

He wanted to *be* his father. The lost years, a fleeting glimpse of Jafir Kamal disappearing through a door at the airport leaving only a whiff of his aftershave behind. Ben sought in life the connection death had denied him by fighting a different battle the same way. Even now, past forty, wanting to make his father proud and live up to the esteem in which Jafir Kamal was still held.

But the only clue he had left to that time was the nameless boy in a tattered black-and-white picture. Good as nothing.

The woods began heading downhill. Ben made out a thinly disguised stretch of barbed wire layered atop a fence. Signs with biohazard symbols and warnings were posted at regular intervals.

As he drew closer, Ben saw that portions of the fence were gone. Judging from the tread marks left in the half-frozen ground, he guessed the fencing had been removed to allow trucks easy passage to the building that came into clear view when he reached the bottom of the rise.

Innocuous, even drab in design, the storage facility had been built bunker-style from layered concrete. A formless square hulk dropped in the otherwise pristine forest. It had been painted an ugly greenish-brown color to better disguise it from the air in the unlikely event anyone was looking. The windows were recessed and small, indicating a single story within, though Ben knew such a facility often contained numerous underground layers.

Nearing one of the breaks in the fence, Ben ducked behind a tree and waited. He had expected some sort of military presence here, but the soldiers must have come and gone.

Satisfied no guards were about, Ben proceeded into the compound and approached the building. There was no evidence of a door, so he swung around to the next side, choosing his steps carefully atop dried mud that smelled like spoiled fruit and listening for any stray sound that might give away the presence of another person in the area.

Ben moved around to the front of the building and found the first sign of something truly amiss. The blackened char marks of blast residue were plainly evident on both sides of the frame and above the door. The door itself was steel, studded with patches of a slightly lighter shade—evidence that it had been repaired recently. The lock also looked new, a basic tumbler variety when one of the electronic variety would have been more appropriate.

Ben searched his pockets for something to use as a tool and came up with the pen he had borrowed yesterday from the rental car counter. He disassembled it and filed the ballpoint against the concrete jam until the tip was sufficiently narrowed to serve as a pick. It took several minutes of trial and error before he got it right, but eventually the ballpoint inserted easily into the lock. Springing the tumblers remained a difficult task that Ben managed only after willing himself to be patient.

The door swung open into a security ante-chamber. Ben recognized the lights as solar variety, explaining why the facility's power was still functioning. He could see no evidence of any gunfire or explosions, as if once they had blown open the main door, the invaders had simply strolled into the facility.

Moving cautiously, Ben entered the first of what could have been any number of secured sections containing the mothballed results of research conducted during the Cold War. A stockpile of weapons from the former Soviet Union that had never been used. Yet it was empty, stuffy with disuse, and looked as if it had been that way for a long time.

The next eight chambers yielded the same results. Ben continued to walk from one to another, listening to the tinny echo of his own steps and trying to put this in perspective with what he knew already.

Anatolyevich, the former KGB and Federal Security Service agent assigned to this facility, had pilfered crates containing a weapon that had been stored here, intending to sell it to a courier for ten million dollars worth of diamonds. But Anatolyevich had been clear on the fact that this had been a business arrangement, ongoing for some time. The invasion that had taken place here more recently, Ben concluded, had not been instigated by Anatolyevich at all. Another party had learned what was stored within these walls and had come here to steal it.

Ben moved on, hoping for some clue. In the woods Victor Stepanski had said the deaths in Dubna had begun six days ago, the very same day, perhaps, the exchange in East Jerusalem between Anatolyevich and Ranieri was supposed to have taken place. And two days after that the *Peter the Great* was raided, its cargo removed.

*What did that all add up to?*

There were too many variables, too many pieces still outstanding.

Perhaps the answers lay within the complex's lower levels, but Ben wouldn't know until he checked those as well. He found a door he believed led downward and thrust it open. Stepping through the door, he found himself at the top of what looked like an endless, dimly lit stairwell.

He heard the door banged shut behind him, followed by a shuffling sound.

"Move and I'll kill you!" a voice said, pressing something cold and hard against Ben's head.

# CHAPTER 61

Two more tapes followed the first one, each of them picturing the trawler's progress north up the Mediterranean. The picture grew even more grainy and less distinct as darkness crept over the sea. The reconnaissance satellites that had tracked the boat clearly had some sort of light-enhancing abilities, but the light wasn't sufficient to allow much on deck to be made out in detail.

Danielle acclimated herself to the terminology scrolling across the screen and found she could follow the boat's progress more easily that way; at least so far as her heading and progress north along the Mediterranean coast were concerned.

"Ain't that the way it always is," Jim Black commented. "There's never an Israeli patrol boat around when you need one. . . ."

"The smugglers' craft is probably outfitted with a device that jams radar. In the night, on the Mediterranean, it would be almost impossible to spot visually."

The final tape was two-thirds finished when a pier came into view. Danielle studied the coordinates scrolling across the screen, trying to get a fix on the position. She was still working on it when a series of jumpy shots showed the boat approaching the pier and then docking.

"What are we looking at?" Borodin asked. He was now standing even closer to the screen than was Danielle, his interest obviously piqued. "What is this place?"

"The Beirut coastline," Danielle said, having just identified it herself. She turned toward Jim Black. "Just down the beach from where my Sayaret team came ashore twelve years ago."

A figure appeared near the end of the pier, his face caught briefly in the spill of a stray flashlight.

"Two miles away from the home of this man," Danielle continued, recognizing him instantly. "Sheik Hussein al-Akbar."

THE GLOW off the screen caught both Danielle and Black in its spill, with Borodin hovering just beyond its reach.

"He'd be dead now, if it weren't for Mr. Black here," Danielle added, glancing quickly at the cowboy.

Black gave her a wink.

"You're saying this sheik is a terrorist?" Borodin asked.

"Not just any terrorist. At last check, he was one of the leaders of the Hezbollah movement dedicated to the destruction of Israel." Danielle tried not to show how scared she felt. She struggled to get her next words out through her suddenly constricted throat. "Looks like I'm going to need more of your help, Mr. Borodin."

"My part of the bargain is completed, Pakad."

"We're not talking about bullets and bombs here," Danielle said, straining to remain calm. "Whatever the sheik took off that freighter could destroy this country. *Your* country. Very bad for business."

Borodin's eyes flickered. His face tightened. "What do you need?" he asked Danielle.

# CHAPTER 62

Ben felt a hand shove him against the wall and spin him around. He smelled gun oil and his head ached where the barrel had dug a cold impression in his flesh.

"Who are you? You're not one of the soldiers," said a man who looked a lot like Victor Stepanski, only frailer and more scared. He stank of unwashed hair and clothes. His eyes swam madly, as if unable to focus.

"What happened here?" Ben asked him. "Who hit this place?"

"*Hit* this place? I don't know what you're talking about!"

Ben realized his translation of the idiom into Russian hadn't worked and tried again. "Someone blew up the door to get in here, didn't they?"

"Are you from the Federal Security Service?" the man asked, referring to the successor of the KGB. "Is that why you talk so funny?"

"You're not a guard," Ben presumed, looking at the man's rumpled and sullied civilian clothes.

"God, no. Far from it."

"You've been hiding."

"Yes."

"From the army?"

The man nodded.

"For how long?"

"Why do you want to know?" the man fumed, the pistol trembling in his grasp.

"Let me see if I can work it out, then. You've been hiding here ever since the facility was raided by the group that stole whatever was left here."

The man steadied his pistol in both hands now. "If you're one of them—"

"I'm not," Ben assured. "I'm not even armed. And I came alone."

"Then you're an even greater fool than I thought!"

"Who did you think I was a part of?"

"I don't know their names, but I've seen men just like them before. I recognized their look, their voices, their accents." Fear flooded the man's eyes. "Arabs," he finished.

"You're telling me it was Arabs who stole what was left here?"

"No, they didn't. The Arabs stole *nothing*, because I stopped them. I had no choice. I knew what the price would be, but I had no choice!" The man's lips trembled. He tried to swallow and failed. "It was all my fault. Dubna. The deaths. *Everything!* Because I let it out. It was the only way to stop them from stealing it, I'm telling you!"

"Steal *what*?"

"The Black Death."

# CHAPTER 63

After viewing the carnage at the Benguema Military Training Center outside of Freetown, President Kabbah thought nothing else in the world could scare him.

He was wrong.

Offering only a sparse explanation of the nature of the emergency, Defense Minister Daniel Sukahamin insisted they return to presidential headquarters at the State House in Freetown, accompanied by an American woman Kabbah had never met before. Someone had set up a television and video recording machine, gifts from the British.

"Mr. President," Sukahamin said as the American woman, whose clothes were dirt-streaked and rumpled, rose stiffly from a chair, "this is Dr. Deirdre Cotter—"

"Professor," the woman corrected.

"*Professor* Deirdre Cotter. Professor Cotter was kind enough to accompany me two days ago to the village of Katani that was the target of a Revolutionary United Front raid not long before that."

President Kabbah looked back and forth between his minister of defense and the American woman, still confused by her presence.

"Professor Cotter is no stranger to our politics," Sukahamin explained. "She came to our country with her husband as part of a U.N. mission. He was killed by the RUF two years ago."

President Kabbah shrugged apologetically.

"Professor Cotter is also an experienced botanist and horticulturist whose expertise I enlisted once the scope of the devastation in Katani became clear."

"I thought we were talking about an RUF raid," the President said to his defense minister, confused.

"We are, sir." Sukahamin and Cotter exchanged a worried glance. "That's why I sought out Professor Cotter's expertise."

With that, Deirdre Cotter moved to the television and switched both it, and the VCR, on.

"What you are about to see, Mr. President," she began, taking the remote control in her hand, "is footage taken yesterday of the village's farmland."

The picture brightened. The VCR whirred softly to life, and President Kabbah stared at the screen in amazement, his lower lip trembling.

"You're telling me *these* are the rice fields of Katani?"

"They used to be, Mr. President," Deirdre Cotter nodded.

# CHAPTER 64

I had no choice," the Russian continued, his voice trembling, eyes turning fearful. "I couldn't let them have the Black Death, no."

"What's your name?" Ben asked him, fighting to remain calm.

"Belush," he said, pronouncing it *Be-looosh*. "Mikhail Belush."

"What exactly did you do?"

"I broke the rules," Belush said, teetering on madness. "I was here alone. Who would know? And this was the last of them. I couldn't resist."

"Keep talking."

"I let the eggs of the final batch thaw out. This was weeks ago. Just a few at first, then all of them."

"Eggs?" Ben interrupted.

But Belush seemed not to hear him. "I was going to destroy the eggs, so the government would have no excuse to keep me here any longer. But I couldn't. I *created* them, after all. I spawned them and bred them and froze their eggs, just as I was instructed so the Black Death would be forever ready if called upon."

"You let them out. That's what you said."

"Not right away. Not until the terrorists came. I thawed them out so I could see one last time the wonder of what I had created. Such masterful work and no credit. The world could never know the miracles I performed here. But I could know, I could see. I thawed them out so I could breed more."

"You just said—"

"That I intended to destroy them? That I wanted to leave? And go where? To what? This is my life; I realized that. Without the Black Death, I'd be nothing."

"Your new breeding program wasn't authorized."

Belush almost laughed. "Look around you. Who else is here? Who else would ever know?" His gaze had gone distant, his ears primed as if listening to other voices. "The KGB, then the FSS, kept me posted here for years to watch over and monitor my creations, just in case they were ever needed again. But they never showed up even to check on my work. They took me for granted, took the Black Death for granted."

"What did you create here, Mr. Belush?" Ben asked, louder to get the man's attention.

"*Doctor* Belush. I'm a geneticist and a biological engineer."

"Okay, *Doctor*. What is the Black Death?"

"It would be better if I show you," Belush said, leading Ben toward the nearest exit.

# CHAPTER 65

President Kabbah took a step back from the television, as if hoping the picture it showed might
change.

Before him on screen was a barren wasteland, an endless
sea of dirt, devoid of any plant life.

President Kabbah had spent much of his youth harvesting
rice, had come to know the simple beauty, resiliency, and
strength of the crop. But the crops the villagers of Katani
had relied on for their livelihoods were . . . gone. As if
washed away by a vast storm, only the ground was left
desert dry and almost absurdly even. A machine couldn't
have leveled it any better.

On screen, the view deepened, the camera adjusted to
peer further into the distance and then refocused. Deirdre
Cotter, who'd done the filming herself, swallowed hard and
decided to let the pictures speak for themselves:

A vast black blanket moved across the rice fields of Katani, edging its way toward the crops that were still standing, utterly enveloping all it passed en route.

"Looks like . . . oil," a shaken President Kabbah managed. "A spreading oil slick."

"No, sir," Deirdre Cotter corrected. "Insects. I examined
a number of samples closely enough to tell you I've never
seen anything like them. Neither has anyone else. These
things aren't indigenous to Sierra Leone; they're not indig-

enous to anyplace on earth. They're a whole new species. Somebody made them."

Kabbah turned from the screen toward her. "I'm sorry, did you say 'made them'?"

"Created them in a lab. Perhaps 'enhanced' would be a better word, because whatever these insects are, they bear many of the same traits and characteristics of ordinary aphids."

"I'm not familiar with . . ."

"Let me try to explain, sir," Cotter said, as the black wave continued to spread across the television screen. "An aphid is an insect in the order of Homoptera. They live in temperate regions as parasites on the roots, leaves, and stems of plants. Their mouths contain organs that are perfect for piercing and sucking plants and consist of four long, sharp prods within a sheath or cover. Accordingly, no plant is safe from them. Not in the fields around Katani, or anywhere else in this country."

Cotter stopped when President Kabbah turned from the screen toward her. He had been listening intently, while following the black wave as it swallowed the last of the village's crops. "I do not need a science lesson, Professor. What I need is an explanation of what happened in Katani."

"I'm afraid the two are very much the same thing, Mr. President," Cotter said, and moved to the hard black sample case she had brought with her to the government building.

She and her husband had bought twin cases prior to coming to Sierra Leone. She had buried his with him just ten miles from Freetown in a grove of Cypress trees. Gunfire had ended his funeral prematurely, sent the priest and few villagers in attendance scurrying, so only Deirdre was left stubbornly behind.

Now she opened her case and removed a glass chest approximately a foot square. Inside, a blanket of black insects crawled over a layer of packed dirt. The creatures were packed so densely they might have been a single organism. The picture on the television screen captured in microcosm, but without any crops to destroy.

"I retrieved these samples from the rice fields yesterday," Deirdre Cotter continued. "I've been studying them ever since." She held the case out to Kabbah, then placed it down atop a table when he refused to take it. "The case was only half full when I began my work."

Kabbah knelt down to better peer inside. "Half?"

"They reproduced, almost doubled their population by my count."

"*In twenty-four hours?*"

Cotter crouched alongside the president of Sierra Leone. "In autumn traditional aphids lay fertilized eggs that survive the winter in crevices and hatch in the spring, producing wingless females that reproduce parthenogenically."

"I don't know what—"

"The process of impregnation does not require fertilization by males. The time of development is so short that the eggs sometimes hatch before they are laid. Often the hatchlings are even born pregnant." Deirdre Cotter tapped the glass, as if trying to attract the attention of the creatures inside. "As near as I can tell, every one of these insects is a female."

"You're telling me *aphids* destroyed Katani's rice fields?"

"No, sir. What I'm saying is that whoever created these things must have started with aphids. This species we're observing doesn't exist. It's never been charted. Someone created it in a laboratory through molecular and genetic engineering, designed with certain goals in mind."

"Like what?"

"To begin with, these insects are up to ten times the ordinary size with metabolisms that operate at least that many times faster than aphids. That means everything increases on the order of a hundred, including their appetites. Whatever these things are, they need to eat constantly in order to survive and fulfill their only other function."

"Reproduction," President Kabbah realized.

Deirdre Cotter nodded. "You are looking at the perfect organism, Mr. President. Traditional aphids often spend their entire lives within ten feet of the spot they were born. But the ravenous appetites of these have made them nomads, wanderers. The more they eat, the more sustenance is made available to their growing eggs, the faster those eggs are laid and the faster they hatch."

"And what do they eat?"

"Grass crops, by all indications. Rice, wheat, barley, rye, corn. I've tried to interest them in other plants, but they've only got an appetite for grass crops."

"Which account for ninety percent of the world's foodstuffs," Defense Minister Sukahamin interjected.

"They don't eat them so much as suck them dry," Deirdre Cotter explained, standing back up. "And that's not the worst of it."

"What could possibly be worse than what you've already told me?" Kabbah asked, rising to join her, glad not to be looking at the glass case any longer.

Cotter frowned. "Common aphids secrete from their intestines a sweet glutinous substance, called honeydew. Our tiny friends in the case secrete a substance, too: a toxically acidic germination inhibitor that will prevent anything in the soil from growing."

"For how long?" Sukahamin asked.

"A year, two years, a decade." Cotter shrugged. "It's hard to say without further tests."

President Kabbah moved close to the television screen again, his motions slow and tentative. He stopped and peered at the last of Katani's crops being swept under the black tide of insects. "And how far will these insects go? How long will they remain on the move?"

Deirdre Cotter shrugged. "So long as there is food in their path."

The room went silent at that and she began thinking of how excited her husband would have been over such a discovery. He was the true insect expert. Instead of being frightened, he would have seen this as the find of a lifetime. Always the scientist. Just as she needed to be now.

"There's something else you need to know," Deirdre

Cotter announced, retrieving the glass case and holding it up for both President Kabbah and Defense Minister Suka-hamin to see.

Almost instantly, one of the black shapes inside seemed to leap up to the case's ceiling.

"Some of them can fly."

# CHAPTER 66

Ben gazed out further into the woods that bordered the western edge of the storage facility where Belush had led him.

*A wasteland . . .*

That's what they looked like; the ground beneath the trees had gone barren and dead, stripped of virtually all its life. The trees alone stubbornly held on. Without sustenance from the ruined soil, they likely wouldn't last long. In fact, a number of their leaves had already browned and been prematurely shed, littering the vacant earth with crisp dark patches.

The Black Death, indeed.

"The bugs you created did this," Ben said to Belush.

"That was the last of the Black Death," he said distantly. "My reason for staying here. Perhaps now at last they'll let me leave. . . ."

"You weren't expecting Anatolyevich to come back for the remainder of the Black Death?"

"I had him fooled. He didn't think there was any left, thought three shipments were all there was."

*"Three?"*

Belush nodded. "Anatolyevich, the asshole. He was one of the ones responsible for keeping me here. Kept promising me I'd be free to leave after the next shipment." The

Russian's eyes widened. "There was always a next shipment."

"And you're saying *three separate shipments* of the Black Death left this lab?"

"Over the course of the past six months. I told Anatolyevich, the shit, it was the last of the Black Death after the last shipment."

"When did you develop these things?"

"The eighties, during the Reagan years in America." Belush almost laughed. "They were our response to the Star Wars missile shield. Much more down to earth, don't you think?" This time he managed a chuckle that emerged as a low, dry rasp and ended in a hacking cough.

Ben frowned. "You contacted Moscow, didn't you? After you released the insects to keep the invaders from stealing them?"

"What choice did I have? Unchecked, the Black Death could . . ." Belush finished his statement with a shrug.

"And that's why the spraying from the air began. To kill the bugs."

Belush's gaze grew distant once more. "I recognized the scent of what they used. Diarbitol, toxic to all forms of organic life, including humans."

"Explaining the rash of sudden deaths that led to Dubna being quarantined. The people were poisoned."

"The government had no choice. I already told you, the bugs had to be stopped before it was too late. Diarbitol might have been the only way."

"You can't even be sure if it worked."

"We'd know if it hadn't, believe me."

"How many in Dubna are going to die?"

"Far, far less than the number would have been in all of Russia if the bugs weren't stopped."

Ben grabbed the man and shook him hard, surprised by his own reaction. "*How many*?"

Belush trembled in his grasp. "Between five and ten thousand. That's why the city had to be quarantined! That's why no one on the outside could learn the truth of what happened!"

Ben released Belush and considered everything he had learned, the chronology. Anatolyevich had arranged to have a third shipment of Belush's bugs sent aboard the *Peter the Great* to the Mediterranean where they would be transferred to the party for whom Ranieri was fronting. Then one week ago an assault team Belush recognized as Arab raided the facility. Once Belush released the last of the bugs, thwarting them, the Arabs must have decided to go after the shipment on board the freighter instead.

It all came together, made sense.

*But what had happened to the other two shipments of the Black Death?*

"These Arabs," Ben started, trying to fill in the last missing pieces, "who were they?"

Belush held his stare, looking more scared than he had when Ben was shaking him. "Followers of Osama bin Laden."

BEN PRAYED Belush was wrong, could tell from the man's eyes that he believed fully in what he was saying. Tried to imagine the remnants of the most dangerous terrorist organization in the world in possession of a weapon that could destroy nations.

"I speak enough Arabic to know what they were saying," Belush explained, even though Ben hadn't prodded him. "It's why I let the bugs out. I had to stop bin Laden's people from getting their hands on them."

"What if you didn't succeed?"

"But I—"

"What if they managed to get their hands on one of the other three shipments that left here instead?"

Belush's face scrunched in anguish. "With that many of the bugs . . ."

"Go on," Ben prompted.

Before Belush could finish, though, Ben heard the crack of a branch breaking behind him. He spun and found himself facing a semi-circle of Russian soldiers training assault rifles on him. Slightly in front of them stood a squat, thick-headed officer holding Victor Stepanski by the scruff of the neck.

"I am Colonel Yuri Petroskov," he snarled. "And you are under arrest."

# CHAPTER 67

You're saying they can *spread*?" President Kabbah managed, after Deirdre Cotter's words had settled in.

"Unless we stop them in their tracks."

"How—how can we do this?"

"Burn them," Daniel Sukahamin answered.

"The two of you have discussed this already."

Cotter and the defense minister looked at each other, then nodded in unison.

"We have developed a workable plan," Sukahamin confirmed, "yes."

As he spoke the defense minister moved to Deirdre Cotter's makeshift terrarium, lit a match, and dropped it in through a small hole in the top. Almost instantly, the case's leafy bed caught fire, spreading to the insects who tried futilely to scurry from the flames' path.

Kabbah considered the ramifications, as he watched them burn. "We both know how many villages are in proximity to the infected fields, Minister."

"They can be evacuated, Mr. President."

*"Entire villages?"*

"The alternative is much worse, by far."

President Kabbah walked over to the television and stopped directly in front of the screen, silhouetted by its shadowy glow. "But we're missing the greater point here, aren't we?" he said to Sukahamin. "You told me the Revolutionary United Front was behind this."

"That's what our intelligence indicates," Daniel Sukahamin acknowledged softly.

"And we have no idea how many more of these . . . things the Dragon has managed to obtain, do we?"

Sukahamin sighed. "I'm afraid we don't, no."

President Kabbah shook his head in disgust. "Plenty to punish us with, I would imagine."

Sukahamin stepped a little closer to the leader of Sierra Leone. "The time has come to take decisive action, Mr. President."

"I quite agree."

"We have several plans drawn up for you to choose among. The American commander—"

"I don't want to hear about the American commander. He doesn't care about us any more than the American government does. What they care about is oil, the light sweet crude they import from Nigeria and Angola. They serve us only to prevent the instability that plagues Sierra Leone from spreading to places where their concerns truly lie. Any plan they suggest is doomed to fail."

"With all due respect, sir, nothing we've come up with has met with any success either."

"That's because we've been trying to defeat Matabu on our terms, instead of hers."

"I . . . don't think I understand."

"Stop listening to the Americans and you will. Now you must listen to me. Can you do that, Minister?"

"Of course, Mister President."

"Good. Now listen closely. There are three thousand of our refugees coming back to Sierra Leone from Guinea."

"Refugees, sir?" Sukahamin asked, perplexed.

"Lost their homes to incursions by the RUF and were turned away at the border by Guinean government officials, I'm afraid. I want them settled in camps outside of Freetown . . ."

"Under the circumstances, Mr. President, I—"

". . . and these camps need to be operational within twenty-four hours," Kabbah continued, without elaboration.

"*Twenty-four hours?*"

"Is that clear, Minister?"

"I can't see what—"

"Is it *clear?*"

Sukahamin nodded, his displeasure with the timing of the task obvious. "I'm sure you know what you're doing, Mr. President."

"Let's hope so, Minister."

# CHAPTER 68

Latisse Matabu stood at the top of the hill, gazing down into the river through the blinding sheets of rain that fell so hard it seemed to choke the oxygen from the air. The storm had begun with rumbles of thunder that sounded like the cracks of artillery shells bursting in the distance, the scent of ozone left to drift through the trees in its wake instead of sulfur and cordite. The thunder had receded quickly, but the torrents had continued to pound the countryside for hours.

Matabu swiped the water from her eyes, glad it hid the tears that fell every time she visited this place where General Treest had dropped the basket containing her baby over the edge. She remembered screaming until her voice went hoarse. The soldiers laughed as they climbed into their jeeps and drove off through the mud, leaving her to scrabble down the hillside, shredding her skin and clothes en route to the river-bank.

She searched for her baby into the night and the next day, until an RUF search party at last found her. And two weeks later she was sent to the United States, where she might still have been had her parents not been murdered. In returning to Sierra Leone after their assassinations, the Dragon had defied the threats by government forces, men like General Treest, to take her life as well.

Her first problem upon returning, though, was the two

incompetent subordinates of her father who had attempted to seize leadership of the Revolutionary United Front by releasing a killing spree on the entire country. They believed fear and intimidation would succeed where politics and strategy had failed. Latisse Matabu had sneaked into their camp in the guise of a prostitute and slain them both, then took their place at a meeting of the RUF's ruling council the next morning. If the remaining generals wanted to kill her, so be it. If not, they would accept her as their leader.

First, though, one more task remained for her. General Treest had risen to second-in-command for the government forces and lived with his family in a villa in the hills above Freetown overlooking the ocean. He came home from a cabinet meeting one night shortly after the Dragon's return to Sierra Leone to find his three personal guards maimed exactly as hers had been a decade before. He found his wife and young son tied up in the living room.

Matabu had unbound the boy first and dragged him across the floor so he faced his father. She held him in front of his father with one hand, while the other whipped from its sheath a Gurkha knife salvaged from one of the British mercenaries brought in to fight the government's war for them.

She thought she might hesitate at that point; after all, this boy, who was no more than nine, had done nothing to deserve this fate. Neither, though, had her parents or her baby.

She had cut the boy's throat without hesitation, watching the terror and agony in Treest's eyes as his son's blood showered him, imagining the din of his screams had she not taped his mouth closed. Her next stroke with the knife severed the boy's head which she placed in Treest's lap angled so the dead glazed eyes were staring up at him. She killed his wife the same way and placed her head alongside their son's so both could watch him die next.

For a moment Matabu considered sparing Treest's life so he might instead know the pain she had lived with since he had murdered her infant son. In the end, though, practical considerations won out and she had killed Treest quickly, wishing almost instantly she had made him suffer more. Before she left, Matabu lined the heads of the general and his family on the mantel over the fireplace as a warning to anyone who came seeking revenge.

Since then the government had remained in chaos, so hopelessly divided that defeat of her forces was a practical impossibility without outside assistance—specifically from the Americans responsible for training the Nigerian forces on the verge of entering Sierra Leone. Matabu's latest plan to seize the government took that into account. And once the RUF had taken Freetown, a new peace agreement would be signed with rebel leaders occupying a majority of cabinet-level positions. By the time new elections were ordered, the people of Sierra Leone would know where the best hope for their futures resided.

Latisse Matabu might live to see that day, but few others, and the prospects terrified her almost as much as defeat. There was no one in the RUF she trusted to be both gracious in victory and compassionate in leadership. The elements of the RUF she needed but despised would run wild in the streets without her to control them. Splintering in the ranks was inevitable. Warring factions would fight over control over various government bodies and functions. Potentially, the situation in Sierra Leone could be more unstable than ever.

She had already slain General Sheku Karim, her greatest rival. Now, as she stood in the pelting rain, it was time to choose her successor.

# DAY SEVEN

# CHAPTER 69

Danielle waited on the pier well until past midnight, having completed her inspection of the boat Borodin had secured for her use. It rested on the water's surface a few feet beneath her, visible through the gaps in the pier's frail, rickety wooden slats. The boat was a sleek, civilian-looking craft, innocuous enough to attract no attention if spotted on the open sea, yet outfitted with equipment sophisticated enough to prevent electronic sightings as well.

It could carry eight comfortably, so Danielle had asked Borodin for seven of his best men. He had several former Spetsnaz commandos in his employ, veterans of Russian special operations who more than fit the bill. They even spoke excellent English, he assured her.

Danielle's nerves wouldn't ease up. Life, her father had always said, had a way of catching up with you. For the better, or the worse. Here she was heading back to the very spot in Beirut that had prematurely ended the service she had been so thoroughly trained to perform. How ironic that regulations prohibited any discussion of operations outside of the Sayaret. She had never shared the details of a single assignment with her father. He had asked a few times, testing her, but Danielle had remained mute. The only mission he had precise knowledge of was Beirut, obtained from a contact who wanted to explain her transfer to Shin Bet.

So her father had never shared in her many successes, only her single failure.

She heard a footstep rattle the rickety pier and turned, her own shoe nearly slipping into a crevice between a pair of decaying boards in the process.

Jim Black was sauntering down the pier, his boots drawing soft echoes from the wood.

"Howdy, ma'am," he greeted and wedged his thumbs into his front pockets.

"You forget to bring something with you, Mr. Black?"

"You must be speaking of Borodin's boys?" He shook his head. "Nah, I didn't forget 'em. Anything but."

Danielle stiffened.

Black hitched his jacket behind him, exposing his pair of twin Sig Sauer nine-millimeter pistols. "I likely did you a favor. They weren't nearly as good as you were expecting."

"Dead?"

"Every last one. And none of them hard. Easy life here had turned 'em soft."

Danielle cursed herself for leaving aboard the boat the pistol Borodin had supplied her.

"You haven't gone soft yet on me, have you, Danny girl?" Jim Black yanked one of his Sig Sauers from its holster. "Catch," he said, and tossed it toward Danielle.

Danielle caught the pistol in midair, stumbling a bit and getting her grip all wrong for the quick shot she needed. Instead she held the Sig angled downward, looking as if she could not possibly hit Black before he drew and fired.

Across from her Jim Black's remaining pistol was still in its holster. "Fair enough for you?"

Danielle kept her gun where it was. "You do this often?"

"Not often enough, if you ask me. Wish I could more. I mean, where's the fucking challenge? Sometimes you've got to know whether you're the best or not."

"Who else are you working for, Mr. Black?"

"Smart woman like yourself, I'd've thought it'd be obvious."

"The diamond cartel," Danielle realized.

Black flashed his annoyingly cocky smile. "Met up with them after I did some work in Antwerp recently. Agreed to keep them informed and take action if it became necessary. As soon as I heard you were involved, I kinda figured it would. See, these diamond folks can't risk the world knowing what you know. It's all about money, Danny girl. And as long as that's the case there'll be plenty of work to keep people like me going."

"What will you tell Borodin?"

"What do you think?"

"That *I* killed the team of men he sent."

Jim Black nodded. "Something like that, yeah." Then he widened his stance enough to further jostle the weakly connected planks. "I'm gonna let you make the call. You know, ladies first and all that sort of shit." His hand edged toward the square butt of the Sig still tucked in one of his holsters, stopping just short of it, fingers coiling. "Man, this is fun. . . ."

Their gazes met and held, each able to take in all of the other, afraid to blink.

Danielle could tell Black meant it. He was letting her make the first move. Small consolation. As soon as she started her gun upward he would draw, and she had seen his work before.

So Danielle never raised her gun.

She pulled the trigger on the angle she'd been holding it, emptying half her clip into the wooden slat at Black's feet. He had just managed to draw his Sig when the slat gave way, Danielle's bullets having chewed through its flimsy rope bonds. She could see the muzzle leveling toward her when Black fell through, the pier seeming to swallow a good portion of him.

Danielle rushed toward Black as the cowboy, half on the pier, half below it, groped desperately for his Sig. He heaved himself further over the wood, his upper body straining to reach it. He managed to get one finger on it, followed by a second.

Black was still dragging it toward him when Danielle kicked him under the chin, her shoe compressing the soft flesh just over his Adam's apple. The blow snapped his head brutally backward. It rocked forward again violently, as Danielle slapped the gun from his grasp. His body slipped slowly through the space between the slats so that only his head and shoulders remained above the pier. Then, before she could launch another blow, Danielle watched Black disappear and heard the plop of his body hitting the water.

# CHAPTER 70

The Russian soldiers had put Ben in a jail cell that reeked of antiseptic and ammonia. No interrogation, no discussion. The one calling himself Colonel Petroskov had confiscated everything on his person, and that was the last contact he'd had with anyone.

Petroskov refused to listen to his warnings about where a portion of the genetically engineered bugs, stored as frozen eggs, had gone. Or perhaps he just didn't care that a weapon capable of destroying any country in the world had perhaps fallen into the hands of a terrorist organization that would most certainly use it.

Distraught, he found himself thinking of Danielle, of the trail of blood diamonds leading ultimately to the Black Death and now the vengeful followers of Osama bin Laden's al-Qaeda organization. Even if she would be no match for them, especially if she had failed to realize the scope of what she was up against.

Ben heard footsteps coming down the long hallway and lurched up from his stone cot. Face pressed against the bars of his cell, he could see a pair of soldiers coming. One worked a key into the lock while the other hung back, rifle at the ready.

"You will come with us," the one with the key said.

"Where?"

"You will come with us," he repeated.

"What have you done with Stepanski?" Ben asked, fearing for the safety of the man who had helped him. "Why were we separated?"

The soldier jerked him out of the cell and aimed him down the hallway. Ben felt the bore of a rifle poke him in the spine, prodding him forward.

"This way," the first soldier said when they reached the end of the hall.

The other Russian thrust open the door, an alley built slightly below ground level visible beyond it.

"Come."

Ben wondered if he was going to be shot. If the soldiers believed he was a spy, or a journalist, it was conceivable under the circumstances.

Outside in the darkness, though, he heard a car engine and then saw a pair of headlights snap on. A car pulled forward, squeezing up next to him.

"You are to get in," the soldier said.

Ben eased the passenger door open and bent his body to slide inside. Colonel Petroskov sat behind the wheel.

"What's going on?"

"We're going for a ride," Petroskov told him. "I borrowed the mayor's car, so we wouldn't attract attention outside the city."

The Russian backed fast up the alley.

"Why are you doing this?" Ben asked him.

"You are Ben Kamal, son of Jafir Kamal?"

"What's the difference?"

"Because that is why I am doing this."

# CHAPTER 71

Danielle settled into the chair before the boat's controls. She had waited several minutes on the pier, Jim Black's Sig Sauer ready in her hand, in case the cowboy reappeared.

When he didn't, Danielle climbed down the ladder from the broken-down pier onto the boat Sasha Borodin had provided. The satellite phone he had given her as well remained in its case; there was no sense calling the Russian now. She doubted he would be willing to help further; and even if he was, Danielle knew he could not possibly get more men to her in time for it to matter. Danielle had estimated she needed a minimum of six to handle the mission in Beirut effectively.

Now she had only herself.

Before sitting down at the controls, Danielle had again catalogued the weapons and equipment Borodin had obtained. He had filled her shopping list perfectly. Everything she had requested was here, as the Spetsnatz commandos would have been had Jim Black not killed them.

Obviously the supply of assault rifles, side arms, extra ammo, and tray of hand grenades were superfluous now, so she turned her attention to the airtight steel, gray-slab shipping container. Inside, the explosives—thirty sixteen-ounce bricks of C-4 plastique—detonators, det cord, and timing mechanisms had been neatly packed.

*Focus! She had to focus!*

A dozen years ago, General Dov Levy had sent eight commandos on the raid of Sheik Hussein al-Akbar's fortress in Beirut. He sent eight because he believed that's how many it would take to do the job effectively. On that night seven Sayaret commandos had died, while she had come home.

Alone.

And now she was going back.

Alone.

Behind the controls of the sleek boat, Danielle tried to tell herself she was doing this because a madman was in possession of whatever had been lifted off the *Peter the Great*. True enough, but not completely.

The rest of the truth lay in the fact that she was returning to finish the job she couldn't a dozen years before.

Danielle thought of Ben and felt her resolve weaken, however slightly. In the morass that had followed her return from New York and subsequent dismissal from the National Police, she had barely missed him; hadn't missed anything, because she'd been able only to concentrate on recovering from her wounds and the child she had lost. She had blamed Ben for the loss, hated him for it, she supposed, to spare her from hating herself. She was afraid to give herself up to him, afraid to surrender to the feelings she fought so hard to deny.

*Because everyone I care about dies.*

She was afraid to care again, preferring a life of isolation to the pain she could no longer take. Afraid to lose any more since one day she might wake up and find herself with nothing left at all.

But she so missed Ben now, wondering if there was a way things could have been different, wishing she had said all she had hidden deep inside herself where she hoped it might be lost. She gazed back at the satellite phone in its shoebox-sized case. Eased herself from the seat and crouched down to open it.

The portable handset inside was slightly larger than a

traditional wireless, and she used it to dial Ben's cell phone number. Wherever he was, though, there must have been no reception available because the call never went through.

*How to get word to him about what she had learned, where she was going, then? An insurance policy in case she failed.*

She thought of Colonel al-Asi, then remembered the colonel's number had been disconnected.

*How else could she contact Colonel al-Asi? There had to be a way. . . .*

Danielle smiled to herself, thinking of something. It took a while for her to track down the number she was looking for, and the person on the other end seemed baffled by her request, spoken in English, before finally relenting and taking her message.

Danielle returned to the controls as soon as the brief conversation was over. She eased the boat away from the pier and kept the engine idling slowly as she slipped into the open water of the Mediterranean. The shores of Israel shrank behind her and then disappeared into the darkness. The wind pressed against her face and stung her flesh with a cold spray lifted off the surface.

The night embraced, swallowed her. Danielle switched on the boat's sophisticated jamming mechanism and its infrared display screen that projected the waters ahead without benefit of light.

Maintaining a speed of thirty knots, she would reach the docks of coastal Beirut just before dawn, en route to the fortress of Sheik Hussein al-Akbar where the past and present would become one.

Your father saved my life. Many years ago," Petroskov continued and produced the photo of Jafir Kamal and the young boy Anatolyevich had given Ben back in Israel. The picture had been confiscated along with all the other papers Sabi had provided. "I recognized Jafir Kamal from the picture. And you . . ." A brief bout of tenderness softened Petroskov's demeanor. "I only saw your father once, but you look just like him."

"1967," Ben managed, a thick lump growing in his throat. His mouth felt pasty, the way it felt when he knew a fight was coming.

"How much do you know?"

"I know that the Palestinian Council voted to accept arms from the Soviet Union to launch guerrilla strikes against the Israelis. My father was the lone dissenter. But the weapons were never delivered."

"Yes, they were," said Petroskov. "You see, I was one of the drivers. . . ."

JAFIR KAMAL *checked his watch. The trucks would be coming from Jordan across the Allenby Bridge any moment. From there they would take the desert road toward Jericho*

*where the weapons inside them would be distributed among two dozen smaller vehicles to confuse any Israeli spies who might be lurking about. A small Jordanian force, Jafir Kamal knew, had set up a security perimeter between the bridge and the desert road on the chance an Israeli patrol should appear on the scene.*

*The contents of those trucks were the best chance the Palestinians had to use the Israelis' own tactics against them. A guerrilla war, an armed* intifada, *would force Israel to concentrate a huge measure of her forces internally, thereby weakening any response to a threat from the outside. The other Arab countries would not sit still if they saw the Palestinians rise up. Not this time. So went the thinking.*

*Jafir Kamal alone knew how wrong that thinking was. The Arab countries held the Palestinians in only slightly higher esteem than they held the Israelis. They would use the Palestinian people while making no move to help them directly. Israel's response to armed rebellion would be swift and excessive. Palestinians would be slaughtered indiscriminately in reprisal, perhaps even driven deeper into the West Bank until they were squeezed against the Jordan River. His people might just as well shoot themselves before the Israelis did.*

*Jafir Kamal had planted his charges strategically across the Allenby Bridge. He had wired them together himself, his fingers scraped raw from the effort that culminated in him peeling the rubber back to twist them around the screws below the plunger. The old detonating device was a relic left over from World War II, crude but effective. He would wait on the other side of the bridge and depress the plunger once all the Russian trucks carrying arms into Palestine had made their way onto the bridge.*

*He waited in the cover of some meager brush, further camouflaged by a mist rising off the Jordan River. The night was cold and Jafir Kamal felt chilled to the bone. He thought of the family he had started here and then raised in the United States, fully believing he would see them*

*again. He did not consider himself a martyr, nor did he
look at this as a suicide mission. The council members
would come to their senses, ultimately realizing he was
right. And if they didn't, Jafir Kamal would recruit new
leaders to take their place and steer his countrymen to an
existence eventually independent of both Israel and, just as
importantly, the corruptive influence of Palestine's Arab
neighbors. Allies whose friendship came with a wink
thrown over their shoulders and fingers crossed behind
their backs.*

*Jafir Kamal never regretted coming back to Palestine,
even though he knew he was leaving the hero he had once
been behind. This was a task more important than any he
had performed fighting the Israelis in 1948 and then helping to hold his people together after they had lost. People
had wept the day he left Palestine. He had left because it
was the best thing for his family. After the Six-Day War
had proved him right six months later, Jafir Kamal had
returned because it was the best thing for his country.*

*He spotted the first Russian truck as it turned onto the
bridge four hours late, closer to dawn than he had been
hoping for. The extra time had left him stiff and freezing,
and he rubbed his hands to flush the life back into them.
The last moments were the hardest of all, the waiting and
hoping that the moist night and sea air would not disable
the wire he had so painstakingly laid after nightfall.*

*The second truck turned onto the bridge and followed
the lead one's measured pace atop the rickety structure,
damaged earlier by stray ordnance. Jafir Kamal twisted the
plunger to the right and drew it upward. A single press down
now would drive metal against metal and blow the trucks
before they reached the other side. The heat of the incen-
diary devices would rupture the tires and shred the trucks'
undersides. With their vehicles disabled, the Russian drivers and accompanying guards would have time only to flee
before the inevitable explosions. No way they would be able
to salvage even a single rifle from the shipment. But they*

would all survive and find their way safely back to their families.

Jafir Kamal found that very important, even as he watched a third truck follow the first two onto the bridge. He was more glad than ever that he had spared his two sons this life they would have inevitably fallen into had he had not taken them to the United States. The curse of living a long life in Palestine would have been to watch one or both of them die. Jafir Kamal knew the odds as well as any man, and those odds had led to his emigration. Someday he would explain it all to his sons. Someday he would explain to them what he had done on this night, too.

The fourth truck dropped onto the Allenby Bridge, the lights of the fifth not far behind it. Jafir Kamal was counting seconds now, tasting the thick air on his breath. He couldn't swallow. His right hand felt stiff again, so he joined his left one over it.

The final truck finally pulled on to the bridge, the lead one just a hundred yards from this side. More spacing than was ideal, but it had to be now.

Jafir Kamal pressed down on the plunger with both hands.

For a long moment nothing happened and it seemed nothing would. Then white flashes erupted all across the bridge a flicker of an instant before the rumble of explosions pierced Jafir Kamal's ears. The percussion of the blasts knocked him backwards and kicked his breath away. He looked up from the ground to see the hoods and undercarriages of all the trucks ablaze, the Russian drivers lunging down from the smoking cabs to run for their lives.

But the driver of the second truck in the convoy tried foolishly to drive on. His truck belching smoke and flames, he grazed the lead truck and squeezed by it before the fuel tank ignited and blew the back end of his truck into the air. It seemed to teeter on its nose briefly before spilling onto its side and collapsing a section of the bridge.

Flames licked at the already blackened steel of the toppled truck. Jafir Kamal rushed toward it in the open, covering his hands with his jacket and pulling himself to the driver's door of the cab which was now parallel to the sky. The thin fabric did little to protect Jafir Kamal's flesh, just enough to mask the pain as he closed his fingers around the latch and yanked the door open.

The driver was inside, still semi-conscious. Jafir Kamal reached down into the building heat and smoke and grabbed him. He raised the man to his waiting second hand and yanked him upward, though not all the way out.

"Push with your legs!" Jafir Kamal ordered him, their eyes meeting for one long moment. "Help me help you! Push!"

He saw the man's feet kick and then push enough for Jafir Kamal to hoist him all the way out and drag him to safety on the other side of the bridge. Exhausted, he barely managed to stagger off into the smoke and confusion, his lungs on fire.

Jafir Kamal made it back to the cover of the nearby brush beyond the bridge and sank his hands to his knees. He intended to rest just for a moment when something with the force of a powerful kick pounded his back. Then he felt something warm oozing through his shirt, instantly cooling in the chilly night. Remembered the sound of a crack that had reached only the edge of his consciousness.

*I've been shot . . .*

That thought registered a moment before the sound of footsteps crunching rapidly over the ground made Jafir Kamal twist painfully round and find the shape of Omar Shaath looming over him.

I did not learn the big man's name until another time,"
Petroskov finished, his fingers bleached of blood from
squeezing the steering wheel so hard through the duration of the story. His teeth ground nervously together.
"Shaath must have been leading the team sent to meet our
convoy. That's why he was in the area."

"You saw Shaath kill my father," Ben said from the passenger seat in what had started as a question. He was surprised the words came out at all. Questions he had posed
all his life finally answered.

"Shoot, yes," Colonel Petroskov told him. "Kill, no."

"You said he was holding the gun, ready to fire again."

"Maybe he did; I'm not sure. I am sure I saw someone
come up behind Shaath and strike him with a branch or a
log in the head. Shaath doubled over. The figure hit him
again. Twice. Shaath went down."

"Did you see who it was?" Ben posed eagerly.

"Someone small."

"A boy?"

"I thought so, yes."

"The one in the picture with my father?"

"I was too far away and it was too dark. I couldn't be
sure."

Ben's mouth felt clogged. He couldn't swallow. "And
my father?"

He could see Petroskov's thick shoulders shrug behind the wheel. "I must have passed out. When I woke up, your father—and the boy—were gone. Where . . . ?" He finished with another shrug, a sadder one that left him looking weak. "This makes me even with him. He saved me and now I have saved you. I will escort you to a military airfield where a plane is waiting to take you back to your country My debt is paid."

"Not yet. Not until you tell me about Dubna."

"You already know everything."

"Does that include you working with Anatolyevich?"

"What makes you—"

"Because you're in charge of security for this sector. And at the storage facility Belush told me it was *soldiers* who carted away the shipments of his Black Death all three times."

Petroskov didn't bother denying the allegation. "In the absence of regular salaries, we of the Russian military have been forced to be creative."

"You knew all along what you were helping to smuggle."

"All the more reason I was glad to see it out of my country."

"Your men drove the crates of Black Death to the nearest port. Loaded them onto the *Peter the Great*, or another freighter like it, as directed by Anatolyevich."

Petroskov's empty stare confirmed Ben's words.

"To be shipped where?" he demanded, resuming. "Who bought them? *Where* were they going to end up?"

Colonel Yuri Petroskov took a deep breath before responding to Ben's staccato burst of questions. "West Africa," he said. "A rebel leader named Latisse Matabu in Sierra Leone."

# DAY EIGHT

# CHAPTER 74

Danielle eased the pushcart down the Corniche, the pedestrian-only promenade that rims the Beirut beachfront to the north. The day had dawned hot and by late morning the sun burned hotter still, steam vapor lifting from stray puddles pooled in a brief rain the night before. Few people paid her any attention and those who did usually shook their heads or frowned in disdain.

The poverty left over from Lebanon's endless civil war had created a new subculture in Beirut: pushcart women. Often homeless or destitute, they roamed the Corniche and the downtown streets between the Christian and Muslim ghettos carrying all their possessions, squeezed in amidst mops, rags, and cleaning products, in search of brief cleaning jobs. They would knock on the doors of homes, apartments, and office buildings in the hope of finding windows to be washed, floors to be mopped, or rooms to be scoured. The women were willing to work for coins and enough people took pity on them to provide the pennies needed to get them through the day.

Danielle had paid the equivalent of roughly ten dollars for this pushcart. Its previous owner had gratefully parted with everything lashed upon it in return, rushing away in glee before Danielle could change her mind.

She had come upon the woman on the Corniche, shortly after venturing up from the docks. Danielle had tied her boat down at an empty slip at the harbor just before dawn, happily surprised by the utter lack of security compared to the frequent patrols she recalled from twelve years ago. In fact, there were few boats of any kind moored as far down as the new marina where the St. George Hotel yacht club had been in 1990. Beyond that the only change of note visible from the docks was a seawall constructed around a huge stretch of beachfront, including the area where Danielle's Sayaret team had come ashore.

The once bustling and noisy downtown streets of Beirut had looked utterly quiet upon her arrival, not a single light burning she could see from the waterfront. Clearly, anyone moving about at night would invite concern and attract suspicion. That meant Danielle's best chance at success would lie in daylight when the sheik's security might be more lax. When an attack would be least expected.

Especially an attack undertaken by a single person.

The means to mount that attack had come to Danielle the moment she first laid eyes on the pushcart. Back in the speedboat's cramped cabin, she inventoried the previous owner's dingy, discolored dresses and chose the largest, the one with the most material. She then tried it on, satisfied that it hung shapelessly over her, billowing to the sides.

Plenty of room to conceal the bricks of plastique explosives supplied by Sasha Borodin. There was ample space on the pushcart to store the detonators and timing mechanisms, plenty to tuck in a pair of submachine guns and pistols, ammo and grenades as well.

The walk along the Corniche to central Beirut where the sheik's compound was located proved much longer than she had remembered. The air felt super-heated and the concrete of the promenade, dappled by cracks and creases, created an oven effect that defied the sea breeze's weak attempts to cool the day down.

The Corniche quickly grew too cluttered with people for comfort, even at this early hour, and Danielle veered to the left. She waited for a man peddling a bicycle with fresh loaves of bread hanging from a rack suspended over his handlebars to pass, before easing her pushcart off the promenade onto the street. A young woman on Rollerblades just missed colliding with Danielle and struggled to keep her balance.

"*Intabih!*" she blared. "Watch out!"

Danielle paid her no heed and shoved her pushcart to the other side of the street. The Beirut sidewalks were in too great a state of disrepair to use, leaving her to cling to the muck-strewn gutters. Occasionally a wheel would get lodged against a piece of debris, or mired in a rut, and it would take all of Danielle's strength to thrust her cart free.

Her cover held all the way across to Allenby Street, nonetheless, past beautiful early century buildings so brilliantly restored as to seem textbook examples of Ottoman or Venetian flair. Fading signs placed in their windows advertised future tenants like Coca-Cola and Merrill Lynch. But these buildings remained as empty as the burned-out shells on the outskirts of town where the renovation efforts hadn't yet reached. The compound of Sheik Hussein al-Akbar lay just a few blocks ahead, across the street from the beachfront hotels. Beyond the compound was a side street called El Sayad where the Sayaret commandos had parked their truck a dozen years before.

The very spot to which Danielle was headed now.

# CHAPTER 75

Ben saw Colonel Nabril al-Asi waiting in the crowded arrivals terminal of Gaza Airport, hastily rebuilt after the recent shelling, as soon as he filed through the door with the rest of the passengers on the plane from Cairo. The colonel looked distinctly uneasy standing amidst so many people. As Ben approached, he saw a man shove his way forward, jostling al-Asi, the colonel suspended between intentions of how to respond.

The flight Petroskov had arranged for Ben in Dubna had gone only as far as a private airstrip in Iran. From there a car drove him to Tehran where he boarded a plane that was like a cattle car for a flight to Cairo, where he transferred again, this time onto an ancient converted military transport for the trip to Gaza.

"You look exhausted, Inspector," al-Asi greeted. Ben realized the colonel's hair had grown more salt than pepper lately, and the cocky, almost insolent sneer was missing from his expression. "I'm sorry to say that you will have no time to rest."

"And you look . . . disguised," Ben returned, making no effort to hide how relieved he was to see him. Petroskov had been true to his word, having obviously managed to contact al-Asi to inform him Ben was on his way home.

The colonel looked down at his own clothes: workman's attire that made him seem a common laborer, instead of the

Armani-clad spymaster who was one of the most powerful men in Palestine. Dried droplets of paint bled down his shirt. His pants were stained with dirt at the knees.

"These? I was painting the walls of the Protective Security Service's new headquarters when your Russian friend's call reached me. I came straight here, glad to have an excuse not to finish."

Ben realized this was the first time he had seen al-Asi without the company of a single guard. But he didn't need Armani to stand out. His gait and demeanor remained enough to make fellow visitors to the airport take a second look and then shrink slightly away.

"Come," al-Asi continued, "I have a car waiting. There are fresh clothes inside. You can change on the way."

"To where?"

"Beirut. And Pakad Barnea."

"I WOULD have talked her out of going, if I'd had the opportunity," al-Asi said, once they were outside the terminal, heading to a parking lot made of hard-packed dirt across the street from the airport.

"Wait, I thought you said you talked to her."

Al-Asi frowned. "Unfortunately, my pissed-off Israeli counterparts must have reached the Palestinian Authority with their tale of my insubordination. Deactivating my phone was my first punishment. Assassination will likely be my second."

"Then how do you know where Danielle is?"

"She left a message, Inspector, at Rafiq's, the building supply store in Ramallah where I have been doing all my shopping."

"WHAT HAPPENED to your driver?" Ben asked when they reached the colonel's Mercedes.

Al-Asi frowned. "He's been reassigned. Another punishment, I'm afraid."

"Your bodyguards?"

"The same," al-Asi said and climbed into the car.

Ben followed, checking the area nervously to see if anyone long intimidated by the colonel's power might be lurking to take advantage of his fall from grace.

"The Russian who contacted me never explained his reason for doing this," al-Asi resumed, after starting the engine. "He told me it would be better hearing the story from you."

Ben pulled from his pocket the now wrinkled, dog-eared snapshot of his father and the boy about to serve Jafir Kamal tea. "He helped me because of this."

Al-Asi looked over at the picture, clearly recognizing it.

"This is the photo you gave to Anatolyevich," Ben finished.

"Because I wanted him to realize I knew things about him no one was supposed to. Makes a man wonder how much more I know."

Ben let his eyes linger briefly on the two faces in the picture. "You knew Anatolyevich would show it to me, of course."

"I was counting on it."

"Because you didn't know how to tell me the truth yourself."

"There are some things that are difficult even for friends to share."

"You can share it with me now," Ben said, and looked across the seat squarely at al-Asi. "You are the boy in the picture, aren't you, Colonel?"

# CHAPTER 76

Al-Asi nodded, ever so slightly.

"I always wondered why you took such a great interest in me," Ben muttered. "Almost from the moment I returned to Palestine. Always my guardian, my protector."

"It seemed the least I could do," the colonel sighed.

"You were there when my father blew up the Russian trucks," Ben said, recalling Petroskov's tale of that night. "You attacked Omar Shaath after he shot my father."

Al-Asi smiled sadly. "It was the first time I ever struck a man, believe it or not. My family always believed I was too weak and frail to fight. I was relegated to the work carried out in back rooms. Perhaps if I hadn't struck Shaath that night, that's where I would still be."

"What happened next?"

*YOUNG NABRIL al-Asi stood trembling over Omar Shaath's body, wondering if he had killed him. But the big man's chest rose and fell, and the boy could hear his breath wheezing. He could have finished the job easily enough, if he had to, glad in any case that it wasn't necessary.*

*Al-Asi then crouched down alongside Jafir Kamal. The*

man's breathing was weak and muffled. He had fallen on his stomach, but his legs must have scrunched up slightly when he tried to move. The boy could see a wide dark stain on the back of Jafir Kamal's shirt and the ground around him was wet with blood.

Around him chaos had broken out. Men shouted and screamed, illuminated by the thickening flames as they tried to reach the trucks burning on the bridge. Someone was yelling for Shaath.

Al-Asi decided to use the chaos to his advantage. He was not strong, being small and frail for his fourteen years, but his first thought was to hoist the unconscious form of Jafir Kamal over his shoulders. The effort failed miserably twice, as the boy's knees buckled under the weight.

Finally he laced his hands beneath Jafir Kamal's armpits and dragged him further into the brush, painting a splotchy trail of blood in their wake. Al-Asi knew where the great hero had left the vehicle he had driven here, because he had hidden himself in the trunk. He had listened to the council members discuss the shipment's arrival and was certain Jafir Kamal would take steps to thwart it. He couldn't say whether he actually agreed with Kamal or not, but he worshipped the great hero, who had treated even such a small boy respectfully despite his youth and poverty.

Al-Asi knew he was betraying the confidence of the council members on this night and that bothered him. They had taken him in, and this was how he repaid them. One of the council members had even brought him into his family, more as servant than surrogate son, yet still a move that put a roof over his head.

Al-Asi wondered if he would still be welcome when all this was over.

He found Jafir Kamal's car in the darkness and, with great effort, managed to haul the great man into the back-seat. The smells of burning oil and charred steel were strong even here and the carcasses of the Russian trucks on the Allenby Bridge continued to burn brightly enough to chase much of the darkness away.

*Climbing behind the wheel, al-Asi realized he had no idea where to go. There had been no reason to think that far ahead since he had never visualized himself in this position. He had accompanied Jafir Kamal merely to watch, not protect him. Attacking Shaath had been an inexplicable and totally unexpected reaction. A sudden explosion of passion stemming from the certainty that the big man was about to shoot Kamal again, shoot him as many times as it took until Jafir Kamal breathed no more.*

*Al-Asi had felt terrified in that moment, yet remained passionate about attempting to save his hero. Shaath became the object of the hate that had been festering inside him.*

*In his imagination the great Kamal would be so grateful for saving his life that he would adopt the boy and take him under his wing. Train him in the ways of the Palestinian warrior so he never need fear anything again.*

*But where to go now?*

*A doctor! Jafir Kamal needed a doctor!*

*The muktar in his old village was a doctor. The muktar was in a refugee camp now, the same one in which the orphaned future head of the Palestinian Protective Security Service had lived until he ran away after being beaten. The refugee camp was several miles from here, a difficult drive at night with Israeli patrols and curfews to consider. But the boy managed to stay clear of the Israelis, in part by driving with his lights off the whole way. His pace was that of a crawl, the car further camouflaged by the utter blackness of the night.*

*He parked on the outskirts of the camp that teemed with bodies squeezed into a muddy flat, living in tents. The stench of raw sewage, spoiled food, and human fear turned al-Asi's stomach, even worse than he remembered.*

*In the car's backseat, Jafir Kamal moaned.*

*He was still alive, that was something anyway, enough to give al-Asi hope. He rushed about the camp until he found his village muktar, a gruff man in his sixties who had gone to school in France. The muktar came carrying his medical bag, his hands dark with the dried blood of several wounded in this camp he had probably not been able to save.*

*"The wound is bad," the* muktar *reported, after a quick examination of Jafir Kamal in the backseat under the spill of a flashlight.*

*"Yes, I know."*

*"Who is this man?"*

*"It is the great hero, Jafir Kamal himself."*

*The* muktar *returned to the unconscious form with renewed enthusiasm.*

*"Can you save him,* sidi*?"*

*"I will do the best I can."*

"IT WASN'T good enough," al-Asi said to Ben in the front seat of his Mercedes, his voice so soft it barely carried over the quiet hum of the air conditioner. "Your father died that night. He never regained consciousness. I was with him— you should know that, at least."

"All these years and you never told me," Ben responded, more shocked than dismayed by the tale.

"I didn't know how to, Inspector."

"The way you just did sounded pretty good."

Al-Asi took in a deep breath and held it briefly. "Would you have looked at me differently if I had told you the truth before?"

"I suppose."

"You would have felt indebted?"

"Of course."

"That's your answer, my friend."

"What?" Ben posed, exasperated.

"I did not want you acting out of debt when around me. You know my position, how I work. Everything I do is based on debt because debt means leverage. When someone owes me something they are far easier to persuade." Al-

Asi's dark, heavy-lidded eyes sought him out. "I did not want you to be just another person for me to persuade. I thought too much of you for that."

"But it explains why you've been looking out for me almost from the day I returned to Palestine."

"No, Inspector, it doesn't. I did what I did out of respect for you, not your father. A man must stand on his own. Early on, I may have tested you to see if you were someone I could trust with my friendship."

"And did I pass?"

Al-Asi's expression didn't change. "I believe there are only two men of integrity in our country, Inspector. You are the second. You can see why I did not greet your pending move back to Detroit with great enthusiasm."

"It wasn't you I was leaving, Colonel."

"Ah, well, my own people have apparently abandoned me, so why not you?" The colonel smiled strangely. "Can I share something with you, Inspector?"

"Of course."

"I owe everything I am to your father, because the day he was killed was the day I realized what it took to survive."

"Omar Shaath recovered," Ben reminded him.

"I should have killed him when I had the chance." The colonel's blue eyes glistened playfully. "But I still had some growing up to do."

"You were never identified?"

Al-Asi shook his head. "No one got a good enough look. Everyone assumed it must have been an accomplice of Jafir Kamal. Who would believe a weak young boy could accomplish so much? I went about my business, playing the dutiful slave while all the time learning how Palestine truly functioned." A sad frown crossed his features. "It is not terribly different now than it was back then, is it?"

"Not yet," Ben agreed.

# CHAPTER 77

Danielle pretended to be resting in the shade of El Sayad Street, seated on the rough sidewalk with her back against her pushcart. In reality she was reviewing her plan.

According to intelligence reports Sasha Borodin had managed to obtain, the sheik had constructed an escape tunnel connected to the crumbling storm drains beneath Beirut that spilled into the Mediterranean. The entrance to those drains, and the sheik's tunnel, was accessible through a square-grated hatch that rested between the pushcart and the sidewalk. The hatch had been made to open only from the inside, but Danielle had spent the last forty minutes using a file to wear down the latch on its underside. She had found the file amidst a collection of rusted tools in a box inside the pushcart that contained the sum total of a person's life, enthusiastically sold for ten American dollars.

Barely an hour before, she had snailed past Sheik Hussein al-Akbar's fortress. Her breath shortened. The pounding of her heart made her ribs ache, as her mind transported her back to the last time she was here. Only then had she come to grips with how much that mission's failure had haunted her. The downward spiral that began then had never really ended. Everything bad that had ever happened to her, it seemed, had its root in that night.

*Unfinished . . .*

So much in her life remained that way. Tenures in the Sayaret, Shin Bet, and National Police. Two pregnancies. Ben. The list went on. No sense of closure. Everything ending before its time, before she was ready.

This was her chance to change all that. To finish what had hung out there uncompleted for more than a decade and change the course of so much which followed it.

That thought filled Danielle with fresh resolve as she continued to ease her pushcart down the street. Drawing even with the front gate on Allenby Street, she had shoved her pushcart further out into the street, skirting perilously close to Beirut's unforgiving traffic. She knew the move was foolish, stupid, but she couldn't help herself. She needed to get closer, needed to see inside the compound. Touch what had been left out of her reach a dozen years ago.

The experience bordered on surreal. The only other time she had viewed this place had been in Sayaret intelligence photos and a grainy picture on a television monitor broadcast from Captain Ofir Rosen's hidden camera.

The grounds within the fortress were lush and magnificent, perfectly kept and manicured. Guards patrolled at regularly spaced distances.

A horn blew. Brakes squealed. Drivers shouted obscenities at Danielle through open windows, gesturing with their hands. They called her a tramp, a whore. Danielle gestured back, spitting their way.

She hit the opposite curb so hard the cart nearly toppled, drawing the attention of the guard poised at the front gate. Danielle ducked her head but tried to look at him as she passed.

The guard was holding a clipboard, lots of names and numbers written in Arabic. A checklist, it looked like.

Danielle headed on, not gazing back.

Now, sitting on the curb of El Sayad Street almost an hour later, Danielle at last felt the latch she'd been filing give way, freeing the hatch to open. All that remained was for her to pry the hatch open and duck down inside the underbelly of Beirut. She rose to her feet and, as unobtrusively as possible, slid the remainder of the equipment she would need into the vast pockets of her shapeless dress.

The detonators Borodin had obtained, standard Israeli military issue, were digitally based and capable of being triggered by a single wireless transmitter. She stuffed timing mechanisms into her pockets as well, still uncertain what she would actually need once inside the fortress. The pistols and extra ammo were easy for her to conceal, the Uzi submachine guns considerably less so. Ultimately, Danielle decided to tote only one of them along.

Satisfied she had everything she needed, Danielle purposely spilled the contents of a box set atop the pushcart and crouched to retrieve them as a ruse to get her closer to the hatch. From this angle the pushcart blocked view of both her and the hatch from the street, but she remained cautious as she wrapped her fingers around the steel grate and yanked upward.

The grate lifted off with minimal resistance. Holding the Uzi under the ragged shawl covering her shoulders, Danielle lowered herself onto the ladder inside. Next she maneuvered the pushcart closer to the grate to better conceal it. Then she dropped a few more rungs before shouldering the Uzi and easing her hands through the hatch to fit the grate back into place. Her angle and the weight she was carrying made it awkward and difficult, but she managed the task and continued her descent.

At the bottom of the ladder, Beirut's storm drains broke off in four directions. Danielle gathered her bearings and chose the one that offered the most direct route to the sheik's fortress. Above her the pushcart had been reduced to a mere shadow concealing the hatchway. Danielle was struck suddenly by the odd certainty she had left something crucial up above and a mental inventory of what she had stuffed on her person did little to alleviate her concern.

Finally she passed it off to paranoia, common for all in such situations, and started off. Her feet sloshed through thin puddles of water, and the sunless cool of the subterranean tunnel chilled the sweat that had coated her face and soaked through her clothes. The air stank of fetid water, mold, and sewage run-off that Beirut's crumbling infrastructure let spill into these drains and, ultimately, the Mediterranean.

Danielle could only hope that the shipment Sheik Hussein al-Akbar's people had stolen from the *Peter the Great* was indeed stored in his fortress. If not she would have to confront the sheik directly to find out where it had been taken. Not a pleasant prospect, and one for which the odds of success were minimal at best.

Danielle continued making her way through the tunnel, knowing it would eventually access the main part of the fortress. From there she would find and destroy the shipment stolen off the freighter and kill anyone who got in her way.

She felt her heart settle in her chest, suddenly calm and composed. She was where she wanted to be, where she should have been a dozen years before.

O sama bin Laden's al-Qaeda group?" al-Asi questioned when Ben got to that part of his story.

"The Russian at the storage facility was certain they were the ones who staged the raid."

"But came away empty-handed when this Belush released these . . . bugs."

"And it was then necessary to switch to Plan B," Ben concluded. "Plan B was to contact this sheik in Beirut and put him on the trail of the freighter that had the last shipment of the Black Death on board."

"And when you arrested Anatolyevich . . ."

". . . his freighter remained at sea long enough for the sheik's people to get there and steal the contents," Ben completed.

Al-Asi nodded in somber understanding. "Which explains why Pakad Barnea set off to destroy this final shipment."

"She'll never succeed alone, Colonel."

"Precisely why we are going to help her, Inspector."

"THERE'S A truck waiting for us just short of Israel's northern border," al-Asi explained. "Loaded with vegetables and fruits and equipped with the United Nations markings that will get us into Lebanon."

"How did you manage all this, Colonel?" Ben asked, amazed, as always, by al-Asi's skills.

"It pays to have lots of debts to call in."

"Have you left any for yourself?"

"Just enough to help my family, if things come to that," al-Asi said, grimly resigned to the possibility. But his voice perked up again almost instantly. "It's been a long time since I've done something like this. I find it refreshing."

"You have friends in Beirut?"

"Not a single one I can call upon, under the circumstances," the colonel beamed. "Totally outside my sphere of influence. Calls for a different strategy. Exciting, Inspector, isn't it?"

THEY CHANGED clothes before climbing into the supply truck that would take them into Lebanon. Ben finished dressing, then moved to inspect the contents of the truck's rear hold. He ran his hands through the bushels of fruits and vegetables, their fresh smells washing over him, expecting weapons, even more men, to be concealed among the crates.

"I told you, Inspector, no tricks today, no surprises," Colonel al-Asi said, drawing next to him. He was wearing an outfit almost identical to Ben's, the worn, shapeless clothes of a laborer. "We'll cross into Lebanon in northern Israel and take the coastal road north to Tyre."

"Why Tyre?"

"You'll see. Come, let's get a move on," al-Asi said, climbing up behind the wheel. "I can hardly wait!"

"You don't have to do this, Colonel," Ben told him, puzzled by the colonel's almost jocular attitude.

"Are you saying you don't want my help, Inspector?"

"I'm saying you're not obligated to provide it."

"You'd so the same for me, wouldn't you? Besides, how do you suppose the Palestinians will come out if this sheik or bin Laden's people lets these things loose on Israel? What will we be left with when the Black Death is finished with the land, our land as well? At best we will have a country that is useless. At worst we will be stuck in the middle of a war that steals what little hope we have left. That's the business the two of us are in, you and I, Inspector."

"Hope?"

"Preserving it. Providing it. Everyone else seems to have forgotten what it means." Al-Asi paused. "Your father knew what hope could accomplish. That's why he came back. You know how often I wonder how things might have been different if I had acted sooner. If I had rushed Shaath *before* he had the opportunity to fire that first shot."

"If it wasn't him, it would have been someone else. Another night, another place."

"And if not we would have Jafir Kamal now instead of Yasir Arafat." Al-Asi started to smile, then stopped. "You would have been your father's heir apparent."

"You'd wish that upon me?"

"Instead, we're stuck with each other."

"And what about *you*, Colonel, had my father lived?"

Al-Asi flashed his devilish grin. "I suspect I would be doing just what I am now."

"You think my father would have made peace?"

"I think he would have faced many of the same pitfalls that our current president has encountered. He would have had to learn to speak out of both sides of his mouth; that much, I'm sure of. He was not one to compromise his principles but politics in this part of the world comprises little else. Sticking irrevocably to one set of principles is the same thing as having none: In either case, you accomplish nothing."

Ben closed the truck's rear flap. "How far would my father have gone?"

"What do you mean?"

"If the Israelis betrayed him, refused to compromise. How far would he have gone, based on how he reacted when the other Palestinian council members disagreed with him in 1967?"

"You're worried he would've taken matters into his own hands, Inspector?"

"I was thinking of these rebels in Sierra Leone who have the other two shipments of the Black Death in their possession."

Al-Asi nodded. "You're wondering whether they will actually use this Black Death on their own nation. Destroy what they cannot control."

"Or destroy *in order* to control. That would be the way they would see it, the way my father would have seen it, perhaps. But why would the rebels need so much?"

"A very good question, Inspector."

Danielle continued moving west through the tunnel, certain Sheik Hussein al-Akbar's property would soon be above her, if it wasn't already. If she couldn't find the stolen crates quickly, she would reduce his entire fortress to rubble. She had enough *plastique* to do it, and it might be the only way she could be sure.

Assuming the crates were still on the premises, that is. If they weren't, if the sheik were hiding them elsewhere, then she was finished and so, perhaps, was Israel.

No, she needed to be sure. Needed to actually see the crates before she destroyed them.

Suddenly the tunnel ended. A dead end. What could she have done wrong? She could double back, retrace her steps until she found a corridor or route she had missed. But she hadn't missed one; she was certain of that much. Was it possible that Borodin's sources in Israeli intelligence were wrong about the sheik's escape route?

Danielle stepped up to the wall before her, touching it with her hands as if to smooth out its rough edges. She tapped on it in various places with the butt of her Uzi and listened for a hollow *ping* beyond. Then she scratched about its surface in search of a depression or ridge indicative of a hidden door.

Nothing.

Futility tugged at her. Had she come this far for nothing?

Was this trip to Beirut about to end in failure just as the last one had?

Danielle looked up, searching for any alternatives.

The ceiling was a patchwork of structural cracks and fissures from a combination of dampness and having to bear more weight than it was built to accommodate. It was darkened by ink blot–shaped leaks in stray splotches, on the verge of collapse it seemed.

Then why wasn't there any debris or rubble on the tunnel floor? She had kicked plenty aside in getting this far. Now in this spot there was nothing.

Danielle used the flashlight she had taken with her from the boat to better scan the ceiling. Sure enough she found a square impression that was perfectly smooth and finished. Not a single mar, crack, or line. Too symmetrical to be simple patchwork.

She must have had it wrong: the storm drain did not link up with the sheik's escape route. The escape route lay *above*, connecting to the storm drain via an access hatch.

Here. Directly above her.

Ten feet up, well beyond her reach. And why not? The escape route would be used only from the inside out. Its builders would have anticipated exactly what she was doing and planned for the eventuality. Even if Danielle found a way to reach it by climbing she was certain she would find the hatchway rigged with explosives or, at least, with electronic sensors that would instantly alert the sheik's security to her presence.

She was a fool not to have considered the obviousness of that before. So what did she have left? Besides a full-frontal assault, she could think of nothing. Wait until night fell and then try slipping past the sheik's formidable security. Succeed where a dozen years ago seven men had failed.

*Think!*

The escape route entry was the key she had to stick with. How to utilize it, though? There had to be something else she could do to gain the access to the compound she so desperately sought.

Danielle pictured the guard posted at the entrance checking the clipboard with notations that looked like names jotted down upon it. The sheik must be expecting guests. That helped explain why security was so heavy and the manicured grounds were so perfectly tended.

Tensions would be running high, Hussein al-Akbar's soldiers ready for anything, the escape route always there if they needed it.

So Danielle would give them a reason to need it, the plan taking shape in her mind as she turned around and retraced her steps down the tunnel.

# CHAPTER 80

Colonel al-Asi clung to the highway without incident through southern Lebanon. The truck's United Nations markings and humanitarian contents allowed for easy passage into the country at an Israeli border crossing known as the Good Fence. Called that for the Israeli medical clinic that continues to treat both Lebanese Christians and Druze, Ben found the checkpoint surprisingly relaxed. Ironically, it overlooked Beaufort Castle, a former stronghold during the Crusades which more recently had become the source of PLO artillery fire.

"I try to make sure the gunmen have the wrong coordinates," al-Asi mentioned, as they had crossed into Lebanon.

An hour later they passed the village of Sarafand and reached the outskirts of Tyre. Ben watched al-Asi tense slightly as he pulled into the parking lot fronting a small group of interconnected shops set before the beginning of the ancient ruins.

"I hope you're thirsty, Inspector," the colonel said, shutting off the engine. "There's an excellent juice bar here."

Offering no further explanation, al-Asi led Ben into a long rectangular shop featuring neat rows of oranges, lemons, limes, and mangoes stored within glass display cases, bushels of bananas and plantains stacked atop them. The juice bar was very bright and modern by any standards.

Ceiling fans spun lazily overhead, cool conditioned air painting a light steam over windows.

Al-Asi ordered blended fruit drinks for both himself and Ben, then turned toward a trio of men seated at one of the juice bar's four round tables. The colonel approached them nonchalantly, Ben falling into step behind him. There was only one chair remaining at the table, and al-Asi sat down and maneuvered it so he was facing the oldest of the three men, his thick hair a strange combination of white and gray.

"*Salammu aleikum,*" the colonel greeted.

"*Aleikum as-salaam,*" the older man returned. "*Al-masaari?*"

Al-Asi's response was to reach into his light jacket and emerge with a thick manila envelope, folded over itself and wrapped with rubber bands. The colonel yanked the bands off and pulled the envelope straight. Then he removed a tightly bound wad of cash Ben recognized as American bills. Without hesitating, al-Asi slid the wad across the table into the eagerly waiting hands of the man with the white and gray hair.

The older man thumbed through them briefly, nodding in satisfaction. He smiled, and Ben noticed he was missing almost all his bottom front teeth when he reached out and squeezed the colonel's forearm with his free hand.

"*Shukran,*" he said, handing al-Asi a wrinkled letter folded into quarters. "Thank you. *Al hamdu illah.*"

"And I thank you for your blessing," al-Asi replied in English. "*Ma' as-salaama.* Good-bye."

With that, the colonel rose with his fruit drink and turned to Ben.

"Come," he said and led the way out of the juice bar.

Back inside the truck, al-Asi took a hearty sip of his drink. "Very refreshing. You haven't touched yours, Inspector."

Ben shifted the cup from his left hand to his right. "Those men were Hezbollah, I assume."

"Local leader. An underling, but a powerful one responsible for a number of incursions into Israel."

"I'm surprised you let him live."

"He always warned me in advance, so I could evacuate any civilians in harm's way."

"How much money was in that envelope, Colonel?"

"A hundred thousand American."

"To make sure we're left alone?"

"If the sheik calls for help, there will be no response now," al-Asi explained.

"So that's what a hundred thousand dollars buys you around here. . . ."

"He gave me a good price, because he knows we are doing him a service: With Hussein al-Akbar out of the way, he moves up in the command structure of Hezbollah. This part of the world is no different from any other, Inspector. It's all about money."

"Which you can ill afford to squander, given the current state of things."

"I keep a rainy day fund for emergencies. This easily qualified."

Ben gazed at al-Asi gratefully, aware that he had done this for Danielle. "And it doesn't bother you, of all people, being beholden to such a man?"

"It's he who's beholden to me, Inspector. If he rises to a new position of power, it is I who will have put him there. Certain to come in handy later."

"What's in the letter he gave you?"

"Credentials, transit documents, to show anyone who stops us."

"I see what you mean about getting your money's worth."

"This is Lebanon, Inspector," al-Asi said, sounding strangely detached. "They lost the dream to which we still cling a long time ago. Replaced hope with currency."

"You bought us protection."

"I bought us the opportunity to help Pakad Barnea, Inspector. We're only an hour from the sheik's fortress now. Get ready."

# CHAPTER 81

What happened?" Latisse Matabu said, bolting upright to find Dr. Sowahy seated by her bedside.

"I gave you a shot."

Matabu's eyes bulged in rage, but the doctor continued before she could speak.

"Your guards summoned me. You were crying out in your sleep, and they couldn't wake you."

Matabu realized her sheets were soaked with perspiration, the monster that ravaged her body twisting and tearing at her blood and spreading with it through her veins. Her skin felt hot. Her hands were flaming red.

"Go. Leave me."

"Not until I've given you another shot."

Dr. Sowahy reached down to the floor for his old, weathered medical bag, laid it in his lap, and unsnapped it. He removed a syringe and a vial, his hand trembling as he inserted the syringe into the vial and extracted the proper amount.

Sowahy rose from his chair and moved to Matabu's bedside where he rolled up the sleeve over the same arm in which he had given her the first injection. The doctor rubbed one of Latisse Matabu's veins down with an alcohol swab. He had started to move the syringe toward the vein when she latched onto his wrist, holding it in place.

"You're not working for the government, are you, Doctor?"

"You're . . . hurting me, General."

Matabu held her iron grip firm. "You wouldn't be getting any ideas of what an easy task it would be to kill me right now, would you?"

Sowahy's face puckered with pain. Sweat rolled down his cheeks. He shook his head.

"That's good, because you have relatives, too, just as General Treest did. I didn't stop with his wife and son, you know. There were his two brothers and their families—all dead now, too. But I enjoyed killing his son most of all. The look on the general's face when I started the blade into the boy's throat—the terror, shock, but most of all the helplessness."

Her grip slackened slightly.

"So do I need to have the contents of that needle checked? Do you want to think twice about giving it to me?"

"That won't be necessary."

"Good," Matabu said and let Sowahy inject the clear liquid into her vein.

"GENERAL."

The voice touched the distant reaches of her consciousness.

*"General?"*

A hand grasped her shoulder. Her eyes burst open.

"I'm sorry, General," a man said, standing before her. "You fell asleep."

Latisse Matabu gazed about her. She was seated behind the rattan desk in her command headquarters, dressed in her uniform.

*How had she gotten there? What time was it? Where had Dr. Sowahy gone?*

The sun burned hot beyond the ramshackle building. It must have been afternoon, yet she had no memory of the hours between morning and now. The right sleeve of her top was rolled up to reveal a small bandage, and she remembered the injections Dr. Sowahy had given her.

"Are you all right, General?" the man before her asked. "Is something wrong?"

Latisse Matabu's mind slowly cleared. The man before her was bent at the knees, staring at her in great concern.

Joseph Tupelo, foreign minister of Nigeria—she remembered now. They had been speaking when she suddenly dozed off. She remembered the diamonds he had come for, and pulled the tightly wrapped pouch from one of the side pockets of her fatigue trousers.

"You have something to report to me about the two battalions the Americans are training in your country," she managed.

Tupelo accepted the pouch gratefully. "They will never arrive in Sierra Leone, I can assure you of that," he said, and started for the door. "I'll see you in Freetown, General."

As soon as Joseph Tupelo had left with his diamonds, Latisse Matabu descended from her headquarters into the vast underground storage bunker where the weapons of the Revolutionary United Front were secretly stored, safe from government raiding parties and the limited aerial surveillance the cursed mercenary forces had begun. The largest of the rooms was empty now, the powerful generators quiet and the crates that had occupied it until just a few days before gone. They had already been shipped to their final destination to await her arrival.

Her bugs journeying, just as Orhan's rats had. Because of the original Black Death, there had been a future for the

Ottoman Empire. Thanks to the current Black Death, there would be a future for Sierra Leone.

"You wanted to see me, General?"

Matabu turned toward the doorway to find her unofficial second-in-command General Yancy Lananga standing there. "Yes, we have some additional matters to discuss, you and I."

"Your meeting with the Nigerian?" Lananga posed, concerned.

"He will be cooperating fully, just as we expected. It is something else we must discuss, General," Matabu explained. "I'm afraid things aren't going to proceed exactly as we planned. . . ."

# CHAPTER 82

Danielle had moved her pushcart to the center of the sidewalk on Allenby Street in front of Sheik al-Akbar's fortress, making sure she was far enough away so as not to attract attention from the guards posted near the gate. She sat with her back against the pushcart, watching, when a white Mercedes sedan approached, its windows blacked out and undoubtedly bulletproof to protect its occupants from scrutiny as well as ambush. The uniformed Hezbollah soldier at the gate checked an item off on his clipboard and waved the Mercedes through.

Danielle left her pushcart against the curb as near the compound as she dared, and walked along the side of Allenby Street, pretending to be begging for money from the drivers as she drifted back toward the corner. She had wedged half her bricks of plastique explosives in amongst the cart's contents and wired their triggers to a single ultrasonic detonator tucked in her pocket. The blast wave created upon detonation was certain to shatter windows and shake the structure of the fortress, hopefully enough to lead Sheik al-Akbar's forces to believe they were under attack and order an evacuation.

Back near the entrance to the tunnels beneath the complex, Danielle readied her weapons, strapped her remaining mounds of C-4 beneath her shabby dress, and then armed the cell phone–sized detonator. It had been thirty minutes since the first car had entered the grounds, certainly long enough for the others to have arrived. There was no reason to delay the process any longer.

Danielle touched her finger to the keypad beneath the single translucent light.

A series of blasts erupted instantly from the front of the compound. From her vantage point behind the cover of the lavish grounds featuring walnut and flowering apricot trees, she could see flames leaping up in the air trailed by black smoke that thickened in the aftermath of a series of secondary explosions.

In her mind, Danielle could picture the windshields of the cars parked inside the gate blowing first, broken shards turned into deadly projectiles that would further confuse the sheik's forces inside and out. They could not be sure of what was happening and would have to assume an all-out attack was underway.

Meaning the escape tunnel was almost certain to be used.

Danielle lifted the grated hatch open once more. She climbed down the ladder into the storm drain and retraced her steps rapidly toward the drain's end, where it was met by the escape tunnel above.

The rumble of numerous additional blasts reached her from the grounds beyond. Gas tanks or engine blocks igniting, Danielle judged, taking the entire remains of the vehicles with them.

She brought the Uzi submachine gun round into her grasp and sprinted down the length of the drain. Minutes passed. Her chest tightened. She slowed to steady her breath, had lowered her hands to her knees to compose herself when the pounding of footsteps, sloshing through an occasional puddle, thundered toward her, converging.

# CHAPTER 83

Danielle rushed straight toward the pounding footsteps, reaching an intersection in the storm drain just as the first shadows appeared. She ducked to her right and pressed herself tightly against the wall, lost enough to the darkness, she hoped, to escape detection.

Just for a few seconds. That's all she needed.

The first white-clad shapes surged through the storm drain's main route. Danielle's mouth had gone bone dry but her vision had sharpened, her focus narrowed on the faces as they rushed by.

She edged forward, still pressed against the wall, Uzi ready.

She glimpsed the sheik surrounded by a quartet of guards at the rear of the pack, his age and infirmity accounting for the lag. Danielle stepped out an instant after they were past her and fired single shots from her Uzi into the backs of the guards bringing up the absolute rear.

The echoes of the silenced shots sounded like firecrackers fizzing through the air. The two guards collapsed. The pair on either side of the sheik swung round to see what had happened.

Danielle shot them as well, two shots for each this time to be sure. Four targets downed without a single bullet fired in return.

The guard on the right slammed into the sheik as he

crumpled, taking Hussein al-Akbar to the floor. He landed with a thud. His head smacked the wet concrete and recoiled.

Danielle lunged toward him, the sound of footsteps rushing back toward her now. She grabbed the sheik by the shoulder and hoisted him effortlessly to his feet. He looked at her in terror, his lips trembling, one of his eyes glazed over by a milky film like a giant cataract.

"You're coming with me!"

Her words emerged with a sneer. Danielle couldn't tell whether the sheik heard her or not. He started to collapse again, his knees buckling, but she thrust an arm under his shoulder for support before she half led and half dragged him back down the storm drain.

She twisted sideways when the thump of pursuing footsteps was almost upon her, Uzi held in her free hand aimed dead center down the concrete corridor. She started shooting when the first shadow turned the corner, but kept her fire restrained to conserve the Uzi's bullets. There would be no time to reload, or perhaps even draw a fresh weapon, under these conditions. If she ran out of ammo too early, she was finished, Danielle thought, as the end of the storm drain came into view. A rope ladder dangled through the ceiling hatch she had spotted earlier, left thankfully in place.

Danielle shoved the sheik behind her and emptied the last of her clip into a pair of guards who fired wildly as they ran.

"Climb!" she ordered, discarding the Uzi and drawing a nine-millimeter Glock pistol in its place.

"No!" the sheik retorted. "I won't!"

She jammed the pistol under his throat and used her other hand to strip a grenade from her belt, then yanked out the pin with her teeth.

"Climb, or we're both dead!" she rasped, her eyes furious.

Then Danielle tossed the grenade and watched it roll awkwardly along the floor, not even flinching when the explosion rocked the corridor and sent chunks of the storm drain ceiling raining down. A jagged shard struck her in the forehead and opened a nasty gash. Danielle felt blood oozing toward her eyes, as she steadied her pistol back down the tunnel and capped off a half dozen shots.

"Last chance," she said calmly, swinging back to Sheik Hussein al-Akbar and jamming her pistol under his throat again. "Climb."

The sheik pulled his flabby neck away from the barrel lodged against it and reached up for the rope ladder.

He had managed three rungs when gunfire erupted from behind the last curve. Danielle could feel the heat of the bullets surging past her, finished the clip on that Glock, and drew her second at the same time she flung her second grenade and heard it thumping out of her line of vision.

The final gunmen ducked for cover before the blast erupted. But Danielle had bought the time she needed and started to climb in the sheik's wake.

Almost to the top, he lashed a foot down wildly toward her, smacking her in the forehead where the blood from her gash had just begun to slow. Danielle fired five more shots down the storm drain with her fresh Glock, then rammed the barrel hard into the testicles floating beneath the sheik's robes.

The sheik gasped, nearly fell.

"Climb!" Danielle ordered, prodding him with the gun.

He clambered up the last stretch, Danielle trailing just behind when gunfire smacked the wall just under her feet. She stuck the Glock in her mouth and scrabbled upward using both hands to propel herself. She surged through the open hatchway a mere moment behind the sheik, ignoring him long enough to draw the rope ladder up and slam the hatch down.

Hussein al-Akbar cowered against the wall, his eyes darting desperately sideways in search of help that wasn't going to come, facing the fact that it was just the two of them now.

Danielle grabbed him by the robes and stared into his eyes. "The crates you stole from the freighter, the *Peter the Great*! Take me to them! *Now*!"

# CHAPTER 84

He was no longer fighting her, terror having trumped all his resistance.

"Where are they?" Danielle demanded, slamming the sheik hard into the wall when he didn't respond quickly enough. The blood from the gash on her forehead seeped into her eyes. She could smell it now, taste the first coppery bits on the edge of her lips.

"Already gone."

Danielle steadied her pistol and shot him in the fleshy part of the shoulder. He screamed and clutched his arm.

"Then you're useless to me! I might as well kill you *here*!" she said, as he stared at the wound in shock, the color draining from his face.

He shook his head madly, fighting for breath. "Loaded in trucks!" Hussein al-Akbar gasped. "In the garage!"

"Take me there!"

Lips trembling violently, Hussein al-Akbar squeezed his shoulder with his free hand, trying to stem the blood flow, but it soaked his robes anyway. He stumbled at first, nearly doubling over, but then found the semblance of a pace. He chose a doorway on the right, then up a slight incline toward the smell of rubber and gasoline.

"Rear entrance," he mumbled, shaking now, his face whitening. "Almost there."

Danielle didn't bother responding; the sheik had conceded, she could tell. The entrance to the garage was a warehouse-style sliding door. She jerked it open and dragged the sheik through with her, before sliding it closed and latching it from the inside.

The garage *was* a warehouse. Cars everywhere, classics every one of them, some of them priceless. Three heavy refrigerated cargo trucks were parked in the middle, one behind another, compressors rumbling loudly to keep the crates lifted from the *Peter the Great* chilled.

Sheik Hussein al-Akbar collapsed to his knees, then pitched over to the floor, unconscious.

Danielle moved on toward the trucks, focused on the task at hand. She stripped off her baggy rag of a dress, exposing the remaining bricks of plastic explosives she wore strapped to her torso. Then she worked fast, removing one charge at a time and affixing them along the bodies of the refrigerated trucks. The tape-glue backing made the C-4 adhere easily once she slapped each in place.

She covered all three trucks with six mounds of *plastique* each in under three minutes. The press of a single button now would destroy the crates stored in the trucks' holds. At the third truck, though, Danielle couldn't resist jerking the rear door upward along its runner to peer at what lay within.

A burst of frigid air struck her, chilling the sweat that had soaked her shirt. She backed up slightly and what looked like an ordinary portfolio case tumbled out, smacking the garage floor. Danielle had started to lean over to inspect it when a loud metallic echo in the rear of the garage made her spin on her heels.

Nothing.

But Sheik Hussein al-Akbar was gone, a thin trail of blood leading back out the way they had come in. Letting him escape didn't really concern her. As soon as she set off the explosives, her mission this time would be complete. She had to find her way out first, though. Trigger the *plastique* as soon as she was on the grounds with the front gate in view.

Danielle had just opened the portfolio when the garage bay door started upward, revealing a short sloped tunnel that led back to ground level. Instinctively, she grabbed the contents of the portfolio and stuffed them under her shirt before ducking between the nearest cars.

Five of the uniformed guards Danielle recognized from the front of the fortress surged in, sweeping assault rifles in all directions. They spoke heatedly in Arabic, exchanging angry shouts and recriminations. The guards ignored the trucks for the time being and continued to probe about. Danielle knew it was only a matter of time, though, before they noticed the explosives she had set in place. She needed to distract them, and at the same time to find a means to escape.

Danielle slid behind the last row of classic cars and eyed the nearest one, a brilliantly restored Bugatti. Hesitating only slightly, she climbed agilely behind the right-hand wheel and felt along the dashboard for the ignition. Not surprisingly, since the engines had to be started on a regular basis, the key was waiting for her. She held her breath in the next instant before twisting it, clinging to the hope that the sheik maintained his cars in perfect working order.

The Bugatti's engine caught and purred instantly to life. Danielle shoved the transmission into gear and pressed down on the gas pedal.

The ancient car shot forward, screeching across the polished pavement, drawing the instant attention of the sheik's guards. Danielle kept one hand on the wheel, the other on her detonator, as bullets blazed toward her. She ducked low beneath the dashboard, feeling the windshield explode over her, spraying glass in all directions.

Danielle hit the sloped ramp with a thud that coughed sparks from the car's underside and pressed the detonator. She imagined she could feel the incredible heat of the blast before the reverberating roar bubbled in her ears and deafened her to anything else. The car buckled, almost seeming to bounce upward. The air burst chased her up the ramp, the world ahead aglow from the light of the flames charging outward, as bright as a flashbulb.

She surged out onto the front of the grounds, the Bugatti's red metallic paint job singed by the flames' touch, its rear end still smoking. She could smell the sickening stench of burned rubber and realized her back tires were on fire an instant before they blew out.

Danielle spun the car to a halt, leaped from the driver's seat, and rolled onto the grass. Guards rushed at her from both sides of the house. Gunshots rang out and she tensed with anticipation of one of the bullets smacking her like a hefty kick. She twisted onto her side and sighted down on a pair of guards who had followed her plunge to the grass. Their bullets hissed through the blades before hers punched them backwards and dropped them on the compound's circular drive.

But guards still surrounded Danielle on three sides, closing upon her even now, as she ejected the spent clip and felt in her pocket for a fresh one. She reloaded, the guards continuing to converge, when a truck roared up to the compound's entrance and slammed through the gate.

The truck drew the fire from the guards intended for her and Danielle turned to see a pair of figures lean out the truck's windows to train twin submachine guns on Sheik al-Akbar's forces, bullets pouring from their barrels.

"Come on!" a voice shouted over the gunshots. *"Hurry!"*

She recognized Ben leaning out the passenger window, and Colonel Nabril al-Asi firing out the driver's with one hand still wrapped around the truck's steering wheel.

*Al-Asi must have gotten the message she had left for him at the building supply store in Ramallah!*

Trusting their fire would cover her, Danielle dashed straight for the truck. Ben thrust the passenger door open for her and she leaped inside. In the driver's seat, al-Asi pulled his right hand from the wheel and jammed the truck into reverse. Still firing with his left hand, he used the other to jerk the wheel around upon hitting the street.

"They'll have the road blocked off!" Danielle warned

desperately. "The sheik will have summoned an army!"

"Not this time," al-Asi said with a strange assurance, as he screeched off. "Relax, Pakad Barnea, everything is under control."

# CHAPTER 85

Despite the fact that al-Asi had bought off Hussein al-Akbar's expected reinforcements, they remained wary as they continued down the road minutes out of Beirut. The front end of the truck rattled badly from the collision with the fence. Fluid bled from the engine and thin clouds of oily smoke drifted through the open windows.

"You're sure you got all of the crates?" Ben asked, after Danielle had related what had transpired inside the fortress. "They were all burned?"

"Yes, I'm positive," Danielle told him, still terrified by Ben's explanation of their contents. "Bugs . . . You're telling me they were bugs."

"Created in a bio lab by Soviet scientists during the Cold War. The Black Death," he finished. "Called that for a reason. . . ."

Danielle could do nothing but shake her head when his tale was finished. "Because they're capable of nearly destroying a city," she said, referring to Dubna.

"No, *the Russians* nearly destroyed the city to stop the Black Death from spreading. With good reason."

"Tell her the rest, Inspector," al-Asi prompted from behind the wheel as the truck's gears ground noisily and the smoke rising from the hood grew more noxious.

"There were two other shipments of the Black Death,

both sold to the leader of a rebel group in Sierra Leone."

"Where the blood diamonds must have originated," Danielle presumed. "But why would the rebels want to destroy their own country?"

"That's the problem. They wouldn't."

Danielle remembered the pages she'd lifted from the portfolio and stuffed under her shirt back in the garage. She pulled the now crinkled pile out, as Ben continued.

"Even if the rebels do intend to use the Black Death, they would have only needed one shipment. They must have other plans. Sell it off or provide it to similar insurgent groups in other African nations."

"No," Danielle said quietly, having unfolded a color map she recognized instantly. "The rebels aren't going to sell or give the Black Death away." She looked up at Ben and al-Asi, her eyes wide with fear. "They're going to use it."

And with that she turned the map toward them.

"On the United States," Danielle finished.

# CHAPTER 86

President Kabbah coughed smoke and soot from his lungs, as he watched his country burn from a hillside overlooking the village of Katani. The fires had been started in keeping with Professor Deirdre Cotter's instructions: a thirty-mile ring in the country's center meant to encircle and, ultimately, envelop the black wave of bugs. Photographs taken by helicopters flying over the region revealed a wasteland spreading north out of Katani, and widening to the east and west as well. The fires would continue to burn inward until they met up with the advancing black tide.

*My God*, Kabbah thought, *it looks like a war*.

And war was exactly what he was preparing for over the course of the next twenty-four hours.

"We cannot fight the Dragon's forces on their territory," he had repeated to Minister of Defense Daniel Sukahamin at their strategy meeting a day earlier. "They control thirty percent of the country now, concentrated in the south and east, along with scattered towns and villages elsewhere. Even with the two Nigerian battalions, dedicating the forces required to launch a major offensive would leave our own strongholds bare. So if we failed against the rebels in the east and south," Kabbah concluded grimly, "they could overrun our remaining forces and drive them straight to the Atlantic."

The men gathered around the table in Kabbah's conference room at the State House in Freetown had gazed emptily at each other.

"Furthermore," Kabbah continued, "the Revolutionary United Front must be crushed here and now. Anything short of that would be a failure."

The President had proceeded with the plan he had come up with himself. Latisse Matabu had left him an opening and he had to seize it. Use the egos and petulance of her commanders against the Dragon. Let them think the poorly disciplined and usually tentative government forces were powerless to stop their advance to the sea. With strongholds in the west, south, and east, the RUF would be able to effect a stranglehold on the government-dominated, densely populated north. The civil war would be over and the government's forces would have lost.

Kabbah knew enough never to underestimate Latisse Matabu again. Her commanders, though, were something else again and Kabbah fully expected them to be unable to resist the bait he would set out.

He watched the swath of Sierra Leone burn from afar, because he dared not risk a helicopter flight himself for fear the rebels would shoot him down with one of the many rocket launchers their blood diamonds had bought them. In the next twenty-four hours, one way or another, the war that had raged for a decade would be decided.

"Mr. President."

Kabbah turned to see Daniel Sukahamin standing just behind him, satellite phone clutched in his hand. "Some news for me, Minister?"

Sukahamin nodded. "We have managed to get all the refugees who were turned back at Guinea settled in the camps around Freetown, sir."

The two men stared at each other for a long moment before Kabbah responded. "Good. Then we should get back to the capital, Minister. We have much work to do."

# CHAPTER 87

natolyevich didn't merely sell the Black Death to his buyers in Sierra Leone," Danielle concluded, after a closer inspection of the maps contained inside the portfolio. "He also sold them the plans for how to use it on the U.S."

"Not very surprising, Pakad Barnea," Colonel al-Asi pointed out, "since the Soviets developed the Black Death specifically to be used against America."

Ben scanned the maps one after another, as they drove across Lebanon toward the West Bank and, ultimately, Jordan. "These show the spread of the bugs depending on placement and volume of release. Mathematical formulas broken down by distance traveled and time sequences. Everything concentrated in crop-rich areas. The heartland, Florida, California."

"Between two and three dozen separate release points for maximum effect," Danielle elaborated. "My God, the Soviet scientists had this timed out to the precise minute and mile."

"You've got to get word to the American government," Ben said to al-Asi.

"And tell them what, Inspector? That African revolutionaries are going to destroy their country's food supply? Cripple the richest country in the world economically for the next decade or so?" The colonel shook his head. "I'm a minister without portfolio now, a pariah. My contacts are gone and, with them, my credibility."

"Then show them the proof," Ben said, flapping the schematics Danielle had given him.

"Relics from the Cold War. And last time I checked," al-Asi continued, his voice laced uncharacteristically with sarcasm, "the Americans maintained no embassy in Palestine. They do not take our intelligence gathering apparatus seriously. And I no longer have access to any of the private channels that matter."

Danielle thought for a moment. "Can you get us there?"

"The United States?"

"No. Sierra Leone."

MAKING SPOT repairs on their truck from time to time allowed them to reach Jordan and the village of Wadi Musa near Petra.

"I still have a few friends in Amman," al-Asi said, by way of explanation, "who might be able to help us."

They checked into the Movenpick Hotel and purchased fresh clothes from a boutique located in the lobby. Colonel al-Asi donned a fresh European suit, and disappeared without explanation, only to return hours later.

"I've done the best I can," he reported to Ben and Danielle in the suite the three of them shared, looking much more like himself. "Jordan maintains reasonably strong diplomatic ties with Sierra Leone and officials from the intelligence service here have agreed to do everything they can to help you reach President Kabbah."

Ben and Danielle looked at each other, grim resolve etched over their features.

"They are having an intelligence file on this Latisse Matabu, also known as the Dragon, delivered to the hotel in the next two hours," al-Asi continued. "But my contact here in Jordan already shared something about her with me I think you will find most interesting. . . ."

# DAY NINE

# CHAPTER 88

For Ben and Danielle, the trip to Lungi International Airport in Sierra Leone, twenty miles north of Freetown, had proved long and exhausting. Multiple legs that had begun nearly twenty-four hours earlier in Jordan's capital of Amman, where they had boarded a South African Airlines flight bound for Johannesburg. They had arrived just after ten that morning and had had to wait an agonizing two hours before their connecting flight on Air Gambia left for Sierra Leone.

Neither of them had realized that the airport in Lungi was located on an island, necessitating a ferry ride from the Tagrin terminal to the Kissy terminal on the mainland just outside of Freetown. They emerged from the terminal to find just three taxis waiting, only one of which was willing to take them into Freetown after dark for five times the price posted on the rear seat.

Even the brief trip down Kissy Road toward Freetown Center, where the State House and governmental offices were situated, revealed the striking contrasts that defined the nation of Sierra Leone. The capital's ancient flavor was no match for either the tension which filled the air or the occasional burned-out husk of a government vehicle left on the side of the road, or the rubble-strewn remains of collapsed buildings they passed regularly. They could see no evidence of any attempts at rebuilding, as if the city had given up, resigned to the inevitability of its own destruction.

Checkpoints manned by Kamajor tribesmen organized by the government into a kind of de facto militia dotted the road. The kamajors, wearing flowing tunics and fishnet shirts, sat in jeeps clutching assault rifles and grenade launchers and mostly ignored the taxi when it passed. Besides the kamajors, Ben and Danielle saw hardly any people. Since the Revolutionary United Front's last failed attempt to seize the capital, movement on the part of Freetown residents had been severely curtailed. Curfews had become routine. And even when they weren't, the inability of government troops and the kamajors to distinguish residents from rebels was more than enough to keep the city inside after dark.

The blackness of the night was broken only by garbage fires speckling the hillsides surrounding the capital until the cab approached central Freetown, passing an abandoned outdoor market by the Susan's Bay beachfront on their right. Ben and Danielle could hear the peaceful sounds of the sea washing over the rocks and sand, providing the illusion of peace until campfires lit by the thousands of displaced residents who now called the beach their home flickered in the narrowing distance. Blazing torches held by the lost forever trying to find their way home.

The cab would drop Ben and Danielle just a few blocks from here at the State House building where the Kabbah government had presided over the country for the last four years and would continue to do so indefinitely, now that the promised elections had been cancelled for the third time. They had no idea what to expect at that point. Everything depended on how successful the Jordanian government was in persuading Kabbah to listen to what they had to say.

Only a few other private vehicles traveled the Freetown roads dominated by government trucks, jeeps, armored personnel carriers, and guns. Guns everywhere, held by troops under the mistaken assumption that bullets could solve everything. Ben and Danielle gazed at each other in silence, realizing how familiar it all looked. Different names, different uniforms, but similar problems. Violence in place of reason and common sense.

"Say again where to leave you," their cab driver requested in the best English he could muster, obviously frightened by the world of Freetown after dark.

"The State House," Ben told him.

"Closed to public and now barricaded," he squealed at them. "No reach. No get close."

"Close as you can, then," Danielle ordered.

The driver had turned toward them to protest when the lights of Freetown flickered once and died.

# CHAPTER 89

L atisse Matabu laid the receiver back on the table. The air in her underground bunker headquarters tasted stale and she suddenly found it hard to breathe.

*So it begins at last. My destiny soon to be achieved. . . .*

The assault on Freetown had started, as planned, with a small team of her best commandos overrunning the power station supplying electricity to the capital. Disciplined soldiers who had learned their trade under foreign flags before signing up with the Revolutionary United Front. Her orders were that the station should not be damaged irreparably; after all, in a few days' time the power would need to be switched back on to reveal a new governing force in place.

Everything so far had gone exactly as planned. Her generals had deployed their squadrons in a ring around Freetown as far south as Kagboro Creek and north to Lungi where the airport would soon be in their hands. The plan was to splinter President Kabbah's government forces in half, allowing General Lananga to drive straight over the range of hills, through the plush village of Gloucester where General Treest had made his home, to Freetown. From there Lananga would seize the harbor, giving the RUF control of the major source of the country's trade.

The plan that had led to her parents' deaths three years

ago had been undermined by bickering and poor discipline on the part of RUF troops more interested in pillaging than politics. From the moment of her return to Sierra Leone, everything Latisse Matabu had done had built toward this moment where her father could be redeemed. Finishing his work. Completing her vengeance on General Treest and those like him in the government for trying to destroy her.

Matabu knew her efforts would fail should the government have the opportunity to marshal the two battalions from Nigeria. The deal she had struck with that country's foreign minister had thus cemented her plan. Not only had the Nigerian troops not arrived in time to launch an attack on the RUF, they would not be coming at all. Her father would have been proud.

She listened to the reports coming over the radio of further advances being made by her generals. They were ahead of schedule. At this rate, Kabbah might well capitulate to her demands before dawn.

But Latisse Matabu was not ready to celebrate just yet. She had dreamed of her grandmother last night. The dream held a warning, a portent of doom represented by an eagle and a hawk flying side-by-side through the sky.

*Two enemies were coming to Sierra Leone to kill her . . .*

Even in death, her grandmother had not abandoned her in this crucial time. Thanks to her, Matabu would be waiting when they arrived.

The Dragon knew her safest bet was to be gone from the country before the eagle and the hawk could find her. Leave to join up with her remaining supply of the Black Death in the United States where her final actions would assure the ultimate freedom of her people.

PRESIDENT KABBAH and Defense Minister Daniel Suka-hamin remained in the heavily fortified State House on

Siaka Stevens Street, as reports of the rebel attacks began to pour in.

Everything was going true to form, exactly as Kabbah had expected.

"How long do we wait?" Sukahamin asked nervously, sticking pins in a wall-mounted map to denote the RUF's advancing positions. The building's emergency generator was not strong enough to power the entire building, and even if it had been, they would have left the lights dim to make for a less inviting target.

"Long enough, Minister," Kabbah said from the window, where he stood, arms clasped behind his back, overlooking the utter darkness that covered Freetown.

"They'll ravage the city."

"And we must let them, if we are to save it."

"You must make the call, sir," Sukahamin implored. "Before it is too late."

"We have already discussed this and settled on a strategy, Minister." Kabbah moved his gaze from the window to a shadowy figure in the room's darkened rear. "There is no going back now."

BEN AND Danielle's driver abandoned them and his cab on Wallace Johnson Street when the blackout occurred, barely a mile from the State House. They didn't bother to call after him as he disappeared into the night, agreeing they would be better off proceeding from here on foot.

"We must've walked straight into a rebel attack!" Danielle realized, pressed next to Ben against a boarded-up building to conceal themselves from the government patrols sweeping desperately through the streets.

"Doesn't bode well for our chances of getting in to see President Kabbah, does it?"

Suddenly the sound of machine gun fire strafed the night. Bright tracer shells lit up the darkness on a major avenue up ahead just in front of the Sierra Leone National Museum. There was a screech of tires, followed by an explosion that sent smoke billowing into the air.

Danielle recognized the sights and sounds all too well, but it was the smells that evoked the clearest memories. The stench of hot, spent shells drifting with gunpowder residue and the scent of scorched metal on the air. War always smelled the same no matter the country.

"Ben," she said softly.

He was pinned back against the wall, trembling slightly. His first experience with a battle of this size and scope.

"Ben," Danielle prodded again, waiting for him to acknowledge her before continuing. "When I move, stay right behind me."

More blasts lit up the night, followed by the sound of glass breaking everywhere.

"Where are we going?" Ben managed to ask.

Danielle gestured toward a set of stairs. "If I've got my bearings right, those steps lead down to the King Jimmy Market just off the waterfront."

"Bad time to go shopping," Ben tried to joke.

"But the fact that it's recessed from the street will keep out the gunfire. Follow it to the end and we'll be just a few blocks from the State House."

"So what are we waiting for?"

What do you mean?" Latisse Matabu demanded of General Lananga by radio.

"You heard me, General. My first assault waves have entered Freetown without resistance."

"That wasn't the plan! You were to *wait* until receiving word that the other sectors were secure and the government troops sufficiently engaged!"

"It's over, General. We're winning. The government troops are running like shit through chickens."

"You have no backup," Matabu warned.

"I don't need it," General Lananga insisted. "The government forces here are looting what's left from the stores. My troops will be at the State House within the hour. We'll have President Kabbah in custody shortly after that."

"Desist, General," Matabu ordered him. "I say again, break off your attack until ordered."

"Too late," Lananga told her.

"Listen to me! There's something wrong. It's *too* easy!"

"No, no. It's all happening just the way I expected it. Next time I call, President Kabbah will be standing at my side. Signing off."

Latisse Matabu held the radio to her ear long after Lananga's voice had ceased. Last night in the dream her grandmother had warned her only of the hawk and the eagle, nothing else. So why did she feel worried? What was going wrong?

*Something . . . Something she had heard recently that should have stuck in her mind, but hadn't. . . .*

The Dragon laid her radio down and sank heavily into a chair behind the rickety rattan table on which a crude map of the western sector of the country, including the coastline, had been drawn with the positions of her various troops highlighted. She tried to think but her head was pounding too much; the pain Dr. Sowahy had warned her about had set in, enveloping her brain. She felt the bottle of pills he had given her rattling around in her pocket. Powerful pills he promised would take away the pain, just as the injections had a few days before. At what price, though? Not only would they soften the pain, they would cloud her head and confuse her judgment.

She wished she could be closer to the war she was directing from afar.

Only then could Latisse Matabu know what it was she couldn't see from the bunker.

DANIEL SUKAHAMIN continued plotting the advancing positions of rebel forces on the wall-mounted maps.

"Well?" President Kabbah asked.

"The rebels have just taken Government Wharf. Our forces are in full-fledged retreat."

"As planned."

Sukahamin frowned. "Faster than we expected, but yes, as planned."

Beyond the well-fortified State House, the firing had intensified. The building shook now with each rocket blast, paint chips and plaster raining downward. Just minutes before, tracer fire had begun streaming past the windows, as government soldiers dug in behind their concrete barricades to meet the charge of the advancing rebel troops.

"It's time," Sukahamin said, in what sounded more like a plea.

"Almost," President Kabbah said, focusing again on the dark figure seated in the room's rear. "Agreed?"

"Yes," nodded Joseph Tupelo, foreign minister of Nigeria, as he rose to his feet. "I am in absolute agreement."

BEN AND Danielle dashed along the cover provided by a dilapidated building called the City Hotel, surprised to find it was still operating, its lobby illuminated by lanterns. Flashes lit up the night, accompanied by the staccato bursts of automatic fire as they clung to the crumbling stone façade. Ben found himself already able to distinguish the heavier caliber fire from that of traditional assault weapons. The difference lay in the center of his ears, the way the sounds reverberated inside his head. He felt the loudest in the pit of his stomach in waves of nausea that made him think he was going to vomit each time.

The M-16 assault rifle felt absurd in his grasp. Heavy and poorly balanced. He and Danielle had sneaked up on a pair of government soldiers cowering behind their patrol jeep as soon as they had emerged from the King Jimmy Market. The struggle had been very brief, ending with Ben and Danielle in possession of the M-16s and the soldiers fleeing toward the sea. The extra clips clinked in Danielle's pocket as she turned to signal Ben it was time for them to move on.

"Where to now?" he asked her.

"Two more blocks to Siaka Stevens Street where the State House is located," Danielle told him. "Just move in my shadow and keep yourself against the buildings."

She felt as free and unencumbered as she had in her days in the Sayaret: so much on the line, but little to lose of herself. The strange thing was that today the only man she had ever felt truly close to, a virtual stranger for months, was now struggling to maintain her pace in a world of violence he didn't understand. What did that say about her life? Had she rediscovered her true purpose, or did she simply lack any semblance of one?

Danielle focused on the mission at hand. A substantially weakened and desperate United States could provide no more help for Israel. Absent the looming retaliatory threat posed by the U.S., Israel's enemies would seize the opportunity to attack. All-out war could break out between Israelis and Palestinians, driving her and Ben apart forever.

They had made it a good way down Siaka Stevens Street, when a familiar sound found Danielle's ears.

*Out here? It couldn't be!*

But her eyes told her that it was, as helicopter gunships followed by Blackhawk troop carriers soared over her head, coming from the sea.

# CHAPTER 91

"We are coming under attack!"

General Lananga's words froze Latisse Matabu's insides. The throb in her head became a pounding, as she struggled to make sense of what was happening, the sudden turn of events in the streets of Freetown.

"Say again, we are under attack! Heavy fire from helicopter gunships! Taking casualties! Enemy troops sliding from the sky on ropes!"

Matabu slammed her fist down on the table, splintering the rattan and just missing the radio. This was why she had ordered Lananga to wait for reinforcements before moving his troops on Freetown. He had rushed the assault and had walked into some sort of ambush as a result.

Suddenly more reports blazed over her radio, barely discernible between the panicked shouts and screams. All her generals, it seemed, were being attacked in a perfectly staged offensive. But neither President Kabbah's troops nor his commanders were capable of mounting such an attack, either in ability or number.

So who was attacking? Where had they come from?

The two Nigerian battalions . . . It had to be them!

But it couldn't be. Her bribing of the Nigerian foreign minister Joseph Tupelo had assured that and, even if it hadn't, the Nigerians had not entered Sierra Leone in the past twenty-four hours. Her spotters and spies assured her of that.

Unless . . .

Matabu squeezed her fingers to her temples, trying to massage out the pain that accompanied the realization that she had been fooled. President Kabbah had used her ambition, and the impetuousness of her generals, against her.

*The Nigerian troops must have been in Sierra Leone for days!*

Hiding in plain sight where no one would think to look. She had even ordered her men to steer clear of them, let them be.

*The refugees who had returned from Guinea, allegedly turned away at the border!*

It was right before her eyes, but Latisse Matabu had missed it. And now her people, as well her cause, would suffer drastically as a result.

PRESIDENT KABBAH watched with unrestrained enthusiasm, as the counterattack proceeded beyond the windows of the State House. This troop, the best trained of the Nigerians, had come in from their staging point well off the beaches aboard commercial freighters leased specifically to provide their cover. On Kabbah's command, the remaining American-trained Nigerian troops had emerged from the strategically placed, and realistically squalid, refugee camps. A sham to get them into Sierra Leone without attracting attention, concocted by President Kabbah and Nigerian Foreign Minister Joseph Tupelo.

It had been Kabbah who suggested to Tupelo the idea of involving himself with the Revolutionary United Front. Let them think he was really working with them when he had covertly supported the standing government all along. Tupelo knew he was risking his life by agreeing to meet with Latisse Matabu. But he also knew that if the Revolutionary

United Front triumphed in Sierra Leone, it would not be long before an offshoot would establish itself in Nigeria as well. No, the tide needed to be stemmed here.

Kabbah had known that the refugee camps were the one thing the Revolutionary United Front would spare in its assault on Freetown and had placed them in a way meant to counter the Dragon's expected plan of attack. Then, once the RUF forces were on the run, the Nigerian troops would sweep eastward, wiping out pockets of resistance and over-running their strongholds. The Revolutionary United Front would be splintered and isolated. Matabu and her commanders would have no choice but to surrender on the government's terms, or flee into the hills, even across the border.

Kabbah remained by the window, watching first-hand the Dragon at the sunset of her time.

THE REPORTS over the radio worsened. Latisse Matabu listened as the largest offensive ever staged by the RUF came to a crushing defeat. Her ragtag troops that fed off the smell of blood panicked when the blood spilled was theirs, returning to their roots as bullies and braggarts, reduced to what they were and had always been. There was nothing her generals could do, since their own roots were little different.

The suddenness of this defeat only increased her resolve, though. Once again it was American guns and training that were responsible for victory. They had killed her parents, and now they sought to kill the dream Matabu had salvaged from the refuse of her parents' lives and her own. The Revolutionary United Front would survive to fight another day, but it would lose again if still faced with the specter of American might and commitment.

That would all change beginning tomorrow. Her escape to the United States through friendly Liberia had been prepared ever since her first purchase of the Black Death. She would leave before dawn along the prescribed route, while the government desperately sought the return of captured U.N. troops and foreign observers the RUF now had no further use for. That would stall Kabbah and his puppet ministers long enough to assure her success in the United States.

Latisse Matabu maintained the presence of mind to order her generals to capture as many more hostages as possible during their retreats to give them the bargaining power the RUF would need to at least survive.

Today's hope was gone.

Tomorrow's remained.

BEN AND Danielle had covered two more blocks, half the remaining distance to the State House located up one final hill. Around them residents streamed into the streets from burning, blast-gutted buildings, scattering in all directions as gunfire reverberated around them.

The firing intensified suddenly, forcing Ben and Danielle to duck into the narrow sliver between the two buildings forming the nation's Law Courts. Barrages from the helicopter gunships strafed Siaka Stevens Street before them without pause, hoping to find rebels. Their barrages resounded with ear-pounding fire that cut through the night and blew chunks of the sidewalks and nearest buildings into the air.

Ben and Danielle clung to their cover between the two buildings, hoping the battle would recede enough for them to mount a rush for the State House.

"My God," Danielle muttered, as a wave of fleeing rebels tried to chase down a horde of civilians.

Instinctively, she spun out from between the Law Courts buildings and fired a burst from her M-16 in the rebels' directions.

"Danielle!" Ben screamed, but she kept firing until her clip was exhausted.

"Help me!" she ordered, leaving no room for doubt.

Ben whirled forward to take her place and opened fire.

He quickly found an eerie rhythm to the shooting, despite his initial unfamiliarity with the M-16.

The first wave of rebels went down without resistance, taken totally by surprise. The civilians ran on, saved for the moment.

But their gunfire had alerted other roaming rebels to Ben and Danielle's position and a wave of dark-clad figures streamed toward the Law Courts. Ben followed Danielle's lead in poking his frame out just enough to offer return fire. Danielle heard his assault rifle click empty and tossed him a fresh clip. It took him a few moments to remember how to eject the spent magazine and snap the new one home, valuable seconds in which rebels gained a foothold behind a building just twenty feet away.

Ben's ears had gone numb from the gunshots. He could hear Danielle shouting something to him between bursts but couldn't discern exactly what. Fought the temptation to sink to the ground, hide in the darkness and cover his ears.

A helicopter gunship soared overhead, pumping staccato bursts from its front-mounted guns. Enough, Ben hoped, to make the rebels retreat, but their fire resumed as soon as the gunship was past, even more intense than before as they drew a bead on his and Danielle's position.

This was his father's world from the first war with Israel in 1948 and then again in 1956. This was the world his father had fled when a third war became inevitable and why Jafir Kamal returned to Palestine in its bloody wake. Ben understood that world truly for the first time; why his father loathed it so much and refused to accept the hero's mantle of leadership his people tried to thrust upon him.

Because war accomplished nothing. Not for Israel, Palestine, or Sierra Leone. Ben didn't want to be Jafir Kamal anymore, didn't want to live in his world.

He wished he could tell his father he understood him

now, didn't hate him for the impossible legacy he had left or for leaving his family behind in the first place. Jafir Kamal lived to stop nights like this from returning to Palestine. And, very likely, the night he had blown up the Russian trucks as they crossed the Allenby Bridge, the night that had cost him his life, he had done just that.

Another helicopter gunship soared overhead, spitting light instead of bullets. The rebels turned their guns up to the air and fired them wildly, futilely, exposing their positions to the second gunship following just behind.

"Now!" Danielle signaled, as the gunship opened fire with its dual-mounted sixty-caliber machine guns. "This is our chance!"

She dashed into the street and rushed away from the gunship's deadly spray. Ben followed, spinning to cover her back. Danielle lunged up onto the sidewalk and pressed her shoulder against the row of buildings as she sprinted along, clinging to the darkness. Ben did the same and felt jagged glass prick him when he drew too close to a shattered window.

Ahead, Danielle stopped at a corner and waited for Ben to catch up.

"Across the street," she huffed, trying to catch breath. "See it?"

"A church . . ."

"Refuge." Danielle gazed through the wafting smoke up the hill toward the ghostly specter of the State House. "We'll never be able to reach Kabbah tonight."

She and Ben exchanged a glance, all they needed. This time they sprinted together, assault rifles at the ready. The stained glass windows of the Anglican St. George's Cathedral had been shattered like all the others in Freetown. Its majestic double front doors were locked from the inside, forcing Danielle to turn her rifle on it from a safe angle. Ben backed off a step or two and covered his ringing ears when she opened fire.

The wood splintered and coughed sideways. The latch

gave. The doors opened inward. Danielle slid through, Ben right behind her.

They both froze.

Around them the pews were full of milling, sobbing Freetown residents. They cowered in fear and clutched loved ones for support.

"It's all right," Danielle said softly, expecting a number of them would understand English, perhaps as many as their native Krio. "We're not your enemy."

She and Ben had just reached the rearmost pew when the clack of assault rifle bolts being jammed back halted them. They looked up toward the balcony to see a dozen Revolutionary United Front rebels angling Kalashnikovs and M-16s stripped from government troops dead on them.

*They had walked straight into the place where hostages had been concentrated!*

Neither Ben nor Danielle could have felt more foolish if they tried.

"Drop weapons! You should drop them now!" one of the rebels ordered in broken English, and Ben and Danielle let their rifles clatter to the floor.

# CHAPTER 92

They were shoved around, passed from rebel to rebel. One of them struck Danielle, and Ben was staggered by a rifle smashed against his skull when he rushed to her aid. He crumpled and she hovered over him protectively to prevent a further attack.

It was easy to tell why they were being singled out. Snippets of conversation revealed that the rebels believed they were part of the international relief forces attached to the U.N. mission, forces thought to be covertly supporting the Kabbah government. Strangely, instead of summarily executing Ben and Danielle, the rebels segregated them along with several captured uniformed members of the peacekeeping force. Blindfolded, gagged, with wrists laced tightly behind their backs, they were led out through the rear of the church and packed into a single Red Cross truck, stolen during a lull in the fighting.

"We're hostages now," Danielle whispered. "To be used as barter."

One of the rebels spoke good enough English to effectively warn them to remain still and silent. The truck rumbled to a start and sped through the streets, dodging bullets and huge depressions blown out of the asphalt, until it slowed upon reaching a dirt road. Then it lumbered along the pitted, unleveled route that led uphill into the higher ground of Sierra Leone's central and eastern regions.

Both controlled by the rebels.

Time had lost meaning what felt like several hours later, when they were yanked harshly from the truck's rear and shoved down a dank tunnel into some sort of underground bunker that chased all the warmth from the night. Only then were their gags and blindfolds removed. Ben and Danielle spent the rest of the night huddled against each other for warmth and later protection, once the tight congestion of bodies had raised the temperature and humidity of the bunker to near unbearable levels.

They shook each other alert when a troop of grim-faced, angry rebels appeared in the bunker and rousted them with the barrels of their assault rifles, then stood at attention as a tall, lithe figure strode in and sized up the motley collection of hostages:

General Latisse Matabu, leader of the Revolutionary United Front.

MATABU'S INSPECTION seemed cursory until she reached Ben and Danielle, both standing now but neither tall enough to look Matabu in the eye. She gazed down as if she recognized them.

"The hawk and the eagle," she muttered, shaking her head in wonder and what looked like recognition. Her expression seemed ironic more than anything else, perhaps the slightest bit fearful. She turned back to her guards. "Bring these two to the bunker," Matabu said, and continued on down the line.

THE GUARDS made doubly sure Ben and Danielle's arms and legs were bound to the twin wooden chairs before complying with Latisse Matabu's order to leave her alone with them in the RUF command bunker. It had been here that she had presided over the failed battle that might well have destroyed her cause forever.

"You have come here to kill me, yes?" the Dragon asked them both.

"Only if we had to," Danielle answered. "Whatever it took to stop you from releasing the Black Death in the United States."

Matabu's eyes narrowed, head tilting to the side curiously. "You know very much."

Danielle stole a quick glance at Ben. "More than you can possibly realize."

"These are among the last words you will ever speak. You should choose them more carefully. Who sent you here to kill me? Speak, and your deaths will be swift."

"We already told you. We came here to stop you from releasing the Black Death," Ben said.

"And why should assassins care about such things?"

"We're not assassins," said Danielle. "We're policemen."

"I'm Palestinian," Ben picked up. "She's Israeli."

Latisse Matabu's expression wrinkled in surprise. "A long way out of your jurisdiction, aren't you?"

"Why America?" Ben posed.

"A *Palestinian* needs to ask me that? You should be rooting for me to succeed in destroying them, for all the good they've done you."

"The Israelis need no help from the Americans in oppressing the Palestinians."

Matabu nodded thoughtfully. "I suppose they don't. They learned their lessons well, I imagine. The oppressed becomes the oppressor. . . . You don't find that strange?" she asked Danielle.

"You make it sound much more cut-and-dried than it really is."

"Of course I do, for all of us, because it *is*. The Jews, the Palestinians, my people—we have all fought, or continue to fight, the same battle. Against tyranny, oppression, brutality."

"Is that why there are thirty thousand maimed civilians in your country, why a million people have been displaced by the civil war you've been waging?" Danielle challenged her. "What battle are you fighting when your troops hack off limbs, General? Please, don't compare us to you."

"Why not, Officer? Aren't you forgetting the efforts of your own Irgun and Haganah, conducted on behalf of your government, in the early years of your state? Were they any less brutal?"

"They didn't slice off the arms and legs of children."

"No, they threw those children out of their homes, turned them into lifelong refugees who lived only to hate. You were just like us then, just as your man friend's people are like us now. We have all faced defeat and refused to succumb to it. We have all fought always with the best interests of our people in mind."

"Us," Ben said, "not you."

"I fail to see the distinction."

"We never deserted our people the way you're about to."

"What's the difference who's in charge so long as the real enemy lies far from our shores?" Matabu hovered over Ben. "The days of passively accepting that as inevitable are gone. Inevitable is something you don't bother to change. I intend to cause change."

"Destroy America's crops with the Black Death and millions, *hundreds* of millions will die," Danielle reminded.

"So let them."

"It won't be limited to Americans," Ben interjected. "Take away the food the United States grows and produces, and a quarter of the world will starve."

"Perhaps as much as half," Latisse Matabu corrected. "The United States controls more than sixty percent of the world's exportable grain and other foodstuffs basic for human existence. The country maintains more of a monopoly on food exports than all of the OPEC nations combined have over oil. So once the Black Death spreads, white bread will end up costing more than caviar. America's balance of trade will cease to exist."

"And that's what you *want*?"

"I want my government back under the control of its people. I want the free elections we have been denied in Kabbah's police state. Neither will ever come to pass so long as the United States has its say."

"That's not what this is about," Danielle said surely, stiffening.

"Who are you to tell me what this is about?"

"A woman who has lost a child, too. To violence, just as you did."

"You know nothing of me! Or my child!"

Danielle glanced at Ben. "We know more than you think. More than you *know*."

Matabu whipped the pistol from her belt and aimed it at Danielle. "I'm going to shoot you myself!"

"Then hear what I've got to say first. Listen to why all this is for *nothing*." Danielle saw Matabu's grasp on her pistol grow tentative and lowered her voice. "You killed General Nelson Treest."

"So you know about Treest. Is that supposed to surprise me?"

"He raped and impregnated you. You gave birth to a son."

"Whom he killed once he learned of the child's existence."

"Treest didn't kill the baby," Danielle said flatly.

"*What?* That is madness!"

"The basket he tossed into the river was empty. He kept the boy to raise as his own. Which he did." Danielle held Matabu's faltering gaze. "Until *you* killed him."

# CHAPTER 93

Matabu stood motionless, the color drained from her face. She opened her mouth as if to speak, but no words emerged.

"General Treest used to boast about what he had done to Jordanian intelligence officers he worked with," Danielle continued, seizing the moment. "That's how we found out."

Before her, Latisse Matabu was trembling, suddenly unsteady on her feet. She stared straight ahead, at nothing, her mind elsewhere.

"You murdered your own son. How does that make you feel?" Danielle challenged, unable to disguise the loathing in her voice.

Matabu didn't seem to hear her. She staggered backwards, looking like a person who'd walked away from a car wreck. She held the pistol lightly, aimed nowhere, as if forgetting it was there.

"You've betrayed yourself worse than anyone else ever could," Danielle said, hoping the futility of if all might stop the Dragon in her tracks when nothing else had been able to.

But Matabu opened the door and called to the guards she had posted there.

"Kill them," she ordered emotionlessly, her eyes locked coldly on Ben and Danielle.

THE GUARDS prodded them up the hastily constructed wooden stairs outside into the cool breeze-blown night. Ben could see Danielle searching for an opening, a weapon, *something*. With their hands still bound, though, there wasn't much even she could do.

From the surrounding landscape of luxuriant foliage and the cascading sound of a nearby river, Danielle guessed this RUF stronghold was located in remote, northeastern Sierra Leone; most likely the Outbamba-Kilimi National Park. The air smelled sweet, lush, and alive—a vivid contrast to the choking, blood-soaked streets of Freetown.

When they were twenty yards from the bunker Danielle caught Ben's gaze, alerting him to be ready. He had barely realized whatever she was going to do was coming fast, when Danielle lashed her left leg backward and crunched one of the rebel's knees. The man screeched in agony and fell, as she wheeled toward the second rebel and kicked the rifle from his grasp before he could fire it. A single shot echoed in the night, all the time Danielle needed to smash a knee into the second rebel's groin, then twist round and tear the knife with her bound hands from the sheath wedged through his belt.

The first rebel had managed to resteady his gun by then and Ben crashed into him with his shoulder. The rebel nearly went down again, but righted himself and cracked Ben in the gut with his rifle's butt. By then, though, Danielle had spun toward the rebel, angling the knife, held blindly behind her, for him. She couldn't possibly have seen where the blade was going, Ben remembered thinking, yet Danielle's slash caught the rebel across the midsection nonetheless. When he started to double over, she rammed the blade into his throat.

Blood burst outward, drenching her, some of it spraying onto Ben. The second rebel scrambled desperately away into the woods, not even bothering to retrieve his fallen rifle.

Ben watched Danielle jam the hilt of the blade into the narrow gap between two tree trunks. Then she angled her wrists behind her and effortlessly sliced the rope binding her hands together.

"We're getting out of here," Danielle said surely, tearing the rope from her wrists. Then she retrieved the knife and slashed Ben's bonds as well.

Ben shook the blood back into his hands and followed her as they raced through the woods, ignoring the branches scraping at his face. He couldn't have said how far they ran, only that his lungs burned and chest ached terribly. He was gasping for breath when all at once a sudden burst of light caught them in its spill.

Danielle froze and threw her arms up instantly, keeping them in view to show the men she recognized as government soldiers that she was unarmed. Ben followed her lead, but the soldiers kept their rifles leveled and ready to fire.

Danielle sank to her knees, closing her hands atop her head. "Friends!" she said in English, hoping for the best. "We're friends!"

"We know who you are," an older uniformed officer said, coming forward. "We've been looking for you."

# CHAPTER 94

I'm sorry we weren't able to locate you earlier," President Kabbah apologized after greeting Ben and Danielle in his office at the State House two hours later, just after sunrise, "and for the confusion when my soldiers came upon you in the woods. But, with all that's been going on, the Jordanian U.N. delegate was unable to reach me until the battle's conclusion."

The State House's hill-like setting provided a clear view of Freetown in the aftermath of the previous night's battle. The city looked as though it had been dumped into a blender and spit out, its streets marred by chunks of debris and its buildings pockmarked and pitted. Martial law had been declared, preventing residents from venturing out to begin clean-up efforts. Instead, only government troops roamed the city, trying to stay ahead of looters and rounding up stray rebels.

"The Jordanian delegate told you about Latisse Matabu's plans for the United States?" Ben asked, speaking loudly enough for his voice to carry over the sounds of power saws and hammering that filled the State House as workers rushed to make the building presentable again.

Kabbah nodded grimly. Save for the armed guards standing vigil on either side of the door, they were alone in the presidential office, the morning sun shut out by boards slapped over windows shattered by blast percussion the previous night.

"I must tell you," Kabbah said, "I saw the work of this Black Death myself."

"Then you understand why you must concentrate all your resources on making sure the Dragon does not leave the country," Danielle interjected.

"I'm afraid it's already too late to stop her," Kabbah told her.

He nodded to one of the guards who proceeded to open the door and signal a pair of men to enter. The first was dressed in a suit, his hair perfectly combed, face freshly shaved—the look of a businessman ready to close a deal. The other, tall and lean, wore a military uniform that was torn at the knees and elbows. Something that could have been blood or sweat stained it in splotches across the midsection. His eyes were bloodshot and puffy. His cheeks were bruised and his nose looked broken. He moved tentatively, as if afraid of where his next step might take him.

"May I present General Yancy Lananga, high commander of the Revolutionary United Front forces," Kabbah said, introducing him. "In the absence of RUF supreme leader Latisse Matabu, General Lananga has generously agreed to act as liaison with the rebels as we strive to work out a comprehensive peace accord. For this, he will be rewarded with an important post in my cabinet." Kabbah turned and smiled at the well-dressed man flanking Lananga. "Isn't that right, Minister Sukahamin?"

"It is, Mr. President."

"Do you agree, General?"

Lananga nodded robotically. His eyes were empty and dazed, twitching from side to side.

"He has also informed me that Latisse Matabu left Sierra Leone, accompanied by two of her soldiers, early this morning following your escape, and entered Liberia where the Taylor government has been supporting her rebels all along." Kabbah turned his attention once more on Lananga.

"We can safely assume she is already en route to the United States, can we not, General?"

Lananga nodded again.

Kabbah kept his eyes fixed upon him. "The general was kind enough to confess that the rest of the Black Death in the Dragon's possession was shipped ahead of her. The original plan was for the crates to be divided up so their contents could be released at strategic points throughout the country. But that changed, didn't it, General?"

Another nod.

"Apparently," Kabbah continued, "the Russians had detailed plans about releasing the Black Death that Matabu never received. This makes sense to you?"

Danielle nodded, recalling the plans that had accompanied the last shipment of the Black Death she had stuffed under her shirt in Sheik Hussein al-Akbar's garage in Beirut.

"Nor did she have the opportunity to dispatch her agents across America. It is just the Dragon and her two soldiers. The general informs me that she still intends to carry out her plan. He informs me that the Black Death has been shipped to the United States for transport down the Mississippi River by barge."

"The center of the country," Ben realized.

"General Lananga says that Matabu's plan is to take possession of the crates in St. Louis. Besides a few other details Matabu shared with him so he could proceed in the event of her death, that is all he knows." Kabbah returned his focus to Lananga. "Isn't that right, General?"

Yet another nod, deliberate and emotionless. General Lananga's eyes looked like blown-out lightbulbs.

"Have you alerted the American government?" Danielle asked the President of Sierra Leone.

Kabbah frowned, started to shake his head, then stopped. "You can see my dilemma, of course. The problems that would result from something so potentially catastrophic must not be linked to my county in any way."

"You've got to give the American authorities a chance to stop it!"

"That's where the two of you come in," Kabbah said, gazing back and forth at Ben and Danielle. "Minister Sukahamin will help you make any arrangements you require, including a government jet to fly you to anywhere in the United States you wish to go. He will also obtain for you any additional resources you request. Is that agreeable?"

Ben and Danielle looked at each other, then nodded, knowing they had no choice.

"Very well, then," Kabbah finished. "I assume you will be flying to Washington."

Ben and Danielle exchanged another glance.

"No," she said. "St. Louis."

PRESIDENT KABBAH dismissed his guards after the foreigners had gone, closing the door behind them before moving to the phone and dialing the number he'd been given in Amman, Jordan.

"It's done," he reported, when the voice answered. "They'll be on their way shortly."

LATISSE MATABU'S plane had barely left Johannesburg for New York when the pain began again. Her head seemed to be expanding, filling with air. She felt queasy and sick, grateful she hadn't eaten anything to vomit up from her stomach. It wasn't just the effects of the disease today, though, it was the words the Israeli woman had tossed in her face, shattering in the truth they held.

*She had killed her own son!*

She wanted to believe it was a trick, a fabrication meant to weaken her and detract from her resolve. But it was the truth; Matabu saw that in the Israeli woman's eyes and knew it in her heart.

Now every time she closed her eyes she saw the terrified look on the boy's—her son's—face before she killed him in view of his father, General Treest. If only she could relive that moment, take him in her arms instead of dragging the blade through his neck. Her throat felt so heavy, she could barely swallow. Resigned herself to keep her eyes open through the entire duration of the flight, because each time she closed the boy's screams haunted her along with those of her parents.

*She deserved to be punished.*

But not yet. First she had to save her country by destroying its greatest oppressor. Provider of the guns that had killed her father. Ally of the man who had raped her and stolen her child.

Matabu sat squeezed in the coach-class compartment in a center seat, dressed in shapeless robes decorated with beads to promote her disguise as a typical West African woman coming to tour the U.S. She had covered her hair with an intricately wrapped turban, and even applied makeup to hide the dry leathery finish the harsh elements of Sierra Leone had given her complexion. In that moment Matabu wished she had the two soldiers accompanying her to America on either side of her. But she had felt it best for security reasons for the three of them to be separated in the cabin to attract less attention to themselves.

The Dragon fought down another wave of nausea and tried not to dwell on the miserable failure of the previous night. Focused instead on her last chance to make amends and come as close as she could to finding peace at the same time.

JIM BLACK showed up at the café in downtown Amman, Jordan, a little early so he could order a beer, only to learn they didn't serve any alcohol. No place in the city did, except the big western hotels where he wasn't in the mood to show his face right now.

He had regained consciousness two nights before, gagging for breath on the surface of the Mediterranean, clinging to a section of dock and recovering his senses in time to search the dock area for Danielle Barnea. Both she and the boat Sasha Borodin had provided, though, were gone. Black couldn't help but smile, in spite of the pain shooting through his head. Nobody had ever outdrawn, or outfoxed, him before. Barnea was even better than he expected and he was almost glad she had gotten away.

He tried coffee at the downtown Amman café and nearly spit out his first gulp, then added a week's worth of sugar to quell the bitterness. When that didn't work, he returned to the counter to get a tea instead and got back to the table to find a man sitting across from his seat wearing a business suit and a *keffiyah*.

"Who'd you say sent you?" Black asked him, bypassing the usual exchange of greetings.

"I didn't."

"Somebody with some clout, be my guess."

"And you would be correct."

Black took a sip from his cup and found the tea only slightly more drinkable than the coffee. " 'Cause you got a serious beverage problem in this country. I'm wondering if your boss could do something about it."

"Don't worry," the man across from him said and leaned forward. "You won't be here long. The man I represent has a job for you."

"I'm expensive."

"He can afford it."

"Where'm I going?"

"The United States."

Jim Black swallowed some of his tea with a grimace. "Normally it ain't wise to shit where you live."

The man slid a photograph across the table. "You know this woman, I believe."

Jim Black found himself staring at the face of Danielle Barnea. "You've got to be kidding me. Man, I just can't get rid of this bitch. . . ."

"Kidding you? I'm afraid I don't—"

"Never mind," Jim Black said, giving up on the tea. "Just tell me where I can find her."

# DAY TEN

# CHAPTER 95

Ben and Danielle flew west aboard a Sierra Leone military jet, an uncomfortable flight that left them grabbing for sleep in the interludes between refueling stops and bouts with turbulence.

During one of the journey's final legs Danielle awoke with a start to find Ben gazing at her.

"We'll be landing in New York soon," he said, not bothering to disguise the irony in his voice. "Good thing we won't have to get off the plane."

"I realized something over the past week," Danielle told him. "I realized New York took more than the baby: It also took my nerve. To be a mother I was resigned to changing my outlook, my priorities. No more risks, no more missions, no more adventures. Everything I'd always been had to change. Then we lost the baby, but it still changed and I couldn't get it back." She stared at Ben more deeply. "I blamed you because I already hated myself too much to bother."

"I understood. I didn't mind."

"You should have. You risked everything to save the child, just like you're risking everything now, and in return I turned my back on you. Sierra Leone made it all clear to me."

"Because of Matabu?"

"I looked at her and saw too much of myself. As bad as

her life's been, she's made it worse. I've been doing the same thing."

"I don't see the comparison."

"Different scale, that's all. You lose hope, you give up, and you become like her. I could have been a step away, I could have been two. But I was getting there and that's not a place I ever want to be. You can't control what happens; only how you deal with it."

"Not true. All that's happened to you may have brought you to the edge, but you never jumped."

"Matabu jumped. I think I was ready to."

"Because you hadn't really changed; you only thought you had. You got caught up in the way Baruch and the other politicians saw you."

"And how do you see me?"

Ben looked at Danielle sitting next to him and managed to smile. "Just where I want you to be."

Three refueling stops, combined with interminable waits for open slots in international terminals, had them on the ground at Lambert Field in St. Louis shortly before dawn. The airport was just opening, the first of the morning passengers beginning to arrive. There was a diplomatic escort arranged by President Kabbah waiting when they reached the arrivals area. The escort had procured a car for them, but Danielle opted not to take it at the last minute, not trusting Kabbah's security nearly enough at this point. Ben and Danielle waited until the escort had departed before slipping out to the front of the terminal where they signaled for a cab and stowed the duffel bag Kabbah's defense minister had provided in the trunk before settling into the backseat.

The problem now was they knew Latisse Matabu and her soldiers were coming in to meet a barge, but not exactly where or when. The hope was the two of them had managed to get to the city ahead of the Dragon, although without any further information that didn't seem to do them much good.

"Where to?" the driver asked.

"The Mississippi River," Ben responded, as much out of frustration with their predicament as anything else.

The driver twisted his head and shoulders back toward them. "You'll have to do better than that."

"How about a freight yard?" Danielle suggested. "Somewhere on the river shipping barges are loaded and unloaded."

"On the Mississippi?" the driver posed incredulously.

"In St. Louis."

The driver shrugged. "Still leaves you lots of choices."

"How many?"

"More than I can count."

"Take us to the largest," Ben said.

"Main Port of St. Louis," the driver said, shaking his head. "It's your dime."

LATISSE MATABU was already awake and walking the decks of the barge when the sun came up. She had chosen the two soldiers who accompanied her, Timo and Dikembe, because they had been born in the same village as she, their fathers killed with the same American-supplied weapons that had slain Matabu's father. They never strayed far from her shadow, forever vigilant and protective, while clearly uncomfortable in western-style civilian clothes.

The insulated crates holding the Black Death were stored in three large refrigerated containers powered by huge compressors located in the barge's stern. Even though the crates could not possibly fill up all three containers, Matabu had rented the entire barge space to avoid complications. The only thing she had failed to consider was the time lag between her arrival and that of the barge's crew. She should have paid them to stay on board. Now she was forced to wait for them to get here before departing. Perhaps in an hour, maybe two or three.

Latisse Matabu tried to be patient, distracting herself

368 / JON LAND

with a review of her plan. During her long stay in the United States, she had seen the Mississippi only once, never imagining the role it would play in her future. She had made a detailed study of the river in recent days, after the third shipment vanished and with it the Russian Cold War schematic plans she had been promised.

North of St. Louis, down to the Chain of Rocks Bridge, the Mississippi was dotted with manmade locks, dams, and channels, evidence of the Army Corps of Engineers' determined efforts to bend and shift nature. South of St. Louis, though, the river remained far more wild and untamed. Narrower, without any locks or dams to impede barge traffic. In fact, Matabu had read of barge tows stretching a half-mile in length. Interconnected monsters generating wakes known to swallow or capsize smaller craft that strayed too close.

The barge she had retained was self-propelled, enabling it to better handle the bends and curves in the river that considerably lengthened the journey south. From St. Louis south to the Gulf of Mexico the river was joined by literally hundreds of tributaries that collectively spanned the heartland of America like a network of veins and arteries. Matabu had already selected two dozen harbors at which to dock long enough to offload a portion of the crates for prearranged cold storage. By the time her journey south was complete, then, the Black Death would have been evenly distributed down the center of the United States. Ready to saturate the nation as soon as she returned to let the frozen eggs at each drop thaw out and then release the creatures to spread.

The bugs would seek out food relentlessly; she had learned that much from the small portion she had tested on the village of Katani nine days before. Matabu had formulated her plan after studying irrigation maps of the farm country that spread outward off the Mississippi. If the Black Death followed the same path as those waterways supplying farms with water, they would end up eventually feeding on land that offered an endless food supply.

Once released, free to spread and breed unchecked, the Black Death would be impossible to stop. The Dragon had not yet worked out the precise timetable for that release; it would be staggered over the course of several days, probably, depending on how long it took her to return to the ports where the insulated crates would be stored.

And she would have her redemption.

JIM BLACK hadn't been back in the United States in nearly two years and it didn't take him very long to figure out why he hadn't missed home much. It was the language, everybody talking and listening in on what other people were saying. Jim Black was a lot happier when he didn't understand what people were saying and they didn't understand him. Made things lots simpler and kept conversation to an absolute minimum. You got your point across and that's where it stopped. No small talk or bullshit.

Places like St. Louis were the worst, the people just too damn friendly. Everybody smiling and expecting you to smile back. It made Jim Black want to draw one of his Sigs and pop the assholes in the center of their foreheads. Teach them to keep to themselves and mind their own business.

He'd like to start with the waitress who ran the coffee shop outside the airport.

"Coffee," he ordered.

"What kind?"

"Black."

"I mean what kind of coffee."

"Anything but the Arab kind," Black told her.

All he wanted was a black coffee and she wouldn't let him leave without a muffin to go with it. Flashing her cigarette-stained teeth as she stuck it in the bag free of charge. Jim Black left her a five-buck tip when he would have much preferred to leave a bullet in her face.

The strange particulars of this assignment made him even

more ornery. He had to be on the move and he wasn't even sure where he had to be on the move to. Everything was vague, when Jim Black thrived on clarity. Connect two points with a fucking straight line and get the hell out of Dodge.

And that wasn't the worst of it. The last person in the world he wanted to meet up with again was Danielle Barnea. But that's what it looked like this day was shaping up towards, as Jim Black dropped his coffee and muffin on the passenger seat of the rental car and headed for the Mississippi River.

# CHAPTER 96

It was just after 7:00 A.M. when Ben and Danielle reached the Port of St. Louis in the shadow of the famed Gateway Arch, glistening in the morning sun. These docks specialized in servicing the industrial barges that routinely traveled the Mississippi River. They'd had the cab stop for breakfast at a fast food restaurant and found themselves so famished from the journey that they devoured the salty egg-and-cheese combinations without tasting them. The coffee was hot and strong, though, reviving them.

The foreman was not expected to arrive for another hour. But a subordinate seemed more than willing to answer their queries, droning on proudly about how river barges remained the eighteen wheelers of the central U.S. Ben and Danielle pretended to be representatives of a foreign conglomerate dissatisfied with their current shipping service and looking to make a change.

The man sipped black coffee from a Thermos cup as he eagerly gave them a tour of the riverfront facilities. Ben and Danielle pretended to pay attention, all the time focusing on the barges they passed in search of the refrigerated one that might have held Latisse Matabu's Black Death.

"We offer full freezer and refrigeration services," he boasted proudly. "And all perishables are one hundred percent guaranteed."

"Anything come in recently?" Ben asked.

"From overseas," Danielle added. "A possible reference for us."

The man drained his coffee and scratched his chin before shaking his head.

The next two barge facilities on the river yielded the same results. Their cab driver was quite happy to keep driving them around so long as they kept paying cash. Danielle and Ben got their act honed considerably better, for all the good it did them.

"Well," said the driver, when they plopped back into their seats after the third facility turned up nothing, "just another dozen or so to go. Hey, could be whatever you're looking for already shipped out."

"Let's hope not," Ben said.

"CRATES?" THE requisitions clerk asked Danielle at the fourth stop on their list.

"Steel, insulated," Ben elaborated, recalling Mikhail Belush's description back in Dubna. "Maybe three or four feet by six. We're supposed to meet the shipment."

The clerk continued scanning his manifests. "Well, you just missed it."

"Missed it?"

"Refrigerator barge shipped out maybe twenty minutes ago, heading south. Checked her out myself. Sorry."

"Any way we can catch it?" Danielle asked, her heart beginning to pound.

The clerk frowned. "Not unless you can get yourselves a faster boat."

Ben and Danielle found the River Patrol speedboat tied up to a dock attached to a small cabin with St. Louis River Authority markings.

"Untie us," Danielle said to Ben, after jumping down onto the deck.

"I hope you know how to drive one of these things," he responded, pulling the rope from the first mooring, "because I don't."

Danielle moved behind the controls, tore some wires free, and joined a pair of them together. "We'll see."

The engine roared to life.

Latisse Matabu clung to the shady side of the barge, the glare of the sun suddenly making the pounding of her head intensify. Timo and Dikembe, the soldiers who had accompanied her, both voiced their concern but she smiled and passed it off to simple fatigue.

*Just let me finish this. Give me that much strength.*

She thought of the Moor Woman as she formed that prayer, wondering if they had more in common than she ever considered. A pair of outcasts, banished from society as punishment for their sins. Her grandmother had never told Matabu what the Moor Woman had done that led to her exile. Perhaps she, too, had killed her own child.

The barge had already cleared the outskirts of the city of St. Louis, and Matabu tried to concentrate on checking her map for the first harbor at which she intended to dock, another fifty miles to the south in Ste. Genevieve. When that effort proved too much, she distracted herself from the painful throbbing of her head by picturing the release of the Black Death along the length of the Mississippi. The eggs thawing out and hatching within minutes, freeing her bugs to ravage the heartland of the United States.

The urban world slowly receded before her on the banks of the Mississippi. Except for other barge and boat traffic, the currents might well have swallowed up the years. On her right, the Missouri side, bluffs and hill formations shaped the landscape, while the Illinois side on her left was dominated by shallows.

Suddenly Matabu's skull felt as if a needle had jabbed it, a flash exploding before her eyes that left her skin broiling on the inside and out. She squeezed her eyes closed in search of comfort and viewed quite the opposite through the darkness. Dikembe and Timo grasped her on either side, their faces taut with worry. But this was not the typical attack she had grown used to. It was different.

*The hawk and the eagle . . .*

She had glimpsed them again, which could mean only one thing: They had somehow escaped death back in Sierra Leone and they were *here*, close by now. Her trackers come to collect the debt she owed to God.

But she wasn't ready to pay up quite yet, not with the victory she had so long sought this close at hand. America had to die, had to pay just as she did.

Standing astern, Latisse Matabu suddenly felt the barge slow and moved out from the cover of one of the refrigerated holds to see why.

# CHAPTER 97

Ben clung to the patrol boat's handholds as Danielle fought the river for speed. From shore the waters had looked calm and easy. In the center, though, drawing away from the St. Louis city limits, the mud-colored river seemed to thicken, battering the small boat with currents that seemed to go in every direction at once. The Mississippi became a creased swell of angry water, determined to fold over itself. Calm pockets, like boils on the water, behaved as whirlpools, forcing Danielle to spin the wheel wildly to compensate for being tossed about.

"I thought you said you knew how to drive this," Ben shouted at her, feeling the boat being smacked around by the currents.

"You could have warned me."

"I've never been on this river before in my life."

Danielle had just swung toward him, about to say something else, when the patrol boat's engine sputtered and died.

THE ONCOMING tow barge stretched six across and as far as Latisse Matabu could see down the river. In the pilot house, her two-man crew had banked the barge sharply toward the shallows, slowing to allow the huge monster to pass while simultaneously angling to stop from being run aground by the powerful vortex of swells.

The barge rocked and swayed. Birds feeding off the Mississippi's surface lurched into the air. Mosquitoes attacked from the swampy lowlands on the Illinois side of the river.

The Dragon gnashed her teeth and waited.

"WE'RE BEING pulled into the shallows!" Danielle blared, tossing Ben one of two paddles tucked against the patrol boat's side. Her efforts to restart the patrol boat had failed and she began to wonder if it had been left tied up against the dock for a reason.

Together they tried to fight the river's powerful flow, succeeding in only slowing the inevitable. Ben strained against the paddle and pushed as hard as he could. They were holding their ground but no more. Going nowhere.

Suddenly the patrol boat flopped upward, listing severely to port.

"What the hell," Ben muttered just before a mighty horn blew and he turned to see a riverboat sliding up alongside them, slowing.

"You folks need a lift?" a man in a captain's suit yelled down from inside a pilot house.

"I DIDN'T know the River Patrol wore plain clothes," the captain of the *Spirit of St. Louis* greeted, when Ben and Danielle joined him up inside the pilot house. "Good thing I was taking her out for a routine test run. I'm Wayne Lockridge."

Ben took the man's extended hand, his own raw from swinging onto the riverboat's rope ladder as it slowed past the disabled patrol boat.

"We need your help, Captain."

"What's on this barge you're looking for that's so important?" Lockridge asked, once Ben was finished.

Ben kept sweeping the area of the river ahead of them with the riverboat's binoculars. "Just help us find it."

Danielle gazed about the pilot house. "How fast can this thing go?"

"How fast do you need it to go?"

"Fast enough to catch a barge that's got a half-hour head start on us, moving south down the river," Ben told him.

Lockridge looked almost hurt. "Mister, this baby's got two Caterpillar 3412 diesel engines that turn 350-kilowatt generator sets. A couple traction motors powered electrically by those generators turn two twelve-inch belt chains, each forty feet in length. My point is the *Spirit* may look like an antique, but don't let that fool you. Full out we can cover fifteen miles per hour and empty, well, let's just say give me a half-hour and I'll have you right along that barge's side."

Latisse Matabu waited anxiously, as her barge came to a near complete halt. The heat built up inside her, boiling her blood and leaving her no choice but to seek refuge in one of the refrigerated holds. She unlatched the rearmost container and stepped inside, the spray of frosty air against her instantly cooling her skin.

She gazed at the dozens of insulated crates stacked within, focusing on the task before her when footsteps sounded against the deck. Matabu turned to find Dikembe and Timo standing in the darkened doorway, holding long hunting knives in their hands.

"I SEE the barge!" Ben said.

They had just rounded a narrow bend in the river when he found the barge with its refrigerated containers idling to one side. He extended the binoculars to Danielle.

She pulled them against her eyes. "Matabu has the door to one of the compartments open. I can see the two RUF soldiers she brought with her." She lowered the binoculars and looked at Ben. "The rest of the Black Death must be inside those holds."

"Black Death?" posed Lockridge.

"Ever serve in the military, Captain Lockridge?" Danielle asked him.

"Damn right, I did. Navy through and through."

"So you know all about fighting for your country. Believe me when I tell you that's what you're doing now."

Lockridge looked at them and nodded. "What is it you want me to do?"

THE TWO soldiers Latisse Matabu trusted as much as any under her command remained stiff and motionless, knives extended toward the deck.

"We are very sorry, General," Timo said.

"We don't have any choice," Dikembe added.

"I understand," Latisse Matabu said with a strange calm. And it was true: She did. Betrayal was the ultimate payment for the terrible sins she had committed. It would end here, just as it should. What right did she have to hope for redemption?

"Just as there was no choice with your parents," Timo finished.

Matabu felt the chilly air press from the hold against her

back, as she stared at Timo. She swallowed hard, her throat suddenly so dry it felt like glass sliding down. "My parents?"

"You blamed the government and the Americans for their deaths. You were supposed to: That is what it was supposed to look like."

"There were too many who did not agree with the plans of your father," Dikembe added. "He was willing to give up too much. And once he lost Tongo and failed to retake Freetown . . ."

"Which of the chiefs, which of my generals is behind this? Which one? *Talk!*"

"All of them," answered Timo, starting to raise his knife. "The battle the other night was viewed as your last chance."

Dikembe's knife flashed in the sun. "We must do this for our country, before you make us a pariah to the world."

"But General Lananga was the only who knows I'm here," Matabu said softly.

"That's right," returned Timo. "He was."

He and Dikembe moved forward together, ready to pounce.

Latisse Matabu sprang before they could. In that instant she was not diseased or dying, nor was she a guilt-riddled sinner who deserved to be punished. In that instant the rage over this betrayal, and the one against her father, filled her with the strength and power that had nearly brought a government to its knees.

Fear filled her soldiers' eyes. Then their long-observed deference to her made them hesitate when she lunged, forgetting the warrior training that had dominated their lives. They slashed with their knives, but missed badly. And, before they could lash out again, Latisse Matabu had control of both their wrists.

Both tried to pull away, but it was too late. Matabu had already twisted the blades toward them. She stared into their eyes and thrust both her hands savagely forward.

Their screams were like sandpaper against her ears. She felt their blood drench her, felt them die.

Traitors!

*Her father had been murdered by those he sought to serve, the ultimate betrayal!*

And if she didn't complete her work here now, her parents would have sacrificed themselves for nothing. Her son would have died for nothing. Treest had infected her with the disease that was killing her, but God had granted her just enough time to complete this one final task.

The huge tow barge finally lumbered past and the Dragon felt her barge start sliding from the shallows.

"IT'S MOVING again!" Danielle realized, as the *Spirit of St. Louis* drew to within a hundred yards of the barge. "Turning back into the river!"

Ben grabbed the binoculars from her grasp, trying to find Latisse Matabu on deck. "Two bodies in the stern. Her soldiers, I think."

*"What?"*

"The pilot house! I can see Matabu in the pilot house!"

The riverboat rocked mightily in the water.

"Better have a look at that tow barge coming straight for us, too," Lockridge advised grimly.

"Steer us around it!" Danielle ordered, the authority clear in her voice.

"Means risking a ride through the shallows."

"It's worth it," Ben said. "Believe me."

"JUST PUT the gun down," one of the barge pilots said to the Dragon. "We'll take you wherever you want to go."

"Just keep moving!" Matabu ordered, a new strategy in mind. "Don't stop unless I tell you!"

She aimed the pistol she had taken from Timo's belt at the radio and fired two shots into it.

"Try to leave this pilot house and I will shoot you. Slow this barge and I will shoot you. Do you understand me?"

Both men nodded fearfully.

BY THE time the *Spirit of St. Louis*'s bow approached the barge's stern, Ben and Danielle had armed themselves with the weapons Defense Minister Sukahamin had packed into the duffel bag for them.

"Let's move," she signaled, taking charge. "You take the second deck, I'll take the top."

Ben squeezed his assault rifle in both hands. "So she can't shoot us both before one of us gets her."

"That's the idea."

*"THEY'RE HERE!*

Her barge was approaching the Jefferson Barracks Bridge when Latisse Matabu heard the voice in her head warn her once again of the presence of the hawk and the eagle, the Israeli woman and Palestinian man who had somehow escaped death in Sierra Leone. On the Missouri side of the river, beyond the bluffs, the barge was passing a sprawling military cemetery.

*Another omen*, the Dragon thought.

After killing the soldiers who tried to betray her, the Dragon saw her only hope lay in releasing the Black Death into the river here and now, by herself. She could summon the strength, even if it was the last she could ever muster. Drag as many of the crates as possible from their refrigerated compartments and let the sun thaw out the eggs. They would then hatch almost immediately, freeing the

Black Death once she emptied the crates overboard.

Now, though, there was the presence of the hawk and the eagle to consider.

Latisse Matabu's head pounded again. Nausea threatened to overcome her. The brief illusion of strength was gone.

*She needed time to make her new plan work!*

She scrabbled forward to the case Dikembe had stowed near the front of the stacked crates, flown to America under the guise of religious materials. She snapped it open and tore aside books and papers until she came to the secret compartment contained beneath them where the Kalashnikov assault rifles were hidden, just as a riverboat angled straight through the shallows for her barge.

BEN STOOD with his M-16 poised over the deck rail, ready to fire as soon as Matabu reappeared. He caught a flash of motion and tried to trace it when a burst of bullets clanged off the rail and shattered the windows at his back. He lost grip on his rifle and strained to reach for it as it dropped off the side. He hit the deck hard, narrowly avoiding the next barrage that just missed his head.

On the deck above, he could hear Danielle answering the fire with bursts of her own. He remembered the pistol tucked into his belt and yanked it free, instantly more comfortable with a weapon he was familiar with. He tried to sight down on Matabu, but she moved too quickly, dancing and darting across the deck of the barge like a phantom.

Danielle's fire from the third deck finally pinned the Dragon down. But their riverboat was sliding past the barge too fast, and Ben realized their best, perhaps only, opportunity would be lost.

He made the decision in the next instant, no time to think or plan further. Time only to lift himself over the rail and leap down for the deck of the barge directly beneath him.

THE DRAGON glimpsed the barge's pilots trying to flee their posts as soon as the shooting started. She rose, aimed her Kalashnikov, and fired off twin bursts. Her bullets slammed into the men and spilled them off the pilot house ladder to the deck.

Almost instantly the barge, now out of control, listed severely to port, angling toward the blackened river bottoms on the Illinois side of the river. Armies of mosquitoes buzzed the air in droves, welcoming her. The Dragon smiled. Land was what she needed.

She rushed to the back of the barge and emptied the rest of her clip into the trio of compressors. Sparks and smoke burst outward. The power instantly died, deactivating the refrigeration units which kept the temperature inside the holds at a constant forty degrees. Beneath the spill of the Mississippi's hot sun, that temperature would begin to rise almost instantly and so would the thawing of the Black Death.

The riverboat was past her now, taking the hawk and the eagle with it. Latisse Matabu reached into her pocket for a spare clip and had just snapped it home when the hawk slammed into her.

She landed hard on the deck with the rifle pinned against her chest and the Palestinian man atop her.

everse us! Get us back to the barge!" Danielle
screamed at Captain Lockridge, shoving her rifle at
him.

"We got bigger problems than getting back to that
barge," he said, gesturing out the window.

A massive tow hauling eight oil barges loaded with the
tanks that supplied fuel to harbors up and down the Mississippi steamed toward them from down river, blasting its horn.

"He's got right of way," Lockridge said. "I don't yield,
and we're all gonna leave this world in a hurry."

"Fine."

"What?"

Danielle shoved the rifle at him again. "Just keep going
and get me as close to that oil barge as you can!"

"That means steering toward the bluffs!"

"That's right."

Lockridge's mouth dropped in shock. "You don't know
this river, ma'am."

She saw the steel emergency kit tucked into a slot next
to the old-fashioned wheel and reached down to open it.
"No, but I'm learning."

BEN HAD landed hard atop Latisse Matabu. He felt her ribs contract violently, certain a few had snapped like pencils. She carried a carrion stench on her, something rotting away as it died. Her breath was stale and hot, coming in long dry heaves. But she somehow managed to twist and spin up on top of him, raking his eyes with her nails, then tearing at his cheek with her teeth.

The intense pain gave Ben the adrenaline burst he needed to kick her from him. His vision clouded, he was still able to see her scrambling for the rifle she had dropped on impact. Ben lunged onto Matabu's back before she could reach the rifle and squeezed his fingers into her hair, trying to slam her face into the wet wood. At that instant the barge ran aground on the river's bottom with a rattling thud and water the color of dirt splashed up on deck.

Matabu uttered a throaty scream and twisted violently, throwing Ben off her. Then she rushed in a crouch to the nearest refrigerated compartment and threw the door open.

"HERE WE GO," Lockridge called out to Danielle from the pilot house, as the riverboat hugged the shore below the bluffs rimming the Jefferson Military Barracks. "Best I can give you is one shot."

"Just get me as close as you can."

Sliding past the bridge, Lockridge managed to brush the starboard side of the *Spirit of St. Louis* against the aft side of the frontmost oil barge in tow, so all Danielle had to do was leap up onto its raised deck. She landed hard and fell deliberately forward to make sure she didn't slip off.

The barge's small crew was oblivious to her presence, all their attention focused on the Illinois side of the river toward the supply barge that had run aground and was perched halfway up the riverbank. Danielle cut between the assortment of tanks, dodging the various thick tubular hoses, as she drew her pistol and chambered a round.

She fired into the air to seize the men's attention, the crew simultaneously turning to look her way, shocked and stunned.

"Get off! Now!" she screamed at them, brandishing her pistol.

"Huh?" one of them managed.

"Get off! Jump! *Swim!*" Leveling the pistol toward the speaker now, her blazing eyes insisting she would use it.

The men backed off, a series of splashes following soon after. A pair of men remained dumbstruck in the control room, and raced desperately to contact the tow to get it to stop. Danielle ignored them and studied the bilge controls, reaching for the nearest hose at the same time.

THE DRAGON could feel the temperature in the compartment rising. It might have been her imagination but she felt certain she could already hear the crackle of the awakened troops of the Black Death fighting through the confines of their eggs, free to wreak havoc as soon as the crates were open.

She would let them loose inside here. They would move instinctively toward the light, toward the heat.

Toward food.

Just open the crates and let fate do the rest.

Latisse Matabu moved to the first crate and unlatched it. She raised the top, as a shadow crossed the hold's doorway.

BEN THREW himself against Matabu, impact knocking over the crate and spilling its contents to the hold floor.

Tiny black insects began scampering across the floor, searching for their bearings. Other eggs remained whole, beginning to crack and open in the brief glimpses he caught before Matabu began kicking at him wildly. She slashed a booted foot into his face and he fell, crawling after her when she moved to another crate.

She had gotten that one open, too, when he latched onto her legs and tried to pull her away. She bellowed, shoved him aside, then retreated from the hold back onto the barge's deck, looking for one of the guns lost in the struggle with the hawk. She caught sight of the Kalashnikov and lurched toward it.

Ben staggered to his feet and wobbled after her. He felt dazed and dizzy. The world was spinning. He tasted his own blood and thought he was going to be sick. The sun burned his wounded eyes when he reemerged into the light.

A huge oil-stained barge drew directly alongside. Ben saw Danielle standing on the edge near the center, holding a black hose in both her hands.

DANIELLE TWISTED the nozzle open and felt the resulting pressure turn the hose into a snake in her hands. She held fast, separating her legs for more balance, and watched the stream of black, noxious liquid pour through the end. It shot slightly into the air and carried over onto the supply barge, coating the holds, spreading across the decks in a thick murky film that left a gray residue hanging in the air.

Danielle maintained her grip as long as she could, feeling the heat of the hose singe her palms, until the slowing oil barge slid past its cousin and an enraged Latisse Matabu appeared in the stern, Kalashnikov steadied dead on her.

THE DRAGON could feel the oil running down her skin in the moment before she fired, the eagle from her dreams directly before her locked in her sights. She caught sight

of the hawk rushing her from the side just as she pulled
the trigger. Impact sent the shot off enough to miss the
Israeli woman.

Matabu tried to right the gun again, but the hawk had
hold of her wrists and wouldn't let go. She struggled with
him and her feet slid out from under her, tumbling both of
them to the slippery deck. This time it was she who landed
on top. Hands on his throat now, squeezing until he died
so she could finish her work.

DANIELLE TORE the flare pistol she'd found in the *Spirit of
St. Louis's* emergency box out of her belt and aimed it at
the stranded oil-soaked barge. She was ready to fire now,
but paused, afraid to shoot off the flare whose flames were
certain to capture Ben once the fire caught.

Agonizing over the fact that she would soon be out of
the flare gun's effective range, Danielle leveled the barrel
toward the barge and squeezed one eye closed.

BEN CAUGHT a glimpse of Danielle well past the grounded
barge now, flare pistol in hand. He knew she was going to
fire, *had* to fire, just as he knew there was no way he could
break Latisse Matabu's grasp in time.

So he stopped trying. Rolled sideways across the slick
deck surface of the barge, locked in a desperate embrace
with Matabu, her hands pressing deeper into his throat, as
they slid closer to the port side of the barge that remained
perched over the river near the stern.

The Dragon realized his intention at the last moment and
tried to pull both of them back. Ben, though, had already
fastened his hands to the wrists that were choking the life
out of him, refusing to let go. Breath bottle-necking in his

throat, he mounted one final surge atop the slippery deck that pitched both of them over the side into the brown, oil-slicked waters of the Mississippi below.

DANIELLE FIRED as soon as Ben dipped below the surface. The flare shot out like a rocket, then lost speed as it neared the stranded barge. For a moment it seemed the flare might drop harmlessly into the water, but it continued to sail through the air on direct line with the craft.

The flare struck a section of the barge broadside and sent a red flaming sheet exploding outward, swallowed almost instantly by a burst of flames. A match striking fluid-soaked charcoal multiplied a million times that pushed its heat into Danielle's face and hair. There was no explosion when the flames caught, the oil fueling the spread of fire that covered the entire barge between breaths while she watched. The fire licked at the water as well, stubbornly clinging to the surface at the same time the flames on the barge spread across the refrigerated holds, certain to incinerate the crates of the Black Death contained within.

Danielle pulled her eyes off the flames, searched the waters for Ben.

No sign of him.

She dove in and swam rapidly toward the shallows already heated by the flaming oil slick.

"Ben!"

She screamed his name futilely, the surface of the water so thick now it was difficult to swim, much less tread on the surface. Black oil coated every inch of her skin and clothing, slowing any motion she tried to make to bring her closer to the flaming barge.

"Ben!" Danielle screamed again as she tried to calculate how long he'd been under, how much air Latisse Matabu might have choked from him before they plunged into the river together.

Danielle heard a popping sound, felt a wave of oily water drench her. She swung and saw Ben gasping for breath just a few feet away. Swam toward him as he writhed and struggled, choking.

LATISSE MATABU sank further away from the amber glow of the waters above, the world darkening around her. She felt strangely peaceful, the pain of the disease that had ravaged her body finally receding.

In her mind she saw the Moor Woman swimming toward her, disappointed that her parents, or grandmother, or even her son had not come to greet her in death instead. But none of them would be waiting in the place where Matabu and the Moor Woman belonged. And in that moment she realized there would be no salvation or happiness in death. The same pain she had known in life awaited her, only for eternity.

The Moor Woman continued toward her, extending a hand. And Latisse Matabu reached out to take it before her eyes closed at last.

DANIELLE, STILL struggling to hold Ben above the surface amidst the flaming swells, turned toward the sound of a racing engine. A river patrol boat raced straight for them, kicking up a wide foamy froth in its wake, its siren wailing. The boat slowed only at the very last moment when a collision seemed inevitable and cut its engine to idle as it bobbed to a stop alongside them.

Jim Black looked down at Danielle and shook his head. "Man oh man, you really know how to throw a party, don't you?"

# CHAPTER 99

Black stretched a hand toward her, revealing the Sig Sauer nine-millimeter pistols dangling at his waist in their twin shoulder holsters.

"I thought you were dead," Danielle said from the water.

"Yeah, well good thing for you and your boyfriend there you were wrong."

Danielle reached up and felt his powerful grasp close on hers. She had barely struck the deck when Black reached back down and hoisted Ben out of the water.

"Your boyfriend's cut up pretty bad, but he'll live," the cowboy said simply and turned back to Danielle. "Something on your mind?"

Danielle raised the Sig Sauer she had plucked from its holster when Black had lowered her on board.

Black smiled. "You gonna give me a chance to draw mine?"

"Go ahead."

"Nah," the cowboy grinned. "I think I'll just see how this plays out."

Danielle swung the gun round and handed it butt first back to Black. "We'll just have to finish it another time."

"Whenever you're ready, Danny girl."

"What are you doing here?" Danielle asked him, hovering over Ben who had just begun to stir on deck.

Black flashed his familiar grin. "I was sent to keep the

two of you alive. Good thing you left me this ride, by the way. We get some time later, I'll teach you a thing or two 'bout engines," he said, and stepped behind the wheel.

"WHO SENT you, Mister Black?" she asked him once they were underway.

"Friend of your boyfriend's back in Arab land. Al something."

"Colonel al-Asi?"

"Yeah, close enough. Sent me here to bring you back safe and sound. I'd say I earned my money."

"I hope you got all of it in advance," Ben said, rising gingerly to his feet next to Danielle. His face was swollen, and he mopped the blood and grime aside with his forearm. "Because we're not going back."

Danielle took his hand tightly and smiled at him.

Jim Black looked confused. "Colonel Al got word to me this morning he'd arranged for your names to be cleared in Israel and Palestine. No questions asked, considering the embarrassment he can cause over all the shit that's gone down. Sounds like he's the kind of man who means business."

Ben and Danielle exchanged a glance, neither showing any enthusiasm for the proposal. Then both of them shook their heads.

"Thank the colonel for his efforts," Ben said, smiling slightly as he thought of al-Asi forever working his strange magic. "But we're not interested."

"Maybe you didn't hear what I said," Black followed, his head cocked a little to the side.

"We heard you just fine."

Black swatted a mosquito on his cheek and flicked it into the river. "You saying you want to stay *here*? Give up the chance to go home and be heroes?"

"We've tried that before," Ben told him. "It didn't work."

The cowboy nodded in bemused admiration. "The two of you are really starting to impress me."

"Just drop us at the next pier," Danielle told him.

"That's it?"

"Unless you want me to reconsider killing you."

Black winked. " 'Nother day, maybe. Shit, there's always tomorrow."

Danielle looked at Ben. "There is now."

Turn the page for a sneak peek at

# JON LAND's

thrilling new novel of
international intrigue

# THE
# SEVEN
# SINS

ONE

Y ou want the cab or not, mister?"
         The voice startled Gianfranco Ferelli, and he swit-
ched his briefcase protectively from one hand to the
other.

"Yes. I'm sorry," he said in broken English and climbed into
the cab's backseat, instantly grateful for the relief the cool air
brought after even such a brief exposure to the scorching desert
heat. The setting of the sun two hours before had clearly provided no respite, and Ferelli mopped his stringy hair back into
place atop his scalp. "Seven Sins Casino and Resort," he told
the driver and felt the car lurch forward into traffic.

The flight from Rome to JFK had been smooth and quiet. But
the next leg out of New York to McCarran Airport in Las Vegas
was packed with loud and boisterous tourists who drank and
gabbed away the hours. Even in first class, Ferelli was left to sit
anxiously with the briefcase held protectively in his lap out of
fear one of the drunken, soon-to-be-gambling revelers might
make off with it if he dared sleep.

A few times he cracked open the case and peered at the
photograph of Michael Tiranno, born Michele Nunziato, resting atop the stack of manila folders and envelopes. Captured
in black and white, the man's face looked to have been
drained of all fat as well as emotion. Lean in shape and sparse
in feeling.

But Ferelli knew enough about Michael Tiranno, things that

few men did, to realize quite the opposite was true. Tiranno might not have shared his passion, or worn it on the exterior. Yet that passion had been the calling card of a rise from orphaned farmboy to fabulously wealthy casino mogul. Along the way, those who had crossed Michael Tiranno had inevitably lived to regret it, and those who had aided him inevitably prospered as a result. It was said he interviewed all of his employees personally and could greet each and every one by name, offering a hundred-dollar, on-the-spot bonus anytime he failed to do so.

Ferelli had been in the company of royalty before; he'd been in the company of fame. But something about Michael Tiranno, captured even in a photograph, transcended both. Something about his eyes, the way he held his smile. Stare at the picture long enough and the eyes seemed to rotate until they locked on to Ferelli's gaze, at which point they would not let go. And that made the task before him all the more daunting because he could not imagine what it would be like to meet Michael Tiranno in person, much less how he might react to what Ferelli had to say.

Because the information contained in his briefcase would change Michael Tiranno's life forever.

Ferelli had spent the bulk of the flight from New York rehearsing lines in his head to explain his discovery. The circumstantial evidence that defied reason. The truth discerned from a terrible lie. Tiranno had never heard of him, and Ferelli was headed to the Seven Sins without benefit of an appointment.

*Just give me five minutes, five minutes, I beg you. . . .*

From there, a glimpse into the briefcase would be enough to guarantee all the time Gianfranco Ferelli needed.

Ferelli felt cold sweat soaking through his shirt and asked the cab driver to turn up the air-conditioning. Thankfully, he had made it this far without incident and had full confidence Michael Tiranno would greatly value him coming all this way to share the secrets contained in his briefcase.

Gianfranco Ferelli knew he had nothing to fear, as his cab fell in behind four virtually identical sedans on Tropicana Avenue.

TROPICANA AVENUE, THE PRESENT

The four sedans clung to the speed limit, McCarran Airport shrinking in the distance behind them. The cars had been left in four different long-term lots the day before, the parking stubs tucked beneath the driver's-side visors. The cars had been chosen for their innocuousness, typical rentals that cruised the Vegas Strip with frequently flashing brake lights as their occupants took in the glitz and glamour they had come to sample.

But the sedans weren't rentals. Rentals might have aroused suspicion. Instead they had been purchased from used car dealerships, where the possibility of a sale dwarfed all other concerns. Even then, added precautions had been taken. The dealers were hundreds of miles apart and none less than five hundred miles from Las Vegas itself. In each instance the buyers were trained to barter before agreeing on a price, then to return the next day with a cashier's check for the agreed-upon amount.

At that point the cars were driven to four designated load points where their trunks were packed with chemical fertilizers stockpiled over a six-month period and dynamite smuggled in through Mexico. The drivers then headed for McCarran Airport and boarded four different flights out of the city during peak travel time.

The four men currently driving the cars had flown in today, arriving within ninety minutes of each other from four separate airports chosen for the least likelihood of delays. The weather had cooperated brilliantly and each of the flights had landed on time.

The drivers were now right on schedule, the lights of Las Vegas twinkling before them in the night.

# THREE

## The Seven Sins, the present

**M**r. Trumbull," Naomi Burns greeted the man seated in a hand-carved chair in the lobby of the Seven Sins Casino and Resort.

"Sorry I'm late," Lars Trumbull told her, rising to his feet. He was tall and gangly, dressed in jeans with designer tears and a loose black Dolce & Gabbana shirt that hung shapelessly over his belt. He was younger than Naomi Burns had expected.

"Actually," she said, "you were an hour early. I imagine you've seen everything the lobby has to offer."

Trumbull's expression tightened a little. His face was thin, showcasing cheekbones that looked like ridges layered into his face. "I'm impressed. Keeping track of your enemies, Ms. Burns?"

"That depends, doesn't it?" As an attorney, Naomi was well versed in answering one question with another. And, as the corporate attorney for both Michael Tiranno and King Midas World, she was equally adept at deciding who would be allowed to meet her employer and who would not. Her attractiveness— dark wavy hair always perfectly coiffed, a tall, shapely frame, and a wardrobe made up of the finest designer names—helped by giving men like Trumbull a false ease. Naomi's graceful manner could be, and often was, misconstrued as weakness, and she enjoyed nothing more than turning the tables on those who took her lightly.

Her navy blue Chanel suit, the same color as Trumbull's jeans, fit the lines of her taut frame elegantly. She wore her hair short, just grazing her collar, a style that complimented a face she had always thought too narrow, further exaggerating her deep-set eyes. A soft, powdery scent, something trusted like Bijan or Samsara, melded into the air around her, refreshing it, in stark contrast to Trumbull's drugstore cologne. Brut, she thought.

"I'm a journalist," Trumbull told her. "I'm only here because of certain information about Michael Tiranno that has recently come to my attention."

"I know what you are."

After wandering about the lobby and retail area for the past hour, Trumbull had phoned her from this chair set just beyond the hotel's entrance of glass doors inlaid between golden archways. The desired effect was one of stepping from the mundane present into a majestic and ancient past offering the spirit of adventure. A forest of golden ionic columns stretched upward from a black marble lobby floor adorned with live exotic flowers, from the radiant golden iris to rare red poppies. Remnants of ropes of amber from Baltic lands, ostrich eggs from Nubia, and a silver stag from Asia Minor covered by a delicate shower of gold rosettes posed amid golden masks, belts, discs, and shields. The lighting, adjusted automatically throughout the day to account for the sun, was soft and easy on the eye: plenty to read by but lacking the overbright glitz of the gaudy. The air, meanwhile, had a fresh rose scent to it, courtesy of carefully concealed automated fragrance releasers.

"Old news, Mr. Trumbull," Naomi told him. "The Nevada Gaming Commission investigated the same allegations and dismissed them as baseless."

"The Gaming Commission doesn't have my sources, Ms. Burns. You'd be wise to keep that in mind."

"Michael Tiranno doesn't take kindly to threats."

"And I thought that's how you must have gotten the job as his corporate counsel. Why else would he hire someone fresh off an embezzlement charge at her prestigious New York law firm?"

"So your article's about me, then."

"You're a part of it, specifically how the charges mysteriously went away after the debt was mysteriously paid. What have you to say about that, Ms. Burns?"

"It all sounds very mysterious to me," Naomi said simply, unflustered.

"Michael Tiranno swooped in and rescued you. Saved your proverbial ass and your career in the process."

"You spoke to my former partners, then."

"It wasn't necessary."

"Of course. Why bother looking for facts when rumors will suffice?"

Trumbull sniffed hard, swallowing mucous. Perhaps he was allergic to some of the exotic flora that adorned the lobby of the Seven Sins.

"Allergies, Mr. Trumbull?"

"Nothing that'll kill me."

"Not yet," Naomi said. Neither moved his or her eyes from the other until a tourist bumped into Trumbull, turning him around into the path of another guest who smacked into him and pushed him backward.

"Your guests always this rude, Ms. Burns?"

"They're always in a hurry to check in, as you can see."

True to Naomi's word, the check-in line behind the eighteen-station marble reception counter wound through an elaborate maze of stanchions strung together by velvet rope. The casino's best customers, identified by a gold medallion, used a separate, lavish VIP room where all their needs were handled. Many of them would be staying in the high-roller suites erected six floors beneath ground level, with one entire wall offering a view into the world's largest self-contained marine environment, prowled by the only great white sharks ever in captivity. Those suites not held back for returning regulars were booked two years in advance at the rate of two thousand dollars per night. One section of the lobby floor was glass as well, allowing strollers a clear view of marine life captured in a perfectly re-created ocean habitat and, if they were patient, a glimpse of a thirty-foot great white.

"Can we cut the bullshit, Ms. Burns?" Trumbull snapped suddenly. "Am I going to get to see Michael Tiranno or not?"

"He asked me to see you first, give him my opinion."

"Have I impressed you so far?"

"Yes, as a hack, a journalistic hatchet man."

"Behaving like a lawyer, in other words."

"Bad lawyers can be disbarred. Bad writers end up in rehab. So," Naomi continued, after a brief pause, "can I get you a drink?"

"What exactly am I doing here?" Trumbull asked, recovering his bravado. "Why grant me an interview with Michael Tiranno if you had all these suspicions?"

"I granted you an interview with me, not Michael Tiranno."

"You said—"

"I said Mr. Tiranno was appreciative of your interest in him and expressed a desire to make sure you had all the facts straight."

"Which means you've already made up your mind."

"That doesn't mean you can't still prove me wrong, Mr. Trumbull. Mr. Tiranno has asked that I give you a tour of the casino," Naomi told him. "Who knows, you might actually like what you see."